About the Author

Bella Bucannon liv[es in] Adelaide with her s[upport]supports her in any[...] dining out and trave[l...] days at sea to relax, plot and write are top of her list. Apart from category romance she also writes very short stories and poems for a local writing group. Bella believes joining RWA and SARA early in her writing journey was a major factor in her achievements.

Nikki Logan lives on the edge of a string of wetlands in Western Australia, with her partner and a menagerie of animals. She writes captivating nature-based stories full of romance in descriptive natural environments. She believes the danger and richness of wild places perfectly mirror the passion and risk of falling in love.

Nikki loves to hear from readers via nikkilogan.com.au or through social media: Twitter: @ReadNikkiLogan Facebook: Nikki Logan

Meredith Webber says of herself, 'Once I read an article which suggested that Mills and Boon were looking for new Medical Romance authors. I had one of those "I can do that" moments, and gave it a try. What began as a challenge has become an obsession—though I do temper the "butt on seat" career of writing with dirty but healthy outdoor pursuits, fossicking through the Australian Outback in search of gold or opals. Having had some success in all of these endeavours, I now consider I've found the perfect lifestyle.'

Australian

AFFAIRS

Australian Affairs: Rescued

BELLA BUCANNON

NIKKI LOGAN

MEREDITH WEBBER

MILLS & BOON

First Published in Great Britain 2019
By Mills & Boon, an imprint of HarperCollins *Publishers*
1 London Bridge Street, London, SE1 9GF

AUSTRALIAN AFFAIRS: RESCUED © 2019 Harlequin Books S.A.

Bound By The Unborn Baby © 2016 Harriet Nichola Jarvis
Her Knight in the Outback © 2015 Nikki Logan
One Baby Step at a Time © 2013 Meredith Webber

ISBN: 978-0-263-27526-1

0219

BOUND BY THE UNBORN BABY

BELLA BUCANNON

Deepest thanks to my husband and soul mate who claims inside my head is the scariest place on earth but loves me unconditionally anyway. Special thanks to the generous, supportive South Australian Romance Authors for their encouragement and steadfast belief in me. And to Flo Nicoll who saw beyond my raw writing and gave me the courage to drastically cut and revise and produce a story worth telling.

CHAPTER ONE

THIRD DOOR ON the left. Why the hell hadn't he given in to his original instinct, phoned the hotel with a refusal, then binned the short letter hand-delivered to his office? He'd never heard of Alina Fletcher—didn't have the time or energy for enigmatic invitations.

Except one phrase, vaguely referring to his family, had captured his interest five weeks after his sister and brother-in-law had died in Barcelona, less than two since his second trip to Spain regarding their estate.

He felt drained. Flying overseas and coping with local authorities while handling the glitches regarding his latest hotel acquisition had been exhausting. The basic Spanish he'd acquired on other trips had helped; deprivation of sleep didn't. He desperately needed a break to enable him to grieve for Louise, and for Leon, who'd been his best friend since primary school. Any additional angst was definitely unwelcome.

The open doorway allowed him a clear view of the woman facing the window. Slim build. Medium height. Short dark brown hair. His gaze slid rapidly over a sky-blue jacket and trousers to flat shoes. Unusual in this time of killer heels.

'Ms Fletcher?' He was curter than he'd intended, influenced by a hard clench low in his abdomen.

She turned slowly and his battered emotions were rocked even more. Pain-filled eyes underlined with dark smudges met his. Widened. Shuttered. Reopened, clear and steady. Whatever had flickered in their incredible violet depths had banished his lethargy. His dormant libido kicked in, tightening his stomach muscles, accelerating his pulse.

Inappropriate. Inexcusable.

'Ethan James? Thank you for agreeing to meet me.'

No welcoming smile. Did he detect a slight accent? He'd have to hear more—wanted to hear more.

He cleared his throat. 'Did I have a choice?' Moving forward with extended hand, he frowned at her hesitation. *She* was the one who'd requested the meeting.

After a cool, brief touch she gestured to the seating. 'Coffee? Black and strong?'

His eyes narrowed at her assumption of his preference, flicked to the wedding ring she wore. Married. Why did he care? The perfume she wore didn't suit her. Too strong. Too exotic. He wasn't thinking clearly—hadn't been since that devastating early-morning phone call.

'What do you want?' No games. Either she told him the reason they were here or he walked. 'You've got two minutes to convince me to stay.'

She met his glare unwaveringly. 'Then you'd better start reading.' Perching on the front of an armchair, she pushed a buff-coloured folder along the low table before pouring coffee into a cup.

His muscles tensed. She appeared confident, was counting on him thinking he'd always wonder if he left without an explanation. He grudgingly picked up the unnamed folder and sat, stretching out his long legs.

Once she'd placed the drink in front of him she took a book from the bag by her side and settled into the chair to read.

He pulled the file out, glanced at the front sheet—and his already shattered world tilted beyond reality. He flipped the pages, studied the signatures. Scowled at the seemingly composed female ignoring him. A fist of ice clamped his gut. His heart pounded. Not true. Not believable. Though the signatures were genuine. He'd seen enough of them in the last few weeks to be absolutely certain.

Why? There'd been no indication.

He reached for his coffee, drained the hot liquid in one gulp while glancing at Alina Fletcher. Not so serene on further scrutiny. The fingers on her left hand were performing a strange ritual. Starting with the littlest, they curled one by one into her palm, with her thumb folding over the top. Dancelike, the movement was repeated every few seconds.

Nervous? She damn well ought to be, hitting him with this out of the blue. He gave a derisive grunt. He'd have been blindsided however she'd informed him.

Reverting to the opening document, he meticulously perused every paragraph.

Alina automatically flicked the blurred pages of her book, her fingers trembling. Her thoughts were in turmoil. This encounter ought to have been straightforward. She'd come to Sydney, acquaint the brother with the situation, and then they'd discuss options in a businesslike fashion. Instead she'd tensed at the timbre of his formal greeting, been slow to take his hand, shaken by her quickening heartbeat.

Please, please, let it be hormonal.

The best scenario was that he'd concur with the logical solution. She'd return to Europe and they'd communicate amicably via email or phone. Living alone would be no hardship. She only shared accommodation when it was required by an employer and rarely maintained friendships, even those forged from seasonal reunions. No roots. No ties. Liking co-workers was a plus. None had been able to break through the wall staying sane had compelled her to build.

She still wasn't sure what had drawn her to Louise on their early irregular meetings. Perhaps an empathy that had enabled her to see behind the sparkling personality and glimpse the hidden sorrow? A feeling that she was a kindred spirit? Seeing the loving relationship Louise had shared with Leon? She'd often thought of them while travelling. Four months ago fate had brought them together at a critical time for Louise, a soul-searching one for her.

She'd stayed away from the funeral service in Barcelona for her own sake, needing time to decide what to do. Contacting Ethan James while he was arranging for his relatives to be transported to Australia for burial would have been insensitive. It was, however, the honourable thing to do now. In the end the only thing she believed would ensure her future peace of mind.

Until she'd looked into those cobalt eyes with their thick black lashes—so like Louise's, except dulled with sadness and fatigue. Unwarranted, almost forgotten heat sensations had flared low in her belly. Immediately squashed. *Never again.* She'd barely survived before—sometimes felt she hadn't.

During the last year she'd slowly, *so* slowly, begun to open up a little to people. Now she was caught in a different nightmare, with far-reaching consequences. It all depended on the man intently scanning the papers she'd given him.

She approved of his neatly trimmed dark hair, his long fingers with well-shaped clean nails. His no-frills attitude to her letter. Leon had described him as astute, pragmatic, and extremely non-sentimental in business. Personally reserved. The very qualities she needed right now.

She sipped her mint tea, praying her guest would agree to her suggestion. Her skin still prickled from his oh-so-fleeting touch. A hint of earthy cologne teased her nostrils every time she inhaled. Unusual and unfamiliar. Definitely not one of the brands she'd sold working in a department store in Rome last summer.

The tension in the room heightened. She looked up, encountered cold, resolute scrutiny, a grim mouth and firmly set jaw. Did he intend to dispute her claim? In October he'd have all the proof he'd require.

Ethan saw fear chase the sadness from her eyes, swiftly replaced by pseudo-cool detachment.

'You're carrying their child.' He didn't doubt the validity of the documents. They were legal, watertight contracts—somewhat alien to his carefree relatives. 'Why?'

'Three early miscarriages with no medical explanation. No trouble with conception. Surrogacy offered them a way to have a baby of their own.' She spoke precisely, as if she'd rehearsed every word.

He swore quietly, fervently. Why hadn't they told him? There'd been no hint of a problem on any of his visits. Or had he been too focused on his growing business empire to notice?

Anger at lost opportunities gnawed at him. Guilt at missing any change in Louise's demeanour flooded him. The urge to strike out was strong. Pity the only one in the firing line happened to be the messenger.

'Why the secrecy? Why *you*?' He ground the words out violently.

She didn't flinch, though faint colour tinged her cheeks. Crossing her arms, she lifted her chin. 'I offered. My choice. My reasons.'

Something in her tone warned him not to pursue the subject. Fine—he'd accept the simplified statement for now. Coming to terms with being uncle to an unborn child conceived by his dead sister and her husband, carried by a stranger, took precedence.

'When's the child due? Did they know?' A myriad of questions buzzed in his brain, making it impossible to prioritise.

'Late October. I'm nine weeks. We did a pregnancy test together.' Her lips trembled. Her gaze shifted to the wall behind him. 'They were so incredibly happy for a few days. Until that goods van smashed into them at that outdoor café.'

Her tortured eyes met his. Anguish ripped through him on hearing those mind-numbing words spoken in her tremulous voice. He knew. He'd received the international call, read the reports. Seen photographs of the mangled wreckage.

Suddenly he craved solitude. And space. He wanted to run from this woman, escape from her predicament. Forget everything and crawl into a cave like a wounded animal to lick his wounds and recover.

Not going to happen.

He ought to stay, talk more. Get more details. How could he? She exacerbated his torment.

Jamming the file into the folder, he stood up. Alina stayed in her seat, her eyes a mixture of sorrow and perplexity, making him feel like a louse. He pulled his mobile from his inside pocket.

'I need time to take all this in. Give me your number. I'll phone you tomorrow.'

She told him, including the Spanish code. 'You can leave a message at Reception so you won't get charged international rates.'

Ethan let out a short, half-choked laugh. She appeared genuinely concerned at the thought of him paying the fees—something his company did every day. 'I can stand the cost.'

A soft blush coloured her cheeks. His gut twisted in remorse.

She rose to her feet, proudly defiant, tightly clasping her book. 'I appreciate what a shock this is. If there'd been an easier way to tell you, I'd—'

'There wasn't. Goodbye, Ms Fletcher.' He spun round and strode out.

The tension drained from Alina's muscles, to be replaced by frightening awareness. Alien. Alarming. His aura still filled the room, surrounding her, challenging her resolve. Threatening what little stability she had.

She tried to equate this barely held together man with the sharp, on-the-ball tycoon described to her. The one who'd always managed to extricate the two friends from escapades usually instigated by the younger one. The one who'd transformed a failing local travel centre into the multimillion-dollar Starburst hotel and tourism empire.

The man she'd just watched hurriedly exit seemed to be operating on stretched nerves.

Pouring another cup of tea, she reproached herself for bringing more trauma into his life, but knew she'd had no choice. The realisation that she'd been banking on him taking charge, relieving her of all major decisions, hit home. She squeezed her eyes shut, stemming the tears. He hadn't rebuffed her completely. There was still hope.

She pictured Louise sobbing in the café the day after the specialist had advised her that any more pregnancies might be detrimental to her health. She recalled walking her home, talking with her, learning about her society-obsessed parents' rigid attitude to social status.

Her sympathy for Leon's and Louise's plight, and her strong desire to help had been understandable; the solution that had popped into her mind had been astounding. And terrifying.

After two days of intense soul-searching she'd offered to be a surrogate. Their initial refusal had given way to grateful acceptance in light of their limited options. Over a supper of fruit, cheese and dips, washed down with local wine, they'd conceived the perfect plan. Almost foolproof. They hadn't counted on brake failure destroying their hopes in the cruellest way possible.

She stroked her stomach. *Their* baby—not hers. She was simply a cocoon. In October she'd have given birth to their son or daughter and then stepped away, allowing them to experience fully the delights and dramas of parenthood.

Ethan *must* consent to her plan. This tiny new life inside her deserved the love and happiness its new family would have shared. Ethan, rather than his parents, was her preferred choice. If they all chose not to… Well, then she'd have to confront and conquer her demons.

Gathering up her belongings, she went to her room, hoping the television would prevent her thoughts from straying to tomorrow's call. And its maker.

She was window-shopping along George Street when her phone rang late the next morning.

'Alina?'

Spoken with a slightly different emphasis, as if personal to him. Silly idea. He'd given her the impression he considered her an intrusive dilemma.

'Sorry I didn't call earlier. I've been juggling my schedule. Are you free tonight?'

'Yes. I came to Sydney for the sole purpose of meeting you.'

'And if I'd refused?' he asked brusquely.

'I'd have posted you a detailed letter with the file and caught the next available flight to Spain.'

'And wha—? No, not now. A hire car will be outside your hotel at five-thirty. I've booked a table. Goodbye, Ms Fletcher.'

He hung up, leaving her startled by his broken-off question. Understanding his scepticism, she swore to be honest—though she'd keep her past to herself unless it concerned the baby. Last night as she'd fallen asleep she'd sensed an elusive unidentifiable memory skip through her mind. Didn't want any more.

Ethan drummed his fingertips on his desk. He'd meant to ask why she wore a ring—if there was a husband or partner in the picture. He'd been distracted by her impassive replies and had accidentally activated an email from Brisbane requiring an urgent reply. Hence his regrettable abrupt ending to the call.

His back ached…his brain spun. An evening on the internet researching surrogacy had raised more questions than it had answered. It hurt that they'd gone through so much heartache alone. Why hadn't they reached out to him? Surely they'd known they mattered to him more than anything?

He'd supported Louise's marriage to Leon against his parents' wishes, happily standing as best man. He had never doubted their love for each other, had admired their courage and steadfast defiance of the demands to wait until they were older. Louise's declaration that they'd have a park wedding in front of a few friends had provoked his mother into grudging agreement. She had then proceeded to turn it into a flash affair for her own social gratification.

From what he'd seen, growing up, those two had been the exception in a world of duplicity and the façade of wedded unity. His own memories of being brushed aside, of days seeing only nannies or cooks, still rankled.

Knowing he carried the genes of two people with no apparent parental feelings had determined his future. Swearing there'd be no children, even if he married in the future, he'd resolved to be the best uncle to any nieces or nephews. Now that vow would be tested in a way he'd never imagined.

Lying awake, contemplating options, he'd finally decided on the best solution for the child and his family. It all depended on that gold ring. Alina Fletcher might not concur with his decision. She was the one who'd offered the use of her body, the one who'd travelled to Australia to meet him. The one who'd spun his world out of orbit with her revelation. She'd committed herself by contacting him.

He'd been disconcerted by his physical reaction to the stranger with the inconceivable news. An effect he blamed on fatigue, combined with his almost celibate life for months. So he'd run—hadn't stayed to find out what *she* wanted, what she expected from *him*.

He'd finally slept restlessly, risen early, and reshuffled his work diary.

Alina spotted Ethan immediately: tall, head-turningly handsome, impossible to miss among the people milling outside the luxurious hotel. His sister had been spontaneous and cheerful; her dinner companion tonight exuded an aura of deliberation and sobriety.

Blaming the prickling sensation down her spine on stress, she steeled herself as she unbuckled the seatbelt. Her door opened, giving her a view of a solid torso clad in an elegant designer suit. She was glad she'd impulsively packed her black dinner dress, bought four years ago in rural France. Rarely worn, it was simple in design, chic enough to give her confidence a boost. Loose enough to conceal any hint of her condition.

She swung her leg out and his fingers curled around her elbow, taking her weight as she alighted. Holding on longer than necessary. As it had yesterday, his touch generated tingles, radiating across her skin.

'Thank you for being so prompt.'

His deep voice sounded less dynamic. The shadows under his eyes were darker. Another too-full day after too little sleep?

Why the let-down feeling at his mundane comment? Quickly followed by a zing of pleasure when he put his arm around her to escort her through the crowd? Heat flared in places that had been winter-cold for years, shocking her into silence.

He released her the moment they entered the elevator

for the short journey up to the restaurant, taken in silence. They were greeted by the maître d', who led them to a window table set apart in a far corner, secluded by greenery. Alina followed, acutely aware of the man behind her and the limited number of diners in the room. She sat, staring in awe at the North Sydney high-rises across the harbour.

'This is incredible,' she said, and sighed, turning her head to take in more. Too far. Their eyes met; warmth flooded her cheeks. He must think her so gauche. To her surprise he glanced out, then smiled at her for the first time, transforming his features, making him less forbidding.

'I guess it is. Over time you get used to the skyline being there.'

'Not possible,' she declared vehemently. 'And it's going to get better as all the lights come on, isn't it?'

CHAPTER TWO

ETHAN'S FATIGUE LIGHTENED at her enthusiasm for something he took for granted. Her eyes gleamed, darkened to the colour of the flowers of the plant on his PA's desk.

His jaw firmed as she returned the smile from the young waiter who offered her a menu. The curt nod he gave him on accepting his was unwarranted, and instantly repented.

Her delightfully intense expression as she carefully read each item restored his good humour. She finally looked up and gestured, palm out.

'How on earth am I supposed to decide? I'm not even sure what some of them are. You choose for me.'

'The lemon sole is particularly good. Or the chef's special if you are in the mood for lamb.' His gaze dropped to her pink, unenhanced lips. Forget food—he wanted to taste *her*. She'd be sweeter than any dessert coming out of the kitchen tonight.

Her voice cut through his inapt thoughts.

'I'll bet they're all delicious. Nothing too spicy or strong-flavoured.' Putting her menu on the table, she laid her arms on top, unintentionally drawing his attention as she leant forward. 'And small portions for me, please.'

The taut fit of the material over her breasts intrigued him. Had being pregnant enlarged them? They'd been hidden under her loose jacket yesterday. Tonight they'd been the first thing he'd visually noticed when she'd stepped from the car—preceded by that perfume so not right for her.

What the hell was wrong with him? The woman opposite him wore a wedding ring and was pregnant. He tamped down his libido, concentrated on selecting their meal.

'Oh, wine...?' Alina's hands fell to her sides as a young

woman carrying a bottle placed an ice bucket and stand next to their table.

'Non-alcoholic,' Ethan hastily reassured her, before addressing the waitress. 'Please allow my guest to sample it.'

She savoured the tangy fruit flavour, drank a little more, and smiled. 'It's very refreshing. Thank you.'

She gazed around while he ordered their meals. A screen of plants, plus a larger than standard space, separated them from the adjoining tables. Little chance of being seen—none of being overheard. Had he asked for it? Or—oh, this upmarket hotel must be part of his Starburst chain.

The waitress left. Alina raised her glass, let the tangy liquid slide down her throat. Her curiosity overrode tact. 'Are these plants and extra space always here?'

He shrugged. 'On request. Some couples find the seclusion romantic. Some men aspire to an elaborate setting with privacy for a proposal.' He paused, a glint of amusement in his eyes. 'In case of rejection.'

She understood the need to keep her presence a secret. An icy shiver ran down her spine. What if he rejected *her* proposal? She had to persuade him it was best for everyone involved.

'Doesn't it invite curiosity from people who might recognise you? Who'll wonder who I am?'

'Few people dine this early. I believe you'll feel more comfortable eating here, then we'll go somewhere quieter to discuss our situation.'

'You're right. Thank you.' Her gaze wandered from the silverware, the fine cut-glass, and the decorative light fittings to the amazing panorama outside the window.

'Fine dining. Romantic setting with harbour lights. They create a wonderful memory for any couple,' he commented.

Like a sandy beach with rippling waves at dawn. Her eyes misted. She bit the inside of her lip. *Don't go there. It's all gone. Gone for ever.*

Ethan wasn't about to let her attention stray. He had too much to learn in too little time. Her history. The reason she'd agreed to be a surrogate. Why she wore that ring. Why a simple piece of jewellery rankled so much.

'Alina?'

Too sharp.

She started, blinked twice, and refocused. 'I'm sorry. I was miles away.'

'I noticed.' He leant an elbow on the table, rested his chin on his hand, and scrutinised her. He sensed her superficial demeanour was a defensive shield, preventing her from revealing anything personal. It was one he aimed to breach for his, and the child's, benefit.

'Relax. Enjoy your meal. You like seafood?'

'Love it.'

Her words coincided with the appearance of their appetiser: creamy pumpkin soup with croutons. They ate in silence, apart from her praise for the country fresh flavour. He signalled for the empty dishes to be removed, requested their mains be held for five minutes.

Once they were alone, he leant forward. 'How long had you known Leon and Louise?'

'Oh. Um… I guess casually for more than three years. If there was a position vacant I worked in a café near their house whenever I was in Barcelona.'

'A waitress?' His eyebrow quirked. *Whenever she was in Barcelona? She was not a resident?*

She bristled at his inference of her pursuing a lowly profession. 'Be careful, Mr James. You're demeaning your staff, who are giving us excellent service tonight.'

He acknowledged her rebuke with a nod. She looked gratified and continued. 'It's a useful skill for a working traveller. I rarely stay anywhere for long.'

'Any other *useful* skills?' This was getting worse by the

minute. Casual worker. Temporary. No profession. Why had they chosen *her*?

Alina fought the urge to challenge his condescending attitude. He was the baby's uncle—ideally its future guardian.

Her choices had been determined by her need to have limited social contact. She toyed with the stem of her glass, drew in a steadying breath. 'Any office work, translating or bar tending. Plus anything seasonal or transient, such as crop harvesting. I have references, if you're interested. It's been my life for seven years—my choice.'

'Not any more. Your foreseeable future will be governed by what's best for the child you are carrying. And I will have an input in every decision.'

His low, inflexible tone added to the challenge in his piercing eyes. She matched him, picturing his relatives' joy—so short-lived.

'The baby *is* my main priority. I'm taking care of myself, eating healthily, exercising sensibly.'

The bite in her voice shamed her. She'd never been confrontational, had always tried to get along with others, even in short-term work environments.

She gulped, tried for conciliation. 'Everything I do is to maintain their dream.'

Their dream—not hers. Talking with Ethan James raked up memories best left forgotten.

'What nationality are you? Where are your legal documents? Birth certificate?' He topped up their wine glasses as he spoke, then watched her as he drank.

Hands hidden in her lap, her spine rigid, she refused to show any sign of weakness. 'I'm Australian, born and bred. Is that good enough for you? For your parents? My passport's in the safe at the hotel.'

She'd done it again. She'd anticipated his questions, prepared herself for suspicion, even rejection. So how did he manage to wind her up so easily?

He waited. His unfathomable dark blue eyes revealed nothing. Inexplicably, she found herself wondering how those firm full lips would feel pressed against hers.

No. No. No! She let out a loud huff of air. Had to be hormonal. Couldn't be the man. It was vital for him to think the best of her.

She tried again. 'Anything not needed regularly is with my solicitor in Crow's Nest.'

'Good. Easily accessible.' He nodded, smiled as if her reply pleased him. 'Here comes our main course.'

He'd chosen grilled lemon sole served with lightly sautéed vegetables and a side salad. It was melt-in-the-mouth scrumptious—the best meal she could remember. Her tension eased as he kept the conversation neutral and light. Because he was satisfied with her answers so far?

Dessert was an unbelievably good strawberry soufflé. She sensed his perusal as she scraped the last morsel from her dish. Didn't care. It was heavenly.

Putting down her spoon, she smiled at him. 'Mmm. Mouth-watering food. Great service. Do you eat here often?'

'I'll pass your approval on to the chef. Apart from dining here, with or without guests, I find it convenient to ring in an order and have it sent to my office or apartment.'

'They home-deliver? Like pizza?' She stared at him in amazement. He regularly ate personally delivered gourmet meals. She occasionally ordered takeaway, saved money by picking it up.

His throaty laugh skittered across her skin. 'Hey, we cater for twenty-four-hour room service. My meals travel a little further in a taxi, that's all.'

'Wow. We *so* live in different worlds.'

His eyes darkened and bored into hers. She couldn't move, couldn't look away. Her lighthearted words had shattered the mood.

Ethan pushed his empty dish aside, annoyed at her emphatic statement. She made it sound like an insurmountable division between them. Although their life in Spain might have been simpler, more casual than his ambition-driven existence, basically his core beliefs were the same as his sister's and brother-in-law's.

He'd enjoyed every moment of the regular visits he'd made to Barcelona, including the noisy, fun-filled meals lasting well into the night. There had always been friends around. So why hadn't he met *her*? Bad timing?

He drank the last of his wine, dropped his napkin on the table. 'Are you ready to leave? We'll have privacy to talk upstairs.' Where he'd be able to override any dissension to his proposition.

'Upstairs?'

Apprehension shaded the striking colour of her eyes, and a strong urge to reassure her rocked him.

'Company suite for family or friends. Leon and Louise stayed here twice; usually they came to my apartment.'

She didn't answer. He came round to hold her chair while she retrieved her bag from the floor and stood, head held high. Courageous. Beautiful.

Taking her elbow respectfully, he guided her towards a door in the side wall. The ever-alert maître d' was there before them. Ethan thanked him, adding praise for the attending staff. A moment later they sped upwards in an exclusive elevator.

They stepped out into a foyer, not the corridor Alina had envisaged. Colourful modern art complemented the light sand-coloured walls between two white doors. He used a key card to open the one on the right, gestured for her to enter.

Her remark rang true as she stared enviously at her surroundings. Different worlds nailed it. She'd cleaned rooms, never luxury suites. And for him this was the norm, his everyday existence.

Floor-to-ceiling windows afforded a spectacular view of the city on two adjoining walls. Perfectly situated to take advantage was a dark wood dining setting, with a centrepiece of bushland flora. A matching coffee table stood in front of a luxurious dark blue three-piece lounge suite, facing a wall-mounted television. Two large bright blue and red abstract paintings hung on light grey walls.

Her companion shrugged out of his jacket, tossed it onto a chair, and gestured towards a hallway. 'The bathroom is the third door along if you need it.'

He walked across to a fancy coffee machine, reaching for two mugs from the cabinet above. She watched the play of his muscles under his navy shirt, chided herself for the sudden appreciative clench low in her belly.

'If not take a seat. Tea? I assume your condition is the reason you didn't drink coffee yesterday?'

He'd noticed. Totally focused on the documents, reeling from shock, he'd still been aware of what she'd drunk. Had he mentally sized her up, judged her, as well?

'Herbal, if you have any, please.'

'No problem. Make yourself comfortable.'

So solicitous. So hospitable. Would his attitude change if they couldn't come to an agreement?

She moved to the settee, kicked off her shoes, and curled into a corner. 'Could you make it fairly weak? Just in case.'

He glanced round, his brow furrowed. 'In case of what?' His face cleared. 'Ah, having trouble with morning sickness?'

She appreciated the concern in his voice, even if it was more for the welfare of his niece or nephew than for her.

'I've been lucky so far—occasional nausea from strong aromas, nothing too bad.'

This polite, bland conversation had no reason to irritate

her—however, it did. There was no one around to hear them. *Let's get on with it.*

'What else have…? Never mind.'

Ethan tamped down his curiosity regarding her history. The current situation had priority. He put the two mugs on the coffee table and sat down beside her, inadvertently too close for detachment. Close enough to smell the fragrance he'd determined to change at the earliest opportunity. Close enough to notice the faded scar almost hidden by her hair. Close enough to inadvertently touch her. He linked his fingers to prevent impulsive movement. To keep it impersonal. *Huh, she's having Louise's child. Can't get much more personal.*

Clearing his throat, he returned to basic facts. 'Has the pregnancy been confirmed medically?' A natural question to open the conversation.

She flicked a non-existent lock of hair from her forehead. A recent change of hairstyle? Cut shorter than she normally wore it?

'No. We did an early home test on February the seventh. Although it showed positive, I repeated it before booking my flight.' Her voice was clear, with no hesitation.

He nodded. 'We have an appointment at eleven-thirty next Monday with Dr Patricia Conlan—reputedly one of Sydney's leading gynaecologists. I've been assured she'll give the best care to you and our baby. She's had a cancellation, otherwise we'd have a longer wait.'

Her pupils dilated, making a stunning display of her violet irises. Her hand moved swiftly to cover her abdomen, triggering a surge of possessiveness in him, alien and disquieting. An instinctive action? Had he imagined the flicker of awareness at his deliberate use of a certain adjective?

'You need your own proof that I'm pregnant. I'll be ready.'

'Not proof. Confirmation that everything is okay.'

She sampled her tea, smiled approvingly. 'It is. Apart from mild nausea, I'm fit and healthy. What else do you want to know?'

All your secrets. She'd been in his thoughts all day, disturbing his concentration at inopportune moments. Every time he'd walked past his PA's potted plant the flowers had conjured up a picture of stunning, sorrowful violet eyes. He'd never been drawn to any woman so fast, so powerfully. Telling himself it was because she carried Louise's child didn't cut it. His body had responded to her on sight, when he'd still suspected a scam.

'I've made frequent trips to Barcelona in the last three years. I don't remember your name being mentioned. How come we didn't meet?' There'd always been noisy gatherings at his sister's, available women and obvious attempts at matchmaking. 'I flew over for a week in January. They were excited and secretive, so I'm guessing it happened around then.'

'I deliberately wasn't part of their social group. Louise and I were casual friends who'd have a chat over coffee sometimes. Occasionally Leon would join us. I'd never been to their home until the day she confided in me. Again, my choice. The embryo was implanted on the twenty-eighth—after you'd left.'

Her gaze drifted to the window, as if she were picturing something from her past. She raised her drink and swallowed. As he watched the movement of her throat his fingers itched to caress her lightly tanned skin wherever it was exposed. Wherever it wasn't.

Draining his mug, he set it down with a sharp clink.

Startled by the noise, she swung round to confront him. 'I told you I travel a lot—mostly Europe. I'm not good at socialising or small talk.'

Merely lack of practice, to be rectified by the new circles he intended to introduce her into—a world involving business dinners and networking. She'd have his support and protection as long as she stayed with him. In return he'd expect her to accompany him to various functions when a partner was invited.

He'd been completely absorbed in her during their meal. Her eyes, her lips, the graceful curve of her neck as she bent her head, even the way she used her cutlery, all fascinated him. The plain gold ring on her left hand—the only jewellery she wore—niggled at his gut.

She still hadn't mentioned a husband or partner. It had always been 'I'. His curiosity had to be satisfied prior to revealing his intentions.

He fisted his fingers on his thigh, braced himself for her reaction. Spoke as she leant over to put her mug down. 'You wear a wedding ring. And my research informs me surrogates are invariably women who have had at least one successful pregnancy.'

She sat immobilised, one arm outstretched, her face in profile.

He couldn't stop the next words forming. 'Where's your child? Your husband?'

Her mug dropped to the table's edge, broke in two. Fell to the floor. Her skin drained of colour. Wide, tormented eyes met his. The truth hit him like a king punch to the solar plexus a split second before she replied.

'They died.'

Flat. Expressionless. Heartbreakingly poignant.

No movement. No sound. Then without warning she erupted from the settee, her desperate eyes swinging towards the door. She took one step. Ethan sprang to his feet and caught her elbow, twisting her round. Her stricken face shook him to the core. He let go.

'I didn't think. I'm sorry, Alina.'

She gulped in a deep, staggered breath that raked her body and silently walked to the hallway.

CHAPTER THREE

THEY DIED. WHY HADN'T he realised? The travelling. The solitary lifestyle. He hadn't connected the facts. Instead he'd acted like a bastard, without consideration for her feelings. An echo of his father.

Somehow he had to make amends, persuade her to stay. The child's acceptance of him depended on her conceding to his proposition. In every way. Alina the woman as much as the child-bearer. *Oh, Louise, what have you started? Why didn't you tell me?*

He picked up both mugs, dropped hers into a bin, washed his, and waited.

Alina sat on the toilet seat lid, hugging herself, rocking rhythmically, trying to quell her shuddering breaths. The cloud in her mind began to clear, leaving behind a mixture of fear and shame. She'd blown it—been ambushed by a question she ought to have foreseen. Ethan James was a man who'd check the information he'd been given—investigate until he knew everything. Or believed he did. And instead of calmly answering, she'd panicked.

She cringed, dreading what his opinion of her would be now—a neurotic female with serious hang-ups who claimed to be pregnant with his niece or nephew. It was essential he be convinced of her emotional stability, so he'd trust her to take proper care of herself and the baby until its birth.

Dampening a cloth from the rail with cold water, she pressed it to her face, ashamed of her abrupt reaction. Her reflection in the mirror was pale and strained—not the composed image she'd hoped to project. *For Louise and*

Leon. She recited her mantra, squared her shoulders, and returned to the main sitting area.

Ethan leant on the counter by the coffee machine, watching her with sympathetic eyes. Guilt also flickered in the cobalt blue, stirring her conscience.

She gave an awkward shrug. 'You surprised me. I anticipated a doctor asking about my history, but I guess I'm not as prepared as I thought. Add my hormones acting crazy, and jet lag—'

'My fault. I didn't mean it to come out so brutally.' He moved forward, gave her plenty of space. 'My only excuse is I'm still trying to come to grips with it all. Forgive me?'

She empathised—had been there. Heck, she was *still* there. Shock upon shock robbed you of lucidity. In the last twenty-four hours, she'd delivered a bundle to him. Not having any option didn't ease her remorse.

She managed a twisted smile. 'Time heals is a furphy. Developing a façade to get through each day is the only way to survive.' And hers threatened to crack with every look, every touch from this man. Her mouth dried; her throat constricted. 'It's not right. They deserved to have their baby. Life *stinks*.'

Fierce and heartfelt.

Ethan concurred that life wasn't always fair, but refrained from admitting it. 'Life's what you make it. Are you up for talking a little longer? If not I'll take you to your hotel and we can continue in the morning.'

'I'll stay.' She ran her tongue over dry lips. 'Could I have another tea, please?'

'Thank you for agreeing. Same flavour?'

With a brave attempt at smiling, she curled into the corner of the settee. When he sat he left a bigger gap between them, avoiding accidental contact.

Space didn't help. Yesterday he'd attributed his reaction to her as the combined effects of disbelief, weariness, and self-enforced celibacy due to his business commitments. Problems with the expansion of his hotel chain into Queensland—on top of his regular heavy workload—had left him little time for a personal life even prior to the accident.

Tonight the desire for physical contact had been—*was still*—much stronger. He'd resisted with effort, knowing it was essential to allay her doubts and resolve some of the essential matters. Every day counted in the agenda he'd formulated.

She drank thirstily, colour gradually returning to her cheeks. Unsure eyes met his and he thought he'd have given almost anything to appease her by bringing the evening to an end.

'That was the reason you kept moving? No ties? No commitments?'

Relief washed over him when she merely nodded before placing her mug down carefully.

'We need to discuss certain issues—the main one being protection for the child. It wasn't random curiosity, Alina. I have a genuine motivation for everything I ask.'

Her jaw firmed, her shoulders hitched. Bracing for what? The sight of her teeth giving a quick tug to the side of her mouth gave him a moment of regret, determinedly squashed. He needed facts.

'What did you imagine would happen when you requested a meeting?'

To his surprise she relaxed, as if she'd feared a different query.

'Springing a newborn niece or nephew on you didn't seem right, even though I don't think you can get DNA proof till then. I figured you'd appreciate time to get used to the idea—time to decide if your family wanted to adopt the—'

'*If* we wanted to adopt Louise's child?' In a second he

was towering over her, six feet of instant fury directed solely at the woman recoiling from him.

A range of emotions flickered across her features. Resentment. Anger. Guilt?

She pushed herself upright, causing him to step back. 'Yes—*if.* You expect me to believe your parents will *welcome* this? Even *with* DNA proof?' She glared up at him, delightfully incensed, daring him to contradict her.

Stunned at her outburst, he felt his temper abate. His mother's perception of social standing... His father's snobbery... Their disapproval of his sister's marriage... All probably the reason Louise's miscarriages had been kept secret.

He spun round to the window, running agitated fingers into his hair. How much more angst was a man supposed to endure?

'Options were limited because of their attitude.'

Her tone was gentle, conciliatory. He turned.

'Louise knew they'd consider adopting a failure, although it *was* to be their last resort.'

'I'm not sure they'd have accepted a surrogate grandchild either,' he grated.

'They weren't going to find out.'

It had slipped out, and Alina couldn't retract the declaration.

A predatory gleam flared in his eyes. He moved quickly, trapping her against the settee, his breath fanning her face. She stood her ground, holding his gaze, hoping he couldn't sense her trepidation.

A long moment later he inclined his head. 'I suggest we sit, so you can explain exactly how the three of you intended to hide it from us.'

She didn't sit. She flopped, desperately trying to regroup. Extremely perceptive, he had a reputation for dealing strictly on the level. Though he might accept his parents' rigid viewpoint had been the incentive for all their secrecy and deception, he certainly hoped the trio hadn't broken any laws. That would definitely test his principles.

He also had a way of undermining her defences, honing in on sensitive secrets. Some were not for sharing.

She watched him settle, folding one leg onto the settee. His features indicated that he was cool, calm, and collected. His right fingers lightly drumming on his thigh proved otherwise.

Crunch time. Next week she'd probably be back in Spain, managing alone until October. She'd learned life's lessons the hard way, already had a plan worked out. There was the trust account Leon had set up, plus an Australian bank account she'd never accessed.

Wriggling into the corner, she tucked her feet up and challenged him. 'Then I can go to my hotel?'

'Yes. Tell me the basics. We'll discuss the rest later.' Milder tone. Persuasive.

He laid his arm along the back of the settee. A normal gesture, yet she had a sudden urge to slide into its embrace, lay her head on his shoulder, and let him take care of everything. Crazy notion. Not for her. *Ever.*

'They made a generous donation to a clinic that caters to low-income couples. The procedure was done under fictitious names, with Louise and me using the same one. We planned to travel around, avoid people we knew. As a patient, I'd use her name.'

She stopped, reluctant to continue as his posture changed. He'd jolted upright when she'd mentioned fictitious names, slowly shaking his head in disbelief. Now he sat still as stone, an incredulous stare in his dark blue eyes. Icy chills ran down her spine; cold sweat formed on her palms. He didn't approve—couldn't comprehend all they'd been through.

'We didn't hurt or cheat anyone. In fact the money we donated gave other couples a chance to realise their dream too.'

His lips compressed. 'What about doctors and scans? The birth? What if something had gone wrong? How many people did you intend to lie to?'

Alina's grip tightened till the ring she wore dug into her flesh. Damn fate and to heck with life. She'd finally found the courage to confront her dark solitude; to try and help someone else in despair. And now she'd been left with the fall-out on her own. *Again.* She curbed the tears threatening to fall. He'd probably dismiss them anyway.

'As few as possible. There was no reason to suppose this pregnancy and birth wouldn't be normal.' Apart from the fact that this tiny person growing inside her belonged to someone else. 'You can't possibly understand. You weren't there.'

He froze. She couldn't even detect any movement from his breathing. His black eyebrows were drawn together, his cobalt eyes dark and fathomless. He was justifiably shaken. Right now she didn't care. She wanted this night to end.

'No, I wasn't. They never gave me the chance to be.'

They were both silent for a moment, then he startled her by reaching out and taking her left hand in his. His thumb stroked over her gold ring.

'How old are you?'

'Thirty.'

'I'll turn thirty-six in December. You're not involved with anyone?'

She shook her head warily.

'No one else is aware of your surrogacy pact?'

A more emphatic shake.

His next words were spoken in a clear, resolute tone. 'Then as far as everyone's concerned, Alina, this child is ours.'

Her heart began to thump wildly. He was claiming the

baby as his own. *Ours. Our baby.* She stared at their joined hands and remembered his earlier words. The best solution of all. More than she'd dared hope for. No need for adoption.

'And it's credible because you were in Spain at the right time.' A whisper…barely audible.

Ethan had still been struggling to make sense of it all even as he'd made his declaration. His sister and his best friend had been prepared to lie, even commit fraud, to become parents. He'd have done everything possible to help. They hadn't asked.

Instead, whatever their original intentions had been, he would now be the father of their child. His tenacious, practical persona, the one that had achieved corporate success, kicked in. He refocused on Alina. He'd give her no choice. She had to accept the optimum scenario he'd envisaged last night.

Her drawn face and drooping eyelids mirrored his own exhaustion. They'd both been bombarded with emotional stress since the accident. Maybe if he carried her into the bedroom they'd sleep peacefully, continue their conversation in the morning. Maybe if he cradled her in his arms they'd find comfort.

Bad idea. He swung his leg off the settee, stretched as he stood. Glanced at his watch.

'It's been gruelling for both of us.' *Like a manic rollercoaster.* 'And tomorrow won't be any easier. This suite has three bedrooms. You can sleep here or I'll escort you to your hotel.'

'I'd prefer my hotel.' She hesitated, bit her lip before resuming doggedly. 'We weren't being reckless. We'd have gone straight to the nearest medical facility at the slightest hint of any problem.'

Her eyes begged for understanding, and she held out her hands, palms up, in supplication. 'I'm not lying. We'd never have risked the baby's health. *Never.*'

'I don't doubt it.' He didn't. They'd concocted a crazy scheme, with holes you could drive a truck through, and yet he found himself believing that with luck on their side they might have succeeded.

He phoned for the hire car. She put her shoes on and went to the bathroom.

A little later Alina stood quietly in the doorway, watching him replace the mugs. For seven years she'd befriended few men, always kept things casual. From the moment they'd met, Ethan James had stirred feelings she tried not to acknowledge. She prayed it was a fleeting thing, caused by her condition. Gone after the birth. Entrusting her shattered heart to anyone would be too great a risk.

So how come that stupid organ was beating faster at the sight of his muscles tensing as he stretched up to the shelf? Why was she gawking at his broad shoulders? Why was she remembering the feel of his hand on her spine?

He turned, as if sensing her presence, smiled reassuringly. She smiled tentatively back. He walked to the door, picking up a laptop bag from the dining table and his jacket on the way.

'Driver's waiting. We'll discuss tomorrow in the car.'

They exited the elevator into an underground car park, where a flashy silver limousine waited. Ethan gave their destination to the chauffeur before joining her on the plush seat. She loved the texture of the soft leather, breathed in its potent aroma, enhanced by her escort's earthy cologne. The brush of his thigh on hers as he twisted to buckle himself in caused her to shift towards the door.

Talk. Any subject. Anything to distract her thoughts from the vitality of the man by her side.

'What happens after I've seen your doctor? Do I leave?' she asked, striving for a casual tone.

The glance he gave her was enigmatic. 'No.' Removing

the computer from the bag at his feet, he placed it on his lap and activated it.

Was he crazy? Her staying would bring embarrassment to his family, cause conflict with his parents. Better she go, returning later in the year. No matter what agreement they made, this baby would be born in Australia.

'You stay with me. You signed a legal contract to carry and give birth to this child. The purpose of your scheme was to prevent that child from suffering any repercussions from its origin or circumstances. Nothing's changed.'

Corporate-speak. Direct. Uncompromising.

He turned the laptop, enabling her to see the document displayed. An insane impulse to laugh shook her. It was an application for a marriage licence, with the groom's details already entered on the left, her name and his address on the right.

She bit back a negative retort. Ethan James didn't play games. He dealt with every situation shrewdly, sweeping aside opposition with logic and unwavering perseverance. And that was what she was to him—a *situation*, to be processed with tact and practicality.

He set the laptop aside, turned towards her. She flinched as his hand splayed across her abdomen, sending a warm glow sliding from cell to cell. She couldn't tear her eyes from his touch.

His voice was honey-smooth, adamant.

'Alina, the baby you carry is my family. I can't—*I won't*—permit this child to be born illegitimate.'

She sympathised, but he had no idea what he was demanding from her. The warmth faded, replaced by a cold chill. Another hand, so like his, had lain there, eagerly anticipating the movement of an unborn baby. Caring. Sharing. Taken from her with no warning.

Somewhere out in the real world a driver beeped his horn. She sensed Ethan studying her, could imagine his brain churning with arguments to reinforce his demand. For him her full compliance was essential. He'd accept nothing less.

His words might come from an innate sense of duty, but the passion in his voice proclaimed a deep brotherly love. She'd been a willing party to the covert plan to protect the baby's name. It was as essential now as it had been then. She consigned her memories to the deep pit where they belonged.

'This explains your interest in my papers. How long is it supposed to last?' It came out wrong. She hadn't meant to sound so cold, so detached. She certainly wasn't prepared for the pained look in his eyes.

'We've got seven months to sort out the future. No one will be surprised if our sudden marriage doesn't survive long-term.' His hand left her stomach and cupped her chin. 'I won't force you to stay, and I swear you won't lose from this arrangement.'

He was right—because she'd already lost everything worthwhile. She'd bought a new gold ring because she hadn't been able to bear the sight or the feel of the original. Wearing it discouraged male attention. He offered a marriage of convenience. No intimacy. No permanency. An expedient arrangement, lasting long enough to convince everyone he was the father.

She couldn't tell him—couldn't tell anyone about the darkness. Remembering the past tore her apart. Speaking of it out loud was unthinkable. His way made sense. If they married, his paternity would be undisputed. He'd give this baby the love she was incapable of feeling.

'You give me your word that I can leave when *I* decide?'

Being nomadic, with no involvements, was the only way to prevent her life from being devastated again. Last year she'd occasionally been drawn into small-town activities. And she'd connected with Louise and offered her help, completely breaking her basic rules. Look where *that* had landed her.

'Yes.' It was blunt. His body was rigid, his features unreadable.

'All right. I'll marry you. When will it be?' So impersonal, so soulless. Why did that worry her?

'Tomorrow morning we'll collect the documents we need from your solicitor for a one o'clock meeting with the celebrant. She'll check the application, lodge it immediately, and the wedding will be a month later.'

He packed the computer into its bag.

As soon as legally permitted. Eleven years ago it had seemed to her like an eternity to wait.

CHAPTER FOUR

ETHAN CONTINUED TALKING as he unbuckled his seatbelt. 'I'll be here at eight-thirty in the morning.'

With a start she realised they'd reached her hotel.

'I'll be in the lobby.'

How did you say goodnight to the stranger you'd promised to marry? The day after you'd met? A man you'd never even kissed.

That last thought rattled her, and she tripped alighting from the vehicle. Ethan steadied her with an arm around her waist. She trembled from his touch—or her own agitation. She wasn't sure which.

'I'll see you to your room.'

He guided her through the foyer towards the elevators.

'It's quicker to walk up one flight,' she said, grateful no one else was there. His aroma mingled with hers, filling the space, heightening her already taut nerves.

He followed her into her room, his sharp, narrow-eyed appraisal of the decor rankling. To her dismay she sensed him making mental note of the mundane fixtures and colours. Her accommodation, definitely lower standard than his hotel, faced the rear of an office block. It was simply somewhere to shower and sleep for a few days.

'It's clean and comfortable,' she retorted. 'It suits my budget. So, if you've finished being critical, I'd like to get some sleep.'

'I'm not judging, Alina. By contacting me you have placed yourself and our child under *my* protection. That's the reason you can't stay here.'

He reached out to her. She stepped back, holding up her hand. She didn't have the inclination to pack even the few belongings she'd brought for a short stay. In addition, she needed some physical space between them to reinforce mental distance.

'Not tonight. I'll check out in the morning.'

His expression disheartened her.

'Please, Ethan,' she begged. 'Give me one night.'

He relented, let out a rough grunt. 'I've been pretty hard on you, haven't I? No more than on myself, I swear.'

He touched her cheek gently. 'I'll see you in the morning. May I have your mobile for a moment?'

He took it and programmed his number in.

'In case you need to contact me. Sometime tomorrow we'll transfer your phone to an Australian plan.' He brushed his lips on her forehead. 'Sleep well, Alina.'

She locked the door behind him. Leant her brow against it, her mind a fuddled whirlpool of everything they'd said and done, everything they hadn't, the way he'd looked, smelt and created minute fissures in her defences.

She filled out the breakfast menu, hooked it on the outside door handle, then sank wearily onto the bed, just for a few minutes. Tomorrow she'd need to be focused. Solicitor. Celebrant. Hazily she wondered what else he had planned.

He'd already booked the celebrant, arrogantly confident that she'd accept his proposal. Not that he'd actually *asked* her. She ought to…

Deep, dreamless sleep claimed her, held her despite the traffic noise. Held her through the alarm's whirl.

Ethan rested his head against the seat, staring unseeing at the city buildings on the drive home. He'd wanted to kiss Alina Fletcher. Not the soft-touch goodnight kiss he'd given her prior to leaving, but full mouth-to-mouth contact. Another unexpected jolt to his system, and the reason he'd let her stay at her hotel.

His primal instinct to relocate her and shield her from

any adverse action was logical. His nephew or niece—no, his *son or daughter*—deserved every resource at his command to ensure a safe and healthy start in life. The sexual attraction was another blindsider.

The women he dated would never settle for 'clean and comfortable' accommodation in any circumstances. The woman he'd coerced into marrying him was an enigma, hiding more than she revealed.

As he lay on his bed, reliving their conversation, the tight rein he kept on his emotions finally cracked. Images flickered through his brain like a movie screening: the secret signals between him and Louise at strict formal meals with his parents, late-night covert snacks watching clandestine television in his room. Her radiant face when she and Leon had confided they were in love. Boyhood games with his best mate, double-dating in their teens. Standing proudly beside him as best man at their wedding.

The dam broke. The tears flowed for his spontaneous, vibrant sister. For his brother-in-law, friend and confidant. For the beloved couple who would never hold and cherish their child.

He rolled over, buried his face into the pillow. Guttural, heart-wrenching sobs racked his body and soul.

Alina was already in the lobby when Ethan arrived fifteen minutes early the next morning. Her treacherous senses responded to his lithe movement as he strode across the pavement. She felt skittish, illogically animated, despite the stern talking-to she'd given herself as she'd showered and prepared to leave.

The delivery of her breakfast at seven-thirty had finally awoken her, still fully dressed on top of the bed. Years of routine had enabled her to shower, pack and be settling her account within an hour. Years of self-enforced solitude had her wishing she could hail a cab and run.

Stylishly dressed in tailored grey trousers and a short-sleeved dark green shirt, Ethan was halfway to the reception desk when he veered towards her. Her pulse skipped at the sight of his tanned muscular arms. Her cheeks flamed at the memory of his touch, his oh-so-light kiss on her brow. *Had* to be hormone madness. She refused to contemplate any alternative explanation.

'Good morning, Alina. You look refreshed. Sleep well?'

She recoiled from the full impact of the 'seduction smile' Louise had mentioned. Quickly recovered.

'Yes, thank you. I'm ready to go.' As she bent to collect her suitcase their fingers collided, adrenaline spiked. She jerked hers away at the same moment his body stiffened.

'Gentleman's prerogative,' he murmured, picking up both pieces of luggage.

She walked silently beside him to the street, where a chauffeur waited by the open boot of a limousine—same car, different driver.

'I'll programme the car hire number into your phone. Use it whenever you go out alone.' He glanced at her as he stowed her luggage. Quickly added, 'I appreciate you're used to being independent, but since Monday you and our child are my family. I take care of what's mine.'

For a moment she resented his over-protective attitude, before realising the baby took precedence. As it should. She'd agreed to live the Ethan James lifestyle so she'd have to adapt and conform.

'I'll try.'

'Thank you. We'll need your solicitor's address.' As they drove off towards the harbour tunnel he offered her his mobile. 'Call his office and arrange to have your papers ready for pick-up.'

'Already done. He'll see us when we arrive.' His surprised expression forced her to explain. More than she'd wanted to. 'I have his mobile number. He dealt with everything after... I was pathetically incapable of doing anything—couldn't make decisions, couldn't think. I...'

'Was reacting normally to grief.' His hand covered hers. 'I understand, Alina.'

'Um... He's a good man. His office is my Australian address.' *I shouldn't find your touch so comforting.*

'It might be expedient to change it to mine. You'll be living with me at least until next year.'

Living with him yet not together. Next year?

Too many decisions in too short a time.

'Can I decide later?' She met his gaze, found mild curiosity not censure.

'Of course. Speak up if you feel I'm rushing you.'

Like the leader of a stampede. Not an opinion he'd take kindly to.

She stared out of the window as the traffic crawled along, reliving the incident in the lobby. Ethan had been looking down when their fingers touched. Had he noticed she'd removed her ring?

From the stories she'd heard, and the photos she'd seen, she'd formed a vague, admirable image of Louise's successful brother—had had no interest in knowing anything more. The man at her side was flesh and blood, solid and real. She was learning to gauge the inflections in his voice, to interpret the messages in his expressive blue eyes. Her body involuntarily responded to him. The image had been far safer for her mental stability.

Ethan held back when the solicitor greeted Alina with a hug and soft words, allowing them privacy. The handshake he received was firm, the assessing gaze slightly disconcerting. Was he being compared to her husband? This man knew the full story of her bereavement, had been there for her when... What about the Fletcher family? Where had *they* been? Where were they now?

He noticed movement at her side as they were led to a

small office, arched his neck to confirm the nervous finger ritual. His heart lurched when her features crumpled at the sight of the archive box on the otherwise empty desk. Once they were alone she drew a long breath, before walking forward and lifting the lid with unsteady fingers.

On their return journey Ethan booted up his laptop. His gaze flicked from the screen to the box containing her life history, on the seat between them. Moved to her left hand. To her bare ring finger.

He was acutely aware of the toll the visit had taken on her. Her fumbling through the box's contents and forced shallow breathing had torn him apart. He still hadn't finished sorting the personal papers he'd brought from Spain.

Gently taking hold of her wrist, and letting what she held fall back inside, he had closed the lid. 'Not here. Not now.'

He'd lifted the box from the desk, then linked his fingers with hers. After speaking to her solicitor for a few minutes they'd left.

She hadn't spoken since she'd introduced him in the office, apart from a mumbled goodbye. Now, as their eyes met, she blinked, swiftly looked away. Primal instinct urged him to dump his laptop on the seat, wrap his arms around her and kiss her till the haunted expression in her eyes changed to—to what? Desire? Passion?

Get real, James. Where the hell is your head?

'I'm not being very helpful, am I? But I haven't needed to access them since probate was granted.'

He heard the slight accent in her trembling voice. Caused by deep emotion?

Putting his computer aside, he clasped her slender hands in his. 'Working hands. Not salon-pampered. Well-cared-for working hands,' he murmured. 'Seven years is a long time to be running and hurting. Finding yourself alone and pregnant so soon after you'd finally begun to connect again must have been traumatic, and yet you found the courage to confront me.'

She let out a tiny huff of a laugh. 'I considered you to be the approachable one in the family. I'd never have been brave enough to tackle your parents alone.'

'That will not happen,' he stated forcefully. 'I won't allow them to interfere, so we'll meet them together after the wedding. I have friends who'll be witnesses. Is there someone you'd like as yours? Family? Friend?'

She had an alluring, pensive air as she pondered his question. *Was* there anyone? There had to be relatives somewhere.

'I have no family. My mother left me with her parents when I was four. Never said who my father was. I haven't heard from her since. Grandma's cancer was quick and aggressive, the year after I finished school, and Grandpa had a heart attack three months later.'

Soulful violet eyes held his for a long, long moment; resolve flickered there, then glowed.

'There are a few people I've kept in touch with. I'll have to think.'

Her tension had eased and her voice was steadier. She appeared to have accepted the reality of their situation. His admiration for her grew, along with another indefinable impression.

'Our next appointment is at one,' he said hastily, not wanting to dwell on the effect she had on him. 'So we have plenty of time.' He released her, reached for his laptop. 'And I think you are brave enough for anything, Alina Fletcher.'

'Thank you.'

He was wrong, but Alina accepted his compliment rather than set him straight. He considered her courageous. Would he believe the same if he knew her decisions were driven by the conviction that she'd be unable to feel any maternal bonding ever again?

'I mean it. Coping with all this must be painful.'

He opened the box.

Excruciating. Like having old wounds ripped open with no anaesthetic. 'It had to happen sometime.' *And it must be now.*

She moved the box closer to her side. 'I'll find what we need.'

Her birth certificate and papers relevant to her mother were on the top, where they'd fallen. Nothing heartrending there. She passed them to him, willed her hands not to shake as she dragged a buff envelope from the bottom. She held her breath, forced herself to focus.

Concentrate on the two you need. Ignore the rest.

Icy fingers fisted round her heart. She clenched her teeth as she carefully removed two certificates. Tucking them under her hip, she waited until he'd finished entering information, then filed away the papers he'd used.

'I'll do the rest.' She heard the tremor in her tone, stubbornly persisted, needing to retain some privacy. Needing to keep the walls up and solid. 'It's *my* past.'

He studied her with an intensity that made her insides quiver. 'If you're sure?'

She wasn't. She had no choice. 'Thank you.'

He settled the computer on her lap, ensuring it was stable. 'I understand.' He paused. 'You haven't eaten a lot this morning, have you? Fancy an early lunch?'

How could he tell? 'I had toast and fruit—enough after that lovely meal last night.' Truth was she'd had to force the food down, and she still wasn't hungry.

His eyebrows twitched almost imperceptibly. His interest wasn't for her alone. She let him win.

'Chicken salad with crusty bread sounds tempting. Will the dining room be open?'

'We'll have Room Service.' He pulled out his mobile.

She tuned him out as she typed names, locations, dates.

She recited, *They are words, figures, nothing more* in her head. Her newly unadorned finger mocked the information she entered.

'Done,' he told her. 'We'll eat, then deal with the celebrant. Changing your phone supplier has to be done in person, so we'll combine that with a visit to the jeweller.'

She met the steely resolve in his eyes. He was locking her into her promise. There'd be no reneging allowed.

His mouth curved into a persuasive smile. 'It won't be so bad, Alina. You'll have time to adjust to life with me until the wedding. Any functions I ask you to attend during our marriage will be quiet occasions, with people I trust.'

'I made a list this morning.' That was better. Keep the conversation on standard stuff.

This time his eyebrows actually arched. 'What sort of list?'

'Things to do. Everyone who'll have to be notified that I'm relocating. Most of my official stuff goes to Crow's Nest.' She couldn't stop the catch coming into her voice. 'Louise used to check the mailbox in Barcelona for me sometimes.'

'We'll need to arrange for it to be redirected. Do you have a base there?'

'No, I rented rooms on a casual basis. When I was away the owner stored my stuff for a small fee.'

'We'll fly over later, so you can decide what to bring back.'

She gave a short, hollow laugh. He made it sound like a day trip to another state. 'Hardly worth a trip. There's just an old suitcase and two plastic boxes.'

His turn to be confounded. 'That's all you have?'

Shoot, she'd spoken impulsively to a very astute man. She pictured the cold steel unit she'd visited once, fought the hard clench in her abdomen. Couldn't lie. Couldn't look into those perceptive eyes either.

'Everything else I own is in storage. I don't go there.'
Mentally *or* physically.

'Too painful.' He made it a statement.

Guilt tempered with empathy overrode her self-pity. His
grief was new, raw, and he had to cope with the aftermath
of the accident. He was processing the estate personally.
She'd let her solicitor take charge.

'I'm sorry, Ethan. I haven't been very sympathetic to
your loss. I've been too wrapped up in myself.' She covered his hand with hers. 'You've had so much to deal with
and still managed to be patient with me.'

'That's easy.' His voice hummed with tenderness. He
flipped his hand to enfold hers. 'You're carrying our
child.' His sudden grin took her by surprise. 'Do you have
a things-to-buy list?'

She responded with a light laugh. 'I've jotted down a
few things. Why?'

'Just wondering. All done?'

She frowned, realised he was referring to the marriage
application, and felt the lightness of the mood change.

'Not quite.' She returned to the keyboard and added the
final data. When she looked up his head was averted, as it
had been when he'd made the call.

'I've finished, Ethan. Thank you for giving me privacy.'

'No problem, Alina.'

The car pulled in to the kerb as he stowed the computer
in its bag.

Their lunch was delivered to a family suite. Afterwards
Alina watched TV while Ethan went to another room to
take a phone call. She viewed without seeing or hearing.
Was he *ever* off duty? Her guilt resurfaced. The time and
effort he was devoting to her meant less for his expand-
ing empire.

The telephone's ring made her jump. Should she answer

it? Thankfully Ethan came through and told Reception to send their visitor up.

Too late to change her mind.

She swallowed the lump in her throat, tamped down her qualms. Steeled herself to act like a newly engaged woman. For his sister and brother-in-law. For their baby.

The celebrant was friendly, bright and efficient. She guided them through the procedure, gracefully declined a drink and promised to lodge the paperwork immediately. The wedding was set for Sunday, April the twentieth at five p.m.

Within fifteen minutes of her departure they were on their way to his apartment.

CHAPTER FIVE

OPULENT WAS THE word that came to mind as Alina stood in her own lavish en suite. *This is my home until the end of the year.*

She ran her fingertips across the marble surfaces—pure, cool luxury—but felt wary of touching the shiny chrome taps in case she left marks.

Bright stunned eyes stared at her from the pristine mirror. Walls the palest of pale mint-green complemented darker green mottled floor tiles, the crystal-clear shower. Matching it all were the softest, fluffiest towels she'd ever snuggled her face into.

She washed her hands, massaged moisturiser into her skin, breathing in its mild perfume.

She loved the beautifully appointed bedroom too. Also with a green theme, nothing bright or glaring, and as tranquil as a country spring morning—including a painting of a clear stream flowing between banks of willow trees. It was her own calming space, where she might be able to achieve meditation.

Sitting cross-legged on the luxurious cream carpet, she rested her elbows on her knees. Shut her eyes. *Black terror.* They flew open. She concentrated on the rural scene. *Breathe in. Breathe out. Count slowly. Count the flowers in the grass. Count the trees or rocks. Block out everything else.* Her inner fears receded—a little.

She stretched, unravelling her legs to lie flat, gazing up at the downlights strategically recessed in the ceiling. By tucking her chin in tight she could see her toes. For how much longer? She rolled over to do twenty push-ups. Did the building have a gym? If she didn't work she'd need to start exercising more.

She brushed her hair and went to join Ethan in the spacious open living area. Too tidy. Too clean. To her, not lived-in. No magazines or books scattered around. No bowls of fruit or nuts. The only personal touches were two framed photos on one shelf of a too organised bookcase.

His dark hair showed over the top of the long red couch, his low, rich voice lured her forward. As if sensing her, he turned, spoke into the mobile held to his ear. 'Hang on a minute.' He covered the mouthpiece, studied her with reflective cobalt eyes. 'Okay?'

Her reward, when she nodded, was a full-blown lethal Ethan James smile that blew her composure sky-high. 'Give me ten minutes. If you're thirsty, I'll have coffee.'

The kitchen area was TV-cooking-show-perfection: black granite benchtops——including an island—with stainless steel appliances. It enforced her earlier assessment. His apartment contained top-of-the-range exclusives with a wood and leather theme. Had he given carte blanche to the same interior designer who'd decorated the hotel?

She hadn't cooked in a kitchen with an island since—since she'd sold the three-bedroom house, mortgaged to the hilt, that she still couldn't bear to see ever again. Not since hired contractors had packed up the contents and put them into storage arranged by her solicitor.

She clamped her teeth together and focused on the coffee machine—top-brand, naturally.

'Bronze pod for me. Biscuits in island cupboard. Top shelf.' His voice floated through the room, accompanied by soft clicks as he dialled another number.

Everything she needed, including a decorative wooden box with the word 'TEA' inlaid on the lid, sat on the bench. She activated the machine for his coffee, then opened the box. A delighted 'Wow...' whispered from her lips. Her blind lucky dip into one of the sixteen compartments of herbal tea—some quite exotic—produced lemon and ginger.

Ethan waited while his project manager verified figures, his eyes tracking Alina as she made two trips, carrying mugs and a plate of biscuits into the lounge. There was nothing hurried in her movements—hadn't been from the moment they met. Except when he'd challenged her about her husband and her child.

His eyes did a slow full-body scan, from the short wavy hair framing her pretty face down to the sleek white blouse, over her still flat abdomen, over slender shapely hips, ending at dainty bare feet. His own body enjoyed every second of the journey.

Quiet and unassuming, she'd have been overshadowed by the vibrant Spanish women he'd chatted up on his visits. Or would she? She disturbed him in a sensual way, new and puzzling, and definitely unwanted in their current circumstances.

'Ethan? You still there?'

The voice in his ear jolted him out of his daydream. Reality ruled.

He gave due praise to his colleague for an urgent problem solved and ended the call. Dropping his mobile by the files on the table, he took an appreciative drink of the strong adrenaline-reviving coffee.

'Thanks for this.' The object of his distracting thoughts was now curled up in one of the lounge chairs with a notebook and pen, completely oblivious to the effect she had on him.

'What's the title of the latest?'

Alina frowned.

He indicated her notebook. 'List?'

'Ah… Personal items. Clothes. What I have won't do for living *your* lifestyle.'

Her voice held an audible hint of resignation that sparked a twinge of sympathy. He understood her reluctance, but couldn't change his stance. He was taking the only course of action he'd be able to live with, irrespective of personal preferences or consequences. Those must be considered collateral damage.

'I've ordered a credit card for you.' He held up his hand to stop her interjecting. 'No argument. Having you here is my decision, so I'll cover any costs you incur because you're living with me.'

'I have money.'

Enticingly stubborn, eyes fiercely defiant, mouth so tantalisingly kissable…

He'd eventually win—just not easily. Every step was a walk in a minefield and they'd hardly entered the paddock. Knowing women as he did, he figured once she began to shop for her growing figure and new social commitments she'd realise he was right.

'Compromise? Accept the card. Use it at your own discretion.'

Her gaze shifted over his shoulder to the photos on the bookshelf. Leon and Louise on their wedding day. With him at a social event. Her eyes softened. She played it down but she'd cared for them too.

He watched neat white teeth bite into a chocolate-covered biscuit, inexplicably imagined them nibbling on his neck. Selecting a plain shortbread, he stretched his legs and crossed his ankles. Wondered what it was about her he found so fascinating.

'Compromise it is. I have final say,' she stated with determination, causing him to chuckle out loud. 'Is there a gym in the building? Or nearby. Until I find a job I'll—'

She stopped as if stunned when his body jerked forward. Coffee dregs splashed onto the table. His eyes narrowed.

A *job*? She wanted to *work*? Hell! He stood, drew in a ragged breath and quelled his exasperation.

'Wait.'

He strode to the kitchen, brought back a cloth and mopped up the mess. She watched him warily. How could he explain his world to a woman who'd depended only on herself for so long?

Sitting by her side, he took her hand in his, felt her resistance. Held on. 'In the social circles I grew up in few women worked. There was always a hint of condescension when my parents spoke of those who did—even those with a profession. My contemporaries are a mixture, mostly by choice. I make no judgement.'

He cupped and tilted her jaw until their eyes met.

'We are different. You've come to me two months pregnant, with limited work skills. Uh-uh.' He quickly placed his thumb over her lips as she stiffened. 'That was not an insult, merely a statement of fact. I admire the diverse ways you've supported yourself, but I'd like you to relax, indulge yourself while you are with me. Accept a little pampering. Let me take care of you both. Please.'

'I'm not sure I know how.'

Her wistful eyes confirmed her words. He waited, liking the way the violet darkened and her brow furrowed as she contemplated the idea.

'Does taking courses constitute work?'

Spontaneous laughter rose in his throat. She was adorable. He hugged her close, pressing his lips to her hair. Wanting to press them to hers.

Rising to his feet, he held out his hand. 'Come with me.'

She hesitated for a second, then accepted his offer. He led her through the kitchen into a short corridor, flicking a hand at two doors on the right.

'Storage and spare.' He opened the door on the left. 'But this is what clinched the deal for me.'

He watched her expression and wasn't disappointed. Her amazement duplicated his when he'd first walked into the not yet finished lap pool/gym area. One glance, one split second, and he'd contracted to buy.

She gawked at the neat array of exercise machines and banks of weights, at the long narrow strip of water. Her lips parted, but he quickly averted any speech with fingers over her mouth.

'Don't…'

Her eyebrows lifted as he spoke.

'Don't you dare say it.'

Her chin lifted defiantly. 'You have no idea what I was thinking,' she claimed into his skin.

He huffed. 'A comparison between our worlds and I refuse to listen to any more.'

She studied the equipment for a moment, then him, and damned if he could define the expression in her eyes. Though he sure as hell knew he wanted to change it.

'Our choices define us, Alina. This is one of my best. My sanctuary from long hours and constant electronic hassle.' He moved behind her, put his hands on her shoulders. 'Now it's yours too. I'll set up lighter weights on any of the machines you want to use. Do you have bathers with you?'

Bathers? Alina's eyebrows scrunched. She'd packed for one or two meetings with a workaholic businessman. The rest of her time would have been spent sightseeing. Depending on the sales, maybe she'd have bought a few bargains. At the last minute she'd thrown in her one evening dress.

She twisted her head to tell him she'd add them to her shopping list. Froze. Her movement had brought her lips close to his. Kissing close. Her legs became jelly. Her mouth as dry as autumn leaves. Her heartbeat a jungle drum message.

His earthy cologne, enhanced by the scent of musky male, encircled her. The hazel rims of his dilated pupils were clearly discernible. Hypnotic eyes drew her in. Heat from his body seared her back, even though their only contact was through his hands. Arousing warmth lured and yet frightened. Distantly familiar. New and alarming.

It was illogical to feel chilled and cheated when he abruptly let her go. Put distance between them.

'Use this area any time you like, though I'd prefer to be here while you do. If the water's too cold I'll up the temperature. Towels are in the cupboard by the door.'

General information, spoken matter-of-factly. He obviously wasn't bothered at all.

Illogical to feel disappointed that his main concern would be the baby's wellbeing. She vowed to make good use of the gym and pool whether he was there or not.

Ethan walked towards the door, berating himself for the rush of desire he'd felt when she'd turned to him. He had to find a way to block this impractical attraction. He chose his women carefully. No homebodies, no clingers. No romantics. Intelligent, beautiful; sometimes both. He shared pleasant evenings and satisfying nights with them. Nothing more.

Alina had no idea how she affected him. She'd probably fly back to Spain tomorrow if she knew what he'd been thinking. How he'd almost kissed her. How much he still wanted to.

Frustrating days, weeks, months loomed ahead. Enforced celibacy with Alina within reach. Limited touching. Yet making their story believable required getting personal, learning each other's personalities and habits. Fast. They had to present a united picture to everyone: a couple mutually attracted enough to have had an ardent fling. It wasn't happening at the moment.

He pivoted round, catching her elbows as she cannoned into him. 'You know something about me, courtesy of my sister. I'm still groping in the dark where you're concerned.

So it's imperative you talk to me, lighten up when we're together.'

He slid one arm around her waist; saw apprehension cloud her eyes.

'We'll let people assume we were lovers…they'll believe I'm the father.' He skimmed his fingertips lightly across her cheek, murmured softly as he lowered his head. 'A man and a woman who've made a baby should at least act as if they've kissed.'

He covered her mouth with his, giving her no chance to thwart him. And his barely restrained libido ran riot. His arousal was swift, unstoppable. Tangling his fingers in her silken curls, he anchored her head while desperately fighting the urge to deepen the kiss.

Willing her lowered eyelids to open, he moved his lips over hers. Pressed a little harder. Her soft lips tasted sweet. Didn't respond.

Nice one, James. Great way to gain her cooperation and trust.

Did he imagine the light tremor under his hands? The tiniest motion of her lips? He eased away. Her eyelids fluttered, opened. His breakneck pulse cranked up another notch at the bemusement in her incredible violet eyes. Lord, he ached to have her even closer, moulded to his hardened form.

Worst idea ever.

He shifted, let his hand slide over her shoulder, down her arm. 'We'll work on it.'

She eyed him with suspicion as she pulled away. 'Yeah, like you need the practice.'

Her offhand comment might have succeeded, if not for its delightful breathless timbre. Deny it all she liked, she'd been affected by his kiss. He rubbed his nape, wishing he could dive into the clear cool water behind him. A few laps fully clothed might diminish his ardour and help regain his sanity. Instead he had another trip in an enclosed car with her by his side. With that too-strong, not-for-her perfume assailing his senses.

With supreme effort he brought the conversation back to household routine. 'The pool is cleaned regularly. The apartment is serviced Monday, Wednesday and Friday mornings. They process any dry cleaning I leave on the kitchen island.'

She looked dazed for a second, then welcomed his change of topic. 'You have security. How do I enter and leave?'

'I've ordered another key card. You can have my spare.' He checked his watch. 'Time to go. Can you be ready in ten minutes?'

Alina wasn't surprised when they were escorted to an exclusive room on the fourth floor above a renowned jewellery store. Entrance to the secure area was gained by virtue of a buzzer and intercom system.

Ethan moved one of the four seats closer to hers, giving the impression of an attentive fiancé. She berated herself for tensing. How could they fool anyone into believing they were a couple?

An elegant, bespectacled man entered, offering congratulations as he placed two ring trays in front of them, another at the end of the cloth-covered table. Alina stared, stunned. Her body involuntarily tried to put distance between her and the brilliant array. The strong arm around her shoulders tightened as if Ethan sensed her agitation.

Dazzling gems in a myriad of colours and settings sparkled and gleamed. Too flashy for her…too many to choose from. There was no comparison to the small diamond in a heart setting that she'd chosen and been kissed over so long ago.

Don't think. Don't remember. This has nothing to do with reality and emotion.

Quiet words were spoken. The jeweller left with the two trays. He returned with a less ostentatious selection. She still couldn't choose, couldn't bring herself to touch.

Ethan caressed her cheek with his knuckles. 'Too much choice, sweetheart? May I?'

Noting his endearment, knowing it was for the benefit of their attendant, she managed a fleeting smile and leant back. She didn't dare speak in case the pain showed in her voice.

Without hesitation he selected an oval amethyst surrounded by tiny diamonds set in gold. Elegant, not showy. Her finger trembled as he guided it on, holding it firmly to stop it sliding off.

Raising her hand, he pressed his lips to her fingers. 'Perfect. Beautiful. *You.*' He kissed her gently.

She knew this was purely for show, knew she had a part to play. So she did what she'd struggled against by the pool. She returned his kiss.

Her heartbeat accelerated. Her body quivered. His hold tightened, his lips firmed. Her fingers crept up his neck, teasing the ends of his hair. She felt giddy, breathless. Cherished.

Until her stomach knotted and fear replaced the floating sensation. Heat flooded her cheeks; she broke away and bent her head to his chest.

Ethan framed her face with his hands, forced her to meet his gaze. Her warm blush was gratifying. Coupled with the soft glow in her violet eyes, it gave an idyllic image of a newly engaged woman.

His own feelings were elusive, and he had no inclination to analyse them here. They were new, overwhelming— might be caused by any one of the upheavals in his life.

He placed the ring to one side, before swapping the tray

for the one at the end of the table. 'Do you prefer a plain or patterned wedding band?'

He'd bet odds that the cross-cut patterned ring she chose was very different from the one she'd worn years ago—not the plain one she'd removed since yesterday. He selected a matching, broader one, then spoke to the jeweller.

'Mine fits. Alina's need to be resized.'

CHAPTER SIX

THEIR NEXT STOP, within walking distance, was his communications supplier. Somehow the end result was a new mobile for Alina with her account bundled with his. Ethan James had a charming way of overruling objections, leaving you feeling as if you'd done *him* a favour.

Like the way he'd cajoled her into an exclusive perfumery store after claiming that he'd noticed her spray bottle was nearly empty. When had *that* happened? Well aware that the one she wore, a Christmas gift, was too strong for her; she was delighted with the new delicate spring fragrance. She'd been aware of the surreptitious looks he'd exchanged with the assistant. What else was he planning?

The arrangements, phone calls, et cetera had all taken time and effort, yet he made it seem simple. To him it was. Decisions were made. Actions followed. Tangible proof of the attributes that had ensured his phenomenal success. Skill and diplomacy would ensure the optimum outcome: a healthy son or daughter.

On their way back to the apartment the car pulled in to the kerb and Ethan unclicked his seatbelt. 'Won't be long.'

He hopped out and the driver moved off. One lap of the block found him waiting to be picked up, now carrying two plastic bags containing rectangular objects with a delicious exotic aroma.

He laughed at her puzzled stare. 'Thai takeaway. Best in town.'

'But…' Of course—the call he'd made while the salesgirl had been demonstrating functions on her new phone.

'Nothing hot or spicy. And what we don't finish tonight

we'll have tomorrow. I've had many a breakfast of reheated Asian food.'

So had she—more from the need to stretch a budget than for pleasure. She laughed as her stomach rumbled. 'I'm hungrier than I thought. Thank you for remembering about the spicy.'

'I remember everything you've told me, Alina.'

His eyes caught hers, held her spellbound. She fought to break the hold, had to stay detached. Letting him in was a risk with too high a cost.

She was happy when he opted to eat in the lounge, claiming casual dining made takeaway taste better. Watching television would provide a break from personal questions and conversation.

At his request she carried two glasses and a carafe of iced water into the lounge, while he brought china, cutlery and the food.

'Tonight it's your choice—apart from reality shows,' he remarked, scooping special fried rice onto two plates.

'I haven't watched much at all these last few years. Hey, not too much on mine.' She stilled his hand, preventing him from overloading the second plate. 'The news is fine by me.'

During the ad breaks they discussed the events of the day—small talk which gave her invaluable insight into the man she'd committed her immediate future to. He wasn't as complimentary about the present government as she'd expected, and spoke sympathetically about lower income earners.

The latter didn't surprise her; she'd experienced his attitude to shop assistants and his own hotel staff. He did surprise her when he patiently explained the intricacies of a technology breakthrough. So she chose a documentary next, figuring it would interest him, knowing she'd like it too. His avid interest in the excavation of an ancient English church which had revealed a former king's remains proved her right.

Ethan's attention strayed during the advertising breaks. Alina would have plenty of time to watch anything she liked in the coming months. It suddenly occurred to him that she'd need something to occupy the hours while he was working. Even if she did sign up for a course or two.

How many people in Sydney had she kept in touch with? Was there anyone she'd confided in? He couldn't imagine how he'd have got through his teens, resisting his parents' expectations, without Leon to confide in. Even Louise, five years younger and flighty as a cuckoo fledgling, had listened and supported him.

Alina had stayed away from Australia. Did that mean there were no close friends here? It was obvious that she carried a deep-seated torment inside. *Damn*, he knew so little about her, but he couldn't bring himself to push too much. He was supposed to be good with people. If he earned her trust maybe she'd confide in him. When he knew the details he was convinced he'd be able to find a way to ease her pain.

Alina stretched as the final credits rolled, then carried their plates to the dishwasher. Ethan followed with the glassware and caught her yawning.

'Ready for an early night? It's been a full-on day for you.' Sympathy showed in his eyes, warmth in his tender expression.

A restful soak in the bath with an intrigue novel appealed more than bed. Did that seem rude? As if she wanted to get away from him?

As if sensing her confusion, he gently took her in his arms, hugged her and let her go.

'Goodnight, Alina. Thank you for being so cooperative. I know it wasn't easy. Sleep well.'

'I survived. Goodnight.' She walked away.

'Alina?'

She turned at the doorway.

'I swear I'll take care of you and our child. Believe me?'

She looked into sincere blue eyes and her doubts subsided. 'Yes, I do.'

This time he didn't stop her, and went back to the lounge. Trying to read reports was a futile exercise. A few strides along the hall was a beautiful woman who stirred him as no one ever had. A woman whose soul-destroying sorrow influenced every decision she made.

Today she'd begun to react naturally—the way he needed her to if they were to convince everyone they'd been lovers. Their supposed affair might have been short, but their mutual attraction had to be evident. On his part it was becoming less of a pretence every time she was near. And from her tentative responses he suspected her buried feelings were beginning to emerge.

Ten past nine. Past morning rush hour. Alina leant on the island, checking her notepad, and glanced down at her well-worn jeans. Added two items to her list. She drank her ice-cold juice, scrunched her nose. Pushed the credit card Ethan had given her in a circle on the granite. Having it didn't mean using it.

He'd knocked on her door early this morning to tell her he was going to his office. Drowsy, needing to use the bathroom, she'd barely acknowledged his remarks. When he'd leaned in to brush her hair from her eyes, his unique smell and the touch of his fingertips had blown her lethargy away, leaving her wide-awake, tingling.

She dropped the pen. This was ridiculous. What could be simpler than writing a list of clothes and accessories to be worn by the wife of a hotshot billionaire? Or was he even richer? Any woman he dated would have no problem filling the page. But she was a nomad, with a meagre pile of cheap, easy-care clothing. Her serviceable underwear would never grace a magazine page or stir a man's libido.

Hey, what was she thinking?

Focus. You only have to buy enough to be presentable for a few weeks.

As she put on weight she'd have to shop again. More expense.

For a second her mind flashed to the investment account. Another buried secret.

Sometime after twelve she sank wearily into a window seat of a busy café. Two bags containing the pathetic results of her attempted retail therapy took the chair beside her. This was hopeless. She'd chickened out every time she'd tried to enter any of the high-fashion boutiques she'd found. Embarrassing Ethan in clothes from the stores she normally frequented wasn't an option. At this rate she'd be in track pants and baggy jumpers right through autumn.

She needed help…didn't know who to ask. She was used to working; now she had all day with nothing to do. Or did she? She'd meant her reference to taking courses as a joke, but now she deemed them a plausible time-filler.

As the waitress walked past, carrying two plates of fish and chips, another idea popped into her head. Taking out her notepad, she began a new list, pushing it aside when her order arrived.

Indulging in a gooey cream-filled pastry didn't solve her wardrobe problem but it tasted good. Drinking Viennese hot chocolate while writing the final items lifted her spirits. Surely he'd give her plenty of notice before expecting her to meet his friends or accompany him to functions?

Ethan sniffed appreciatively as he entered the apartment—later than he'd intended due to an impromptu meeting with his second-in-command. The sooner he implemented the new changes in his workload, the better.

It was a surprise to find the table set for two, even though he'd called, asking her to order dinner from the hotel. There was a bowl of fresh garden salad in the centre, and a bottle of Shiraz waiting to be opened. His home was warm and welcoming—a pleasurable new experience. He shed the trials of his day and moved forward.

'Mmm, smells good. Mushroom sauce, if I'm not mistaken.'

'Hi.' Alina came around the island, carrying water and glasses. 'Dinner will be ready by the time you wash up.'

Placing his laptop on the end of the table, he moved nearer, breathed in flowers and sunshine—perfect for her, enthralling for him. If this were real...

It wasn't.

This morning she'd been dreamy-eyed, and he'd come close to kissing her. He hadn't thought, had merely acted, something he'd need to curb if they were to build a trusting relationship.

'Give me five minutes.'

Alina arranged steak with foil-wrapped baked potatoes on warmed plates, placed hot crusty rolls in a serviette-lined basket. Smiled with satisfaction. Everything looked appetising, hopefully tasted as good. If she could convince him to let her cook and clean she'd feel so much better about their arrangement. Support for the child was one thing—her being totally dependent on him another.

No way was she going to compete with his qualified chefs. She'd serve recipes she felt capable of, even if they weren't gourmet standard. The cookbook she'd bought was for inspiration.

Ethan had already poured his glass of wine when she set down his plate, along with the gravy boat. When she returned with her meal he was waiting by her chair, studying his food across the table. She held her breath while he took his seat.

The sparkle in his eyes when they met hers was unnerving. 'This didn't come from my hotel kitchen, did it?'

'No.' She broke eye contact, her heart sinking. Took a sip of water. If the difference was so obvious she'd already lost.

'Hmm…' He poured gravy, put sour cream on his potato and began to eat.

Her breath caught behind the lump in her throat. Her whole body felt primed for his reaction. She so wanted his approval.

'It's good.' His smile caused her lungs to deflate, the lump to dissolve.

'Not what you're used to?'

'Better.'

She bristled. She didn't need or want pseudo-compliments. 'You don't have to butter me up. I know there's no comparison.'

'I promise I will always tell you the truth, Alina. Since the accident I've ordered meals. They came. I ate often while still working, usually too focused on facts and figures to taste or enjoy it. At home I lived in a void. My way of blocking out the grief, I guess.'

That she understood. 'And I made it worse with my bombshell.'

'No—no way.' He dropped his knife, reached across and took her hand. 'It was as if nothing had real purpose. I avoided thinking about Louise and Leon because then I'd have to accept they were never coming back. I hated knowing I should have been there for them much more than I was.'

She laid her free hand on top of his, subconsciously acknowledging its male texture.

'You felt guilty? Oh, Ethan, there was never, ever, in any conversation I had with them, the slightest hint that you had been anything but a loving and supportive brother and friend. One who'd be there for them in a heartbeat if they needed you. I don't know why they kept their problem a secret. Maybe because shielding those you love from worry goes both ways.'

'Maybe. I keep wondering if there was anything else I could have done for them. All I know is that you've given my life meaning again. I wake in the morning knowing my sister and best friend aren't completely lost to me. I feel—'

He broke off, slowly withdrew his hand, as if unsure of revealing too much emotion.

'Best we eat while it's hot. What other culinary delights do you have planned?' He helped himself to a serving of salad.

'You mean it? You'll really need more than one meal to make a sound judgement.'

'Bring them on.'

His smile as he raised his drink ignited trails of heat along her veins, threatening the solid barriers she'd sworn to maintain.

'Here's to many more home-cooked dinners together.'

They clinked glasses. Alina let her water slide, cool and refreshing, down her throat.

'It's on the understanding that you tell me if it's not good or not to your taste. If I take over the housework as well it'll fill my days. I'm rethinking the courses idea.'

'I'm locked into a cleaning contract, so that's a different proposition. Anyway, in a few months you might be grateful for the help.'

And with the purchase he'd arranged today she might also reconsider.

She pondered his statement as she cut into her steak. 'You may be right. It's not easy work, but it pays the bills. Losing their hours here may cause hardship for someone.'

'You discuss what you'd like done with whoever comes. I'll notify the company that you have the authority.'

'Thank you.'

So she'd also done cleaning during her nomadic life, had not been too proud to accept domestic employment. Showed consideration for other manual workers. Every conversation gave Ethan more insight into her—thankfully without her realising how much she revealed.

'Are you a sports fan?' she asked. 'I know Leon and Louise were Sydney Swans supporters and watched the games on the internet. You don't appear to have much free time.'

'We never missed a home game when they were here. I'm still a fully paid-up member of the club, and get to go occasionally. It wasn't the same without them, and the Starburst Group has been growing, demanding more time. I often wind down at night watching whatever sport's being televised. Clears the mind.'

He asked which countries she'd been to as they ate fruit and ice cream for dessert. She revealed that she'd become fluent in Spanish, Italian and French, got by in other languages, and considered it no big deal. His Spanish was basic, so to him it was an enviable achievement.

He made hot drinks while she stacked the dishwasher.

Alina struggled to keep awake during the short late newscast. Had to stop herself from falling against his shoulder and nodding off.

'Do you mind if I go to bed? I'm not usually so tired… It has to be the change of environment or the pregnancy, so hopefully it won't last long.'

'We'll check if you need extra vitamins on Monday. You go and rest.'

'Thank you.'

Admitting her failure at clothes shopping when he'd been so complimentary about her meal seemed a backward move. She'd try again tomorrow.

She had no idea that her disappointment showed in her face, but Ethan noticed, and couldn't resist drawing her into his arms for comfort.

'Dinner was delicious, Alina. I know this isn't easy for you, but I promise we'll work out any problems that arise. Tell me if anything bothers you and I'll try to put it right.'

Her eyes were bright as she accepted his vow, and without conscious effort he bent his head to kiss her, moving his lips softly over her mouth. He felt a slight movement in her lips, heard a muted sound from her throat. Reluctantly raising his head, he encountered bemusement tinged with sadness.

He relaxed his hold, stepped back and tried to keep his voice stable. 'Sleep well, Alina. I should be home earlier tomorrow.'

Watching her go, he cursed himself for his lack of restraint. Tonight they'd really begun to connect, and he feared she might rebuild her barriers overnight. He cursed his parents for the hang-ups that governed his thinking, tainted his ability to feel deep emotion with others apart from Louise and Leon.

His short, raw, ironic laugh was spontaneous. Those two had had no qualms about showing their love—privately or in public. Eye contact, touching, kissing—all had been as natural to them as breathing. He'd never, ever seen either of his parents show any tenderness for each other, never seen a sympathetic gesture like the one Alina had given him tonight.

Not wanting to dwell on why kissing Alina made him feel less alone, he reasoned doing it when they could be seen would substantiate their story of a short and overwhelming passion. But it had to be believable—from both of them. No holding back, no tension. He was a grown man, well able to curb any sexual urges.

* * *

Today had been better. Alina placed her special purchases on the coffee table before carrying the other bags into her bedroom. She'd still avoided high-fashion boutiques and exclusive salons, but with her more positive attitude she'd had some success.

In a big department store she'd found two summer dresses and a lightweight jacket to go with either of them on cooler days. The shoes and bag she'd bought also went with both. She had limited her new underwear purchases, knowing she'd soon outgrow them.

After showering and changing she settled in the lounge to be productive. She had a cup of tea, a block of nut chocolate and a home renovation show on the television. There was plenty of time before Ethan was due home.

His consideration might be because of the baby she carried, his attention and kisses might be to make their relationship more believable, but she had to admit she found them nice. Nothing more. She hadn't been cared for since she'd fled from Australia, too cowardly to face anyone or anything that raised painful memories.

Mentally planning tonight's dinner, she opened her present to herself…

CHAPTER SEVEN

SUBDUED NOISES CAME from the lounge as Ethan opened the front door—the earliest he'd been home for months. Putting his briefcase and packages down, he strode in. He hadn't let Alina know he was on his way, meaning to surprise her. Instead he was the one who stopped short, spellbound by the vision in front of him.

Alina was ensconced on the settee, her eyes lowered, completely absorbed in the material in her hands, her tucked-up legs hidden by a flowing pleated floral skirt. He took in the sleek line of her neck, the satin glow of her cheeks, the sweep of her dark brown lashes. A perfect picture of natural beauty, and for the rest of this year she was his to admire.

He stepped forward, willing her to look up, anxious not to startle her. Her own subtle aroma enhanced her new perfume, making his nostrils flare, stirring his blood. She sensed his presence, gave him a shy glad-to-see-you smile that zinged straight to his heart.

With two paces, completely forgetting his mental declaration of self-control, he was beside her, his arms around her. He bent his head, glimpsed the reticence in her eyes and somehow managed to pull back. Couldn't stop his grip intensifying, though.

'Ouch.' His left leg jerked. He massaged his thigh and chuckled. 'I've been slapped a few times. Never stabbed.'

Alina paled, staring at the small metal needle in her fingers. 'I… I'm sorry. I…you… I was sewing. You made me forget I…'

He took the offending weapon and placed it on the coffee table alongside an array of coloured thread. 'My fault. I was distracted by the entrancing sight on my settee. Didn't allow for hidden danger.'

She blushed at the compliment. 'It's not sharp. Do you want to check if there's bleeding?'

The nervous tremor in her voice, plus the remorse in her eyes, acted like a dousing of cold water. He'd shocked her, shamed himself. This macho being, acting on impulse, wasn't him. He couldn't explain even to himself, didn't know why.

He moved away, dragging his fingers through his hair, trying to concentrate on the essential reason for her presence in his apartment. Five days ago he'd had no idea she existed. To her he was the preferred solution to a situation she didn't want long-term.

Boardroom strategy—that was what he needed. He had to get back to his original plan. Convince everyone they'd been lovers. Keep his distance in private. Best solution for everyone—especially the woman observing him now with dark, cautious eyes.

He picked up the cloth stretched over a round wooden hoop from her lap. Various shades of green thread had already been woven into the outline of a country cottage garden.

'Interesting. Pretty scene.'

'Small, light, fits into my backpack and challenging enough to keep me occupied in the evenings.' She took it from him and laid it on the table. 'It's absorbing—stops me from thinking too much.'

'And you have a weapon handy if you're attacked,' he teased, standing up and pulling her to her feet. 'New dress? Beautiful.' His scroll from head to foot was deliberately quick, yet he still felt an appreciative clench. 'Good shopping trip?'

Her smile faded. 'Not my favourite occupation. Having

no idea what size I'm going to be in a few weeks doesn't help. How was *your* day?'

'Busy. I received a delivery today. Let's sit down.'

She tensed as he reached into his inside pocket and brought out a small black box.

Taking her left hand in his, he slid the amethyst ring onto her finger. 'Perfect fit.'

She stared down at their joined hands. Her posture slumped.

'Alina.' Her head came up. He had a quick glimpse of sorrow, then it cleared. 'Remember why we're doing this. Who it's for.'

'I know.' She freed her hand then crossed her arms, hugging her body. 'It's… All this isn't what I expected.' Her mouth tried to form a smile. Didn't quite make it. 'I won't let you down.'

So brave, so determined to do the right thing, no matter how heart-wrenching her memories. So delightfully confused by her physical reaction to him.

Basic instinct urged him to hold her, protect her from more pain. But it wouldn't work for either of them. She wasn't going to stay. She had emotional baggage that his expectations of her were exacerbating. He had an agenda, an empire to build. He'd have a young child completely dependent on him.

He accepted he'd never be as approachable as his sister. She'd rebelled outwardly against their parents' attitude, defied them to marry the man she loved, and emigrated to escape their continued interference. He'd channelled everything into developing his company, determined never to emulate his parents and end up in a cold, loveless marriage.

Better to stay a bachelor, to enjoy female company without emotional entanglements. Strict rules and no pain when it ended. Becoming a single father at this stage might throw his life out of whack, testing him to the full, but he'd cope, adjust and succeed.

And on the topic of interference, Alina needed to be aware of a major factor.

'My parents won't be invited, so please don't wear the ring in public until after the wedding.'

She frowned, not understanding his meaning.

He explained. 'I've gathered Louise mentioned their attitude on social standing and—unbelievable in today's world—"breeding". They take snobbery to a new height. You're in or you're out, no middle ground.'

His gut clenched as he recalled their fights with Louise, their turning on him when he had defended her and Leon.

'They were never happy with Leon being my best friend because, although he was wealthy enough to give his children the best education affordable, his father had begun his working life as a bricklayer. His building firm is my main contractor, always will be. When Leon asked their permission to marry Louise they practically threw him out, forbade him from seeing her.'

'Which obviously didn't work. Couldn't they see how happy they were? How much he…he adored her?' Her voice faltered over the last few words.

'That didn't factor in their thinking. Our wedding may not be conventional, but I'd like it to be an occasion you'll remember fondly. There'll be no one there who might upset you in any way. Telling them afterwards gives them no choice but to accept that we're married.'

'I understand.' She began to slip the ring off. He stopped her.

'Keep it on at home. For me.' He brought her fingers to his lips for a second, then stood up. 'I've also got something to help occupy your time. Close your eyes.'

Alina had no fear of natural darkness. It was her own internal black world that tormented her. So, as soon as she sensed him leave she covered her eyes with her hands and opened them.

Shame at the way she'd swayed forward for his kiss, had almost succumbed to him, fizzed in her stomach. At the time she'd seemed to be weightless, floating, with no power over her limbs or her actions. She didn't resist. Didn't participate.

When he'd sprung away the bewilderment had had her blathering like a drunk, made worse by his shocked expression and deliberate retreat, putting distance between them. He'd recovered first, bringing normality back to the conversation, seemingly putting their embrace behind him.

That was what she had to do—act like a mature woman. She took long deep breaths, calming her stomach. Her defensive shields were solid. Mind you, if they began to crumble…

'Keep them shut.'

He'd returned.

'Or covered.'

Must be looking at her.

She heard some clunks, and the drag of the coffee table. The cushions dipped as he sat next to her. Now her stomach sizzled with suspense.

'This is for you.'

She stared in astonishment at the red laptop with matching mouse and butterfly motif pad. Alongside lay a hardcover notebook plus a boxed set of pens. Her hand flew to her mouth.

Grinning broadly, Ethan gently lowered it, then lifted the computer's lid. 'The password's "bluesheen" at the moment.'

'You bought this for me?' Her incredulous gaze swung from his face to the laptop. Twice. She'd never had a computer of her own. Not with the nomadic life she lived.

Though lately she'd been considering one of those light-weight notepads.

'All yours. Complete with bag so you can take it anywhere.'

She touched the keyboard cautiously, her fingers tripping across the keys. He caught one and pressed it on 'start'. The screen lit up and her eyes eagerly followed the process.

This was *hers*. Really hers. She turned to the man watching her with dark, hypnotic eyes. Swayed towards him again. Stopped. Touched his arm.

'Thank you.'

She was lost for words.

So was Ethan for a moment. His heart pumped and the lump in his throat threatened to choke him. He'd seen the intent to kiss him in those sparkling violet eyes, and perversely he rued her change of mind.

'You're welcome. Mouse or touch?' The connection for the wireless mouse was already in the port.

'I've always used a mouse. I'll have to learn to touch.'

Learn to touch him?

His chest tightened. He obviously hadn't listened to his own pep talk.

She quickly bent forward and began to type in the password; her hair only partially covering her reddening skin. He wasn't fooled by the action, and surmised she'd had the same thought.

'Why "bluesheen"?' The catch in her voice spoke volumes.

'Came out of the air.' *She'd been wearing blue the day they met.* 'Easily changed.'

'I love it. What are all these icons for?'

Her eyes shone with excitement, heightening his own pleasure.

'Finding out is part of the fun. I've added the internet, an email account and cloud backup.' He opened the notebook. 'All the passwords are written in here, plus relevant names with phone numbers—including my IT guy, who set it up. He's offered to give you one-on-one lessons if you like. I'm not too bad—he's brilliant.'

'Why? You know I won't be staying, so why are you doing this?'

He shrugged. 'Don't argue—just accept it. You can enrol for online courses…there's plenty to choose from.' He lightened the mood by joking. 'Imagine all the lists you'll be able to create. And you know you'll enjoy finding recipes.'

'You may not think so when you have to eat my weird concoctions.' She smiled back.

'I'll take my chances.'

His mobile rang. Bad timing. She was more at ease with him now than she'd ever been. Muttering a light curse, he wrenched the offending instrument out of his pocket, checked the caller. With a grimace he stood up.

'I have to take this. Do you have dinner planned?'

'Yes, but not started.'

'Save it for tomorrow. I'll book somewhere quiet where we can talk.' He got to the end of the lounge and glanced back, his dazzling smile sending heatwaves to every region of her body.

'You really do look exquisite, Alina.'

Another genuine compliment that gave her confidence another boost. It was hard to believe he'd bought her such a thoughtful gift she'd use in so many ways. The expense hardly registered with him. The time and effort he'd taken meant so much more.

Shutting down the laptop, she watched each process avidly, wanting to take in every little detail before carefully closing the lid. When she packed everything into the bag she found a charger and a set-up manual.

She'd intended to try shopping again tomorrow—now she'd rather stay home and browse. Anything she didn't understand would go on a list to be shown to Ethan. Although at least one session with his IT specialist was a must.

After putting her embroidery into a craft bag, she went to her room to give her minimal make-up a light touch-up.

As she walked along the hall the muffled mingling of running water with what sounded like a mistuned radio came through his door. Curiosity made her stop and press an ear to the wood. The slightly off-key singing persisted, too indistinct for her to recognise the vaguely familiar song.

The shower stopped. She scurried away, her cheeks burning. If he caught her would he be angry or amused?

She couldn't get that tune out of her head…couldn't remember the title. Couldn't ask him.

For Alina the family-owned restaurant with its discreet booth tables was ideal. She hadn't asked the name of the suburb; that would be making it a memory for keeping. Though, perversely, she knew she'd never forget the tasty meal, the restful music from the live band…her attentive escort.

Couples were moving on to the small dance floor and she watched them with envy. She had once known how it felt to be held tenderly, barely moving in a traditional lovers' slow shuffle. Without warning, images of all the women Ethan might have entertained here broke into her daydream. Stunning. Polished. Fashion connoisseurs who'd dance faultlessly.

'Hey.' His deep voice cut through her thoughts and she turned to meet his amused gaze. 'You're very pensive. Care to share?'

Not in a million years. The predictable warmth stole up her neck. 'Just enjoying the music. The meal was delicious. Is this a favourite haunt of yours?'

'A friend brought me here last year. I kept it in mind,

waiting for a special occasion.' He put his hand invitingly, palm up, on the table. 'Never found one until today.'

Mesmerised by his incredible dark blue eyes, she laid her hand in his. He began to stroke her knuckles with his thumb. She dismissed the danger signals in her head. Her skin tingled from his touch. Her throat dried up, and liquid wasn't the solution.

Had she been so sensitive to male contact before? Had her hormones gone this crazy ten years ago? Those memories were locked away, never, ever to be revisited.

Ethan had seen her wistful expression as she watched the couples moving around the floor, her body swaying in time to the music. She was in another world. A long-lost world? He wanted her in the here and now, totally focused on *them*.

She'd provoked an acute rush of satisfaction when she'd given him her hand. His heartbeat had spiked, unaccustomed yearning snaking through him. The eons-old urge of man to protect his child? Or primitive gratification that its mother trusted him to safeguard them both?

'Dance with me, Alina.'

She glanced across the room, shook her head. 'I'll embarrass you. I only do modern stuff with no touching. Nothing like this.' She gestured towards the dancers. 'They are so graceful.'

'No touching *ever*?' His eyebrows rose in disbelief. 'Or only since…?' He left his question unfinished, didn't need a reply.

She tried to free her hand, merely succeeded in twisting it so that his thumb pressed into her palm. Stopped resisting when he resumed his slow caress. Was he playing fair? Touching and kissing hadn't been mentioned when they'd first made their agreement. There'd been no reason in that emotionless civil conversation.

'You're denying something you really want, Alina. Trust me. You'll regret it if you don't.'

Cautious eagerness dawned in her sceptical eyes. 'Your toes might regret it if I do.'

He laughed, walked round the table without letting her go. 'Let's find out.'

Drawing her to her feet, he led her onto the dance floor. He placed her left hand on his shoulder, his right hand on her waist, then clasped her free hand in his, over his heart. Each movement was slow, deliberate. Non-threatening to her peace of mind.

'Look at me, Alina.'

Alina did.

'Trust me.'

She did.

'Let me guide you.'

He held her firmly, murmured in her ear and directed her steps with his thighs. His breath tickled her earlobe, his cologne filled her nostrils. Heat radiated from his touch as he compensated for her initial stumbling. She let her muscles go loose, giving him full control of her movements.

They glided round the room as if floating on air. Her eyelids fluttered. The music combined with the man to create an ethereal realm she wished she could stay in for ever. No more sorrow. No more loneliness. She gave a soft sigh, glanced up—into a searing wave of cobalt desire.

Their feet stopped moving; their bodies swayed in time with the rhythm of the music. She couldn't swallow, couldn't breathe, yet she felt his deep intake of air. Felt...

Guilt—as strong and shattering as when she'd been the only survivor.

The magic dissolved into stark reality. She began to shudder—couldn't stop. She tried to pull away, found herself being ushered to their table and gently settled into her seat. The strong arm stayed around her, supportive, grounding.

A moment later there were muffled words in a concerned tone, a deep reply. Deep as Ethan's voice but clipped, disconnected, not like him at all. She did know that it was his fingers lifting her chin, and hazily wondered why they trembled.

'Alina?'

She blinked, saw his pale face, his brow creased in concern. She bent her head, unable to find words to explain.

His hand dropped. 'Let's go home. We'll talk there.'

'No.' Plaintive, even to her own ears.

'We have to.' Soft-spoken. Decisive.

They drove home in silence. Alina counted cars as they passed, timed their stops at traffic lights—anything to keep from dwelling on the talk ahead. Could she feign a headache? Believable in the circumstances, but delaying the inevitable.

If Ethan James wanted to talk, they'd talk—sooner rather than later.

CHAPTER EIGHT

ETHAN KEPT HER hand in his after locking the car, only letting go to allow her to enter the apartment first. How come she'd not only become used to that small intimacy but welcomed it? She dropped her bag onto the island, walked round to make hot drinks.

'Would you like coffee?' She reached for a bronze pod.

'Make it a black pod. I need a strong kick.' He was already walking towards the hall, discarding his jacket as he went.

Good idea. She picked up her bag and headed for her room to change. Jeans and a casual top were more conducive to a serious discussion.

In the few minutes it took her he'd returned, and their drinks were ready in the lounge.

'Biscuits?'

She shook her head. 'No, thank you.'

His lips twitched at the corners, just a tad. 'Chocolate?'

So he'd noticed the wrappers in the bin and her stash in the cupboard. Again she declined. Why the heck was she being so formal? Last night the atmosphere had been light and friendly. Today even better. Until that moment when the past had reasserted its claim on her.

She sat in the corner of the settee, drawing her legs up tight when he chose one of the armchairs, putting extra space between them. She stared at the mug in her hands, dreading the words she might hear, fearing he might be annoyed if she couldn't or wouldn't answer.

'We have to talk, Alina.'

The sombre tone of his voice brought her head up. His eyes had the sharp intensity she remembered from when she'd taken over filling in the marriage application. As if reading her inner thoughts was the only thing that mattered at this moment.

'This isn't going to work the way we are now. I've never had a problem with women before, but now I'm second-guessing what to do. For our baby's sake we have to convince everyone we've had a passionate affair.'

'And I'm failing miserably. I'm sorry, Ethan. I don't know how… There was only ever… I…' The words wouldn't come. She bit the inside of her lip, looked down at her white knuckles gripping the hot mug.

His hollow laugh snapped her gaze back to his face.

'I'm not doing much better, Alina. I never knew grief could be so overwhelming, so soul-draining. You brought some light into my dark world. Now you're here—so sweet and beautiful, so vulnerable.'

He leant forward, hands clasped between spread knees.

'I can't deny the physical attraction. Can't fathom whether it's linked with knowing you're carrying Louise's baby. Tonight—the music, dancing with you in my arms— I was in a new world. I frightened you, and I'm sorry—'

'No. It wasn't you,' she cut in. 'There've been so many first-for-a-long-times for me, it's bewildering. I feel like I've been thrown back into mainstream city living without a guidebook.'

She suddenly realised she was mimicking his stance, sharing his desire for their plan to succeed. Something shifted inside her, as if the extra tightening around her heart that had come when she'd heard about Louise and Leon had slipped a few notches. The old pain remained. She'd accepted only death would bring *that* to an end.

'It's only been four days. I didn't expect to stay in Australia—much less with you.' She smiled, watched as his eyes softened and his brow cleared. His answering smile lifted her heart. 'I'm rusty in all the social niceties of sharing a home and…and things.'

He shifted as if to stand, sank back. 'I don't have a good track record there. I've only had two live-in relationships, neither here, and neither lasting more than five months. Both confirmed my belief that I'm not cut out for domesticity. I'm too pragmatic—and, as one of them pointed out, I've no romance in my soul. Assuming I *have* a soul.'

'That's better for us, isn't it?' Although did she really want him to stop his gentle touches, his scorching looks? His kisses?

'No.' Sharp. Instant.

He came to sit at the other end of the couch, folding one leg up, spreading one arm along the back. She wriggled into her corner and listened.

'We need to create an illusion of instant attraction and overpowering passion. I've never been demonstrative with girlfriends in public. Little more than hand-holding and social greetings. So a good way to convince people our affair was different is to show affection in front of them.'

'You mean kiss if someone's watching?'

'Alina, we're implying that we had a short, tempestuous affair that resulted in your becoming pregnant. That you're here with me now will tell everyone you mean more than any other woman I've dated. Which is true in the nicest way. Our limited knowledge of each other doesn't matter—displaying our irresistible attraction does.'

'So somewhere between how we've been and how Louise and Leon were?' Not a hard task, considering the way she reacted to him each time they touched. As long as she kept her heart secure.

'Definitely less blatant—though I envied them their intimacy. I can't imagine having such a close bond with anyone. I'm aware I'll have to change the way I think and act, make it credible to friends and family. It's not only me who'll be affected by our success.'

She locked eyes with his. 'The baby.'

'*Our* baby. It's essential my parents believe that. You have to be comfortable with me as your partner, alone and in company.'

'I can.' She heard the slight tremor. 'I will be.' Better. Stronger.

Ethan slid his leg off the couch. 'Come here.'

That persuasive honey tone. Those compelling cobalt eyes.

She sidled along until there was barely a hand's length between them. His fingers lightly traced her cheek. His arm slid around her, loose yet secure.

'Any time you feel uneasy, tell me.'

His slow smile had her leaning in closer.

'Any time you feel like taking the initiative, go right ahead.'

He stroked her hair, laid her head on his shoulder and cradled her against his body. His heart beat strong and steady under her hand, an echo of hers. His voice, his cologne, everything about him was becoming familiar, safe. It was a feeling she refused to analyse.

'We'll keep to ourselves for a couple of weeks. When you're ready I'd like to arrange dinner with the couple I hope will agree to be our witnesses. If we're out and meet anyone I know I'll introduce you only by name. After the wedding I'll tell my parents, and then the whole world can know.'

'All at once?' she teased, liking the way his eyes crinkled at the corners when he laughed down at her.

She also liked the sound of the couple he went on to describe—friends he'd known for years, who'd also known and visited Louise and Leon.

They made small talk, sat in quiet contemplation, still in

an amicable embrace. When it was time to retire it was she who raised her face for his tender goodnight kiss.

Ethan leant against the wall, his gaze fixed on the light under her door, not quite sure what had happened tonight. A week ago he'd have claimed the scenario he'd suggested held no qualms for him, apart from the discomfort of their public displays.

He'd have bet his finest hotel that his romantic emotions would not have been involved, and still didn't quite believe they were. The trauma of losing his sister and best friend, the shock of Alina's pregnancy, plus his determination to take responsibility for the child were a formidable combination. It was enough to scramble anyone's senses.

He still believed his decisions had been made with logic and foresight, with the child's future wellbeing his main consideration. Main? He meant *only*. He'd be a single father, with all the problems that entailed. Public displays had to be kept objective—surface emotion only.

Yet he couldn't deny that Alina slipped under his guard whenever they were together, popped into his thoughts when they weren't.

The light went out. He whispered, 'Pleasant dreams…' and went to his big, lonely bed.

Alina woke early, had coffee brewing and the table set for breakfast by the time Ethan walked down the hallway dressed for work.

'Good morning.' He sat opposite and poured his favourite sugarbomb cereal. 'Do you want a lift anywhere this morning?'

'No.' Too quick. Too sharp.

Last night their decision had sounded plausible, simple to put into practice. This morning, as water had cascaded over her in the shower, she'd decided she wanted some alone time, to mull it over and fully accept its implications in her head.

'I'd like to practise on the laptop. I bet there are functions I've never heard of.'

'There are probably programs I've never used either. Any questions you have I'll try to answer later. With luck, and few interruptions, I might only need a few hours at the office.'

'Don't you usually work all day on Saturday?'

'Ah, that was the *old* me in the *old* days.' His sparkling eyes belied his self-critical tone. 'A pre-baby workaholic. Now I'm in training to be the best daddy ever.' His voice roughened over the last sentence, and the sparkle dimmed a little.

Alina covered his hand with hers. 'You will be, Ethan. You'll be everything they'd want their child to have in a father.'

'And mother.'

She jerked her hand away. He caught it.

'There won't be any other. I sure as hell won't marry again just to provide maternal comfort or for the public two-parent image. I've learned from experience how a marriage held together purely for society standing can influence a child.'

That was why he'd have no problem letting her go, would never try to persuade her to stay.

There was no justification for the dejection that washed over her. No reason for the retort that burst from her.

'Louise turned out fine. She was generous, warm-hearted and open. Even through her medical traumas there was always a genuine welcome for anyone at their home. You know how everyone loved her because she was…was… *she was Louise.*'

'And I'm not like her?' He released her hand, picked up his spoon.

'I'm sorry. That's not what I meant.'

'No, but it's true. She never changed from the sweet, wide-eyed creature the nanny at the time put into my arms when I was five. She grabbed my finger, gurgled, and I immediately forgave her for not being the brother I wanted.'

His light laughter was tinged with remorse.

'I wish I'd been as courageous as her—constantly rebelling against the rigid conformity of our upbringing, openly making friends with people she liked, whether they were deemed acceptable or not. My way was quiet avoidance rather than personal confrontation.'

'You kept Leon's friendship, and championed them when they wanted to marry.'

He huffed. 'My parents didn't like that. I don't think they've forgiven me for supporting Louise's declaration that she'd happily have a park wedding without them. Not the "done thing" in their circle. It would have been embarrassing, so they capitulated.'

'Do you see them regularly?'

'We have little in common—different standards. They'd like me to be more involved in their close-knit elite group. I dislike the way they boast about my success to elevate their own status. They are, however, the only parents I have, so we maintain a polite relationship.'

He ate for a moment, eyes downcast. Pondering. Then looked up and spoke with determination.

'Forget them for now. Cutting down my office hours is essential to my being available for appointments right now, and planning for our baby in the future. So I've been reorganising my staff.'

'You're delegating?

'Even better—I've promoted. My second-in-command now has two assistant managers. Between the three of them they'll take most of the day-to-day load off me. By the time our baby comes everything should be working smoothly enough for me to take paternity leave.'

'Decision made. Action taken. Problem solved.'

'You don't approve?' He sounded disappointed.

'I do. Very much. It's so much a part of who you are. And it's been a long time since I've felt secure enough to depend on anyone for anything.'

She was paying him a compliment, saying what he should want to hear. Ethan shouldn't feel aggrieved, but he did. She admitted to trusting and relying on him—both important to their relationship. But he wanted something different, something more. Something indefinable.

He pushed back his chair, picked up his bowl.

'I'll clear. You head off,' Alina said, buttering a piece of cold toast.

'Okay. I should be home early afternoon. Did you buy bathers?'

'Yes, haven't worn them yet.'

He hadn't used the gym since Sunday. Or the pool since Tuesday evening, after their talk. He was normally a creature of habit and liked his routine, which included daily exercise and swimming early morning or evening. The less disruption, the less stress. If she worked out at the same time he'd know she was okay. It would be a start to getting his life back in control.

'How about when I get home? We'll work out, then swim.'

Her face lit up. 'That sounds good.'

He went to his room, planning a positive day. A few minutes later he collected his briefcase from his study, and left.

Alina ate her toast and honey, mulling over her every encounter with Ethan. She'd developed a habit of deep thinking over people and situations during her solitary lifestyle. Sometimes she created fictional stories about them in her mind to pass the time.

This was real. The attraction between them was real—had been since the moment she'd turned from that window. She could understand *her* reactions. Suddenly thrown into enforced proximity with an attractive, virile man after seven years alone... Pregnant, with rampant hormones playing havoc with her emotions...

His puzzled her. She appreciated the need for them to give the impression they'd been lovers, so kissing was essential. The first kiss had been experimental, to judge her response, the second for show. The others... She wasn't sure. Yet she'd sensed tension in him every time—right from the initial touch of his lips on hers. As if he was keeping a tight rein on his actions. Or on emotions he claimed not to have.

She sipped her camomile tea, pulled a face. Cold toast was okay—cold tea was not drinkable. It was time to get cracking.

She clicked on the kettle, cleared the table and set herself up for a morning's exploration of the internet.

The sound of the front door opening had Alina's head swinging round. A quick check of her watch surprised her. Ten to three. How could it be that late?

'Hi, you've set yourself up pretty well, there. Good use of the dining table.'

How did this man's smile make a good day seem brighter?

'Better than leaning over the coffee table. Did you get what you wanted done?'

'Finally—it took longer than I'd hoped.' He leant over her shoulder to check her screen. 'Agassi Falls? Planning a trip, Alina?'

'Just having fun surfing,' she replied. 'I checked out some courses, then spent some time finding out what all the icons stand for.'

'I trust you've been taking breaks and eating properly?'

Banana peel lay in a small dish, alongside an empty mug on the table.

'Yes, sir. I've stretched every hour…done other stuff in between.' She arched her back and smiled up at him. 'This morning I went out for a short walk; this afternoon I went through your kitchen cupboards to see what's there before looking up some recipes. I found a few meals we might enjoy, but—'

'You can't print them out. We'll fix that on Monday, along with a desk and chair.' He held out a red USB. 'In the meantime copy and use mine.'

'Thank you.' She surprised both of them by rising up on her toes to kiss his cheek. 'This is all I need. You don't want to be left with excess stuff.'

Ethan opened his mouth to refute her claim. Changed his mind. Words weren't going to change hers.

'That's my concern. Right now I'm psyched up for the session in the gym we agreed on.' He took her hands, held her at arm's length. 'Hmm, nice tracksuit—you look as good in green as in blue. Give me five minutes.'

'I'll meet you there.'

He strode to his room, fantasising about the bathers she might be wearing under that outfit as he hastily pulled on T-shirt, bathers, track pants and sneakers. She was waiting for him, sitting on the press-ups bench. The lights were brighter than he usually set, the music a pleasant background sound.

'Bike or treadmill for warm-up?' she asked, offering him a bottle of water. 'I don't mind either.'

'I'll take the bike.' It was still set up for him. 'Twenty minutes okay?'

She agreed, and he selected a programme for mid-range difficulty. Settling into his normal pace was easy—resisting the temptation to watch Alina not so easy. She moved smoothly, gracefully.

'I promise I won't fall off.' She'd caught him checking her out.

'It's been a while since anyone's been here with me.'

Solitude in this special area had always been a plus. It was his private time, for releasing tension. Only occasionally had he invited anyone to join him. To his surprise, he didn't mind Alina being there at all. In fact he felt downright glad to have her running alongside him. A feeling that unnerved him a little, causing him to switch back to getting-to-know-you mode.

'What sort of keep-fit do you do on the move?'

'Depends on the current job. Crop-picking, dog-walking or waitressing are usually enough. If it's in an office I run, or do casual sessions at pools or gyms.'

'Whoa—back up. Dog-walking?'

Her laugh, the first genuine one she'd given, zipped through him. Musical and light, it was a sound he wanted to hear again. Often.

'It's fun, challenging or downright exhausting, depending on the size or number of pooches. And always available in any city, any country.'

'Ever lose any?' The more he learned, the more fascinated he became.

CHAPTER NINE

'No. I HAD one Labrador who didn't want to go back to his owner, but I didn't blame him. The woman's perfume was so overpowering it clogged my throat.'

She blushed and bent her head. So delightfully embarrassed he wanted to jump off and comfort her.

'Hey, yours just didn't suit *you*. On another woman it'd be different.'

'Someone more flamboyant? More "out there"? It was a Christmas gift from a temporary boss, probably recycled. The box had been opened.'

'Now you have the perfect fragrance for you—delicate, reminding me of sunshine and flowers. Ethereal…' He chuckled. 'Maybe not the last one. Though sometimes you *do* drift off into another world.'

Alina was grateful for the distinct ping announcing the end of her programme. She stepped off as the machine slowed down. Moved over to the weights.

For the next thirty minutes they rarely spoke, each concentrating on their own exercises. She'd have been completely relaxed if she'd been able to block out the male effortlessly lifting weights alongside her, built well enough to play A-league football.

He smiled whenever their eyes met in the huge wall mirror, disconcerting her. His T-shirt moulded to his sculpted chest and muscular upper arms. Her breath hitched every time his biceps firmed as he curled or lifted weights. She felt hot, sweaty, much more than she ever had while exercising before.

Deciding she'd done enough, she walked over to the pool. Discarding her tracksuit, she used the ladder, shivering as she descended into the cool water. Made a mental note to ask him to up the temperature. Taking a deep breath, she ducked under, sinking to the bottom, then shooting up. She grabbed the rail, shaking her head, refilling her lungs... Found herself staring at a pair of slender feet attached to tanned legs with a light covering of black hair.

She tilted her head for a slow scan past firm calves to the muscular thighs that had steered her round the dance floor last night...and a pair of black swimming trunks that left no doubt as to his manhood.

Her mouth dried; her pulse raced. Her body heat overrode the chill from the surrounding water. She didn't dare meet his eyes, chose the coward's path and swung into a freestyle stroke away from him. Quickened her pace at the sound of a splash behind her.

Ethan overtook her, touched and turned at the end. He was still below the surface as they passed again. She recovered her composure, slowed to her normal leisurely pace. This wasn't a contest.

Six laps were enough for her.

She sat on the top of the ladder, wrapped in a towel, her feet dangling. She ought to leave. Shower and dress. Think about dinner—no, too early for that. She stayed. Not sure why, except that it was mesmerising, watching Ethan churn through the water, hardly making a ripple. The way he went through life: single-minded, controlled.

He swam like a machine—clean, even strokes, powering along the pool, flipping like a seal at the end. She timed his push-offs. Always constant. So precise. So coordinated.

She frowned. He'd dipped in front of her on his last turn, hadn't resurfaced. Suddenly he burst upward from the water, making her jump. His chest skimmed her legs as he rose, catching hold of the rail for stability.

'Waiting for me?' He grinned, spraying her with tiny drops as he shook his head.

'Hey!'

He levered himself higher so they were on eye level. 'It's only water. Anything special you'd like to do tomorrow? We'll have all day.'

'Oh. No work or commitments?'

'None. I'm all yours. Stay home, and relax. Go for a drive. Walk on the beach. Your choice.'

How was she supposed to make an instant decision with him so close that there was a hint of his cologne in the chlorine-scented air? With his glistening muscled torso inches from her twitching fingers? With his appealing blue eyes offering her something she refused to name?

'A ferry ride.' Out of the blue. From somewhere in her past.

His eyebrows almost met his dripping hairline. 'You want to go on a ferry?'

She nodded. 'The Manly Ferry across the heads. I used to love it during the winter in rough weather.'

His smile shot into a scowl. 'No *way* are you going out in a storm.' Grated out. Possessive.

She laughed, recognising the over-protective tone. 'They don't cross in really rough weather. I don't get seasick. And it's spring.'

He relented, didn't look convinced. 'We'll decide at Circular Quay.'

He twisted, hoisted himself out onto the pool side and picked up the towel he'd left nearby. Alina stood, heading for the door as he patted excess water from his body. He caught her arm and took her towel from her.

'Stand still.'

He moved behind her, began to dry her hair, firmly yet gently. It was soporific, soothing. She arched her neck in pleasure, sighed when he dropped the towel and began to massage her neck and shoulders. Trembled when his hot breath teased the pulse under her ear.

'Your muscles are taut as a drum. A proper massage might help.'

From *him*? Considering he was the main reason for their tension, she doubted it, but his offer was tempting.

'There's a beauty parlour in the next block. Make an appointment.'

Why had it suddenly become less appealing?

After Alina had retired for the night Ethan turned off the television and dimmed the lights. Then, sipping brandy, his feet up on the coffee table, he tried to make sense of the mayhem his normally ordered life had become.

He was committed to becoming a short-term husband and a lifelong father. He was becoming attached to a woman whose heart and love belonged to a dead guy. Her response to him was merely physical. His carefully planned future was now a day-by-day unknown.

Ethan suggested they put light coats, plus anything else she wanted to take, into her backpack—which *he'd* carry. He deliberately lingered over breakfast, determined to use their outing to ease any tension between them, make this a day for light conversation with no conflict.

It was mid-morning as they strolled towards Circular Quay. After guiding her across the first road he linked their fingers, claiming it would prevent them from being separated by the crowds already building up. She didn't argue, seemed content to let him be protective. He was rapidly becoming more comfortable with the feeling.

Had to curb it when, while drinking water and watching the boats, she declared she'd love to do the Harbour Bridge climb.

Alina hadn't *forgotten* the sheer joy of crossing the heads to Manly on a windy day in choppy seas. She'd purposely blocked it from her mind. Now she realised how much she'd missed the city she'd lived in for so many years.

Today it was fairly mild, until they reached the gap leading to the ocean. She felt alive, leaning on the rail, facing into the breeze, letting it prickle her skin and tease her hair. Nautical toots and engine noise, calls from yachts as they sailed past, all combined with the sounds of circling seagulls to fill her world.

'There's nothing like this anywhere—nothing so exhilarating.' She twisted her head to smile up at Ethan, braced behind her, his hands on the rail either side of her.

His expression said he didn't quite agree. She turned back, leant well forward, as if searching, unsure how to express the way she felt. He repeatedly said that he owed her, but she hadn't expected him to show it so personally, to spend so much time with her. Covering her living costs would have been ample.

'Hey.' One arm wrapped round her. 'It's a long way down.'

'I'm looking for dolphins.'

'Wrong area for them. Wrong season for whales.'

Husky tone, hot breath fanning her ear.

'Some friends and I did a whale-watching trip along the coast a few years ago. Mid-June, I think. If you're feeling up to it, we'll go.'

'I'd love it.' She let him draw her back against his chest. Breathed in the salty air. And him. Let herself live in the moment.

Ethan wondered if she knew how captivating she looked. Genuinely happy, with flushed cheeks and sparkling eyes, she was irresistible. He made a mental note to arrange a day's sailing with friends.

He cupped her cheek, bringing her face round to his. 'Nothing like it. Definitely no sight more beautiful,' he murmured, dipping his head to capture her mouth. He saw her eyes darken. Felt her tremble. Silently agreed: it *was* exhilarating.

The ferry lurched, breaking them apart. He grabbed the rail again, trapping her safely between his arms. They rocked in unison as the boat ploughed through the rough swell. General conversation might be safer.

'I have to confess the only ferries I've been on for years have been for corporate evening events with catered food and drinks. My friends and I used to think day-old pies and cold cans of drink were the ultimate meal.'

He realised how many other simple pleasures he'd left behind as he built his Starburst chain. Pleasures Alina understood and still enjoyed. His adrenaline surged at the thought of her helping him rediscover them. Then she'd go, leaving him to share them with their child. He trembled at the challenge.

Alina felt it and looked round.

'That wind's cold. Do you want to go inside?' he said.

He wasn't lying. It went right through the jacket he'd put on before boarding. Hers wasn't much heavier.

'You're kidding? Inside is for sensitive people, small children or the wuss breed. There's hot drinks and delicious fish and chips waiting near the docks.'

She turned back to watch their approach into Manly.

Ethan nestled his head against hers. 'Okay, but if I catch a chill you have to nurse me.'

The sound she gave was suspiciously like a giggle. 'No chance. No virus would dare attack you without an appointment.'

He stiffened. Was that the impression he gave? Good humour won him over. A week ago she'd been wary of him, anxious about his reaction to her pregnancy. Ready with a plan to have the baby alone if he denied her. He felt a warm glow deep in his gut. If she liked him enough to bait him he must be doing something right.

So he had a reputation for being hardnosed in business? He also was known for being fair and trustworthy.

Late on Monday morning Alina walked through the foyer, trying to pep-talk away her apprehension. Exercising hadn't helped. The line between truth and tacit lies seemed so tenuous. She was not the biological mother—had to persuade everyone she was. She and Ethan had never been lovers, had shared only a few kisses—one long one for an observer's benefit. Were required to act as if they'd had a passionate affair.

Her trepidation had increased when she'd realised he'd been rescheduling appointments to accommodate her and the problems she'd brought him. This morning he'd left early for a meeting postponed from Wednesday. Thirty minutes ago he'd phoned to ask her to come down and meet the car as he'd be running late.

For the baby. For Louise and Leon.

Repeating her mantra silently, she went outside to wait in the shade, praying he wasn't stuck in a traffic jam. The vehicle pulled in to the kerb as if summoned by her plea. She hurried forward, not giving the driver a chance to alight. Scrambling in, she dragged the door shut, leaving Ethan leaning forward awkwardly with his arm extended.

'Oh, sorry.' She gulped in a quick breath, inhaled his distinctive cologne. Flicked him an apologetic grin. 'I'm not used to having someone take care of me.'

'That lesson I'm learning.' Cobalt eyes appraised her as the car moved off. 'You look anxious, Alina.' He caressed her jaw line, tilted her chin.

'What do you expe—?'

He cut off her rebuke by firmly pressing his lips to hers. Her heartbeat hiccupped, doubled in speed. Sent her blood racing along her veins.

The kiss lasted less than a moment. Or for ever. Too

long. Too short. She slumped against the seat and stared at him, too befuddled to think coherently. The piercing eyes holding hers hostage showed no sign of the turmoil he'd inflicted.

She consciously steadied her breathing. 'You should warn me.' It came out like a husky plea for more rather than a reproach.

Ethan gave a low chuckle that resonated over her skin and skittered down her spine. 'So it's okay to kiss you any time as long as I don't surprise you?'

His amusement stretched already taut nerves. 'That's not what I meant.' She scrunched her eyes and bit on her lip.

'I'm not insensitive, Alina.' He lifted his hand. Let it drop. 'Every time I touch you I'm very aware of how you feel. Remember we need to portray a couple who can't resist each other?'

For him it was all for public image, so his declaration should please, not disappoint. Stupid hormones. She *so* had to check with the doctor why they were affecting her this way. In private.

'I can handle the pretence.' *Liar.* 'I'm getting used to it.' *Double liar.* 'It's… The doctor might ask for information I can't…can't give.'

'Ah…'

As if he understood. She shook with frustration. 'No, you don't get it. I can give her the dates she'll need, fudge the method of conception. It's… She's bound to ask…'

It had been bad enough writing details on the clinic's patient information forms he'd accessed on Friday. She'd thanked him for his considerate action in allowing her to fill out her medical history privately. It was the idea of it being voiced out loud that was eating at her. There was no way to explain the dark place where she'd buried the unbearable pain and heartbreak.

He wrapped his arms around her, drew her into his warmth. His hands began a soothing caress over her spine.

His voice was gentle, as if speaking to a child. 'You're not alone, Alina. I'll be with you.' His hands stilled. 'Unless you *want* to see her alone.'

Of course she did.

'No, that's cowardly. I can handle it.' Her quivering voice proved otherwise.

'Are you sure?'

He meant it. And the compassion in his blue eyes and the generosity of his offer gave her strength.

'You may have questions too. Besides, the father has the right to be there.' With a jolt of amazement, she realised a simple truth. 'I'd *like* you to be there.'

'I am the father...' His large hand covered her abdomen. 'My baby. Our child.'

She didn't protest and he appeared satisfied. She'd never be able to use that phrase, never be able to care that way again. Hearing it resonate from him relieved her. He was going be a great father.

Ethan linked his fingers with hers as they entered the light, hospitable clinic. Her anxiety was palpable and he had no remedy. Give him a struggling business to rescue any time.

'Relax, Alina. It's only a preliminary examination.'

At least his words earned him a faint smile. He steered her into an empty elevator and pressed the button. The compulsion to comfort her and drive the shadows from her soulful eyes rippled through him.

'We're bending the truth for our child's sake, Alina. The book claims doctors need dates and medical history— nothing more. No one's going to pry into your personal history.'

Her eyes widened in astonishment. 'What book?'

'The one I bought Tuesday morning, specifically written for expectant fathers.' His mouth twisted. 'Very informative and downright scary.'

They stopped and he guided her out.

She handed in the forms and her obligatory urine sample at Reception and were directed to an empty waiting room. Light classical music played softly in the background. Alina sat idly flipping the pages of a magazine. Ethan filled two plastic cups from an orange juice dispenser and offered one to her.

She accepted it with a noticeably shaky hand and his heart sank. He noticed her agitated finger movements, half hidden by the bag on her lap, finishing in a clenched fist. Hoping their appointment wasn't delayed, he put his cup on the low table and wrapped steadying fingers around her hand.

'Patricia Conlan has a very good reputation.' He raised the hand clasping the cup to her lips. 'Now, drink. Slowly.'

Alina obeyed, emptying the cup. He drained his, took both cups to a bin, then returned to sit beside her, studying a poster on the wall opposite.

She kept her eyes downcast, wishing she had his self-discipline. He'd been predictably shaken by her initial bombshell, and angry a few times during subsequent conversations, but he'd rapidly recovered his composure every time. She, on the other hand, had trouble keeping any control over her emotions.

She glanced sideways, surprised to find him looking more nervous than he'd let on. The long supple fingers of his right hand thrummed on his thigh, and she recalled them spanning her stomach. The image of them sensuously exploring her body flashed into her brain, and she couldn't stifle a throaty gasp.

He jerked round. 'Alina, are you all right?'

'Alina Fletcher?'

She jumped up, willing her burning cheeks to cool,

grateful for the interruption from the uniformed woman in the doorway.

They were ushered into the consulting room.

'Dr Conlan will be with you in… Ah, here she is.'

'Alina, Ethan. It's nice to meet you.' The fortyish woman with slightly mussed brown hair and bright blue eyes clasped her hands, then Ethan's, in genuine welcome.

'Let's sit down and get acquainted.' She emanated compassion and invited trust.

'Thank you, Dr Conlan.' Alina took a seat, placing her handbag on the floor as a folder was opened and perused. Even Ethan's reassurance couldn't dispel her feeling of foreboding at the thought of queries about her past. An occasional note was written, an occasional 'hmm' mouthed.

She noticed a slight resemblance to her husband's Aunt Jean, triggering a pang of guilt. She'd only kept in token touch with everyone, had avoided personal contact. In a few weeks she'd have to notify them that she was living in Sydney. Remarried. Having another baby. The latter when Ethan decided to make the announcement.

Sneaking a peek at him, she met genuine concern. Whatever he saw caused him to take her hand, link their fingers and squeeze. He had no idea how calming those slight actions were.

Dr Conlan laid down her pen and glasses, placed her elbows on her desk and linked her fingers. She smiled sympathetically.

'I appreciate this must revive painful memories for you, Alina, and I sincerely hope your new baby brings you happiness.'

Ethan squeezed her hand again.

'The sample you brought in officially confirms your pregnancy. If you'd like to go into the examination area, I'll be in shortly. We'll talk after.'

Alina went to the open doorway indicated. The faint

murmur of voices drifted in as she prepared and lay down on the examining table. She stared at the ceiling, silently chanting her mantra.

CHAPTER TEN

NICE AS THE doctor was, Alina felt relieved as they left. A referral for an ultrasound and an appointment card were in her handbag. Ethan held the door open, his free hand clasping the pamphlets they'd been given.

She'd seen his surreptitious peek at his watch in the elevator. Catching his arm she stopped them both. 'You need to get back to the office, don't you?'

'There's always work to be done. We can—'

'Hail a taxi and I'll drop you off. The sooner you get back, the less chance of staying late.' And she'd have some quiet contemplation time to mull over the doctor's advice, read those pamphlets, and fully accept the path she'd chosen.

His cobalt eyes gleamed with gratitude. His fingers rested gently on her cheek for a moment. 'Spoken like a true corporate wife.' He looked round. 'There's a snack bar over there. I'll grab a sandwich to eat at my desk.'

He made one call during the taxi ride to his office, booking the ultrasound for Monday the twenty-first of April at ten. She wrote the date and time in her notebook as he repeated them for confirmation, realising it was the day after the wedding. When she would be recorded as his wife.

Ethan sensed a change in her. Was she too beginning to realise the enormity of their agreement, so simple in words, so complex and mind-boggling in reality? In front of the doctor he'd claimed to be the father of her child. He'd said 'our baby', 'our child' so easily. Now he had to fulfil the promises he'd made to Alina and his sister's memory.

His pragmatic nature demanded everything be put in place quickly, privately. Nothing left to chance, no hesitation that might give anyone cause to believe he doubted his paternity. Even before she'd agreed he'd set up appointments without considering the effect on her. Even after learning of her loss he hadn't deviated from his plan.

He hadn't allowed for the reality—hadn't understood the impact it would have on them both.

He reached for her hand, breathed in her sweet fragrance. She didn't react; lost in a world he had no right to access.

The taxi was nearing his office. He tilted her chin, took in her subdued expression and almost told the driver to keep going. What could he say or do? Nothing until she was ready to confide in him. A quick kiss on her forehead produced little response. He had no right or reason to be disappointed. Only a week ago he'd walked out on her.

Alina's head was inside the kitchen island cupboard when the intercom buzzed at about eleven the next morning. She'd just managed to reach the small can in the back corner and jerked at the sound, banging her head.

She walked over to the front door. Hesitated. Ethan hadn't mentioned anyone coming. Would he want her to answer? Another buzz. She pressed.

'Hello.'

'Good morning. Is Ethan at home?'

The hairs on the back of her neck lifted at the high-pitched, cultured voice. Her mouth dried. She swallowed twice, rubbed her neck. Finally managed a croaky reply. 'No, I'm sorry, he's not.'

'I'm Sophia James. May I come up?'

His mother—judgemental to the nth degree. Far worse than the ex-girlfriend she'd suspected. Should she let her in? What would she do if Alina refused her entry?

'Hello? Are you still there?' Slightly peeved.

'Please come up.' Denial only delayed the inevitable.

In three weeks Sophia would be her mother-in-law. For a short time anyway.

She raced to her bedroom to check her appearance. After brushing her already neat hair she went slowly back, taking long lung-filling breaths. Waited, slowly counted to nine after the bell rang before opening the door.

Sophia James was the epitome of a stylish, sixtyish woman with all the resources to fight any sign of ageing. From her coiffured dark hair to the handmade high-heeled shoes colours matched, everything fitted perfectly. There was nothing soft about her at all. Not a trace of warmth in her red lips or in her flat brown eyes.

Alina felt an irrational zing of satisfaction that both this woman's children had expressive blue eyes, clearly inherited from another family member.

'Please come in,' she said, standing aside.

Sophia walked in with an air of entitlement, scanning the area as if it were her territory. Scanning Alina as if she were an applicant for a lowly household position.

'You are not the cleaner. Why isn't Ethan here with you?'

Spoken as if she couldn't be trusted to be alone in his home. She felt a twinge of insecurity, then pride came to her rescue. She lifted her chin, squared her shoulders. *She's Ethan's mother. Treat her with respect. She's the baby's grandmother.* That last thought eased her resentment. This lady would *not* take kindly to any of the traditional titles given to a grandmother.

'I'm Alina Fletcher. Would you like coffee or tea? Ethan's at work.' She held back on saying, *But I'll bet you know that*.

'Mild coffee, thank you. White. No sugar.' As if she were ordering from a waitress in a café.

Alina watched as Sophia stopped before entering the lounge, giving the area a thorough scrutiny before selecting one of the armchairs. Giving the impression that she had never seen the decor before. After popping a pod into the machine Alina joined her, staying on her feet to attend to the drinks.

'You're the girl with Ethan in the photograph a friend texted to me. You were kissing in the street, and now you're acting like this is your home. Are you *living* with him?' Blunt and insulting.

She made a point of staring at Alina's bare left hand, made no attempt to hide her displeasure. Alina's attitude swung again. How dared this woman question and insult her?

'I don't discuss my private business with strangers.'

Sophia's lips thinned, almost disappeared. Her back stiffened. 'I'm his mother. I have a right to know.'

'Then perhaps you should ask *him*. Next time we're in contact I'll ask him to get in touch.'

It was a definite dismissal. Forget coffee. Alina wanted her gone.

The scathing look Sophia gave her was defused by the dull shade of red flooding her face. She rose stiffly to her feet.

'Be warned, Ms Fletcher. You don't fit. You may have him fooled for a short time, but his contemporaries will see through you as easily as I do.'

Her movement to the door was as near to a stomp as Alina had ever seen anyone do in heels. She followed, far enough behind so that Sophia had to open the door herself.

She turned for a parting shot. 'Even suitable girls don't seem to last long with Ethan. Your novelty will quickly pall for a man of my son's impeccable taste.'

She swept out, leaving the door open.

Alina closed it, shaking with disbelief. She uncurled her clasped fingers to enable them to rub the back of her neck, tilted her head to the ceiling. What had she done? Apart from insulting his mother, and practically throwing her out of his home, she'd given the impression she had authority here.

Ethan hadn't wanted his parents to know about her yet. A public kiss hardly equated domestic cohabitation. Should she have lied?

Her head reeled.

Should she wait 'til he came home to tell him, when she'd be able to see his reaction? What if Sophia rang him first with a distorted version of events?

Taking bites of some dark rich chocolate for courage, she debated the pros and cons…

'She *what*?' The outrage in Ethan's voice seared down the phone line. She'd got no further than telling him his mother had visited before he'd exploded.

'I'm sorry, Ethan. I didn't know whether to let her in. I—'

'She's never been there before—never been invited. What did she want?' Barked out, agitating her even more.

'Someone sent her a photo of us kissing. I didn't know what to tell her.'

She'd screwed up. No, he'd put her in that position by keeping her a secret. It was *his* family who had the issues.

'You should contact her. I… I… I'll see you tonight.'

She hung up.

'Alina?'

She'd gone. Ethan realised his knuckles were white from his grip on the mobile phone. His free fist ground onto his desk. She'd sounded distressed. What the hell had his mother said to her?

He'd never been so angry. Or so worried when Alina didn't answer his call back. He selected his mother's number.

'Ethan, we haven't heard from you for a while.'

Not since they'd criticised the wording for the gravestone. Lucky for her there was half a city between them else he'd be tempted to throttle her.

'So you thought you'd pop into my home when you knew I wasn't there?'

She spluttered. He gave her no chance to refute his claim.

'Don't bother denying it. My receptionist logged the same female voice yesterday, saying she might call in. Your voice is quite distinctive.'

It wasn't said as a compliment. Anyone who truly knew him would have been wary of his low, controlled tone.

'I was worried. I'd received a photograph of you with that girl I met in your apartment.'

He almost lost it at her throwaway reference to Alina. Gritted his teeth, needing to know how his mother had discovered she was there. He waited for a long, tense moment.

'Okay, I described her to an acquaintance who lives a few floors below you. She said she'd seen her—sometimes alone, sometimes with you. I'm only looking out for your welfare, Ethan. There's something not quite right about her. She just about ordered me out.'

'After, I'm guessing, you began to interrogate her. Listen carefully, Mother. You'll have no more contact with me at all if you bother Alina again. Understand?'

'Ethan, you—'

'Goodbye, Mother.'

He dragged his fingers through his hair. *Alina, sweetheart, you didn't deserve that. I made a mistake—should have known she'd start digging at the slightest rumour I might be dating.*

He tried the apartment. No answer. Tried Alina's number twice more. It went to voicemail each time.

There was no sound in the apartment, no sign of Alina. Her mobile lay on the kitchen island. *She has to be here. Has to be.*

Ethan strode to her bedroom. The breath he felt he'd been holding for ever whooshed out at the sight of her handbag by her dressing table. Her bathroom door was open. Not there. One place left to check.

The gym area was silent apart from the low hum of the water pumps. The lights were dimmed, giving him limited vision of the figure floating in the pool. The only movements were slight flicks of her feet, gently propelling her along towards him. A rush of relief swamped his body. He sagged against the doorjamb, his heart racing. He'd had no reason to think she would run, yet he'd feared she might.

Wiping his hand over his mouth, he wondered why this fragile, damaged woman stirred him as no one ever had. It went deeper than the embryo she carried. His anger towards his mother had been at her treatment of Alina. His concern had been solely for Alina's feelings.

He toed off his shoes, stripped to his boxer shorts, watching her slow progress through the water. Not wanting to startle her, he walked along the side, meeting her halfway. Felt his lips curl. How did she keep a straight line with closed eyes?

They flew open, though he'd swear he'd never made a sound. Her head turned. One look into sorrowful violet and he dived in, surfacing next to her. He hauled her into his arms, the anxiety he'd experienced giving his action more force than he'd intended.

He buried his head in her neck, his lips seeking her pulse, his heart rate lifting at the feel of its erratic beat. The feel of her hands clasping his shoulders, her legs brushing his as they trod water, the tantalising aroma from her skin—all heightened his senses.

Her wrists stiffened, preventing him from drawing her closer. He raised his head, meeting censure in her eyes.

'Alina, I…' Where the hell were the words he needed? 'You hung up on me. Didn't answer your phone.'

Indignation flared, making the colour of her eyes even more stunning. Her hands lifted and slammed onto his skin, clearing his mind. He huffed out air, drew in fresh breath, regained control.

'I'm not angry, Alina—not at you. You sounded so upset. When you didn't pick up I was...' *Admit it .Tell her how you felt.* 'I'm not sure what I felt. Just knew I had to see you, hold you.'

'Your mother—'

'Had no right to come here. If I'd even suspected she might I'd have told you not to grant her entry. I'm sorry, Alina—and, believe me, so is she right now.'

'You've talked to her?'

His chest tightened. Hadn't she believed him when he'd said he'd protect her?

'More like a short, angry lecture. Plus her one and only warning. I made it clear if she upsets you again I'll have even less contact with them.'

'That's a bit drastic. They're your family, Ethan. I knew about her attitude, so I shouldn't have overreacted—though she certainly lived up to her reputation.' Her tone softened with regret. 'I'm really messing up your life, aren't I?'

He shook his head. 'Quite the opposite, Alina Fletcher. You enrich my life every day. You and our baby have changed my world.'

Her hands relaxed, allowing him to tighten his hold, bringing them into full body contact. Her fingers traced a featherlight path up his neck, across his chin. A glimmer of desire flickered in her eyes. It was satisfying for a few seconds—until his body responded to the flimsy barrier of cotton bathers and silk boxers between them, to the press of her breasts on his bare chest. To the flesh-on-flesh contact of their thighs.

His mouth crashed down on hers. No preamble, no gentle brush of lips—this was need, satisfying a hunger that had been building for days. From that first gut-clench, that first look into her haunted eyes.

He tilted her head for better contact, took what she offered, his tongue caressing hers, tangling, tasting the sweetness he'd dreamt of. And she was an active participant, giving and receiving, her fingers weaving into his hair, holding his head to hers.

His heart thumping, pulses pounding at every point, his lungs screaming for air, he had never felt so gloriously alive.

Reluctantly breaking the kiss, still holding her close, he gazed into violet eyes as bright as the stars in a moonless night, stunned and bewildered by the ardency of their kiss. He'd crossed an unspoken boundary, knew he should apologise. Knew it would be a lie.

'Do you want another apology?'

How could Alina ask an apology of him when she'd willingly contributed to the kiss? When she'd seen the concern in his eyes as he'd surfaced beside her? When it had been him she'd been thinking of as she'd floated in the semi-darkness, lost in a hopeless fantasy?

There'd been no sound—only a crackling in the air surrounding her skin. She'd opened her eyes and dream had become reality. A splash and a moment later she'd been enveloped in strong arms, his lips nuzzling her neck.

As if nothing had happened. As if his mother hadn't treated her with contempt. She'd bristled, hit him in an effort to get away.

His sincere contrition had chastened her; his defence of her had quelled her resentment. His claim that she enhanced his life had spun her back into her daydream and his kiss had been everything she'd imagined and more. She could no longer deny that she wanted him—rampantly hormonal or for real. Where that took them, she had no idea.

'I don't ever want you to say sorry unless you truly mean it. I'm the one who ought to apologise, for acting like an immature schoolgirl. I should have kept calm this morning and placated her.'

She was blurting out waffle, keeping back the words she really wanted to say.

The incongruity of the situation suddenly hit her. She was in a dimly lit pool, treading water with an almost naked, definitely aroused man whose very presence threatened her safe, isolated, unemotional existence.

'Ethan, I… I can't… Oh, hell, I can't shop.'

Ethan's eyes widened when she swore. His hold loosened, giving her the chance to paddle backwards, putting distance between them. He caught her at the steps, his touch light yet compelling. His hand framed her cheek. His little finger lifted her chin, enabling him to study her face with the intensity she no longer found intimidating. Especially when the warm, caring gleam in his dark blue eyes said he'd wait as long as it took for her to confide in him.

She quivered: from his look, from his hold, from her fear of his reaction. From everything about him.

His lips curled in reassurance. 'If I let you go now, will you explain what that meant when you're dry and dressed?'

When she'd had time to rethink, time to decide to try again. When he'd be corporately attired, in his business persona again.

Her eyes blurred with tears. She needed help—the sooner the better.

'Of course I can shop—that's ridiculous. It's buying stuff to wear when I meet the people in your world that's so daunting. Those fancy boutiques scare me; even the upmarket department stores are discouraging if you don't follow the latest trends. Reading magazines doesn't help, because I have no idea what's suitable for what event.'

'I like you in blue.' Instant and believable. He gently wiped the corners of her eyes with his thumb. 'And your new dresses look great.'

'They were easy. Summer daywear. Once I start meeting people you know I'll be judged on how I look, what I wear. How I speak. I'm afraid I'll fail you.'

Her mouth stayed open, unable to form more words as her brain seized on her last thought. Failing Ethan, having her unsuitable image impact on him, was her number one fear. Perhaps an avoidable situation if one woman had behaved as a loving mother should.

'Why couldn't your mother be more like Louise? Then I'd be able to ask *her* for help.' As soon as the words were spoken she wished them back. Gave a choked snort of a laugh.

'Stupid question. If she were we wouldn't be having this conversation. I need to manage by myself.'

CHAPTER ELEVEN

ETHAN HAD LOST track of the number of times he'd been racked with guilt these last several weeks. There'd been days when it had been as prevalent as breathing.

He'd given Alina a credit card, assuming she'd enjoy shopping. A lot of the women he knew—including his mother—considered having unlimited credit their due right, an essential element in their pursuit of looking stunning on the arm of their partner at any public or private function.

Alina was different. No demands, no preconceived notions. Absolutely no idea how beautiful she was.

He placed his hands on her waist, lifted her onto the side of the pool, and checked his watch.

'We'll meet in the lounge in, say, thirty minutes?'

'For what?'

His pulse hiked at the endearing way her brow wrinkled and her eyes narrowed, as if she expected a reprimand.

'A shopping trip. If I'm the one you're dressing for, I guess I ought to help in the selection.'

His reward was a beaming smile and sparkling eyes—worth any amount of waiting outside changing rooms or carrying umpteen promotional bags. The single experience he'd had accompanying a female shopper had left him disinclined for a repeat, but this was for Alina.

'You mean it?'

He ran his finger down her cheek. 'I told you—I take care of what's mine.'

She was on her feet in an instant, grabbing a towel on the way to the door. He followed, hoisting himself from the water, giving himself a quick dry-off before retrieving his clothes.

* * *

It wasn't working. Ethan felt way out of his depth, wished he'd offered to find someone else to help her. He knew when a woman looked chic, understood the way it transformed her inner attitude. The selected clothes weren't having that effect on Alina. They were in the third boutique, and she'd modelled the tenth outfit.

The assistants had been helpful, yet there was an edge to their attitude he couldn't fathom. Was it him? His obvious antipathy to this environment? Was it sweet, shy Alina, who hadn't looked comfortable at all, posing awkwardly as if she'd rather be anywhere else?

If she lifted her chin, held her shoulders back and stood proud, the effect would be so much better. He groaned inside. He'd promised to help her—failure wasn't an option.

'This isn't working, is it?

Her voice echoed his thoughts as she came up behind him, wearing the dress she'd left home in. He swung round, ready to protest.

Alina stopped his words with two fingers on his lips, ignoring the tingles her action generated.

'You're uncomfortable with it all, and I'm as helpful as seagulls at a beach picnic. I can tell what clothes *aren't* right on me. Others…' She shrugged. 'I have pictures in my head of women attending special events, can't put myself there. Maybe if you lend me some of your confidence it'll solve the problem.'

He gave her a crooked grin and took her hand. 'Not such a good suggestion, huh? I overestimated my expertise with all this. Louise was never a fashion slave, she—'

His eyes lit up, and his smile turned into a heart-stopping grin.

'I'm an *idiot*. Though, in my defence, I've had a few distractions.' He brushed his lips over hers. 'You being number one. Wait here.'

He was back in a few moments, after talking to the head saleswoman. As they left he pulled his mobile from his inside pocket.

'Got your notepad and pen?'

By the time she'd found them, his call had been answered.

'Thanks, Tanya…we're getting there. How are you? Definitely—we'll make it soon. Right now, I need the names of a couple of boutiques Louise patronised. It's for someone special who's recently moved to Sydney.'

He repeated three names and numbers for Alina to write down, promised to arrange a foursome dinner soon, then said goodbye.

'Don't know why I didn't think of her earlier.' He gently flicked her chin. 'Like I said—distractions. She recommends the first one, says the woman there has an uncanny knack of finding the perfect outfit for her customers. Let's ring—find out if she can see us today.'

Maralena's displays were simple, yet very effective, with one model in an appropriate setting in each window. Alina's fingers gripped Ethan's as they entered. She had no doubt how she'd be perceived, how the sales staff would wonder what he saw in her, why he was with her. She received an encouraging squeeze. What she needed was a little of his innate self-assurance.

Inside, there was room to move easily around the minimal racks of clothing, or along the walls containing full-length gowns. The blonde woman who came to meet them was everything Alina wished she was: poised and perfectly groomed, yet clearly approachable. She dispelled any fears with her genuine smile.

'Welcome to Maralena's.' She held out her hand to Ethan. 'Mr James, please accept my deepest sympathy for your loss. Louise always brightened our day when she came shopping, whether she purchased or not.'

'Thank you, she's very much missed. Please, call me Ethan.' He drew Alina forward. 'This is Alina Fletcher, her friend from Spain.'

'I'm Marlena—I tweaked the name a little for business. I'm pleased to meet you, Alina.'

She shook hands, then stood back, giving her new customer a quick and thorough appraisal. Unlike Sophia's critical gaze, it was a professional assessment which didn't bother her at all. To her surprise, the eyes that met hers were approving.

'It will be a pleasure to help you, Alina. Do you have any particular style in mind? Any colour preferences?'

All doubt dissipated, as if Alina's whole body gave a sigh of relief. She'd found the help she so desperately needed.

'I have a list of what I *think* I need.' She sensed Ethan's lips curling. Was tempted to nudge him in the ribs with her elbow. 'I've been backpacking through Europe for a long time, so I'm out of touch with what's in fashion.'

'What suits you is more important. Do you have a time limit today?'

'No.' Emphatic from Ethan. 'Take all the time you want.'

A few minutes ago Alina might have begged him to stay. Now she had no qualms about placing herself in Marlena's hands.

She put her hand on his arm, drew him aside. 'Thank you, Ethan, this is just what I've been hoping to find. You can go back to your office now. I'll be fine.'

His eyes narrowed. He didn't seem convinced.

'Did you leave work unfinished and come home because you thought I was upset?'

'No, because I *knew* you were.'

'I'm not now. The quicker you get back, the earlier you'll come home.'

He grinned. 'Can't fight feminine logic. Okay, I'll go. Call the hire car when you've finished.'

'I promise.'

He kissed her, slow and tender, seemingly oblivious to anyone else in the shop. Her fingers tightened on the strap of her bag, her other hand lifted to cradle his neck. Her lips moved in unison with his.

She felt his muscles tense. Wasn't this a kiss for show? To her it seemed the perfect place. Maybe he didn't, so she broke away.

'I'll see you later.'

'Mmm…' He blinked and his head jerked. Still holding her, he nodded to Marlena. 'Take care of her.' With a final squeeze of her hand, and a husky, 'Tonight…' he walked away.

'Okay, Alina, let's see your list.'

She was escorted into a dressing room. Within minutes she'd confided her lack of success and doubts of her fashion abilities to an empathetic Marlena.

Ethan's mobile rang as he walked into the apartment building a few minutes before seven. Things were settling into place, with the agenda set for a breakfast meeting with his new management team in the morning. Once they were clear on their roles he'd be able to reorganise his working hours.

'Good evening, Father.'

'Ethan. I believe you have a new girlfriend?'

'Yes.' He wondered what spin his mother had put on today's events.

'We'd like to meet her. Does dinner on Saturday night suit you?'

'I'll check with Alina.'

'We'll look forward to seeing you. Goodbye, Ethan.'

He stood in front of the elevator, staring at his mobile,

his gut twisting in regret. He had more cordial conversations with the people he spoke to regarding aspects of renovation or trading with his hotels. Was he destined to be as impersonal as his parents, considering he had their combined DNA?

The idea appalled.

He stabbed at his floor number, tapped his thigh on the journey up and strode purposely to the door. Alina came through from the lounge as he dropped his briefcase on the floor. His mind registered her sweet smile in the same instant as he wrapped her in his arms, burying his face into her silken curls, breathing in their citrus aroma. He relished her warmth, her softness, the way she stood still in his embrace, her only movement being to slide her arms around his waist.

Seconds ticked by. Holding her wasn't enough.

He lifted his head. 'Hi.'

Their kiss was gentle, a mutual giving and taking. So soul-soothing he kept it short rather than risk pushing for more. This was new—something to build on. She was beginning to trust him as a man. He was beginning to reassess who he was.

She leant back in his arms to study his face.

'You caught up?'

Warmth radiated through him. This felt *right*. This was the way homecoming should always be. 'As good as. How did you go?'

'Two outfits which I love. One's here, the other needed some alteration, so I'll pick it up on Friday.'

'Only two?' He grinned down at the face she pulled and kissed the tip of her nose. 'Whatever you feel comfortable with, Alina.'

'The new season stock's arriving in a week or two. By then I'll be bigger. Common sense says to buy what I need as I need it.'

His laughter shook his body. 'Since when did common sense become aligned with fashion shopping?'

'Hey!' She swatted his arm playfully, then froze as she realised what she'd done, eyes widening in shock.

Alina couldn't believe what she'd done. One second he'd been teasing her, the next she'd reciprocated. Completely spontaneously. Without thinking, she'd hit him, as if they'd been friends for a long time. The incredulous look on his face made it worse.

'I...' She tried to break free, suddenly found herself being lifted and carried backwards, to be plonked unceremoniously on the kitchen island. His hands gripped the bench either side of her. His impassive features gave no indication of his thinking. It was like their first meeting, but without the angst filling the room.

'Ethan, I—'

'Alina Fletcher,' he cut in. 'I do believe you are starting to let your true self sneak out from its constrictions.'

She dropped her head. He lifted it with his finger, his thumb grazing her skin. His eyes sparkled with amusement, daring her to act again. The very fact that she wanted to scared her, holding her back. She trembled, held her breath. Then, as if of its own accord, her hand lifted, her fingers covering his on her chin.

The air around them seemed hot and heavy. She couldn't think straight His eyes darkened. His lips curled. Did his body sway closer? Did hers?

He abruptly withdrew his hand, pushing himself upright, shaking his head. 'A cool dip in the pool before dinner?'

Her body flopped. Gratefully, she seized on his suggestion. 'Yes. *Yes.*'

'Don't sound so eager to run, my sweet.' He swung her to the floor, keeping hold for a moment. 'And don't be afraid to show the woman you really are. I like what I've seen so far.'

Not trusting her voice, she gave a quick nod before turning away.

He stopped her with a gentle hand on her arm. 'My father's invited us to dinner on Saturday. I'm so angry with my mother I'm inclined to say no.'

'Delaying the inevitable? I think I'd rather face it now.'

'The way you did with me? I won't let them demean you, Alina.' A softly spoken declaration that demanded compliance. A firm hold she didn't want to break. Commanding blue eyes that enthralled.

'*You* were receptive,' she said. 'They're bound to think I'm trapping you. You're not the type to lose control and forget protection.'

Ethan never had. Even in his testosterone-driven teens he'd always been disciplined. Now, being with Alina every night, inhaling her essence, having her within easy reach, he appreciated how overpowering desire could be.

Anger ground in his gut. At his parents, who judged everyone by high, rigid standards and dismissed any contrary opinions. At himself for allowing them to influence his life, his behaviour. At the fates who had taken his sister's life when the best times were just beginning.

Yet those same fates had brought Alina and his future son or daughter to Sydney. To *him*.

Taking a short step forward, he manoeuvred her into his arms. In the simple act of holding her and stroking her hair he found solace as he reassured her.

'That's all the more reason for us to convince them of the undeniable magnetism between us. If we show them we're happy they'll have to accept it.'

'*Are* you happy?' A muffled plea into his shirt.

He tilted her chin to gaze into lovely despondent eyes and swore silently. Didn't she realise how much her being here meant to him?

'How can I *not* be happy? You've given me the most

precious gift I'll ever have. You are giving a part of Louise back to me. Her child. You had easier options, yet you came to me not knowing how I'd react. You *did* know how my parents would.'

She took a long, shuddering breath, drawing his eyes to her full pink mouth. His body vibrated in response. She had no concept of what she was doing to him. He wasn't sure himself.

'Can we go this week? I'd prefer less time to dwell on it.'

His mobile rang before he could answer her. He grimaced at the caller ID. 'I agree. I've got to take this, so I'll meet you in the pool.'

He walked to his room, trying to focus on building regulations instead of smoky violet eyes and full, inviting lips.

Alina walked away, didn't look back. His words had woven a soothing path through her mind, into her heart. Diminishing her qualms.

You've given me the most precious gift.

So similar to the phrase she'd heard from Louise when those two blue lines had materialised on that vital stick. Validation that she'd made the right decision to contact him now rather than after the birth.

Seven minutes to six on a Thursday evening and his desk was clear. Ethan felt pumped at an achievement he determined would become more routine than not. He conceded that the new promotions, which would become official at midnight on Sunday, made it possible.

He stopped on the way home for handmade chocolates to celebrate. Trying to quell the rush of anticipation, he entered the apartment, silently chuckling at the sci-fi epic music coming from the speakers.

Alina was preparing dinner at the kitchen counter. His eyes drank in her brunette curls, her enticing curves—soon to be curvier. Alluring. Desirable. This attraction was unlike any he'd ever experienced. Because of the situation? Her condition? His unexpected paternity? None of them explained that initial gut-clench when the only knowledge he'd had of her was her name.

She continued working, oblivious to his presence. How near did he have to be before she sensed him?

She had. The moment he'd opened the front door. Trying to quell her quickening heartbeat and ignore the prickling at the back of her neck was a futile exercise. There was nothing to account for her sudden heat rush.

Darn hormones. Why pick *this* pregnancy to play up? The first time—she couldn't prevent the comparisons surfacing—there'd been occasional morning sickness, a few cravings, and manageable backache in the last trimester. She'd been blissfully content, cherished, and pampered by…

She gripped the vegetable peeler till it stung, fought the tears threatening to spill.

His cologne seeped around her. Still no sound or greeting. Was he playing games, waiting for her to acknowledge him? She put down the peeler, pivoted.

Her lungs seized up. Her mouth dried. She sucked in her cheeks and swallowed, trying unsuccessfully to form moisture. Ethan stood there, gazing at her as if she were priceless, unique. When he walked round the island, smiling at her, she couldn't have moved if someone had tossed a grenade.

'You were so engrossed I didn't want to disturb you.' He cupped her chin, restarting her lungs in a short sharp gasp. He drew her to him as if their future was limitless and she leant into him, wanting to be closer. Wanting whatever he was offering.

He kissed her lightly, then deeper when her lips moved under his. When they parted of their own accord he accepted the tacit invitation. The tip of his tongue found hers.

Heat flooded every cell. She tasted a hint of wine, coffee, tightened her hold on his neck, hungry for more.

Her stomach lurched. She wrenched free, clapping her hand over her mouth. Holding an arm across her belly, she bent double, trying not to throw up.

'Alina, what's wrong?'

The anxiety in his tone penetrated her brain. The support of his strong arms steadied her.

'Alina?'

The nausea hit again. Breaking free, she stumbled to the bathroom, crumpled beside the toilet bowl and dry-retched repeatedly. Didn't have time to worry about privacy.

CHAPTER TWELVE

WATER SPLASHED IN the basin and then Ethan was kneeling beside her, offering a damp cloth. She pressed it to her skin, letting the coolness soothe the heat from her humiliation. He'd kissed her and she'd practically thrown up on him.

Why? She'd eaten nothing, done nothing to trigger it. She shivered, couldn't stop, couldn't stem the shame churning in her belly.

'Alina?'

She looked up into blue eyes dark with concern. For the child? A tiny pang of regret hit her heart.

'I'm sorry, Ethan—so sorry. I've no idea what triggered that.'

He gently removed the cloth, tossed it into the sink, then cradled her to his chest.

'Hey, I've got friends with children. Over the years I've heard plenty of stories about so-called morning sickness. Including the fact that it should be named any-time-anywhere-for-no-apparent-reason sickness. Feeling better?'

She touched the stubble on his chin, managed a rueful half-smile. 'I think so.'

He helped her up, waited until she'd rinsed her mouth, then aided her walk back to the lounge. Sat beside her, his arm around her shoulders.

'Do you want some chocolate to take away the taste? I brought a box home.'

'Peppermint tea with plain biscuits will be more settling. I can get them.'

'You stay put. You're sure you're all right?'

For his sake she nodded, forcing a smile.

His eyes narrowed as if he wasn't convinced. 'My book

contains a whole chapter on morning sickness, and its triggers. I think I'd better reread it.'

She put her hand on his thigh. 'Thank you for…for being there.'

'Always.' He kissed the top of her head. 'I'll be right back.'

Ethan went to the kitchen, turned on the kettle and sank against the bench, taut hands rubbing his face. He'd had to fight for composure in the bathroom; he still shook inside.

Seeing her sickly pallor as she'd hunched over the toilet had scared the hell out of him. Hearing the rasp in her voice had affected him in a way nothing had before. Because he'd feared for their baby? Or because Alina had been hurting? Both had ripped him apart.

On his return, he felt the taut knot in his gut ease at the tinge of colour in her cheeks. He gave her the tea and biscuits, scrutinised her as he drank his tea, the same flavour. If he had to he'd make herb tea his regular drink at home. Just in case.

'I feel better. Thank you.' She started to rise.

He stopped her, catching hold of her arm. 'You're sure?'

Her smile was steadier. 'I'm fine.'

Alina went to the kitchen, where the salad she'd been preparing waited, not realising he was behind her until he spoke.

'What can I do to help?'

Help? He hadn't offered before. She'd never been sick before. 'I can manage. You go do whatever you had planned.'

He hesitated, his cobalt eyes gleaming with an emotion she didn't dare try to decipher. The new upheaval in her abdomen had nothing to do with her being pregnant.

'Go. I can handle kebabs and salad.'

Why did it take so much effort to drag her eyes from him? She forced herself to concentrate on the half-finished carrot.

'I'll call you when it's ready.'

The grunt he made was unintelligible and utterly male. It tickled the edge of her memory. Was quickly relegated to the clouds, where it belonged. She sneaked a peek as he left, wished she hadn't.

His grey shirt was moulded to muscles toned to perfection from swimming and working out. Her gaze was drawn down past his trim waist to firm buttocks that flexed with each step. Her breath quickened. This was crazy. She was checking him out like a teenager.

Her knees shook. She flattened her hands on the bench-top for support, barely aware of the peeler handle digging into her palm. She craved ice-cold water, cursed the heat flooding her body. Daren't risk walking to the tap.

He spun round, catching her off guard. 'By the way…' His mouth stayed open. His eyes widened. He grinned—a conspiratorial I-know-what-you're-thinking grin. Moved slowly towards her, holding her spellbound with captivating blue eyes.

The music from the speakers reached a dramatic crescendo, heightening the atmosphere. It had hardly registered until then. Now it filled the space between them. The width of the room. The breadth of the kitchen island. The length of his arm.

She faced him, her brain in a quandary as warnings of danger sparred with reminders of his kisses. He halted at that arm's distance, his eyes now sombre, his features composed. A façade. She noted his rigid stance, the way he'd fisted his hands.

'Are you game to try again?'

She heard the caution in his voice. The kiss? He'd initiated it; she was the one who'd allowed it to become more intimate. This time there'd be no intoxicating flavour of wine or coffee. She guessed he'd used mouthwash, had seen him drink peppermint tea. Just in case.

Until Tuesday's highly emotional embrace in the pool

his kisses had been mostly tender—a gentle way of gradually familiarising her with his touch. Their intimate kiss, though interrupted, had been a giant advance in their relationship. A definite declaration that he found her attractive. Desired her.

There'd been no mention of their sleeping together, but she couldn't deny her body responded to his virility, couldn't stop his image invading her thoughts. Oh, Lord, had her nausea been triggered by guilt, by feelings of infidelity?

He quietly waited for her answer. They both knew there was only one way to resolve the issue.

'Yes.'

Her single husky word had him enfolding her and gently covering her mouth with his. The music faded. The air around them crackled. Time stood still. His lips moved slowly, persuasively over hers. His hands stroked unhurriedly, without pressure. He kept space between their bodies.

Her fingertips inched up his chest until they touched his skin. His body trembled. His earthy Ethan aroma filled her lungs, clouding her brain. Dominating her will. Freeing her will. Her fingers twisted into his hair. Her lips parted.

Ethan held his breath, every muscle tensed in a supreme effort not to sweep his tongue inside to explore the sweetness he'd sampled earlier. Being restrained with a woman was a new experience for him. Mutual attraction led to equally satisfying sex. No strings. No commitment.

This was different. For indefinable reasons. After the initial spontaneous jolt everything he'd done had been influenced by the fact she was pregnant. Or had it? When they were apart she was in his head. When they were together he couldn't stop looking, touching and inhaling her essence, fresh as spring.

He slowly traced a line with his tongue around the soft,

moist inside of her lips. She gasped, taking in his breath. Quivered under his roaming hands. His body hardened and he shuffled his feet, widening the gap. Sliding his tongue in deeper, he cautiously stoked hers, fully prepared to stop at the slightest hint of distress.

There was none—only a timid response that almost had him hauling her closer. There was no sense of time. It felt as if he were standing on the edge of a precipice, knowing there was something wonderful waiting if he'd just let himself fall. With a rough shuddering breath he lifted his head to gaze into clear, shining eyes.

'I guess it was one of those inexplicable pregnancy things, huh?'

Her spontaneous laugh zapped his already strained senses.

'Seems like it.'

To double-check, he kissed her briefly, firmly. 'So— you feel okay?' His pulse kicked up even higher when she flick-licked her bottom lip and smiled, as if she'd tasted something delicious.

'Go—or you won't be eating dinner tonight.'

He went, deeming it an option he'd happily choose.

On Saturday morning Alina paced restlessly round the apartment. Something was itching at her brain—wouldn't surface, wouldn't go. She'd booted up her computer. Closed it down. She'd changed, walked into the gym, turned, walked out. Changed back into jeans and a top. Curled up with her embroidery, packed it away after a few stitches. Every room was tidy; everything was clean.

She glanced at the kitchen calendar and the notation for tonight: *Dinner with parents.* An unavoidable ordeal to be endured. She was convinced they wouldn't be adding her to their regular guest list unless they wanted Ethan there too. And he'd given her the impression he'd happily miss most of their organised events.

A picture flashed into her head at the sight of today's date. She quickly blocked it out. She didn't do special days.

Tenuous, ghost-like memories nipped at the edge of her mind, wouldn't be dismissed. Tears welled in her eyes as memories crashed back. Her mother-in-law's birthday. *Mum.* Unlike Sophia, she'd welcomed Alina, drawn her into the family and loved her as a daughter. She'd be lucky if Sophia tolerated her for the time she was here.

Ethan had family and friends for support. She didn't begrudge him any of them; he'd need all the help available next year. She had no one. Unless…

You only have to reach out. There'll be no recriminations, only love and understanding.

Her thumb trembled as she scrolled through her phone for the name and number. A short tear-choked conversation later she grabbed her handbag and ran out the door, heading for the one person she could tell anything. Though she wouldn't reveal the whole truth.

Where was she? Ethan drummed his fingers on his office desk, forced himself to focus on the computer screen, re-reading figures he hadn't taken in before. They were good. His mindset wasn't. He exited the program, scowling. Why hadn't she returned his calls?

He hadn't been concerned when she hadn't answered her mobile or the apartment phone at first, assuming she was in the gym area. Now, however… He checked his watch for the umpteenth time. Ten past twelve—over two hours since his first call.

He rotated sideways, staring at the city skyline, seeing only her face, wondering why she'd been so subdued this morning after they'd spent two enjoyable evenings together. Maybe it was one of the mood swings detailed in his book.

He grabbed his phone again, hesitated with his hand in mid-air. It rang, vibrating in his palm. Wrong caller ID. After quickly dealing with the matter, he went to the coffee machine. With refilled mug in hand he paced the floor, trying to convince himself it was normal trepidation given her condition.

In truth, she'd triggered something inside him from the moment they'd met—something incomprehensible. She didn't fit his long-term plan in any way. Grieving and haunted, she was determined not to stay in Australia. He wouldn't stop her leaving, though he'd give her support for as long as she wished. He wasn't perfect, but the child she carried needed a parent as hang-up-free as possible. And right now *he* needed her to answer her damn phone.

Grabbing a printed report on his Gold Coast hotel, he sprawled on the long sofa, his mug and mobile on the low table by his side. Normally he'd have been elated that the renovations were on schedule and under budget.

Startled by his ringtone, he almost knocked over his coffee in his haste to grab his phone. His adrenaline spiked when he saw the caller ID. He sucked in air, tried to project a calm he definitely didn't feel.

'Alina.'

'Ethan, I'm sorry.'

Her distressed voice chilled his heart. Feigned calm flew out of the window. He was on his feet, striding to grab his jacket as he spoke.

'What's wrong? Where are you? I'll come for you.' Hell, he felt as desperate as he sounded.

'No! It's nothing. I'm an idiot, that's all.' Breathless. Anxious.

He stilled. Wished he was there so he could see her face, read how upset she really was. 'Tell me.'

'I went to visit my husband's aunt. We sat in the garden and my bag was inside, on her sofa. I missed all your calls.'

Spontaneous laughter surged up his throat and burst out at the simple explanation. She was all right. She was safe. He perched on his desk, torn between pure relief and self-reproach for worrying so much.

'It's not funny. I've got six messages from you.'

Her slightly miffed tone was endearing.

'I'm just glad you're okay. Where are you now?'

'Sitting on a bus.'

He wanted her here, wanted to hold her. Wanted to shake her for scaring him. Kiss her until she melted in his arms.

'Why were you calling?' she added.

'My father rang, asking if we could arrive half an hour earlier tonight.'

She was always ready on time—he could have called when he left the office. Then he wouldn't have had two hours of angst. Or heard her sweet, apologetic voice.

'No last-minute reprieve, huh?'

'I'm afraid not. You're sure you're okay?' He sure as hell hadn't been, two minutes ago.

'I'm fine. I'm truly sorry for worrying you, Ethan.'

'Worrying me? You, my sweet, are putting me through emotions I can't even name.'

He ended the call, huffing the air from his lungs as he tossed his phone onto his desk. He wasn't normally prone to panic. If there was a problem he coolly and methodically searched for a solution.

Was this new apprehension going to be part of his future? A normality of being a parent? He'd probably be overloaded with advice and disaster stories once his friends found out about his impending fatherhood. Knowing they'd be there for him and his child, he'd take it all in the spirit it would be given.

Alina had said she had no family, and yet there was this aunt—her husband's aunt. And maybe other relatives? How close was she to them? Close enough to want to re-establish contact. Why deny them before? Why turn to them now?

Hell, he'd hardly learnt anything about her; she kept her guard up tight. That hadn't been an issue when they'd met and agreed to marry for the child's sake. Now she was real to him, she was special in a way he'd never felt before. *He* wanted to be the one she reached out to for support.

Alina wriggled uneasily on the bus seat. Unflappable, down-to-earth Ethan had been rattled until she'd explained. If that teenager texting with his head bent hadn't bumped into her, she wouldn't have thought to check her phone. An incident she'd skip mentioning. She accepted his reasons for being over-protective, preferred not to give him cause to be more so.

She replayed his words in her mind. He'd seemed genuinely concerned for her. The tenderness in his voice during that last remark had almost had her saying, *Ditto*.

Once he'd recovered from the initial shock of her pregnancy he'd been very supportive. He hadn't pressured her for the details of her life she'd rather keep private. And, while his physical attraction to her was obvious, his manner had been conciliatory, letting her set the boundaries.

It was parent confrontation time. Ethan glanced at the dashboard clock and eased his foot on the accelerator. Alina sat quietly, hadn't said much at all since he'd arrived home. There'd only been time for him to grab a quick shower and change before leaving. He'd still had the reality of her having relatives on his mind, hadn't wanted to talk either. Even if he could figure out how to bring up the subject, now was not the time.

He glanced over. She was staring ahead, pale and rigid, as if being driven to the guillotine. Her left hand was hidden but he'd bet it was doing that finger dance. His heart wrenched. Sweet, brave Alina, with demons he could only imagine, was prepared to confront his ultra-judgemental parents for *his* benefit, and he was jealous because she'd called someone who'd be on her side.

Jealous! No, he couldn't be. He flicked her another look, felt a deep surge of tenderness. Accepted the reality of that emotion, new for him.

Taking his hand from the wheel, he gently covered hers for a few seconds. 'You are beautiful, Alina Fletcher. I'm proud to have you by my side—any time, anywhere.'

His reward was a tentative smile. He wanted more.

Alina toyed with her hair, smoothed her skirt over her slightly rounded belly. Was it too late to ask him to take her home? Too late. Too cowardly. They were the child's nearest relatives, next to him. Maybe they'd mellow with age; grandparents often did. She'd be gone soon, so any adverse judgement on her shouldn't impact on Ethan or the baby.

The vibes she'd picked up from Ethan had exacerbated her tension, turning the butterflies in her tummy to turbulent judders. She wished she were anywhere else—like on the Manly Ferry, steaming across the heads, wind blowing her hair, spray cooling her cheeks. And Ethan surrounding her, his chest at her back, arms at her sides. Shielding her. Protective.

Her eyes widened and she pressed back in her seat as they drove through the gates of the formidable James couple's opulent home. It was a two-storey, luxurious mansion, like something out of a magazine, set in flawless landscaped gardens. The back area was as impressive as the front.

They pulled up. Reluctant to leave the security of the vehicle, she sat, vaguely aware of him moving around the front of the vehicle, opening her door and hunkering down beside her. Gentle fingers stroked her arm. Empathetic eyes met hers when she looked up.

'Remember, this is all for show. The house. The decor. Their attitude. Real life is you, me and our baby.'

His hand splayed protectively over her stomach, radiating warmth with his touch, diminishing her fears. A little.

'You won't be left alone with either of them. They can insinuate all they like; they'll only learn what we choose to tell them.'

Unbuckling her seatbelt, he helped her out. She gripped his hand, felt his flesh dent under her nails. 'I'm worried I'll let you down.'

He shook his head. 'Impossible. You're the bravest woman I've ever met. Our marriage, our lives, are exactly that. *Ours.* Don't forget, it's they who are on notice.'

Giving her that special Ethan smile, he raised her hand and pressed his lips to her palm. Electrifying quivers sped along her veins, through her, settling in her stomach. A lovely, if slightly scary feeling. She smiled back and he led her round to the front steps. She was thankful her flowing dress hid her condition, grateful for the strength of his fingers entwined with hers.

CHAPTER THIRTEEN

ETHAN RANG THE DOORBELL, wishing they were home…
alone. Alina's trembling vibrated through his palm and
his heart twisted. Taking her into his arms, he kissed her
for comfort, keeping it tender. Until he heard her contented
sigh. Until she softened into him.

'Try to contain yourself, Ethan. There's no excuse for
a public exhibition.'

Alina flinched. Ethan barely stirred at the caustic remark from behind him, though his gut tightened with irritation. Then he reluctantly lifted his head, scanning the
large empty garden before grinning wryly.

'Hardly public, Father.'

His chest expanded as he smiled down at Alina, seeing her sweet blush and the glow in her eyes. *He'd* done
that—taken her from apprehension to desire. With a kiss
that contained a promise for later.

'Alina, this is my father—Martin James. Father, I'd like
you to meet Alina Fletcher.'

His father inclined his head towards her. 'Please come
in, Ms Fletcher.'

Embarrassment flooded Ethan at the stilted remark. He
stiffened, quite prepared to walk away. Alina forestalled
him, moving forward, hand extended. Leaving his father
no choice but to accept her greeting.

'Thank you, Mr James. It's very kind of you and your
wife to invite me.' Deliciously tongue in cheek.

The air whooshed from his lungs. He stared in admiration at this poised woman whom he'd sensed had been ready
to bolt a few minutes ago. She'd been surprising him from

the moment they met. Anticipation of the months ahead zipped along his veins.

They entered together, Alina's hand in his once more. Was she comparing the cold, immaculate decor to the welcoming, comfy atmosphere of Louise's courtyard home in Barcelona? He did—every time he came here.

A sharp intake of breath at his side made him aware he was crushing her fingers. He loosened his grip, gave her an apologetic glance—and was completely thrown when she winked her left eye at him. A simple act that triggered a fuzzy memory of something shared. Of concealed laughter.

Alina noticed his startled expression, but had no time to jog his memory. Sophia James was waiting for them. She lifted her chin, quite prepared to confront the woman who would one day take great pleasure in telling her son, *I told you so.*

He knew it, accepted it, and would handle it with his natural diplomacy. At least he'd have the consolation of his son or daughter.

Why the sudden depression? She'd asked for her freedom—had to have it. Had to keep moving. No ties. No commitments. Keep the memories blocked out. She feared there was now going to be so much more she'd have to not remember.

Sophia was standing regally, ready to be greeted. She reminded Alina of the titled women of history—so proud, so extremely conscious of their presumed status in life. With another quick squeeze of her hand Ethan led her forward, not letting go as he greeted his mother with a light kiss on her proffered cheek.

'Mother, you've already met Alina—though I understand it was a brief encounter.'

Alina hoped she was the only one who heard the nuances in his introduction. Felt a flush of warmth at his championship.

'Yes, it was quite a surprise. Welcome, Alina.' Sophia gave her an obligatory social air-kiss on both cheeks. 'Shall we all sit for drinks?' She raised a perfectly trimmed eyebrow at Alina. 'Do you have a favourite cocktail, my dear?

'Iced water, thank you. I don't drink.'

Spoken so woodenly she didn't recognise her voice. She cringed inside at the pointed look exchanged between the older couple. This wasn't a family dinner; it was a formal… She didn't know what it was.

She *did* know she had the support of the man whose firm hand now guided her to the deep-cushioned sofa. For as long as she stayed in Australia—maybe even longer. His innate integrity ensured that he'd never betray or disown her. Life would have been so much better if only this staid, society-obsessed couple had appreciated the genuine affable qualities of their children.

Ethan kept his arm around her, even after a pointed scowl from his father when he gave them their drinks. He now fully comprehended the primitive male urge to protect a mate. It reinforced his determination to have everyone believe that he had married for love.

'How is the Gold Coast hotel coming along, Ethan? Is the projected opening still viable?'

'Yes, Father, but I'd rather not talk business. This is family time. Mother, I hear the charity night at the opera house you helped organise was a great success?'

'Thank you, Ethan. I'd hoped to see you there.'

'Not my scene. To support your cause I did buy three double tickets, as a bonus for ardent followers at work.'

'Opera's an acquired taste. You never gave it a chance,' his father stated.

'Simone attended with her parents,' his mother chimed in. 'She was very gracious with her condolences, and apologised for missing Louise's funeral due to a modelling assignment in New York.'

Her voice slowed as Ethan's head jerked up. His brow furrowed as a powerful surge of emotion ripped through him. *Louise. The wink.*

He flicked a quick glance at Alina, whose gaze was focused on his mother.

His sister's favourite ploy as a child—and sometimes in adulthood—had been winking, always with the left eye, to defuse a tense situation. It was one that had so often had them squirming in their seats, trying not to laugh. Alina had deliberately given him a reminder of happy times.

'Simone is the daughter of friends, Alina. She and Ethan have been close for *years*. Now, tell us about yourself. Do you have a profession?' Sophia's words were syrup-sweet, politely phrased with a definite hint of disdain.

Alina met her condescending brown eyes full-on, thought of how Louise had suffered because of this woman's attitude, and remembered her happiness when the procedure had worked. In less than a heartbeat all her apprehension evaporated.

'No. I've never needed one. I speak three languages fluently; get by in a few others. Travelling through Europe has taught me more than I'd have learnt at any university. Hands-on life is a great teacher.'

'Oh, so how do you make a living?' Slightly more acidic.

'By accepting honest casual work in a variety of places and industries.'

She felt disapproval radiate through the room. Should she continue? She hated deceit, even when it was warranted or unavoidable. This wasn't.

'Barcelona was my base. That's where I became friends with Leon and Louise.'

'So that's where you two met? Ethan...' Sophia stopped talking, flashed a wary look at her son.

'Please continue, Mother.' Ethan's arm tightened around

her shoulders. His flat, calm tone should have served as a warning. His mother missed it.

'I realise dealing with everything was paramount, but you never mentioned meeting anyone there. It hasn't even been two months since the accident, and she's...'

Another hesitation. Alina guessed it was very unusual for this very outspoken woman.

'She's what?' Harsher. A definite signal to back off.

'Oh, come on, Ethan. What do you expect?' Martin James obviously couldn't contain himself. 'You chose not to tell us about her, when you met or how. She's obviously led a nomadic life, with no ties or responsibilities. Now she's moved in with you. I assume she's not working?'

Alina's heart pounded; her stomach heaved. She heard the words, understood the implications but not the undertones. They seemed to be talking of someone or something else, using her as the target. She'd been prepared for personal questions or subtle jibes—not this blatant hostility.

No one had ever treated her this way—as if she weren't good enough to be in their company. Swinging her head from wife to husband, she saw only harsh dissatisfaction. She wanted out. She turned to Ethan—and froze.

Cold chills swept over her as she recalled his pained features after he'd read the surrogacy documents, his fury when she'd suggested his family might not want the baby. Right now he was rigidly controlled, icy. Much more intimidating.

Ethan had never been angrier. Not when a trusted friend had betrayed his loyalty. Not when a long-time girlfriend had cheated on him. Not even when a stupid, avoidable thing like a faulty brake had taken his sister and his best friend from him.

The rage building inside him was a culmination of years of their haranguing him to conform to their views, virulent criticism of his own choices. Their deplorable treatment of Leon and Louise. Plus a deep conviction that defending Alina was paramount—above anything he had ever done. Or ever would.

He rose to his feet, taking her with him, acutely aware that his teeth had ground together and his free hand had balled into a fist. One glance at Alina's face and his only thought was to get out of there, so he could beg her forgiveness for subjecting her to this poisonous atmosphere.

'This charade is over.'

'Ethan, we—'

He flicked his hand, silencing his mother, dismissing both parents. Tenderly brushing a curl from Alina's brow, he kissed her forehead. 'Let's go home, darling.'

He turned his head as they reached the door, subliminally noting their gobsmacked expressions.

'Stay away from our home. Any calls will not be answered or returned.'

The son who'd always been the mediator had finally rebelled.

Ethan refrained from gunning his car as they left the property. The fierce urge to put distance between him and his parents was tempered by the knowledge that he had the most precious cargo.

He had no doubt they'd blame Alina, having always previously claimed to their friends that it was business commitments that had caused his withdrawal from their social world. *Damn. Idiot.* He ought to have insisted their first meeting be held in a restaurant, where they'd have had no choice but to be socially polite.

Probably wouldn't have changed the end result.

He glanced across, met wounded eyes in an ash-white face and hit the brake, swinging into the kerb. He flung off his seatbelt, hauling Alina into his arms as he fumbled for her clasp. Holding her against his heart, breathing in her subtle aroma, was so liberating after the overpowering room they'd left behind, his anger began to dissipate.

'I needed this. Needed your sweetness.' He stroked her back, brushed her hair with his lips. 'I'm sorry, Alina—forgive me for taking you there. You've done nothing to deserve the way they treated you. Nothing.'

She gave a muted sound suspiciously like a sob into his chest. He threaded his fingers thorough her hair and tilted her head up. Wanted to wipe the deep sorrow in her eyes away for ever. Hated that he didn't know how. Her trembling lips broke his heart.

'Why are they like that? No one's ever treated me as if I'm nothing, not good enough to be polite to. *No one*—in all the places I've been.'

'And they'll never get another chance.'

'No.' She pushed away, shaking her head. 'They're your parents, Ethan, your family. Don't lock the door. Life can change in a split second and then it's too late to go back. We both know that.'

He threw his head back against his seat, closed his eyes. He did know, and it hurt like hell. Her self-deprecating laugh penetrated the anguish.

'I think, somewhere deep in my head, I expected them to accept me the way Colin's parents did.'

His eyes flew open at the mention of her husband. She sat, half turned towards him, hands in her lap, eyes downcast. He held his breath, didn't dare move a muscle.

'We met when he was twenty, still at uni. I was only seventeen, and a major distraction to his studies, yet his parents welcomed me, treating me like a loved daughter. They were so thrilled when…'

Lord, it was so hard not to reach for her as she painfully struggled for the next word.

'When M… M… Michael was born. We were a real family.'

She went silent. Seemed immobile. Waiting was excruciating, but he sensed there was more she wanted to say. For her own sake.

'They're all gone. I'm not.' Her head came up, eyes big and dark with despair. 'Why just me?' She began to tremble violently.

Now he moved, spurred by the stabbing pain that raked him. He enfolded her into his warmth. Desperate to comfort her, desperate for comfort himself. She'd been the only survivor. She might have died too.

Headlights lit up the windscreen. Alina pulled back, blinking, trying to regain composure. She hadn't spoken about the accident since it had happened. Why now? Why to Ethan?

'Take me home. Please.'

He didn't move, kept a loose hold on her, his features grey and heartrending, his eyes dark and tortured.

'Ethan?'

His shoulders shook as he shuddered. His eyes refocused.

'Home. Yes, let's go home.'

When they arrived at the apartment Alina stayed Ethan's hand when he reached for the light switch.

'Leave them off.'

The lights from the city gave the room a soft glow, a more confiding atmosphere. He'd defended her against his parents' insinuations; he deserved to know more than the half-reveal she'd given him. At least the meagre details she hadn't been able to avoid learning.

She poured herself a glass of water, and took her defensive place on the settee. Ethan followed with a cold beer— the drink he usually favoured in afternoons. When he saw the way she was huddled in the corner his brow furrowed, but he chose the other end, folding one leg up, his body towards her.

She drank half the glass to clear her throat, then fixed her gaze on the window. There was no emotion in her flat, detached voice.

'We'd been on a week's holiday, touring places near the New South Wales and Victoria border. The plan was to stop for the night, then drive home. Colin and his dad were both careful drivers, changing over whenever we stopped. It was getting dark, and I heard them talk of the next town being about thirty minutes away before I fell asleep.'

Ethan gripped the cold metal can so hard it began to buckle. His throat was so tight he could hardly breathe. He knew what was coming, didn't want to hear it. Couldn't avoid it. Couldn't take his eyes from her pale, impassive face and blank, unseeing eyes. He watched her drain her glass, swallow with difficulty, and shiver as she drew in breath.

'Everything's a blur after that. Screams, thuds, screeching metal. Voices and sirens. That hospital smell. I don't remember who told me. Someone in the corridor mentioned a kangaroo and a semitrailer. I didn't want to know—never want to know.' Her voice broke. 'I had concussion from a head wound, lots of cuts and bruises. And they all died.'

Her empty glass fell into her lap. She hunched over, covering her face with her hands.

Ethan's hand shook as he put down his drink and automatically moved her glass to the table. Her words had torn an agonising path into the depths of his soul. A tiny twist of fate and he'd never have known her.

Would she push him away if he reached for her? His confidence faltered.

'Alina?' Desperate. Begging to help her. 'I'm here. Whenever you want or need me.'

She lifted tortured eyes that stared at him as if she won-

dered who he was, why he was there. Then her face cleared
and she flung herself into his arms.

'Ethan. Hold me.'

He cradled her as close as humanly possible, needing to
reassure her. Needing reassurance himself. *She was meant
to live. Meant to have this baby with him. Meant to love
again one day.*

'Hold me tight, Ethan. Hold me. Please don't let me be
alone.'

He held her. For as long as she'd let him, he'd hold her.

'You're not alone any more, darling. I'm not going anywhere. Not without you. I'll be here to hold you, comfort
and care for you. You, my beautiful, courageous Alina.'

He caressed her back, murmured words from his heart,
knowing she might not understand. Knowing only that he
needed to voice how much she'd come to mean to him. The
baby she carried was an added joy.

He kept talking, even after her body softened in sleep
against him. He had no idea when she'd be ready to hear
his admission in the cold light of day.

A long-forgotten sensation infiltrated Alina's brain, enticing her to wake; less pleasant ones held her in limbo. A familiar earthy aroma surrounded her. A light breeze stirred
her hair. She moved, yet the warm wall at her side stayed.
Warmth spread from the weight on her stomach.

Her senses kicked in. Her eyes fluttered, flew open. She
was lying on her back, early-morning light allowing her
to see an unknown painting on the wrong wall. A white-
sleeve-covered arm stretched out from under her neck. She
was in Ethan's arms. In his bed. Still wearing her dress.

Her last recollection was of Ethan twisting them both so
they lay prone on the settee, of his hands soothing her to
sleep. He'd done as she'd pleaded, had cradled her. Hadn't
left her on her own.

She turned her head. He lay on his side, his chest moving in steady rhythm. Hassle-free in sleep, his features were softer, the tiny lines at the corners of his eyes less obvious. His stubbled jaw was strangely appealing. He slept so peacefully for a man whose world had been blown apart. By her.

She arched her neck. To wake the sleeping Prince with a kiss? Crazy notion. She rolled towards the edge of the bed.

'Alina?' Slumber-rough and drowsy.

His hand caught her arm, slipped off, and she slid onto the floor.

'It's late. I have things to do.'

Like run from an awkward situation.

CHAPTER FOURTEEN

ETHAN HAD THE table set when Alina arrived in the dining area, calm and guarded. She quickly sat down without speaking, not giving him the chance to be polite. He understood her reticence, hoped she'd still feel able to talk about her family.

She flicked a glance at him as he put a mug of peach tea in front of her. A delicate rosy hue coloured her skin. Where was the feistiness she'd shown in the past?

He felt her gaze follow him as he took his seat, grabbed his favourite cereal and filled his bowl.

'That was cowardly of me.'

Subdued tone. Why was she so nervous? Waiting for her to elucidate, he prayed her confession hadn't caused a regression in their growing relationship.

'When I woke up in your bed I bolted like a naive teenager.'

He nodded. 'A natural reaction after your revelations, Alina.'

She filled her bowl with fruity nut muesli, kept her head down while she ate, as if mulling over an important issue.

'Was there a woman in your life when I came?'

He spluttered on his coffee. Hell, she kept finding new ways to surprise him.

'There hasn't been anyone for a long time. I swear there will be no one as long as you are with me.'

Her nod was barely perceptible. She swallowed as she averted her gaze, reinforcing her apprehension. Hidden under the table, her left hand would be performing its ritual dance.

'Do… Do you expect… Want me to move into your room after the wedding?'

She completely took his breath away with that one. His jaw dropped; adrenaline zapped through his veins. He'd been trying to work out how to introduce the topic gently; she'd come right out with it. He leant back, studying her, wondering if she realised how courageous and strong she was.

'Alina Fletcher, you are amazing. I've bulldozed you into agreements you'd rather run a mile from. My actions have rekindled harrowing memories you'd prefer were left buried. Yet you offer compromises which will reinforce our child's parentage.'

Her eyes widened as he spoke. The soft blush he'd begun to anticipate and adore tinged her cheeks. Across the table was too far a distance. Pushing his chair away, he walked around it, took her hand and lifted her to her feet. Cupped her cheek.

'Having you in my arms as I fell asleep felt better than anything I can remember. As if protecting you and our baby gives my life true meaning for the first time. I'd like to feel that way every night, but the choice is yours, Alina. Now, after we're married or never. I want you there only if it's where *you* want to be.'

She placed her hand over his heart, her lips curling into a sweet smile and a warm glow flickering in her eyes.

'It felt nice.' She glanced away, breathed in, then met his eyes again. 'Can we talk about Colin's aunt and uncle? Jean and Ray?'

Any subject was fine by him. Every conversation revealed a little more of who they were and brought them closer. He settled her back into her seat.

Alina gathered the thoughts that had tumbled through her mind as she'd showered and dressed. Looking into Ethan's sympathetic eyes, she suddenly found it easy.

'They were the ones who held it all together for me after… Well, you know. They and the solicitor arranged everything—cleared the house and sold it, put everything in storage.'

She stopped, turned her head to stare at the floor. Looked at him again.

'They took me in and cared for me, even though they were grieving too. I owed them so much and I ran. Fled the country. I phoned or wrote occasionally, and sent postcards of the places I visited. Yesterday she was so welcoming… refused to let me feel guilty.'

'Because she understands. You needed time and distance to heal. I'd like to meet them. And I think you'd like them to be at our wedding.'

'Yes, very much.'

'After we've eaten, ring and see if they're home today.'

Unlucky to see the bride before the wedding? *Yeah, right— that had really worked for her before.*

Sophia James had probably insisted that Louise follow tradition. And Alina hadn't been able to deny Jean's request after she'd been so supportive, even promising to keep the wedding a secret.

Ethan had won Jean and Ray over with his charm and sincerity, convincing them that Alina was the only woman he'd ever wanted to marry. Jean truly believed he loved her. Only Alina knew he wanted to ensure the baby's right to his name.

After a teasing protest he had agreed to let Alina and Jean spend two nights in the hotel suite in order to shop and prepare. His compromise had been being allowed to have a short time alone with Alina the night before the ceremony.

He'd sat beside her in the lounge, took her hand and pressed his lips to her knuckles.

'Everything had to be arranged so quickly we didn't follow many of the usual traditions. This one I can make right.'

Before she could speak he stunned her by dropping to one knee without relinquishing his hold.

'Alina Fletcher, will you marry me tomorrow? Be my wife for as long as you feel you can?'

Her heart lurched at the hitch in his voice on the second question. Her eyes misted; her throat choked up. She looked into sincere cobalt eyes and her answer came easily.

'Yes, I'll marry you, Ethan.' She refused to think about the time limit right now.

He pulled a flat black box engraved with a familiar jeweller's name from his jacket. The exquisite amethyst pendant was a flawless match for her engagement ring. Another thoughtful gift she wasn't sure she deserved.

She stared wide-eyed at this man who'd so drastically changed her life, pushed and cajoled her in matters he deemed important, eased off and given her freedom in others. Like where she slept. Knowing she was attracted to him, yet still unsure of herself, she hadn't slept with him again. As promised, he hadn't mentioned it.

Over the last two weeks they'd slipped into an easy friendship she wanted to maintain though it was inexplicably frustrating sometimes. Hormones again?

'It's lovely, Ethan. Why…?'

'Because I wanted to.'

His lips covered hers in a long tender kiss. She slid the box onto the couch, leant in and wound her arms around his neck. Somehow she ended up in his lap on the floor, wishing he could stay.

When he left his whispered, 'I'll miss you…' was as tender as his kiss.

The wedding party was waiting for them in the roof garden. She had no reason to stall. Her hair shone with new highlights, its longer length framing her face and curling on her neck. The make-up applied by a beautician was light and perfect. Her long chiffon dress, shimmering with shades of lilac and silver, fell softly over her burgeoning bump. Her new necklace completed the illusion.

This wasn't the shy girl in a white princess gown who had trembled with eager anticipation eleven years ago. The woman staring at her today was a mature stranger, fulfilling a vow to friends. No wildly beating heart. No dreams of eternal love. Strip off the trappings and tonight's ceremony was just a formal recognition of the decision Ethan had made to remedy a family dilemma.

Everything changed the moment she stepped out of the elevator. He was watching for her, impeccably dressed in a dark suit, white shirt and dark blue tie, his brilliant cobalt gaze immediately zoning in on hers. A dashing knight waiting for his princess.

Her feet refused to move forward. Sensations cascaded through her brain, impossible to separate. Except for the one certainty she'd clung to since consenting to his scheme—her trust in this man, and her absolute belief that he'd never hurt or betray her.

Her palms began to sweat as they gripped her orchid and fern bouquet. Her insides melted in a rush of heat while her heartbeat crashed into a rock 'n' roll drum rhythm.

A gentle nudge came from behind her. 'He's waiting for you, Alina.'

Not any more. He strode forward, eyes gleaming, his radiant smile just for her. Taking her hands, he drew her to him, the rough timbre of his voice revealing his emotion. 'Exquisite. Unforgettable.'

Through misty eyes she was vaguely aware of Jean moving past her to join the others, glimpsed a photographer beside the celebrant. The city noises faded until there was only Ethan holding her, surrounded by a neon-enhanced darkening blue sky.

His lips touched hers lightly, reverently. In an instant her mind cleared. Her reservations dissipated. She kissed him back, standing on tiptoe for deeper contact. The tremor that shook his body echoed in hers. They walked together to the flower festooned arch where she relinquished her bouquet, allowing them to join hands as they stood face to face.

At this service the male response was calmer, clearer than the one so long ago. It ought to be impassive. Yet there was something in the resonance of his voice, in the pressure of his grasp and in the depths of his eyes that chipped at the barricades guarding her heart. She replied with the vows that would bind her to him in kind, without qualms or hesitation.

'I pronounce you husband and wife.'

Not waiting for permission, Ethan kissed her with all the fervour of a loving groom. Hugs and kisses were exchanged, and after the certificates were signed they all moved to a small lamplit marquee.

The first toast was to the bride and groom, wishing them a long and happy life together. As they clinked glasses Ethan's piercing eyes sent a message for her alone. His distinct, 'To us!' triggered a pleasurable shiver.

The celebrant left and then their entrées were served. The wine waiter refilled their glasses and moved discreetly away.

Ethan spoke next. 'To those who will always be remembered, living on in our hearts.' He held out his glass to Alina, dropped his gaze to her stomach and mouthed *Louise and Leon*. She reciprocated, touching her glass to his.

Then *her husband*—a phrase she'd believed she'd never think or say again—surprised her even more. His fingertips gently lifted her chin and his eyes darkened with intensity as he repeated the salute. Her eyes misted as she understood his generous gesture. For Colin, his parents and Michael.

The sweet liquid caught in her throat as she suddenly realised there'd been only a numbing sorrow as she'd thought their names. Had she come through the darkness, as Jean had suggested this morning? Not really. Ethan found it so easy to believe in *our* baby. Her maternal feelings had died on a dusky country road.

She was definitely appreciative of the delicious specially prepared courses, making a mental note to send a written thank-you to the chef and his staff. Everyone in the know had been loyal and discreet—a tribute to the man by her side.

Ethan fiddled with his new gold ring. The sun had set. Hot drinks and handmade chocolates had been served. He was married—something he hadn't envisaged in his foreseeable future. If he ever had, he would have imagined his choice would be one of his peers—a successful woman with interests they'd share, who had no desire to procreate.

Circumstances and his code of honour had dictated otherwise. Yet to his amazement he felt satisfied, content, as if he'd found a unique treasure he hadn't realised he'd been searching for. The vows he'd made to her were real. Her vows had been defined and strong.

As if sensing his attention, Alina turned to meet his gaze. When she smiled shyly contentment morphed into something earthier, lustier. He'd never had the urge to swing any other woman round and then drag her into a mind-blowing kiss. Never had an impulse to sneak away at a family function for a kiss and a cuddle—maybe more. Now he stared into enticing violet eyes and imagined it all happening.

Tonight there were no shutters; her wide-eyed open expression raised the hairs on his nape. Tingled his spine.

Flipped his heart. *Alina James*. The name rolled sweetly off his tongue.

'Well, Alina James, do I call for the car or do you want more dessert?'

'I'm full. It was all so delicious.'

The tip of her tongue licked her lip, as if searching for a final taste, sending a fiery jolt to his groin.

They were alone apart from the limousine driver. Ethan wrapped his arms around his bride and kissed her, slow and deep. His body responded with a sharp tug, low in his gut. She tasted sweet—pavlova-sweet. He craved more. He craved pure Alina taste.

His wife. They were legally one. She…

He was doused in a cold shower of reality. He could do nothing that might remind Alina of her first wedding night. Nothing she might regret in the morning.

He settled back holding her close, murmured, 'We'll soon be home, Mrs James,' into her ear.

Home. The word echoed in Alina's head. Her home—for as long as she chose to stay. Ethan had given the impression he meant every word of his vows. Only she knew he didn't.

'Tired, sweetheart?' The tenderness in his eyes melted her misgivings.

'Just thinking. Thank you for making tonight so wonderful, even if it's n—'

His mouth cut off the rest. Powerful and firm. Punishing. 'It's as real as any other,' he grated, tilting her face, his flashing dark eyes boring into hers. 'Don't ever forget that.'

Her body chilled, as if she'd dived into icy water. She'd offended him—the last thing she'd intended. Tears prickled in her eyes as she struggled for words to put it right.

Suddenly she was crushed against him and kissed, with a thoroughness that left her body alive and burning.

He looked dazed when he broke away, bemused and

aroused. She knew he'd see the same in her. Complete obliviousness to their surroundings.

Ethan's fingers shook as they cradled her cheek. 'Alina, darling…' He trembled as he drank her in. His reaction when she'd denied their marriage was real had astounded him. He'd endeavoured to show her how valid it was to him. Succeeded spectacularly. With a kiss like none he'd ever known.

He struggled to draw air into empty lungs, fought to clear his brain. He'd been lost in a fantasy world where the only reality was the taste of Alina on his tongue and the softness of her in his arms. Heaven.

Her stunning eyes were dark and bewildered. His stomach twisted. Bewitched by her beauty, and by her response to his kisses, he'd allowed his own ardour to override the need for restraint. Only noisy revelry out on the street as the vehicle stopped had thrown him back to reality.

He leant his forehead on hers and sucked in air scented with spring and his wife. 'I'm the one who's apologising now. Not for the kiss. Never for the kiss as long as I live. Not for anything we've shared—especially tonight. I have no right to be angry when you've complied so willingly with everything I've asked of you.'

He helped her from the car, thanked the driver and hugged her to his side as they walked to the elevator, squeezed tighter as they flew upward. When the ping announced the opening of the doors he scooped her into his arms—ignoring her protests—and stepped out.

'This is for me, sweetheart.'

Her pupils dilated, making her eyes even more alluring.

'This will be my once in a lifetime.'

He jiggled her body onto his chest as he used his key card, pushed open the door, and covered her lips with his as he carried her over the threshold. She slid her arm around his neck, her fingertips curling into his hair.

After kicking the door shut he continued the kiss, slowly letting her slide down until her feet were on the floor. Clasping her hands, he stepped back, imprinting her into his memory.

'Tonight was special in so many ways, but this is the memory I'll keep for ever. You—so incredibly beautiful, so enticingly sweet.'

Alina watched his Adam's apple bounce as he swallowed his emotion. She'd been right in thinking their relationship might change—wrong to believe that it was a bad thing. Hormones or not, she couldn't deny she cared about Ethan James.

'You made it special, Ethan. I was… Oh, I don't know how to explain. Then you were there, and everything was right.'

'And now I have to let you go to bed.'

She heard the desire in his voice, saw it in his eyes. For a second she wondered why she wasn't pulling away and running. Then she gave her answer without any qualms.

'I'm your wife.'

She felt his tension flow out, even though their hands were their only contact. Heat flared in his eyes, quickly softening to concern.

'And much more than I deserve, Alina James. Turn around.'

He unclasped her necklace and trailed light kisses across her neck. Slipped his arms around her and drew her close, his breath teasing her earlobe.

'Go to bed, darling. While I can still let you leave. Tonight I want no regrets.'

Her cheeks burned. She'd refused to think of *that other* first night, and yet he'd understood how it might come flooding back. She'd blatantly offered herself, denying the possible—probable—consequences.

Twisting to face him, she touched her fingertips to his

lips. 'I'm sorry, Ethan, I'm being selfish. I thought if you held me it wouldn't—'

'It still might. But I'll hold you in whichever bed you choose. Tonight we'll sleep. Tomorrow we'll start our honeymoon.'

She raised up onto her toes and pressed her lips to his, kept it brief.

'Thank you, Ethan.'

Her final thought as sleep overtook her was I'm Mrs Alina Paulette James…

CHAPTER FIFTEEN

ETHAN STOOD BY the lounge window, swirling his brandy in its glass, oblivious to one of Australia's most iconic views. He was reliving the emotional rollercoaster he'd ridden since the elevator doors had opened to reveal his exquisite bride.

The moment she'd seen him her stunning eyes had seemed to fill her face. She'd stopped, giving him the chance to take in every gorgeous centimetre of her. His heart had hammered; his stomach had clenched. His brain had ceased to function logically.

Her tongue-tip had flicked nervously over her tempting lips. With her bouquet held defensively over her baby bump, she'd been like a frightened animal, captured in a hunter's spotlight, unable to move. So adorable. So courageous.

He'd made no conscious decision; his movement towards her had been instinctive, as natural as breathing. Drawing her close and kissing her had eased the unaccustomed ache from being apart from her. The brightness in her eyes as they'd stood face to face, hands joined for the ceremony, had given him cause to hope.

Yet as she'd sworn, ''Till death do us part...' her fingers had lain cool in his, her voice had been calm and steady, making him wonder if she still had no intention of honouring that vow. Then she'd returned his kiss with a fervour that had made his head spin.

His cognac was failing to have its usual satisfying effect. His complete focus was on Alina.

He rinsed the glass and went to find her. She lay on her side, in *his* bed, one hand tucked under her cheek. His wife—for as long as he could persuade her to stay.

Sliding in beside her, he cradled her into his body and splayed his hand on her belly. *Alina James. Baby James.* His family. Here in his arms where he could protect them. All was right with his world.

With a deep sigh of contentment, he fell asleep.

Inching carefully out of Ethan's arms, Alina sat up, curbing the impulse to stroke his stubbled jaw. With his long dark lashes and tanned muscular body, plus a secret smile as if he were dreaming of hidden delights, he created a magazine picture that would have women lining up to buy it.

His brand-new gold ring caught her eye. She glanced down at hers, bright and shiny, a symbol of hope. She was *married*. Tendrils of the past crept into her head, were dismissed immediately. The future was unknown, not to be thought about. The now...

Her skin tingled. Lifting her head, she met Ethan's wide-awake gaze and sensual smile.

'I was looking forward to waking you with a kiss, Mrs James.' Husky. Thick.

'From your expression, whatever you were dreaming must have been better,' she teased.

A second later, she was flat on her back, drowning in dark cobalt contemplation.

'Nothing could be better than kissing my wife good morning.'

Appropriate action swiftly followed his declaration. She closed her mind, and surrendered to the ardour of his skilful lips. Everything was changing. Every day the fine line between role-playing and reality became more blurred. No longer a solitary entity, she was once again joined with someone.

'I meant to wake earlier. We have a full day in front of us, Alina.'

His rough inflections as he gulped air while trying to talk amused and thrilled her.

'Then you'd better let me go.' Teasing, half hoping he wouldn't.

He braced himself on his arms, blue eyes gleaming with suppressed delight. 'Ultrasound, then lunch. Okay?'

She nodded, not quite sure where he was going with this.

'After that my visit to tell my parents we are married will take a couple of hours. Which gives you plenty of time to pack. I've booked a holiday house in the Blue Mountains until Sunday.' He grinned like a magician who'd pulled off an amazing trick.

If an open mouth and wide eyes was the reaction he'd hoped for, he got it. Alina's heart pounded as she realised that their recent discussion on Australian tourist spots had been him info-gathering. He'd taken note of the places she'd never been to, ensuring his plans didn't clash with her memories. Another chink in her armour widened.

'Just the two of us, alone in the Blue Mountains. Time to get to know each other better without any distractions.'

'What about work?' He'd be getting calls all day.

'All fixed. Emergencies only.'

The pavements were crowded. Alina stared through the tinted glass at people living normal lives, fiddled with her two rings. It wasn't nerves. Heck, she'd been through this procedure three times. Truth was, she was scared she might begin to care for the life inside her once she'd seen an active image on the screen. Feared she wouldn't. She wasn't sure which would be worse.

'Try to relax, Alina.' Ethan covered her restless hands with his. 'With new technology the imagery will be enhanced.'

So they'd see everything more clearly. She'd prefer vague and fuzzy.

'This was meant to be a happy time…the three of us were supposed to be together at every stage.' Her voice cracked. She bit her lip, refusing to cry.

'Now you only have me,' he remarked wryly. 'A poor substitute, but I'll do my best.'

Hearing the sorrow in his voice, she felt contrite. They were both in need of comfort.

'I wish I could talk about them without being torn apart. About the way Leon's face lit up when he saw the blue lines, their laughter when he picked Louise up and spun her round… It hurts that their happiness only lasted a few weeks.'

'Happiness *you* gave them. For that alone I'll always be in your debt.'

He let go of her hands, hugged her so close she felt his ragged breath rumble up his chest. She thanked her lucky stars—not that there'd been much evidence that she had any—that she'd made the decision to come to him earlier rather than wait until after the birth.

A short time later Alina lay on the examination table, gripping Ethan's hand, staring at the blank monitor. He brushed his lips across her cheek.

'Our baby, Alina. An individual person.' His compelling dark eyes held her spellbound. 'Created by Leon, Louise and you. Unique in its own right.'

The technician breezed in, all smiles and goodwill. Showing soon-to-be parents images of their babies must be one of the best jobs ever.

'Hi. Alina and Ethan James, right? I'm Gary.' He grinned as he sat on the stool, checking her chart. 'Ready for some hi-tech wonder. Tuck your top up and brace yourself. Maybe one day they'll develop a lotion we can apply warm.'

He squeezed the cold gel onto her abdomen, causing her to wince and screw up her nose. Making Ethan laugh.

'Same reaction from all the dads,' Gary mused. 'Funnily enough they always refuse the offer to try it. Now, do you want to know the sex?'

'No!'

Two voices in unison. Their eyes met: hers grateful, his in accord.

'Thanks for asking,' Ethan added, his thumb moving reassuringly over her knuckles. 'We'd like to be surprised in October.'

'Lots of people still would, myself included.' He noted their refusal.

Alina watched avidly as images formed on the screen. Goosebumps peaked on her skin as she made out a moving shadowy form floating on a black background. From the dark recesses of her mind voices begged her to shut her eyes. She didn't.

The picture became clearer, the image bigger, as Gary manipulated the mouse, mouthing quiet satisfactory grunts as he worked.

'Okay, we have two arms, two legs, good proportion of head to body. Right size for fourteen weeks…' He jiggled something, the clarity increased, and then the cursor pointed to a tiny pulsating blob. 'There—can you see?—your baby's good, strong heartbeat.'

Her breath caught in her throat. Tears for her friends who would never experience this wonder filled her eyes.

A strangled gasp resonated at her side.

She swung her head and her own heartbeat stilled. Ethan's lips were parted, his eyes big and glowing with amazement. His body leant forward as far as the table permitted. His rapt expression rebooted her heartbeat into aching double time. A lifetime ago she'd seen the same wonder on another face.

She watched his Adam's apple bounce as he tried to

swallow, heard his deep indrawn breath and emotional gruff tone.

'Our baby. Gives a whole new meaning to the word "daddy", doesn't it?'

'This is the moment it all becomes real,' replied the technician.

'Oh, yeah.' Ethan's smile could have lit up the city and then some. 'Thank you, Alina.'

His misty eyes chipped at her defences. His next words, whispered by her ear, tugged at her heart.

'Thank you for allowing me to be part of this incredible experience.'

She wiped a tear from his cheek and let her fingers rest on his skin. 'It's amazing, isn't it? I know the baby's there. I can see it moving. Yet I can't feel anything.'

Her brain wouldn't be forced into accepting 'our' or 'my'. That was the plan. No caring. No bonding. The right to return to her solitary life with no past, only an uncertain future. The day she'd flown to Australia she'd had no doubts it was the best possible outcome.

Since meeting Ethan certainties were becoming cloudy and convictions ambiguous. Somewhere in the clump of wool that masqueraded as her decisive mind was the niggling certainty that this was being caused more by the man who was regarding her now as if she was all the treasures he'd ever dreamed of rolled into one than by her condition.

Ethan's gaze swung from the monitor to Alina and back. He didn't know whether to holler out loud or cry. That indistinct wriggling blur was his niece or nephew—living proof that he hadn't totally lost the two people he loved most. Five weeks ago unpredictable and unbelievable. Now an almost touchable actuality.

In less than one of those rapid heartbeats he lost his heart. Utterly. Irrevocably. For ever. *Our baby.* Now he truly believed what he'd originally claimed for appearances' sake. At that instant he became a father, silently vowing to become the kind of daddy his friend would have been.

His interest in the technology vanished. He was filled with reverent awe, seeing life as it began. In six months this tiny creature would emerge as a living, breathing person. *His* child, *his* responsibility for life. He wondered how he'd ever believed he was as unemotional as his parents. His heart had swelled fit to burst.

Alina brushed away tears he hadn't realised he'd shed. Touched his cheek. A new softness shone in her beautiful eyes, curved in her smile. However deep she'd buried her maternal instincts, it wasn't enough. The natural mother he suspected her to be was going to surface, no matter how hard she fought it.

His mouth felt dry, his chest tight. His heartbeat powered up. Whether because of their baby or her it didn't matter. From this moment they really were a family. The voice in his head was telling him to somehow keep it that way.

'Okay, Mum and Dad, I've got the information I need.'

Ethan blinked as the monitor clicked off. Over already? He wanted to watch longer, see more.

'Check with the receptionist for your photos and DVD.' The technician handed Alina a box of tissues. 'Good luck. I might see you when you come in again.'

Ethan took the tissues and began to wipe off the gel, desperate to be physically involved, not wanting to come down from his euphoria. He concentrated on her stomach, absurdly self-conscious after revealing a side of him few people had ever seen.

Coward. He'd said thank you—a pathetic reward for the miracle she'd brought to him.

Throwing the tissues in the bin, he turned to meet compassionate violet eyes. A deep yearning, alien to his normal awareness, flowed through him. Along with the desire to cherish and protect as long as he lived. He shook with its intensity.

'Ethan, are you all right?'

Her fingers rested on his arm. For her a friendly gesture. For him, much more.

'Better than I've ever been.'

He smoothed her top down and helped her from the bench. Kissed her tenderly until he ran out of breath, needing her gentleness, her sweetness. *Her*.

'Let's go home, darling.'

After an early lunch Ethan drove to his parents' home alone, psyching himself up for the confrontation. He'd always been the mediator, acting as a buffer for others. Not any more. Today he was the activist.

His parents' judgemental nature along with their unachievably high standards had caused so many problems. He was convinced their agreement to Louise's marriage had been motivated only by the idea of hosting a flash high society event. It was their interference that had motivated the newlyweds to move to Barcelona. Now they'd gone he had no one else to champion. Except the quiet beauty he'd left alone in their apartment, and the grandchild he *might* inform his parents was on the way.

He walked round the house, growling in frustration. It was ridiculous that their offspring had to use the front door like guests once they'd left home, that he had to ring the bell even though they must know he'd arrived. His greeting to his father was polite, yet clipped, the reply mundane.

'This must be important, for you to take time off from work. Is it something to do with the estate?'

As expected, no welcome.

'No.'

He walked straight to the lounge. His mother sat in her chair, perfectly groomed. Just once he'd like to see her in casual clothes, with mussed-up hair. His thoughts flew to the heart-warming image of his wife in the blue chainstore outfit she'd worn at their first meeting.

'Good afternoon, Mother. I won't be stopping. I have an appointment.'

To take my bride on a honeymoon I hope will bring us even closer than we've become.

She frowned at his lack of physical greeting. He compared her barely touching air-kiss for Alina with the loving embrace he'd received from Jean when they'd met. Didn't feel the slightest guilt.

'Good afternoon, Ethan. Is there something wrong?

His father was now seated in an armchair. There was no mention of that disastrous visit, nor the fact that there'd been no further contact until yesterday morning, when he'd phoned them. They'd never deign to make a conciliatory move, and he was only here for Alina's sake.

He took the settee, placing a long envelope on the coffee table.

'I have something to tell you prior to an official announcement. If you don't approve, that's hard luck. It's a done deed.'

They both stiffened. He paused. This was for his sister, his friend. *Their baby.*

'Alina and I were married yesterday evening.'

'What?' His father sprang up.

'Sit down, Martin.'

Sophia's curt tone had its effect. He obeyed, glaring at his son. She continued, her censure radiating through the air.

'Is this some sort of warped joke because you took umbrage at our concerns over her background? I know application forms need to be lodged a month before, so…'

'It was done. We had a quiet wedding, with friends as witnesses.'

His mother went rigid, unusually lost for words. It was his father who spoke.

'Really, Ethan. We coped with immature dramas from your sister. Never expected any from *you*. You've always been practical and reasonable—'

'Maybe too much so,' Ethan cut in brusquely. 'I lost precious time with Louise and Leon because you would not accept they were meant for each other. Time I'll never get back now they're gone.'

Dismissing the protests that erupted from both of them, he leant forward, balanced his elbows on his knees and clenched his hands together.

'I love Alina.' Not a lie. It wasn't the same as being *in* love. How could he not love someone who'd given him the most priceless gift he'd ever have? 'And anyone who upsets or disrespects her will be out of my life. I don't give a damn what people think or say. Accept it or not—she's my wife, my priority.'

He waited, quite prepared to walk out. The looks they exchanged didn't faze him. He didn't care what explanation they gave their social acquaintances for his hurried secret wedding. Their society image mattered only to *them*. Tragedy had taught him that there were far more important things in life.

His mother finally found her voice. 'How are we supposed to explain this rushed event to our friends?'

All they cared about was how it would affect their image. He almost laughed out loud—couldn't remember when he'd last heard genuine amusement from either of them. Alina had a quiet sense of humour, enjoyed quirky comedies, and encouraged him to see the fun in them too.

'That's not my concern.' He flicked the envelope with his finger. 'This is a copy of the notice that will be placed in the paper on Saturday, plus a list of friends and relatives whom I will inform later this week. I would prefer you to wait until then to tell anyone else. We'll be away on our honeymoon until Sunday, so I'll only be answering urgent calls.'

'What about the Starburst chain?' His father sounded shell shocked.

'Under control.'

'I see. As usual, you've covered everything.'

He wasn't fooled by his mother's resigned tone.

'Will we see you when you return?'

He hesitated. Dared he trust them around Alina, especially as her pregnancy would soon be apparent?

'That depends on your attitude. Our baby's due in October.'

Ignoring their gasps and aggrieved expressions, he stood up.

'I'm happier right now than I have ever been in my life, and thrilled that my wife is carrying my baby. Anyone who isn't can just stay away.'

He said goodbye soon after, breathing a sigh of relief as he went through the gates. He ought to feel guilty for the subterfuge. Instead his head was filled with Alina—her beguiling smile, the way her violet eyes revealed her emotions. Her extraordinary courage.

My wife. The simple yet profound phrase kept repeating in his brain. As he drove, singing along off-key with the radio, he felt giddy and irrationally happy. He was going home to claim another long kiss, as sweet as the one they'd shared before he left.

CHAPTER SIXTEEN

'TURN RIGHT IN four hundred metres. Clifftop Lane.'

Ethan obeyed the GPS instruction, grateful for the hassle-free drive. He pulled up in front of a white weatherboard house, switched off the engine and checked the time.

'Twelve minutes short of the two-hour estimate. You feeling okay, darling?'

'Apart from needing to stretch. This car rides much smoother than most of the vehicles I've travelled in.' She opened her door.

He was there to help before her foot touched the ground. Arching his back, he drew in a deep breath. 'Ahh…'

Alina followed suit. 'Eucalyptus. Invigorating! True Australian aroma.'

His heart sang. Could she look any more beautiful, any happier? 'Shall we take a look inside?' He jingled the keys he'd picked up on the way through Katoomba.

'Can we go for a walk first? I'd like to see the sun set on the mountains.'

They walked along the path behind the house. Through the trees they saw glimpses of brown, green and gold against a darkening blue sky, dotted with pink-tinged clouds.

'Picture-perfect.' Alina sighed, stopping to implant it into her memory.

'I agree,' Ethan replied, ignoring the scenery and embracing her from behind. He trailed soft kisses over her neck, revelling in the way she quivered with each one. Trembled himself when she twisted round, wrapped her arms around his neck and pressed her lips to his.

He inhaled the spring essence that was Alina. Fought

the craving to show her how much he wanted her. His heart pounded into his ribs. And darn near exploded when her lips parted, inviting more intimate contact.

Without hesitation he accepted, loving her with his tongue, aligning their bodies with pleasurable strokes of his hands, letting her know how blatantly he was aroused. His world shrank to the two of them. It was all he needed, all he desired.

Alina arched into him, letting his heat simmer through her, returning his kiss with a passion that shook her. Her anticipation had been building since they'd arrived, diminished by the expectation of guilt. When it hadn't come, she'd pushed the boundary by kissing him.

Danger signals abated to an almost inaudible buzz. Painful consequences were a long way in the future. For the moment she was caught in the *now*. Yearning overrode everything, holding the darkness at bay.

Necessity for air broke them apart. The transparent desire in Alina's eyes told Ethan all he wanted to know.

He swung her up, cradling her close to his chest. 'Mine.' Hoarse with emotion.

'Yours…' Hot. Breathless. Murmured into the skin above his polo shirt.

He strode back to the house, king of his universe.

The sun's rays teased Alina's eyelids open. She blinked, snuggled further under the cover, trying to recapture the magic of her dream. Reached out for…

Her eyes flew open.

She was cradled by a solid wall of naked muscle, moving to a gentle rhythm. Warm breath tickled her earlobe. Firm fingers lay on her hip. A delicious glow spread from her core to every extremity at the memory of Ethan's ardent lovemaking. She turned over to look at him.

Ethan. Her husband. Her lover. Her lips curled as she recalled the tension in his muscles as he'd held his own need in check, caressing and soothing her until her barriers had finally exploded in a fiery burst of passion.

A wave of shyness engulfed her. He was a mature man who'd made love to many women. She'd only known the gentleness of first love before. Ethan had awakened the woman in her, freed her heart. But did he want it? Swearing to care for her and protect her was an abyss away from loving her.

He made a low contented sound in his throat, rolled onto his back and arched. Lazy cobalt eyes opened, widened. His lips curled in a slow, satisfied smile that held such tenderness it tugged at her heart.

'This is the perfect way to wake in the morning.'

He reached out for her, covering her mouth with his, his tongue tempting her lips to open for him. How could they not when she'd hardly recovered from the dizzy heights he'd taken her to during the night? In this big bed that she'd never forget.

'Ethan, I…' Where were coherent words when she needed them? 'Last night I…'

'Last night was more than I'd dreamt it would be…so much more than I'd fantasised.' He stroked her tousled hair, tangled his fingers through her curls. 'Promise me you won't regret what we shared. I sure as hell won't. Never. Not for a second as long as I live.'

Alina yearned to drown in the dark blue pools of his eyes, longed to share it all again now. Couldn't say the words.

Ethan ached to make love to her again, but saw the confusion in her bemused violet eyes. Knew he'd have to wait. Knew he'd have to find the right moment to tell her he wanted to make this marriage real in every way. Wanted her to always be his wife.

'Go shower.' Sometime soon he'd share one with her. 'I'll get breakfast, then we'll go sightseeing.'

She nodded, shuffled to the edge of the bed and hesitated. He smiled, loving her shyness even though she'd been married before. Was married *now*. He couldn't contain his chuckle as she shot from the bed. Paid for it as his body reacted to the sight of her running naked to the en suite. Pulling on his boxers, he headed for the kitchen, planning their day, their evening. Their night.

'Ethan!'

The panic in her voice froze his blood, sending him racing for the bathroom, his heart pumping. A heart that screeched to a halt at the sight of her huge frightened violet eyes. He dropped to his knees in front of her, hunched forward on the toilet lid, wrapped in a white towel, her arms clasping her stomach. Dragged her to his chest, fighting his own gut-wrenching fear.

'Alina, darling—tell me. What's wrong?'

She shuddered. A pain-filled cry jarred against his bare skin. 'It h-h-hurts. In my stomach—'

Her stuttering stopped with a sharp sound that cut through him.

For a second his mind went blank, refusing to process the horror her words evoked. Then it cleared. Alina needed a practical, take-action man. Lifting her as if she were delicate china, he carried her to the bed, brushing his lips across her forehead. Telling her everything would be all right. Silently cursing the fates for putting her through more torment.

Grabbing his mobile, he opened Alina's unpacked suitcase, rummaging for underwear and a dress with one hand, thumbing his phone with the other. He wrestled into the jeans and polo top he'd worn on the trip and slid on his sneakers one-handed, holding the phone to his ear with the other.

His answers to the operator's questions were clear and precise. Details could wait. Alina was frightened. His heart wrenched every time she shuddered and cried out. Their tiny baby might be in danger. He didn't dare think beyond getting them to the hospital—thankfully not too far away.

With a plan in action, he helped Alina into her clothes. He murmured reassuring phrases he'd never be able to recall, trying to ignore the resurging irrational fear gnawing at his insides. He told them both how cherished they were. He couldn't, *wouldn't* lose either of them. They were so close to becoming a family, and he'd fight like hell to keep that prospect attainable.

True to the operator's word, a medical team and trolley were waiting at the emergency entrance of the hospital. They whisked her away, leaving him to find a place to park.

Walking through the front doors, he was confronted with corridors, signs, and not a trace of Alina. Now she and their baby were in good care his composure crashed. His life, his future, was somewhere in this building and he wanted to be close to them.

He needed them. They needed him.

There'd be a path from his prowling back and forth worn into the waiting area if they didn't come for him soon. How far away was she? Had she asked for him?

He repeatedly checked his watch, matched it with the clock on the wall, tensed when anyone in hospital garb walked in.

The guilt gnawing at him now was worse than he'd felt after Louise and Leon had died. This time he'd been actively to blame. Last night when Alina had welcomed him with kisses and caresses he'd loved her with a passion that had shaken him to his core. Emotions he'd have claimed not to be any part of him had surfaced, taking them both soaring to the edge of ecstasy and tipping them over.

This was *his* fault. That book said sex was safe after the first trimester as long as there were no problems. He hadn't considered that there might be. He slammed a fist into his other palm. Prayed to all the gods that anyone believed in not to let Alina suffer another loss.

'Mr James?'

He swung round and locked eyes with a man who hardly looked old enough to be an intern.

'I'm sending your wife for an ultrasound and she's asked for you to be with her. This way.'

They fell into step and he continued. 'The physical examination shows nothing wrong. There's no bleeding, and your child's vital signs are strong.'

Ethan's brain filtered out whatever came next. Tension whooshed out of him, leaving him loose and vulnerable. *Nothing wrong. Strong vital signs.* Their baby was a fighter. It didn't lessen his culpability.

'Doctor, last night we made love. Could that have been the cause?'

'Alina told me. It might have some bearing, maybe not. Even if the ultrasound shows all's well I'd like to keep her in at least overnight, so we can monitor them both.'

'Do whatever's necessary to keep them both safe.'

Ethan sank into a chair in the private room, his eyes glued to the monitor recording their baby's heartbeat. He tried to swallow the lump in his throat as he watched that life-affirming pulse—faster than his, normal for an unborn child.

He hadn't let go of Alina's hand the whole time, needing the contact more than he needed air to breathe. His fingers caressed her knuckles. His free hand brushed strands of hair from her forehead. It tore him apart to see her so pale, so still, with a drip inserted in her wrist. He didn't know what it was—didn't care as long as it helped. Her breathing was steady; his was as erratic as leaves in a windstorm.

'If you'd like a break I can sit with her while you go for coffee.' A nurse laid a comforting hand on his shoulder.

'No, I have to be here. I have to be with them.' He wasn't going anywhere.

Ethan wasn't going anywhere. He'd even walked alongside the trolley, his hand wrapped around hers, but for the first time his warmth hadn't been able dispel Alina's icy chills. Everything had been a blur since he'd carried her from the en suite, his soft words unintelligible through the fog in her mind.

Her barricades had crashed back up with the first stab of pain, sucking her into the dark void of bereavement and despair. Resisting the impulse to cling to him, she'd lain passive in his arms as he'd carried her to the bed and the car, desperately trying to close down her nightmare.

During the ultrasound she kept her eyes closed, blanked out the technician's voice and Ethan's replies. Didn't comprehend what he said to her, only realised by the squeeze of her fingers and his kiss on her forehead that the baby was okay. For now.

Then something deep inside her shifted, shimmied through her, releasing a long-denied emotion. She gasped at the overwhelming surge of love for the tiny child fighting for survival inside her.

'Alina, does it hurt?'

The anguish in his voice focused her thoughts. She looked up, saw the furrows in his brow, the clench of his jaw, and stared into anguished eyes. Cobalt blue eyes in a captivating face that, without her realising, had become as dear to her as Colin's. She loved him—loved him *and* the baby.

No! To love was to risk everything. Mind-numbing. Terrifying. She'd fought her way back once. If she lost again she'd *never* recover.

Scrunching her eyes shut, she forced her mind to think of the remote places she'd escaped to before. Anything but him, his eyes, his touch, the way he'd loved her last night. She forced herself back to the emotionless detachment that had kept her heart safe for seven years.

Two days later Ethan took her back to the holiday house.

The next morning they returned to Sydney.

She'd done it again. Slipped away while he still slept. In the four weeks since her stay in hospital Alina had drifted into an abstract world Ethan wasn't privy to. She lay apathetic in his arms at night, rarely initiated conversation and almost never smiled. He'd built an empire with persuasion and action—now nothing he said or did helped.

He'd ensured she had time with Jean and with Dr Conlan, hoping she'd open up to one of them, or both. Giving her time and space, he hadn't pressed her, had kept their daily life as normal as possible while letting her know he'd change his schedule any time she needed him. He'd encouraged her to use her computer, knew she didn't, tried to be reassuring without crowding her.

At night he cradled her and caressed her until she fell asleep in his arms. Every day he let her know how precious she was to him in words and actions. He was determined that she'd understand how much he cared for and wanted her, even though he made no attempt to make love to her. For her sake and their baby's.

More than anything he ached for what might have become a special part of his day: waking with Alina nestled against him, her hand over his heart, her breath soft on his chest. He longed to start each morning by kissing her awake, his heart soaring as she reacted sleepily, returning his ardour as her senses awoke.

This morning he found her in the kitchen, making herbal tea. His pulse raced even as his heart twisted at the sight of her slumped posture. He lifted her chin, dipped his head, watching for a flicker in her sorrowful eyes. The same flicker that had raised his hopes time after time, only to dash them as it quickly died.

He stepped away, ran agitated fingers through his hair. He'd been patient, willing to try anything to reach her, knowing she wasn't to blame. Today he'd run out of ideas.

'Alina, talk to me. We can work through this together, but I need to know how you feel, what you're thinking.'

She backed away, fuelling his frustration. 'I don't feel anything. Nothing.'

'Try, darling. For me. For our baby.'

She shook her head, squared her shoulders in defiance. Raised her voice. 'I can't. *I can't.*'

He bunched his fingers to prevent himself from hauling her close and kissing her hot and hard in an attempt to melt the ice that held her prisoner. Knew he was close to doing just that.

'Forget breakfast. I need space to think.' He strode to the door, grabbing his keys on the way.

His stormy departure stunned Alina, leaving her breathless, mouth gaping, fingers curled tight. She sank to the floor, leaning against the cupboard. That was the same expression she'd seen once before, when he'd walked out of their first meeting, angry, shattered.

Then she'd been unsure if she'd see him again. Now the same feeling washed over her, so much stronger. She felt desolated. Abandoned. Alone.

Wrapping her arms around her swelling stomach, she hugged herself and rocked, chest tight and body trembling. Suddenly she stilled. She wasn't alone. Her hands were cradling their baby. *Their baby.* Ethan was right: it was easy to say it once you believed.

She also believed he'd never desert Louise's child. It was his prime consideration.

He'd given his word to take care of them both. Since her stay in hospital he'd been gentle, compassionate, treating her as if she were fragile. He cuddled her close at night, whispered comforting words she hardly heard, and never attempted to make love to her.

Because he was protecting her and their baby? Because Dr Conlan had advised him not to?

She'd driven him away—maybe lost him. One night of loving might be all she'd have to remember…a magical night that…

He'd said it had been more than he'd dreamt, more than he'd fantasised. She closed her eyes and pictured his face when he kissed her, always with open eyes.

Now she recognised the love that shone in that darkening blue. Every act, every caress had been for love. For her. For their baby.

A wave of serenity washed over her. She went to the window, seeing only his smile, his quirky eyebrow rising. His cobalt blue eyes, so suspicious at first. So frustratingly angry when he'd left today because of her withdrawal, her stupidity in not sharing her fears and giving him the chance to help her.

Could he ever forgive her?

Please let him come home soon so she could tell him how much she loved him *and* their baby. She'd try to explain the mind-numbing grief, beg for his understanding and help. If he still wanted her she longed to stay, to be his wife and this baby's mother. The three of them could become a real family…

CHAPTER SEVENTEEN

TURNING LEFT AT ground level, Ethan walked aimlessly without stopping, crossing streets or turning corners depending on the traffic lights. His brain spun; his gut churned. He was the mediator, the one who found solutions. Why not for Alina? He'd broken her barriers down before—now he seemed to be the reason they'd been rebuilt.

He sidestepped a toddler, squirming in his mother's grip, quirked a smile at them both. Hopefully that was his future—an active, adventurous child with Louise and Leon's DNA. Their love of life, their loyalty, their... His throat tightened. Would there be anything of Alina? How could there not be when she'd nourished and cocooned their baby for nine months?

A red light. He swung left. Ahead lay Circular Quay and the Manly Ferry.

Alina's eyes had sparkled that day; her smile had enthralled him. He'd loved her sweet response to his kiss. Loved her... *Loved her.*

He stopped short, barely registering the stroller slamming into the back of his leg or the young father's apology.

'Not your fault, mate. I stopped.'

And he'd stopped being an idiot. He moved over to the building, his body trembling as he acknowledged how much of one he'd been. That original tightening in his gut, his complete trust in her from the start and the primal urge to protect her... His desire to know her would have been as strong whenever, *however* he'd met her.

Alina had captured his heart from the moment he'd stood in that doorway. He hadn't realised it because he hadn't believed he was capable of the feeling. For weeks he'd been following a nightly ritual in secret, not comprehending he'd truly meant it for both of them. If he'd let himself believe he might have prevented the rebuilding of her barricades.

He began to run—back to the apartment, back to claim her for his own. Back to offer her his love and life.

Opening and then closing the door silently, he moved forward, muscles tense, pulse racing. Heart praying.

Alina stood by the window, staring out. It was an echo of their first meeting, only this time he rejoiced in the gloriously familiar gut-clench.

Alina stroked her stomach, whispered words of encouragement, letting their baby know everything was going to be all right.

'Your daddy's temper flares quickly…cools almost as fast. He'll ponder the problem, think out a solution. Come home to take action.'

The back of her neck tingled.

'Alina?'

She turned, her heart flipping at his voice. Cobalt blue eyes set in impassive features scanned hers with the deep intensity she knew so well. His muscles were taut, as if prepared to ward off a devastating blow. His lips twitched.

Her mouth dried. Chills ran down her spine. She couldn't move.

He came towards her. His arms swung out, fingers spread. 'I can't go on like this.'

She froze. He couldn't mean it. He couldn't leave her. Or send her away. Her legs felt like jelly and yet they refused to buckle.

Her brain screamed. *Tell him you want to stay. Tell him you love him.*

The words wouldn't come.

One more step brought him close enough to caress her baby bump. He didn't.

'Can you imagine what it's like, waiting for you to fall asleep every night before I can tell you how much I love you?'

Grated out as if in protest.

Heat raced through her veins. Her legs crumpled. Ethan caught her, crushing her to his chest.

'You *do* that?'

He'd been saying he loved her. *He did love her.* Her arms wrapped around his neck, holding fast.

'Every night for weeks. I believed I was incapable of loving the way Leon and Louise did, so I told myself it was for our baby. Persuaded myself the physical attraction was because you were so beautiful, so sweet and courageous.'

His eyes sparkled. His hands soothed her. His brilliant smile was for her alone.

'I love you, Alina James. Probably from the moment I saw you. Recognising it took my head longer than my heart. Stay with us. I swear—'

'I love *you*, Ethan James. There's nowhere else I want to be.'

Ethan's lips sought hers tenderly, lovingly, savouring the taste of her, becoming more fervent as she responded in kind. He heard a low groan of desire, wished it were hers. Knew it came from him.

Breaking the kiss, he scooped her up, settling on the settee with her in his lap, her head on his shoulder, his hand splayed over her growing baby bump.

'I'm sorry for not trusting you to help me, Ethan. I've been so scared of losing you, losing you both. So fearful of getting trapped in the darkness again, being alone with no way out this time. You saved me and I pushed you away.'

'We're together now, and nothing's—'

His heart lurched as she suddenly sat up, eyes vivid and wide, a delighted smile lighting up her face.

'Our baby *moved*! Like a tiny ripple. Ethan, our baby's letting us know we're not alone.'

He kissed her softly, reverently. 'I promise you'll never be alone again, my love.'

September thirtieth.
Baby active.
Kept Alina up most of the night.

Ethan closed the diary and stretched. Alina was resting in the lounge, at his insistence, after rising early, claiming she couldn't get comfortable in bed.

He was just about to check if she wanted anything, tell her he'd work from home today, when she waddled in.

Her concerned expression had him on his feet in an instant.

'Do you need something, darling?'

'I didn't tell you earlier—thought it might be a false alarm.'

His body hit full alert in a heartbeat. He crossed the room, clasped her arms and pinned her with a warning glare.

'The contractions started before dawn. I've been timing them and—'

'Don't say it.' If it was voiced out loud it might happen. 'We've got three weeks to go. Must be a Braxton-Thick false alarm thing.'

Please let it be.

She gave him an indulgent smile. 'Braxton-*Hicks*—and that's why I waited until I was sure. I finished packing the bag, in case, then phoned Dr Conlan. She said she'll meet us at the hospital and to drive carefully.'

'No ambulance? No paramedics, trained in case the baby comes en route?'

'We have plenty of time, Ethan. I promise. The hire car's on its way.'

He strode from the room. Came back frowning.

'We need to…um…*hell*!' His mind was a fuzzball.

The hospital bag. He walked to the door, pivoted at the musical sound he normally loved to hear. His gorgeous wife was laughing at his indecision—a moment after telling him she was in premature labour.

He did the only thing a man could do in the circumstances: pulled her close to stop her mirth with his mouth. A breathless eternity later he lifted his head. It was time to man up. Or daddy up. He knelt to kiss her stomach, then splayed both hands there.

'Okay, bub, your timing's out, but you're in charge. Unless you want to reconsider and stay where you are, nice and cosy for another three or four weeks.'

His response was a firm kick. With a wry grin he straightened up.

'I guess we're gonna have a baby, Mrs James. You keep timing the contractions. I'll get the bag.'

'You'll have to call your mother on the way.'

His features hardened. 'Why the hell would I do that?'

In five months he'd only occasionally seen them socially, phoned them when necessary. Refused to give them any chance of upsetting Alina.

'Jean and I bumped into her at a baby shop last week. We talked for a few minutes, then arranged to have lunch today. I was going to tell you how it went tonight.'

'My mother was in a *baby shop*?' An unbelievable event. She ordered gifts online from exclusive stores.

His features softened and he drew Alina as close as their baby allowed.

'You agreed to meet her after the way they treated you? You are a very special lady, Alina James, and I'm a very lucky man.'

* * *

Dr Conlan was waiting for them. As Alina was wheeled away Ethan caught her arm.

'It's too soon. You said late October.'

She patted his hand and smiled. 'Babies don't always follow our planning chart, Ethan. This one's decided to-day's its birthday, whether we're ready or not.'

He wasn't. This was his woman. Their baby. He desperately wanted to take her home, where he could keep them both safe until the due date.

'Can't you delay it? At least until our baby's bigger?'

'Too late for that. Looks like your child's made an executive decision. Welcome to fatherhood, with all its unpredictability.'

It was happening. Louise's baby. Louise who'd hated being late for anything, who had always been early, eager to savour the first moment, the overture. His little miracle was about to be born.

Adrenaline pumped through his veins. It was like that exultant moment in a business deal when he knew he was on the cusp of victory. Only a thousand times better.

It wasn't the exclusive birthing suite he'd booked. Didn't matter. They were in the safest place possible. Dr Conlan was there, there were paediatric specialists within call. He could see the special incubator, positioned discreetly by the wall.

He rubbed Alina's back and encouraged her to puff and blow. Wiped the sweat from her brow, kissed her and repeatedly told her how much he loved her. He wished he could take the pain for her, and didn't flinch when her nails dug into his hand.

'Okay, Daddy, let me take over here.'

The nurse was there, nudging him aside. He growled. 'No.'

This was *his* place. *His* prerogative.

'Go help deliver your baby.'

Deliver? Him? He looked at Alina, who nodded.

'Go.'

Her reassuring smile filled his heart to bursting point.

An urgent, 'Come on, Ethan!' had him scrambling to the doctor's side.

He obeyed instructions, his eyes totally focused on the thick thatch of damp dark hair emerging. A whoosh of movement and suddenly his arms were full of a squirming, slippery, wrinkled creature. He intuitively hugged the red-faced newborn to his pounding heart, fascinated by the petite button nose and bow lips.

When a delightful squeak became a distinctive howl of objection he blinked away his tears of joy. They had a daughter. He was a fair dinkum father.

'Hi, bub. We've been waiting for you.'

To his amazement, as if soothed by his voice, her crying was tempered to a whimper and the cutest hiccup. He gazed into unfocused cobalt blue eyes, a reminder of Louise, then looked at Alina, who lay with her head back, face pale and eyes closed. And loved her even more.

He watched impatiently as this miniature of his sister was weighed and checked, exulted when her fingers wrapped around the one he used to touch her palm lightly. Scowled when she gave a tiny mew as they took a blood sample from her heel.

With the doctor's all-clear he carried their baby to the woman he adored beyond reason. His hopes soared as her eyes opened to reveal misty love-filled violet. As he gently lowered their little girl into her arms he held his breath, praying this little angel would finally erase the last vestige of her grief.

'We have a little girl, my darling. A beautiful daughter.' He said it proudly, aloud for the world to hear. His next whispered words were for her alone. 'As beautiful as her mothers. *Both* of them.'

Still cradling his daughter's head, he wrapped his arm around his wife. He believed his emotions had peaked until her finger softly caressed the tiny cheek, and they zoomed even higher. His heart threatened to burst through his chest as she pressed her lips to the ruddy pink forehead. She gazed down in wonder, her lips curled into the most beautiful smile he'd ever seen.

When she looked at him, her eyes shone like diamonds. 'We have a daughter, Ethan. I love you both so much,' she said huskily.

Her words thrilled him. Her kiss echoed her spoken words.

Alina had welcomed his tender caresses, his declarations of affection as he'd tried to ease her pain. Had seen his disconcertion at the nurse's attempt to take over. She'd always treasure the memory of his startled expression when their baby had slid into his hands, quickly replaced by one of wondrous awe as he tenderly gathered the precious bundle to his chest. She saw a tiny fist waving in protest and felt her breasts respond to the plaintive cry.

Her heart had blipped when he'd nestled the baby into her arms. Blipped and then beaten steady and strong as she saw dark hair, cobalt blue eyes, bow lips and long fingers: the perfect blend of her natural parents. As she'd touched the soft rosy cheek the last trace of anguish had faded, leaving only the gentler sorrow for what might have been.

She choked up at the sight of Ethan's hand cradling their daughter's head—protective, loving. The way he'd cradled *her* from the start. With tenderness and patience he'd demolished her defences, allowing her to recall the good memories without pain, allowing her to love again.

She kissed their daughter's brow and guided her searching mouth to her breast. Rejoiced at the ecstasy of this unique moment of bonding. *Their daughter.* How wonderful it sounded now.

Gazing at her husband she wondered if a heart could burst with joy. She stretched her neck to kiss him, luxuriating in the knowledge that he was hers. Basking in the glow from his darkening cobalt eyes.

'Louisa.' He stroked their daughter's hair. 'A priceless gift. Very much wanted and loved.'

'Louisa Leona James,' she countered. 'A mother has naming rights too.'

* * * * *

HER KNIGHT IN
THE OUTBACK

NIKKI LOGAN

For Mat

Acknowledgements

With enormous gratitude to Dr Richard O'Regan
for his help with the pharmaceutical aspects of
this story, which were integral to its resolution.
And with deepest respect and compassion for the
families of *'The Missing'*.

CHAPTER ONE

IT WAS MOMENTS like this that Evelyn Read hated. Life-defining moments. Moments when her fears and prejudices reared up before her eyes and confronted her—just like a King Brown snake, surprised while basking on the hot Australian highway.

She squinted at the distant biker limping carefully towards her out of the shimmering heat mirage and curled her fingers more tightly around the steering wheel.

A moment like this one might have taken her brother. Maybe Trav stopped for the wrong stranger; maybe that was where he went when he disappeared all those months ago. Her instincts screamed that she should press down on her accelerator until the man—the danger—was an hour behind her. But a moment like this might have *saved* her brother, too. If a stranger had only been kind enough or brave enough to stop for him. Then maybe Travis would be back with them right now. Safe. Loved.

Instead of alone, scared…or worse.

The fear of never knowing what happened to him tightened her gut the way it always did when she thought too long about this crazy thing she was doing.

The biker limped closer.

Should she listen to her basest instincts and flee, or respond to twenty-four years of social conditioning and help a fellow human being in trouble? There was probably some kind of outback code to be observed, too, but she'd heard too many stories from too many grieving people to be particularly bothered by niceties.

Eve's eyes flicked to the distant motorbike listing on the side of the long, empty road. And then, closer, to the scruffy man now nearing the restored 1956 Bedford bus that was getting her around Australia.

She glanced at her door's lock to make sure it was secure.

The man limped to a halt next to the bus's bifold doors and looked at her expectantly over his full beard. A dagger tattoo poked out from under his dark T-shirt and impenetrable sunglasses hid his eyes—and his intent—from her.

No. This was her home. She'd never open her front door to a total stranger. Especially not hours from the nearest other people.

She signalled him around to the driver's window instead.

He didn't look too impressed, but he limped his way around to her side and she slid the antique window open and forced her voice to be light.

Sociopaths make a decision on whether you're predator or prey in the first few seconds, she remembered from one of the endless missing-person fact sheets she'd read. She was not about to have 'prey' stamped on her forehead.

'Morning,' she breezed, as if this wasn't potentially a very big deal indeed. 'Looks like you're having a bad day.'

'Emu,' he grunted and she got a glimpse of straight teeth and healthy gums.

Stupidly, that reassured her. As if evil wouldn't floss. She twisted around for evidence of a big damaged bird flailing in the scrub after hitting his motorbike. To validate his claim. 'Was it okay?'

'Yeah, I'm fine, thanks.'

That brought her eyes back to his glasses. 'I can see that. But emus don't always come off the best after a road impact.'

As if she'd know...

'Going that fast, it practically went over the top of me as it ran with its flock. It's probably twenty miles from here now, trying to work out how and when it got black paint on its claws.'

He held up his scratched helmet, which had clearly taken an impact. More evidence. She just nodded, not wanting to give an inch more than necessary. He'd probably already summed her up as a bleeding heart over the emu.

One for the prey column.

'Where are you headed?' he asked.

Her radar flashed again at his interest. 'West.'

Duh, since the Bedford was pointing straight at the sun heading for the horizon and there was nothing else out this way *but* west.

'Can I catch a lift to the closest town?'

Was that tetchiness in his voice because she kept foiling him or because hers was the first vehicle to come along in hours and she was stonewalling him on a ride?

She glanced at his crippled bike.

'That'll have to stay until I can get back here with a truck,' he said, following her glance.

There was something in the sag of his shoulders and the way he spared his injured leg that reassured her even as the beard and tattoo and leather did not. He'd clearly come off his bike hard. Maybe he was more injured than she could see?

But the stark reality was that her converted bus only had the one seat up front—hers. 'That's my home back there,' she started.

'So…?'

'So, I don't know you.'

Yep. That was absolutely the insult his hardened lips said it was. But she was not letting a stranger back there. Into her world.

'It's only an hour to the border.' He sighed. 'I'll stand on your steps until Eucla.'

Right next to her. Where he could do anything and she couldn't do a thing to avoid it.

'An hour by motorbike, maybe. We take things a little more easy in this old girl. It'll take at least twice that.'

'Fine. I'll stand for two hours, then.'

Or she could just leave him here and send help back. But the image of Trav, lost and in need of help while someone drove off and left him injured and alone, flitted through her mind.

If someone had just been brave…

'I don't know you,' she wavered.

'Look, I get it. A woman travelling alone, big scary biker. You're smart to be cautious but the reality is help might not be able to get to me today so if you leave me here I could be here all night. Freezing my ass off.'

She fumbled for her phone.

His shaggy head shook slightly. 'If we had signal don't you think I'd have used it?'

Sure enough, her phone had diminished to *SOS only*. And as bad as that motorbike looked, it wasn't exactly an emergency.

'Just until we get signal, then?' he pressed, clearly annoyed at having to beg. 'Come on, please?'

How far could that be? They were mostly through the desert now, coming out on the western side of Australia. Where towns and people and telecommunications surely had to exist.

'Have you got some ID?'

He blinked at her and then reached back into his jeans for his wallet.

'No. Not a licence. That could be fake. Got any photos of you?'

He moved slowly, burdened by his incredulity, but pulled his phone out and flicked through a few screens. Then he pressed it up against Eve's window glass.

A serious face looked back at her. Well groomed and in a business shirt. Pretty respectable, really. Almost cute.

Pffff. 'That's not you.'

'Yeah, it is.'

She peered at him again. 'No, it's not.'

It might have been a stock photo off the Internet for all

she knew. The sort of search result she used to get when she googled 'corporate guy' for some design job.

'Oh, for pity's sake…'

He flicked through a few more and found another one, this time more bearded. But nothing like the hairy beast in front of her. Her hesitation obviously spoke volumes so he pushed his sunglasses up onto his head, simultaneously revealing grey eyes and slightly taming his rusty blond hair.

Huh. Okay, maybe it was him.

'Licence?'

A breathed bad word clearly tangled in the long hairs of his moustache but he complied—eventually—and slapped that against the window, too.

Marshall Sullivan.

She held up her phone and took a photo of him through the glass, with his licence in the shot.

'What's that for?'

'Insurance.'

'I just need a lift. That's it. I have no interest in you beyond that.'

'Easy for you to say.'

Her thumbs got busy texting it to both her closest friend and her father in Melbourne. Just to cover bases. Hard to know if the photo would make them more or less confident in this dusty odyssey she was on, but she had to send it to someone.

The grey eyes she could now see rolled. 'We have no signal.'

'The moment we do it will go.'

She hit Send and let the phone slip back down into its little spot on her dash console.

'You have some pretty serious trust issues, lady, you know that?'

'And this is potentially the oldest con in the book. Broken-down vehicle on remote outback road.' She glanced at his helmet and the marks that could be emu claws. 'I'll admit your story has some pretty convincing details—'

'Because it's the truth.'

'—but I'm travelling alone and I'm not going to take any chances. And I'm not letting you in here with me, sorry.' The cab was just too small and risky. 'You'll have to ride in the back.'

'What about all the biker germs I'm going to get all over your stuff?' he grumbled.

'You want a lift or not?'

Those steady eyes glared out at her. 'Yeah. I do.'

And then, as though he couldn't help himself, he grudgingly rattled off a thankyou.

Okay, so it had to be safer to let him loose in the back than have him squished here in the front with her. Her mind whizzed through all the things he might get up to back there but none of them struck her as bad as what he could do up front if he wasn't really who he said he was.

Or even if he was.

Biker boy and his helmet limped back towards the belongings piled on the side of the road next to his disabled bike. Leather jacket, pair of satchels, a box of mystery equipment.

She ground the gears starting the Bedford back up, but rolled up behind him and, as soon as his arms were otherwise occupied with his own stuff, she unlocked the bus and mouthed through the glass of her window. 'Back doors.'

Sullivan limped to the back of the Bedford, lurched it as he climbed in and then slammed himself in there with all her worldly possessions.

Two hours…

'Come on, old chook,' she murmured to the decades-old bus. 'Let's push it a bit, eh?'

Marshall groped around for a light switch but only found a thick fabric curtain. He pulled it back with a swish and light flooded into the darkened interior of the bus. Something extraordinary unfolded in front of him.

He'd seen converted buses before but they were usually pretty daggy. Kind of worn and soulless and vinyl. But this…

This was rich, warm and natural; nothing at all like the hostile lady up front.

It was like a little cottage in some forest. All timber and plush rugs in dark colours. Small, but fully appointed with kitchenette and living space, flat-screen TV, fridge and a sofa. Even potted palms. Compact and long but all there, like one of those twenty-square-metre, fold-down and pull-out apartments they sold in flat packs. At the far end—the driving end—a closed door that must lead to the only absent feature of the vehicle, the bed.

And suddenly he got a sense of Little Miss Hostile's reluctance to let him back here. It was like inviting a total stranger right into your bedroom. Smack bang in the middle of absolutely nowhere.

The bus lurched as she tortured it back up to speed and Marshall stumbled down onto the sofa built into the left side of the vehicle. Not as comfortable as his big eight-seater in the home theatre of his city apartment, but infinitely better than the hard gravel he'd been polishing with his butt for the couple of hours since the bird strike.

Stupid freaking emu. It could have killed them both.

It wasn't as if a KTM 1190 was a stealth unit but maybe, at the speed the emu had been going, the air rushing past its ears was just as noisy as an approaching motorbike. And then their fates had collided. Literally.

He sagged down against the sofa back and resisted the inclination to examine his left foot. Sometimes boots were the only things that kept fractured bones together after bike accidents so he wasn't keen to take it off unless he was bleeding to death. In fact, particularly if he was bleeding to death because something told him the hostess-with-the-leastest would not be pleased if he bled out all over her timber floor. But he could at least elevate it. That was generally good for what ailed you. He dragged one of his satchels up onto the sofa, turned and stacked a couple of the bouncy, full pillows down the opposite end and then swung his abused limb up onto it, lying out the full length of the sofa.

'Oh, yeah…' Half words, half groan. All good.

He loved his bike. He loved the speed. He loved that direct relationship with the country you had when there was no car between you and it. And he loved the freedom from everything he'd found touring that country.

But he really didn't love how fragile he'd turned out to be when something went wrong at high speed.

As stacks went, it had been pretty controlled. Especially considering the fishtail he'd gone into as the mob of emu shot past and around him. But even a controlled slide hurt—him and the bike—and once the adrenaline wore off and the birds disappeared over the dusty horizon, all he'd been left with was the desert silence and the pain.

And no phone signal.

Normally that wouldn't bother him. There really couldn't be enough alone time in this massive country, as far as he was concerned. If you travelled at the right time of year—and that would be the *wrong* time of year for tourists—you could pretty much have most outback roads to yourself. He was free to do whatever he wanted, wear whatever he wanted, be as hairy as he wanted, shower whenever he wanted. Or not. He'd given up caring what people thought of him right about the time he'd stopped caring about people.

Ancient history.

And life was just simpler that way.

The stoic old Bedford finally shifted into top gear and the rattle of its reconditioned engine evened out to a steady hum, vibrating under his skin as steadily as his bike did. He took the rare opportunity to do what he could never do when at the controls: he closed his eyes and let the hum take him.

Two hours, she'd said. He could be up on his feet with her little home fully restored before she even made it from the front of the bus back to the rear doors. As if no one had ever been there.

Two hours to rest. Recover. And enjoy the roads he loved from a more horizontal perspective.

'Who's been sleeping in my bed?' Eve muttered as she stood looking at the bear of a man fast asleep on her little sofa.

What was this—some kind of reverse Goldilocks thing?

She cleared her throat. Nothing. He didn't even shift in his sleep.

'Mr Sullivan?'

Nada.

For the first time, it occurred to her that maybe this wasn't sleep; maybe this was coma. Maybe he'd been injured more than either of them had realised. She hauled herself up into the back of the bus and crossed straight to his side, all thoughts of dangerous tattooed men cast aside. Her fingertips brushed below the hairy tangle of his jaw.

Steady and strong. And warm.

Phew.

'Mr Sullivan,' she said, louder. Those dark blond brows twitched just slightly and something moved briefly behind his eyelids, so she pressed her advantage. 'We're here.'

Her gaze went to his elevated foot and then back up to where his hands lay, folded, across the T-shirt over his midsection. Rather nice hands. Soft and manicured despite the patches of bike grease from his on-road repairs.

The sort of hands you'd see in a magazine.

Which was ridiculous. How many members of motorcycle clubs sidelined in a bit of casual hand modelling?

She forced her focus back up to his face and opened her lips to call his name a little louder, but, where before there was only the barest movement behind his lids, now they were wide open and staring straight at her. This close, with the light streaming in from the open curtains, she saw they weren't grey at all—or not *just* grey, at least. The pewter irises were flecked with rust that neatly matched the tarnished blond of his hair and beard, particularly concentrated around his pupils.

She'd never seen eyes like them. She immediately thought of the burnt umber coastal rocks of the far north, where they slid down to pale, clean ocean. And where she'd started her journey eight months ago.

'We're here,' she said, irritated at her own breathlessness. And at being caught checking him out.

He didn't move, but maybe that was because she was leaning so awkwardly over him from all the pulse-taking.

'Where's here?' he croaked.

She pushed back onto her heels and dragged her hands back from the heat of his body. 'The border. You'll have to get up while they inspect the bus.'

They took border security seriously here on the invisible line between South Australia and Western Australia. Less about gun-running and drug-trafficking and more about fruit flies and honey. Quarantine was king when agriculture was your primary industry.

Sullivan twisted gingerly into an upright position, then carefully pulled himself to his feet and did his best to put the cushions back where they'd started. Not right, but he got points for the effort.

So he hadn't been raised by leather-clad wolves, then.

He bundled up his belongings, tossed them to the ground outside the bus and lowered himself carefully down.

'How is your leg?' Eve asked.

'I'll live.'

Okay. Man of few words. Clearly, he'd spent too much time in his own company.

The inspection team made quick work of hunting over every inch of her converted bus and Sullivan's saddlebags. She'd become proficient at dumping or eating anything that was likely to get picked up at the border and so, this time, the team only found one item to protest—a couple of walnuts not yet consumed.

Into the bin they went.

She lifted her eyes towards Sullivan, deep in discussion with one of the border staff who had him in one ear and their phone on the other. Arranging assistance for his crippled bike, presumably. As soon as they were done, he limped back towards her and hiked his bags up over his shoulder.

'Thanks for the ride,' he said as though the effort half choked him.

'You don't need to go into Eucla?' Just as she'd grown used to him.

'They're sending someone out to grab me and retrieve my bike.'

'Oh. Great that they can do it straight away.'

'Country courtesy.'

As opposed to her lack of...? 'Well, good luck with your—'

It was then she realised she had absolutely no idea what he was doing out here, other than hitting random emus. In all her angsting out on the deserted highway, she really hadn't stopped to wonder, let alone ask.

'—with your travels.'

His nod was brisk and businesslike. 'Cheers.'

And then he was gone, back towards the border security office and the little café that catered for people delayed while crossing. Marshall Sullivan didn't seem half so scary here in a bustling border stop, though his beard was no less bushy and the ink dagger under his skin no less menacing. All the what-ifs she'd felt two hours ago on that long empty road hobbled away from her as he did.

And she wondered how she'd possibly missed the first time how well his riding leathers fitted him.

CHAPTER TWO

IT WAS THE raised voices that first got Marshall's attention. Female, anxious and angry, almost swallowed up by drunk, male and belligerent.

'Stop!'

The fact a gaggle of passers-by had formed a wide, unconscious circle around the spectacle in the middle of town was the only reason he sauntered closer instead of running on his nearly healed leg. If something bad was happening, he had to assume someone in the handful of people assembled would have intervened. Or at least cried out. Him busting in to an unknown situation, half-cocked, was no way to defuse what was clearly an escalating situation.

Instead, he insinuated himself neatly into the heart of the onlookers and nudged his way through to the front until he could get his eyeballs on things. A flutter of paper pieces rained down around them as the biggest of the men tore something up.

'You put another one up, I'm just going to rip it down,' he sneered.

The next thing he saw was the back of a woman's head. Dark, travel-messy ponytail. Dwarfed by the men she was facing but not backing down.

And all too familiar.

Little Miss Hostile. Winning friends and influencing people —as usual.

'This is a public noticeboard,' she asserted up at the human mountain, foolishly undeterred by his size.

'For Norseman residents,' he spat. 'Not for blow-ins from the east.'

'Public,' she challenged. 'Do I need to spell it out for you?'

Wow. Someone really needed to give her some basic training in conflict resolution. The guy was clearly a xenophobe and drunk. Calling him stupid in front of a crowd full of locals wasn't the fastest way out of her predicament.

She shoved past him and used a staple gun to pin up another flier.

He'd seen the same poster peppering posts and walls in Madura, Cocklebiddy and Balladonia. Every point along the remote desert highway that could conceivably hold a person. And a sign. Crisp and new against all the bleached, frayed ones from years past.

'Stop!'

Yeah, that guy wasn't going to stop. And now the McTanked Twins were also getting in on the act.

Goddammit.

Marshall pushed out into the centre of the circle. He raised his voice the way he used to in office meetings when they became unruly. Calm but intractable. 'Okay, show's over, people.'

The crowd turned their attention to him, like a bunch of cattle. So did the three drunks. But they weren't so intoxicated they didn't pause at the sight of his beard and tattoos. Just for a moment.

The moment he needed.

'Howzabout we find somewhere else for those?' he suggested straight to Little Miss Hostile, neatly relieving her of the pile of posters with one hand and the staple gun with his other. 'There are probably better locations in town.'

She spun around and glared at him in the heartbeat before she recognised him. 'Give me those.'

He ignored her and spoke to the crowd. 'All done, people. Let's get moving.'

They parted for him as he pushed back through, his hands full of her property. She had little choice but to pursue him.

'Those are mine!'

'Let's have this conversation around the corner,' he gritted back and down towards her.

But just as they'd cleared the crowd, the big guy couldn't help himself.

'Maybe he's gone missing to get away from you!' he called.

A shocked gasp covered the sound of small female feet pivoting on the pavement and she marched straight back towards the jeering threesome.

Marshall shoved the papers under his arm and sprinted after her, catching her just before she re-entered the eye of the storm. All three men had lined up in it, ready. Eager. He curled his arms around her and dragged her back, off her feet, and barked just one word in her ear.

'Don't!'

She twisted and lurched and swore the whole way but he didn't loosen his hold until the crowd and the jeering laughter of the drunks were well behind them.

'Put me down,' she struggled. 'Ass!'

'The only ass around here is the one I just saved.'

'I've dealt with rednecks before.'

'Yeah, you were doing a bang-up job.'

'I have every right to put my posters up.'

'No argument. But you could have just walked away and then come back and done it in ten minutes when the drunks were gone.'

'But there were thirty people there.'

'None of whom were making much of an effort to help you.' In case she hadn't noticed.

'I didn't want their help,' she spat, spinning back to face him. 'I wanted their attention.'

What was this—some kind of performance art thing? 'Come again?'

'Thirty people would have read my poster, remembered it.

The same people that probably would have passed it by without noticing, otherwise.'

'Are you serious?'

She snatched the papers and staple gun back from him and clutched them to her heaving chest. 'Perfectly. You think I'm new to this?'

'I really don't know what to think. You treated me like a pariah because of a bit of leather and ink, but you were quite happy to face off against the Beer Gut Brothers, back there.'

'It got *attention*.'

'So does armed robbery. Are you telling me the bank is on your to-do list in town?'

She glared at him. 'You don't understand.'

And then he was looking at the back of her head again as she turned and marched away from him without so much as a goodbye. Let alone a thankyou.

He cursed under his breath.

'Enlighten me,' he said, catching up with her and ignoring the protest of his aching leg.

'Why should I?'

'Because I just risked my neck entering that fray to help you and that means you owe me one.'

'I rescued you out on the highway. I'd say that makes us even.'

Infuriating woman. He slammed on the brakes. 'Fine. Whatever.'

Her momentum carried her a few metres further but then she spun back. 'Did you look at the poster?'

'I've been looking at them since the border.'

'And?'

'And what?'

'What's on it?'

His brows forked. What the hell *was* on it? 'Guy's face. Bunch of words.' And a particularly big one in red. MISSING. 'It's a missing-person poster.'

'Bingo. And you've been looking at them since the border

but can't tell me what he looked like or what his name was or what it was about.' She took two steps closer. 'That's why getting their attention was so valuable.'

Realisation washed through him and he felt like a schmuck for parachuting in and rescuing her like some damsel in distress. 'Because they'll remember it. You.'

'Him!' But her anger didn't last long. It seemed to desert her like the adrenaline in both their bodies, leaving her flat and exhausted. 'Maybe.'

'What do you do—start a fight in every town you go to?'

'Whatever it takes.'

Cars went by with stereos thumping.

'Listen…' Suddenly, Little Miss Hostile had all new layers. And most of them were laden with sadness. 'I'm sorry if you had that under control. Where I come from you don't walk past a woman crying out in the street.'

Actually, that wasn't strictly true because he came from a pretty rough area and sometimes the best thing to do was keep walking. But while his mother might have raised her kids like that, his grandparents certainly hadn't. And he, at least, had learned from their example even if his brother, Rick, hadn't.

Dark eyes studied him. 'That must get you into a lot of trouble,' she eventually said.

True enough.

'Let me buy you a drink. Give those guys some time to clear out and then I'll help you put the posters up.'

'I don't need your help. Or your protection.'

'Okay, but I'd like to take a proper look at that poster.'

He regarded her steadily as uncertainty flooded her expression. The same that he'd seen out on the highway. 'Or is the leather still bothering you?'

Indecision flooded her face and her eyes flicked from his beard to his eyes, then down to his lips and back again.

'No. You haven't robbed or murdered me yet. I think a few minutes together in a public place will be fine.'

She turned and glanced down the street where a slight *doof-*

doof issued from an architecturally classic Aussie hotel. Then her voice filled with warning. 'Just one.'

It was hard not to smile. Her stern little face was like a daisy facing up to a cyclone.

'If I was going to hurt you I've had plenty of opportunity. I don't really need to get you liquored up.'

'Encouraging start to the conversation.'

'You know my name,' he said, moving his feet in a pubward direction. 'I don't know yours.'

She regarded him steadily. Then stuck out the hand with the staple gun clutched in it. 'Evelyn Read. Eve.'

He shook half her hand and half the tool. 'What do you like to drink, Eve?'

'I don't. Not in public. But you go ahead.'

A teetotaller in an outback pub.

Well, this should be fun.

Eve trusted Marshall Sullivan with her posters while she used the facilities. When she came back, he'd smoothed out all the crinkles in the top one and was studying it.

'Brother?' he said as she slid into her seat.

'What makes you say that?'

He tapped the surname on the poster where it had *Travis James Read* in big letters.

'He could be my husband.' She shrugged.

His eyes narrowed. 'Same dark hair. Same shape eyes. He looks like you.'

Yeah, he did. Everyone thought so. 'Trav is my little brother.'

'And he's missing?'

God, she hated this bit. The pity. The automatic assumption that something bad had happened. Hard enough not letting herself think it every single day without having the thought planted back in her mind by strangers at every turn.

Virtual strangers.

Though, at least this one did her the courtesy of not referring to Travis in the past tense. Points for that.

'Missing a year next week, actually.'

'Tough anniversary. Is that why you're out here? Is this where he was last seen?'

She lifted her gaze back to his. 'No. In Melbourne.'

'So what brings you out west?'

'I ran out of towns on the east coast.'

Blond brows lowered. 'You've lost me.'

'I'm visiting every town in the country. Looking for him. Putting up notices. Doing the legwork.'

'I assumed you were just on holidays or something.'

'No. This is my job.'

Now. Before that she'd been a pretty decent graphic designer for a pretty decent marketing firm. Until she'd handed in her notice.

'Putting up posters is your job?'

'Finding my brother.' The old defensiveness washed through her. 'Is anything more important?'

His confusion wasn't new. He wasn't the first person not to understand what she was doing. By far. Her own father didn't even get it; he just wanted to grieve Travis's absence as though he were dead. To accept he was gone.

She was light-years and half a country away from being ready to accept such a thing. She and Trav had been so close. If he was dead, wouldn't she feel it?

'So…what, you just drive every highway in the country pinning up notices?'

'Pretty much. Trying to trigger a memory in someone's mind.'

'And it's taken you a year to do the east coast?'

'About eight months. Though I started up north.' And that was where she'd finish.

'What happened before that?'

Guilt hammered low in her gut for those missing couple of months before she'd realised how things really were. How she'd played nice and sat on her hands while the police seemed to achieve less and less. Maybe if she'd started sooner—

'I trusted the system.'

'But the authorities didn't find him?'

'There are tens of thousands of missing people every year. I just figured that the only people who could make Trav priority number one were his family.'

'That many? Really?'

'Teens. Kids. Women. Most are located pretty quickly.'

But ten per cent weren't.

His eyes tracked down to the birthdate on the poster. 'Healthy eighteen-year-old males don't really make it high up the priority list?'

A small fist formed in her throat. 'Not when there's no immediate evidence of foul play.'

And even if they maybe weren't entirely healthy, psychologically. But Travis's depression was hardly unique amongst *The Missing* and his anxiety attacks were longstanding enough that the authorities dismissed them as irrelevant. As if a bathroom cabinet awash with mental health medicines wasn't relevant.

A young woman with bright pink hair badly in need of a recolour brought Marshall's beer and Eve's lime and bittes and sloshed them on the table.

'That explains the bus,' he said. 'It's very…homey.'

'It is my home. Mine went to pay for the trip.'

'You sold your house?'

Her chin kicked up. 'And resigned from my job. I can't afford to be distracted by having to earn an income while I cover the country.'

She waited for the inevitable judgment.

'That's quite a commitment. But it makes sense.'

Such unconditional acceptance threw her. Everyone else she'd told thought she was foolish. Or plain crazy. Implication: like her brother. No one just…nodded.

'That's it? No opinion? No words of wisdom?'

His eyes lifted to hers. 'You're a grown woman. You did what you needed to do. And I assume it was your asset to dispose of.'

She scrutinised him again. The healthy, unmarked skin under the shaggy beard. The bright eyes. The even teeth.

'What's your story?' she asked.

'No story. I'm travelling.'

'You're not a bikie.' Statement, not question.

'Not everyone with a motorbike belongs in an outlaw club,' he pointed out.

'You look like a bikie.'

'I wear leather because it's safest when you get too intimate with asphalt. I have a beard because one of the greatest joys in life is not having to shave, and so I indulge that when I'm travelling alone.'

She glanced down to where the dagger protruded from his T-shirt sleeve. 'And the tattoo?'

His eyes immediately darkened. 'We were all young and impetuous once.'

'Who's Christine?'

'Christine's not relevant to this discussion.'

Bang. Total shutdown. 'Come on, Marshall. I aired my skeleton.'

'Something tells me you air it regularly. To anyone who'll listen.'

Okay, this time the criticism was unmistakable. She pushed more upright in her chair. 'You were asking the questions, if you recall.'

'Don't get all huffy. We barely know each other. Why would I spill my guts to a stranger?'

'I don't know. Why would you rescue a stranger on the street?'

'Not wanting to see you beaten to a pulp and not wanting to share my dirty laundry are very different things.'

'Oh, Christine's dirty laundry?'

His lips thinned even further and he pushed away from the table. 'Thanks for the drink. Good luck with your brother.'

She shot to her feet, too. 'Wait. Marshall?'

He stopped and turned back slowly.

'I'm sorry. I guess I'm out of practice with people,' she said.

'You're not kidding.'

'Where are you staying?'

'In town.'

Nice and non-specific. 'I'm a bit… I get a bit tired of eating in the bus. On my own. Can I interest you in something to eat, later?'

'I don't think so.'

Walk away, Eve. That would be the smart thing to do.

'I'll change the subject. Not my brother. Not your…' *Not your Christine?* 'We can talk about places we've been. Favourite sights.' Her voice petered out.

His eyebrows folded down over his eyes briefly and disguised them from her view. But he finally relented. 'There's a café across the street from my motel. End of this road.'

'Sounds good.'

She didn't usually eat out, to save money, but then she didn't usually have the slightest hint of company either. One dinner wouldn't kill her. Alone with a stranger. Across the road from his motel room.

'It's not a date, though,' she hastened to add.

'No.' The moustache twisted up on the left. 'It's not.'

And as he and his leather pants sauntered back out of the bar, she felt like an idiot. An adolescent idiot. *Of course* this was not a date and *of course* he wouldn't have considered it such. Hairy, lone-wolf types who travelled the country on motorbikes probably didn't stand much on ceremony when it came to women. Or bother with dates.

She'd only mentioned a meal at all because she felt bad that she'd pressed an obvious sore point with him after he'd shown her nothing but interest and acceptance about Travis.

facepalm

Her brother's favourite saying flittered through her memory and never seemed more appropriate. Hopefully, a few hours and a good shower from now she could be a little more socially appropriate and a lot less hormonal.

Inexplicably so.

Unwashed biker types were definitely not her thing, no matter how nice their smiles. Normally, the *eau de sweaty man* that littered towns in the Australian bush flared her nostrils. But as Marshall Sullivan had hoisted her up against his body out in the street she'd definitely responded to the powerful circle of his hold, the hard heat of his chest and the warmth of his hissed words against her ear.

Even though it came with the tickle of his substantial beard against her skin.

She was *so* not a beard woman.

A man who travelled the country alone was almost certainly doing it for a reason. Running from something or someone. Dropping out of society. Hiding from the authorities. Any number of mysterious and dangerous things.

Or maybe Marshall Sullivan was just as socially challenged as she was.

Maybe that was why she had a sudden and unfathomable desire to sit across a table from the man again.

'See you at seven-thirty, then,' she called after him.

Eve's annoyance at herself for being late—and at caring about that—turned into annoyance at Marshall Sullivan for being even later. What, had he got lost crossing the street?

Her gaze scanned the little café diner as she entered—over the elderly couple with a stumpy candle, past the just-showered Nigel No Friends reading a book and the two men arguing over the sports pages. But as her eyes grazed back around to the service counter, they stumbled over the hands wrapped around *Nigel's* battered novel. Beautiful hands.

She stepped closer. 'Marshall?'

Rust-flecked eyes glanced up to her. And then he pushed to his feet. To say he was a changed man without the beard would have been an understatement. He was transformed. His hair hadn't been cut but it was slicked back either with product or he truly had just showered. But his face…

Free of the overgrown blondish beard and moustache, his eyes totally stole focus, followed only by his smooth broad forehead. She'd always liked an unsullied forehead. Reliable somehow.

He slid a serviette into the book to mark his place and closed it.

She glanced at the cover. *'Gulliver's Travels?'*

Though what she really wanted to say was…*You shaved?*

'I carry a few favourites around with me in my pack.'

She slid in opposite him, completely unable to take her eyes off his new face. At a loss to reconcile it as the under layer of all that sweat, dust and helmet hair she'd encountered out on the road just a few days ago. 'What makes it a favourite?'

He thought about that for a bit. 'The journeying. It's very human. And Gulliver is a constant reminder that perspective is everything in life.'

Huh. She'd just enjoyed it for all the little people.

They fell to silence.

'You shaved,' she finally blurted.

'I did.'

'For dinner?' Dinner that wasn't a date.

His neatly groomed head shook gently. 'I do that periodically. Take it off and start again. Even symbols of liberty need maintenance.'

'That's what it means to you? Freedom?'

'Isn't that what the Bedford means to you?'

Freedom? No. Sanity, yes. 'The bus is just transport and accommodation conveniently bundled.'

'You forget I've seen inside it. That's not convenience. That's sanctuary.'

Yeah…it was, really. But she didn't know him well enough to open up to that degree.

'I bought the Bedford off this old carpenter after his wife died. He couldn't face travelling any more without her.'

'I wonder if he knows what he's missing.'

'Didn't you just say perspective was everything?'

'True enough.'

A middle-aged waitress came bustling over, puffing, as though six people at once was the most she'd seen in a week. She took their orders from the limited menu and bustled off again.

One blond brow lifted. 'You carb-loading for a marathon?'

'You've seen the stove in the Bedford. I can only cook the basics in her. Every now and again I like to take advantage of a commercial kitchen's deep-fryer.'

Plus, boiling oil would kill anything that might otherwise not get past the health code. There was nothing worse than being stuck in a small town, throwing your guts up. Unless it was being stuck on the side of the road between small towns and kneeling in the roadside gravel.

'So, you know how I'm funding my way around the country,' she said. 'How are you doing it?'

He stared at her steadily. 'Guns and drugs.'

'Ha-ha.'

'That's what you thought when you saw me. Right?'

'I saw a big guy on a lonely road trying really hard to get into my vehicle. What would you have done?'

Those intriguing eyes narrowed just slightly but then flicked away. 'I'm out here working. Like you. Going from district to district.'

'Working for who?'

'Federal Government.'

'Ooh, the Feds. That sounds much more exciting than it probably is. What department?'

He took a long swig of his beer before answering. 'Meteorology.'

She stared. 'You're a *weatherman*?'

'Right. I stand in front of a green screen every night and read maximums and minimums.'

Her smile broadened. 'You're a weatherman.'

He sagged back in his chair and spoke as if he'd heard this one time too many. 'Meteorology is a science.'

'You don't look like a scientist.' Definitely not before and, even clean shaven, Marshall was still too muscular and tattooed.

'Would it help if I was in a lab coat and glasses?'

'Yes.' Because the way he packed out his black T-shirt was the least nerdy thing she'd ever seen. 'So why are my taxes funding your trip around the country, exactly?'

'You're not earning. You don't pay taxes.'

The man had a point. 'Why are you out here, then?'

'I'm auditing the weather stations. I check them, report on their condition.'

Well, that explained the hands. 'I thought you were this free spirit on two wheels. You're an auditor.'

His lips tightened. 'Something tells me that's a step down from weatherman in your eyes.'

She got stuck into her complimentary bread roll, buttering and biting into it. 'How many stations are there?'

'Eight hundred and ninety-two.'

'And they send one man?' Surely they had locals that could check to make sure possums hadn't moved into their million-dollar infrastructure.

'I volunteered to do the whole run. Needed the break.'

From...? But she'd promised not to ask. They were supposed to be talking about travel highlights. 'Where was the most remote station?'

'Giles. Seven hundred and fifty clicks west of Alice. Up in the Gibson Desert.'

Alice Springs. Right smack bang in the middle of their massive island continent. 'Where did you start?'

'Start and finish in Perth.'

A day and a half straight drive from here. 'Is Perth home?'

'Sydney.'

She visualised the route he must have taken clockwise around the country from the west. 'So you're nearly done, then?'

His laugh drew the eyes of the other diners. 'Yeah. If two-thirds of the weather stations weren't in the bottom third of the state.'

'Do you get to look around? Or is it all work?'

He shrugged. 'Some places I skip right through. Others I linger. I have some flexibility.'

Eve knew exactly what that was like. Some towns whispered to you like a lover. Others yelled at you to go. She tended to move on quickly from those.

'Favourites so far?'

And he was off... Talking about the places that had captivated him most. The prehistoric, ferny depths of the Claustral Canyon, cave-diving in the crystal-clear ponds on South Australia's limestone coast, the soul-restoring solidity of Katherine Gorge in Australia's north.

'And the run over here goes without saying.'

'The Nullabor?' Pretty striking with its epic treeless stretches of desert but not the most memorable place she could recall.

'The Great Australian Bight,' he clarified.

She just blinked at him.

'You got off the highway on the way over, right? Turned for the coast?'

'My focus is town to town.'

He practically gaped. 'One of the most spectacular natural wonders in the world was just a half-hour drive away.'

'And half an hour back. That was an hour sooner I could have made it to the next town.'

His brows dipped over grey eyes. 'You've got to get out more.'

'I'm on the job.'

'Yeah, me, too, but you have to live as well. What about weekends?'

The criticism rankled. 'Not all of us are on the cushy public servant schedule. An hour—a day—could mean the difference between running across someone who knew Travis and not.'

Or even running into Trav himself.

'What if they came through an hour after you left, and pausing to look at something pretty could have meant your paths crossed?'

Did he think she hadn't tortured herself with those thoughts late at night? The endless what-ifs?

'An hour afterwards and they'll see a poster. An hour before and they'd have no idea their shift buddy is a missing person.' At least that was what she told herself. Sternly.

Marshall blinked at her.

'You don't understand.' How could he?

'Wouldn't it be faster to just email the posters around the country? Ask the post offices to put them up for you.'

'It's not just about the posters. It's about talking to people. Hunting down leads. Making an impression.'

Hoping to God the impression would stick.

'The kind you nearly made this afternoon?'

'Whatever it takes.'

Their meals arrived and the next minute was filled with making space on the table and receiving their drinks.

'Anyway, weren't we supposed to be talking about something else?' Eve said brightly, crunching into a chip. 'Where are you headed next?'

'Up to Kalgoorlie, then Southern Cross.'

North. Complete opposite to her.

'You?' His gaze was neutral enough.

'Esperance. Ravensthorpe. With a side trip out to Israelite Bay.' Jeez—why didn't she just draw him her route on a serviette? 'I'm getting low on posters after the Nullabor run. Need an MP's office.'

His newly groomed head tipped.

'MP's offices are obliged by law to print missing-person posters on request,' she explained. 'And there's one in Esperance.'

'Convenient.'

She glared at her chicken. 'It's the least they could do.'

And pretty much all they did. Though they were usually carefully sympathetic.

'It must be hard,' he murmured between mouthfuls. 'Hitting brick walls everywhere you go.'

'I'd rather hit them out here than stuck back in Melbourne. At least I can be productive here.'

Sitting at home and relying on others to do something to find her brother had nearly killed her.

'Did you leave a big family behind?'

Instantly her mind flashed to her father's grief-stricken face as the only person he had left in the world drove off towards the horizon. 'Just my dad.'

'No mum?'

She sat up straighter in her seat. If Christine-of-the-dagger was off the table for discussion, her drunk mother certainly was. Clearly, the lines in her face were as good as a barometric map. Because Marshall let the subject well and truly drop.

'Well, guess this is our first and last dinner, then,' he said cheerfully, toasting her with a forkful of mashed potato and peas. There was nothing more in that than pure observation. Nothing enough that she felt confident in answering without worrying it would sound like an invitation.

'You never know, we might bump into each other again.'

But, really, how likely was that once they headed off towards opposite points on the compass? The only reason they'd met up this once was because there was only one road in and out of the south half of this vast state and he'd crashed into an emu right in the middle of it.

Thoughtful eyes studied her face, then turned back to his meal.

'So you're not from Sydney, originally?'

Marshall pushed his empty plate away and groaned inwardly. Who knew talking about nothing could be so tiring? This had to be the greatest number of words he'd spoken to anyone in weeks. But it was his fault as much as hers. No dag-

ger tattoo and no missing brother. That was what he'd stipu-
lated. She'd held up her end of the bargain, even though she
was clearly itching to know more.

Precisely why he didn't do dinners with women.

Conversation.

He'd much rather get straight to the sex part. Although that
was clearly off the table with Eve. So it really made a man wonder why the heck he'd said yes to Eve's 'not a date' invitation.
Maybe even *he* got lonely.

And maybe they were now wearing long coats in Hades.

'Brisbane.'

'How old were you when you moved?' she chatted on, oblivious to the rapid congealing of his thoughts. Oblivious to the
dangerous territory she'd accidentally stumbled into. Thoughts
of his brother, their mother and how tough he'd found Sydney
as an adolescent.

'Twelve.'

The word squeezed past his suddenly tight throat. The logical part of him knew it was just polite conversation, but the
part of him that was suddenly as taut as a crossbow loaded a
whole lot more onto her innocent chatter. Twelve was a crap
age to be yanked away from your friends and the school where
you were finding your feet and thrust into one of the poorest
suburbs of one of the biggest cities in the country. But—for
the woman who'd only pumped out a second son for the public benefits—moving states to chase a more generous single-
parent allowance was a no-brainer. No matter who it disrupted.

Not that any of that money had ever found its way to him
and Rick. They were just a means to an end.

'What was that like?'

Being your mother's meal ticket or watching your older
brother forge himself a career as the local drug-mover?

'It was okay.'

Uh-oh…here it came. Verbal shutdown. Probably just as
well, given the direction his mind was going.

She watched him steadily, those dark eyes knowing something was up even if she didn't know exactly what. 'Uh-huh…'

Which was code for *Your turn next, Oscar Wilde*. But he couldn't think of a single thing to say, witty or otherwise. So he folded his serviette and gave his chair the slightest of backward pushes.

'Well…'

'What just happened?' Eve asked, watching him with curiosity but not judgment. And not moving an inch.

'It's getting late.'

'It's eight-thirty.'

Seriously? Only an hour? It felt like eternity.

'I'm heading out at sunrise. So I can get to Lake Lefroy before it gets too hot.'

And back to blissful isolation, where he didn't need to explain himself to anyone.

She tipped her head and it caused her dark hair to swing to the right a little. A soft fragrance wafted forwards and teased his receptors. His words stumbled as surely as he did, getting up. 'Thanks for the company.'

She followed suit. 'You're welcome.'

They split the bill in uncomfortable silence, then stepped out into the dark street. Deserted by eight-thirty.

Eve looked to her right, then back at him.

'Listen, I know you're just across the road but could you… would you mind walking me back to the bus?'

Maybe they were both remembering those three jerks from earlier.

'Where do you park at night?' He suddenly realised he had no idea where she'd pulled up. And that his ability to form sentences seemed to have returned with the fresh air.

'I usually find a good spot…'

Oh, jeez. She wasn't even sorted for the night.

They walked on in silence and then words just came tumbling out of him.

'My motel booking comes with parking. You could use that if you want. I'll tuck the bike forward.'

'Really?' Gratitude flooded her pretty face. 'That would be great, thank you.'

'Come on.'

He followed her to the right, and walked back through Norseman's quiet main streets. Neither of them spoke. When they reached her bus, she unlocked the side window and reached in to activate the folding front door. He waited while she crossed back around and then stepped up behind her into the cab.

Forbidden territory previously.

But she didn't so much as twitch this time. Which was irrationally pleasing. Clearly he'd passed some kind of test. Maybe it was when the beard came off.

The Bedford rumbled to life and Eve circled the block before heading back to his motel. He directed her into his bay and then jumped out to nudge the KTM forward a little. The back of her bus stuck out of the bay but he was pretty sure there was only one other person in the entire motel and they were already parked up for the night.

'Thanks again for this,' she said, pausing at the back of the bus with one of the two big rear doors open.

Courtesy of the garish motel lights that streamed in her half-closed curtains, he could see the comfortable space he'd fallen asleep in bathed in a yellow glow. And beyond it, behind the door that now stood open at the other end of the bus, Eve's bedroom. The opening was dominated by the foot of a large mattress draped in a burgundy quilt and weighed down with two big cushions.

Nothing like the sterile motel room and single country bed he'd be returning to.

'Caravan parks can be a little isolated this time of year,' she said, a bit tighter, as she caught the direction of his gaze. 'I feel better being close to...people.'

He eased his shoulder against the closed half of the door

and studied her. Had she changed her mind? Was that open door some kind of unconscious overture? And was he really considering taking her up on it if it was? Pretty, uptight girls on crusades didn't really meet his definition of uncomplicated. Yet something deep inside hinted strongly that she might be worth a bit of complication.

He peered down on her in the shadows. 'No problem.'

She shuffled from left foot to right. 'Well…'night, then. See you in the morning. Thanks again.'

A reluctant smile crossed his face at the firm finality of that door slamming shut. And at the zipping across of curtains as he sauntered to the rear of the motel.

Now they were one-for-one in the inappropriate social re-action stakes. He'd gone all strong and silent on her and she'd gone all blushing virgin on him.

Equally awkward.

Equally regrettable.

He dug into his pocket for the worn old key and let himself into his ground floor room. Exactly as soulless and bland as her little bus wasn't.

But exactly as soulless and bland as he preferred.

CHAPTER THREE

'THIS BUS NEVER stops being versatile, does it?'

Eve's breath caught deep in her throat at the slight twang and comfortable gravel in the voice that came from her left. The few days that had passed since she'd heard his bike rumble out of the motel car park at dawn as she'd rolled the covers more tightly around her and fell back to sleep gave him exactly the right amount of stubble as he let the beard grow back in.

'Marshall?' Her hand clamped down on the pile of fliers that lifted off the table in the brisk Esperance waterfront breeze. 'I thought you'd headed north?'

'I did. But a road train had jack-knifed across the highway just out of Kal and the spill clean-up was going to take twenty-four hours so I adjusted my route. I'll do the south-west anti-clockwise. Like you.'

Was there just the slightest pause before 'like you'? And did that mean anything? Apparently, she took too long wondering because he started up again.

'I assumed I'd have missed you, actually.'

Or hoped? Impossible to know with his eyes hidden behind seriously dark sunglasses. Still, if he'd truly wanted to avoid her he could have just kept walking just now. She was so busy promoting *The Missing* to locals she never would have noticed him.

Eve pushed her shoulders back to improve her posture,

which had slumped as the morning wore on. Convenient co-incidence that it also made the best of her limited assets.

'I had to do Salmon Gums and Gibson on the way,' she said. 'I only arrived last night.'

He took in the two-dozen posters affixed to the tilted up doors of the bus's luggage compartment. It made a great road-side noticeboard to set her fold-out table up in front of.

He strolled up and back, studying every face closely.

'Who are all these people?'

'They're all long-termers.' *The ten per cent.*

'Do you know them all?'

'No,' she murmured. 'But I know most of their families. Online, at least.'

'All missing.' He frowned. 'Doesn't it pull focus from your brother? To do this?'

Yeah. It definitely did.

'I wouldn't be much of a human being if I travelled the entire country only looking after myself. Besides, we kind of have a reciprocal arrangement going. If someone's doing something special—like media or some kind of promotion—they try to include as many others as they can. This is something I can do in the big centres while taking a break from the road.'

Though Esperance was hardly a metropolis and talking to strangers all day wasn't much of a break.

He stopped just in front of her, picked up one of Travis's posters. 'Who's "we"?'

'The network.'

The sunglasses tipped more towards her.

'The missing-persons network,' she explained. 'The fami-lies. There are a lot of us.'

'You have a formal network?'

'We have an informal one. We share information. Tips. Successes.'

Failures. Quite a lot of failures.

'Good to have the support, I guess.'

He had no idea. Some days her commitment to a bunch of

people she'd never met face to face was the only thing that got her out of bed.

'When I first started up, I kept my focus on Trav. But these people—' she tipped her head back towards all the faces on her poster display '—are like extended family to me because they're the family of people I'm now close to. How could I not include them amongst *The Missing*?'

A woman stopped to pick up one of her fliers and Eve quickly delivered her spiel, smiling and making a lot of eye contact. Pumping it with energy. Whatever it took…

Marshall waited until the woman had finished perusing the whole display. *'The Missing?'*

She looked behind her. 'Them.'

And her brother had the biggest and most central poster on it.

He nodded to a gap on the top right of the display. 'Looks like one's fallen off.'

'I just took someone down.'

His eyebrows lifted. 'They were found? That's great.'

No, not great. But at least found. That was how it was for the families of long-timers. The Simmons family had the rest of their lives to deal with the mental torture that came with feeling *relief* when their son's remains were found in a gully at the bottom of a popular hiking mountain. Closure. That became the goal somewhere around the ten-month mark.

Emotional euthanasia.

Maybe one day that would be her—loathing herself for being grateful that the question mark that stalked her twenty-four-seven was now gone because her brother was. But there was no way she could explain any of that to someone outside the network. Regular people just didn't get it. It was just so much easier to smile and nod.

'Yes. Great.'

Silence clunked somewhat awkwardly on the table between them.

'Did you get out to Israelite Bay yet?' he finally asked.

'I'll probably do that tomorrow or Wednesday.'

His clear eyes narrowed. 'Listen. I have an idea. You need to travel out to the bay and I need to head out to Cape Arid and Middle Island to survey them for a possible new weather station. Why don't we team up, head out together? Two birds, one stone.'

More together time in which to struggle with conversation and obsess about his tattoos. Was that wise?

'I'll only slow you down. I need to do poster drops at all roadhouses, caravan parks and campsites between here and there.'

'That's okay. As far as the office is concerned, I have a couple of days while the truck mess is cleared up. We can take our time.'

Why did he seem so very reluctant? Almost as if he was speaking against his will. She scrunched her nose as a prelude to an *I don't think so.*

But he beat her to it. 'Middle Island is off-limits to the public. You can't go there without a permit.'

'And you have a permit?'

'I do.'

'Have you forgotten that this isn't a tourist trip for me?'

'You'll get your work done on the way, and then you'll just keep me company for mine.'

'I can get my work done by myself and be back in Esperance by nightfall.'

'Or you can give yourself a few hours off and see a bit of this country that you're totally missing.'

'And why should I be excited by Middle Island?'

'A restricted island could be a great place for someone to hide out if they don't want to be discovered.'

The moment the words left his mouth, colour peaked high on his jaw.

'Sorry—' he winced as she sucked in a breath '—that was… God, I'm sorry. I just thought you might enjoy a bit of down-time. That it might be good for you.'

But his words had had their effect. If you needed a permit and Marshall had one, then she'd be crazy not to tag along. What if she let her natural reticence stop her and Trav was there, camping and lying low?

'I'll let you ride on my bike,' he said, as though that made it better. As if it was some kind of prize.

Instantly her gut curled into a fist. 'Motorbikes kill people.'

'People kill people,' he dismissed. 'Have you ever ridden on one?'

If riding tandem with a woman in the midst of a mid-life crisis counted. 'My mother had a 250cc.'

'Really? Cool.'

Yeah, that was what she and Travis had thought, right up until the day it killed their mother and nearly him.

'But you haven't really *ridden* until you've been on a 1200.'

'No, thanks.'

'Come on... Wouldn't you like to know what it's like to have all that power between your legs?'

'If this is a line, it's spectacularly cheesy.'

He ignored that. 'Or the freedom of tearing along at one hundred clicks with nothing between you and the road?'

'You call that freedom, I call that terror.'

'How will you know until you try it?'

'I'm not interested in trying it.'

He totally failed at masking his disappointment. 'Then you can tail me in the bus. We'll convoy. It'll still be fun.'

Famous last words. Something told her the fun would run out, for him, round about the time she pulled into her third rest stop for the day, to pin up posters.

'There's also a good caravan park out there, according to the travel guides. You can watch a west coast sunset.'

'I've seen plenty of sunsets.'

'Not with me,' he said on a sexy grin.

Something about his intensity really wiggled down under her skin. Tantalising and zingy. 'Why are you so eager for me to do this?'

Grey eyes grew earnest. 'Because you're missing everything. The entire country. The moments of joy that give life its colour.'

'You should really moonlight in greeting-card messages.'

'Come on, Eve. You have to go there, anyway, it's just a few hours of detour.'

'And what if Trav comes through in those few hours?' It sounded ridiculous but it was the fear she lived with every moment of every day.

'Then he'll see one of dozens of posters and know you're looking for him.'

The simple truth of that ached. Every decision she made ached. Each one could bring her closer to her brother or push her further away. It made decision-making pure agony. But this one came with a whole bundle of extra considerations. Marshall-shaped considerations. And the thought of sitting and watching a sunset with him even managed to alleviate some of that ache.

A surprising amount.

She sighed. 'What time?'

'How long are you set up here for?'

'I have permission to be on the waterfront until noon.'

'Five past noon, then?'

So eager. Did he truly think she was that parched for some life experience? It galled her to give him all the points. 'Ten past.'

His smile transformed his face, the way it always did.

'Done.'

'And we're sleeping separately. You know…just for the record.'

'Hey, I'm just buying you a sunset, lady.' His shrug was adorable. And totally disarming.

'Now go, Weatherman—you're scaring off my leads with all that leather.'

Her lips said 'go' but her heart said *stay*. Whispered it, really. But she'd become proficient in drowning out the fancies of her heart. And its fears. Neither were particularly productive in keeping her on track in finding Travis. A nice neutral... nothing...was the best way to proceed.

Emotionally blank, psychologically focused.

Which wasn't to say that Marshall Sullivan couldn't be a useful distraction from all the voices in her head and heart.

And a pleasant one.

And a short one.

They drove the two hundred kilometres east in a weird kind of convoy. Eve chugging along in her ancient bus and him, unable to stand the slow pace, roaring off ahead and pulling over at the turn-off to every conceivable human touch point until she caught up, whacked up a poster and headed out again. Rest stops, roadhouses, campgrounds, lookouts. Whizzing by at one hundred kilometres an hour and only stopping longer for places that had people and rubbish bins and queued-up vehicles.

It was a horrible way to see such a beautiful country.

Eventually, they made it to the campground nestled in the shoulder crook of a pristine bay on the far side of Cape Arid National Park, its land arms reaching left and right in a big, hug-like semicircle. A haven for travellers, fishermen and a whole lot of wildlife.

But not today. Today they had the whole place to themselves.

'So many blues...' Eve commented, stepping down out of the bus and staring at the expansive bay.

And she wasn't wrong. Closer to shore, the water was the pale, almost ice-blue of gentle surf. Then the kind of blue you saw on postcards, until, out near the horizon it graduated to a deep, gorgeous blue before slamming into the endless rich blue of the Australian sky. And, down to their left, a cluster of weathered boulders were freckled by a bunch of sea lions sunning themselves.

God...so good for the soul.

'This is nothing,' he said. Compared to what she'd missed

all along the south coast of Australia. Compared to what she'd driven straight past. 'If you'd just chuck your indicator on from time to time…'

She glanced at him but didn't say anything, busying stringing out her solar blanket to catch the afternoon light. When she opened the back doors of the bus to fill it with fresh sea air, she paused, looking further out to sea. Out to an island.

'Is that where we're going?'

Marshall hauled himself up next to her to follow her gaze. 'Nope. That's one of the closer, smaller islands in the archipelago. Middle Island is further out. One of those big shadows looming on the horizon.'

He leaned half across her to point further out and she followed the line of his arm and finger. It brought them as close together as they'd been since he'd dragged her kicking and cursing away from the thugs back in Norseman. And then he knew how much he'd missed her scent.

It eddied around his nostrils now, in defiance of the strong breeze.

Taunting him.

'How many are there?'

What were they talking about? Right…islands. 'More than a hundred.'

Eve stood, staring, her gaze flicking over every feature in view. Marshall kept his hand hooked around the bus's ceiling, keeping her company up there. Keeping close.

'Trav could be on any of them.'

Not if he also wanted to eat. Or drink. Only two had fresh water.

'Listen, Eve…'

She turned her eyes back up to his and it put their faces much closer than either of them might have intended.

'I really am truly sorry I said that about your brother. It was a cheap shot.' And one that he still didn't fully understand making. He wasn't Eve's keeper. 'The chances of him being out there are—'

'Tiny. I know. But it's in my head now and I'm not going to be able to sleep if I don't chase every possibility.'

'Still, I don't want to cause you pain.'

'That's not hurting, Marshall. That's helping. It's what I'm out here for.'

She said the words extra firmly, as if she was reminding both of them. Didn't make the slightest difference to the tingling in his toes. The tingling said she was here for him.

What did toes ever know?

He held her gaze much longer than was probably polite, their dark depths giving the ocean around them a run for its money.

'Doesn't seem a particularly convenient place to put a weather station,' she said finally, turning back out to the islands.

Subtle subject change. *Not.* But he played along. 'We want remote. To give us better data on southern coastal weather conditions.'

She glanced around them at the whole lot of nothing as far as the eye could see. 'You got it.'

Silent sound cushioned them in layers. The occasional bird cry, far away. The whump of the distant waves hitting the granite face of the south coast. The thrum of the coastal breeze around them. The awkward clearing of her throat as it finally dawned on her that she was shacked up miles from anywhere—and anyone—with a man she barely knew.

'What time are we meeting the boat? And where?'

'First thing in the morning. They'll pull into the bay, then ferry us around. Any closer to Middle Island and we couldn't get in without an off-road vehicle.'

'Right.'

Gravity helped his boots find the dirt and he looked back up at Eve, giving her the space she seemed to need. 'I'm going to go hit the water before the sun gets too low.'

Her eyes said that a swim was exactly what she wanted. But the tightness in her lips said that she wasn't about to go wandering through the sand dunes somewhere this remote with a virtual stranger. Fair enough, they'd only known each other hours. Despite having a couple of life-threatening moments between them. Maybe if she saw him walking away from her, unoffended and unconcerned, she'd feel more comfortable around him. Maybe if he offered no pressure for the two of them to spend time together, she'd relax a bit.

And maybe if he grew a pair he wouldn't care.

'See you later on, then.'

Marshall jogged down to the beach without looking back. When he hit the shore he laid his boots, jeans and T-shirt out on the nearest rock to get nice and toasty for his return and waded into the ice-cold water in his shorts. Normally he'd have gone without, public or not, but that wasn't going to win him any points in the *Is it safe to be here with you?* stakes. The sand beneath his feet had been beaten so fine by the relentless Southern Ocean it was more like squidging into saturated talcum powder than abrasive granules of sand. Soft and welcoming, the kind of thing you could imagine just swallowing you up.

And you wouldn't mind a bit.

His skin instantly thrilled at the kiss of the ice-cold water after the better part of a day smothered in leather and road dust, and he waded the stretch of shallows, then dived through the handful of waves that built up momentum as the rapid rise of land forced them into graceful, white-topped arcs.

This was his first swim since Cactus Beach, a whole state away. The Great Australian Bight was rugged and amazing to look at right the way across the guts of the country but when the rocks down to the sea were fifty metres high and the ocean down there bottomless and deadly, swimming had to take a short sabbatical. But swimming was also one of the things that kept him sane and being barred from it got him all twitchy.

Which made it pretty notable that the first thing he *didn't do* when he pulled up to the beautiful, tranquil and swimmable shores of Esperance earlier today was hit the water.

He went hunting for a dark-haired little obsessive instead.

Oh, he told himself a dozen lies to justify it—that he'd rather swim the private beaches of the capes; that he'd rather swim at sunset; that he'd rather get the Middle Island review out of the way first so he could take a few days to relax—but that was all starting to feel like complete rubbish. Apparently, he was parched for something more than just salt water.

Company.

Pfff. Right. That was one word for it.

It had been months since he'd been interested enough in a woman to do something about it, and by 'interested' he meant hungry. Hungry enough to head out and find a woman willing to sleep with a man who had nothing to offer but a hard, one-off lay before blowing town the next day. There seemed to be no shortage of women across the country who were out to salve a broken heart, or pay back a cheating spouse, or numb something broken deep inside them. They were the ones he looked for when he got needy enough because they didn't ask questions and they didn't have expectations.

It took one to know one.

Those encounters scratched the itch when it grew too demanding...and they reminded him how empty and soulless relationships were. All relationships, not just the random strangers in truck stops and bars across the country. Women. Mothers.

Brothers.

At least the women in the bars knew where they stood. No one was getting used. And there was no one to disappoint except himself.

He powered his body harder, arm over arm, and concentrated on how his muscles felt, cutting his limbs through the surf. Burning from within, icy from without. The familiar, heavy ache of lactic acid building up. And when he'd done all the examination it was possible to do on his muscles, he focused on the water: how the last land it had touched was Antarctica, how it was life support for whales and elephant seals and dugongs and colossal squid and mysterious deep-trench blobs eight kilometres below the surface and thousands of odd-

shaped sea creatures in between. How humans were a bunch
of nimble-fingered, big-brained primates that really only used
the millimetre around the edge of the mapped oceans and had
absolutely no idea how much of their planet they knew nothing about.

Instant Gulliver.

It reminded him how insignificant he was in the scheme of
things. Him and all his human, social problems.

The sun was low on the horizon when he next paid attention,
and the south coast of Australia was littered with sharks who
liked to feed at dusk and dawn. And while there had certainly
been a day he would have happily taken the risk and forgotten the consequences, he'd managed to find a happy place in
the *Groundhog Day* blur that was the past six months on the
road, and could honestly say—hand on heart—that he'd rather
not be shark food now.

He did a final lazy lap parallel with the wide beach back
towards his discarded clothes, then stood as soon as the sea
floor rose to meet him. His hands squeezed up over his lowered lids and back through his hair, wringing the salt water out
of it, then he stood, eyes closed, with his face tipped towards
the warmth of the afternoon sun.

Eventually, he opened them and started, just a little, at Eve
standing there, her arms full of towel, her mouth hanging open
as if he'd interrupted her mid-sentence.

Eve knew she was gaping horribly but she was no more able to
close her trap than rip her eyes from Marshall's chest and belly.

His *tattooed* chest and belly.

Air sucked into her lungs in choppy little gasps.

He had some kind of massive bird of prey, wings spread and
aloft, across his chest. The lower curve of its majestic wings
sat neatly along the ridge of his pectorals and its wing tips
followed the line of muscle there up onto his tanned, rounded
shoulders. Big enough to accentuate the musculature of his
chest, low enough to be invisible when he was wearing a

T-shirt. It should have been trashy but it wasn't; it looked like he'd been born with it.

His arms were still up, squeezing the sea water from his hair, and that gave her a glimpse of a bunch of inked characters—Japanese, maybe Chinese?—on the underside of one full biceps.

Add that to the dagger on the other arm and he had a lot of ink for a weatherman.

'Hey.'

His voice startled her gaze back to his and her tongue into action.

'Wow,' she croaked, then realised that wasn't the most dignified of beginnings. 'You were gone so long...'

Great. Not even capable of a complete sentence.

'I've been missing the ocean. Sorry if I worried you.'

She grasped around in the memories she'd just spent a couple of hours accumulating, studying the map to make sure they hadn't missed a caravan park or town. And she improvised some slightly more intelligent conversation.

'Whoever first explored this area really didn't have the best time doing it.'

Marshall dripped. And frowned. As he lowered his arms to take the towel from her nerveless fingers, the bird of prey's feathers shifted with him, just enough to catch her eye. She struggled to look somewhere other than at him, but it wasn't easy when he filled her field of view so thoroughly. She wanted to step back but then didn't want to give him the satisfaction of knowing she was affected.

'Cape Arid, Mount Ragged, Poison Creek...' she listed with an encouraging lack of wobble in her voice, her clarity restored the moment he pressed the towel to his face and disguised most of that unexpectedly firm and decorated torso.

He stepped over to the rock and hooked up his T-shirt, then swept it on in a smooth, manly shrug. Even with its overstretched neckline, the bird of prey was entirely hidden. The idea of him hanging out in his meteorological workplace in a

government-appropriate suit with all of that ink hidden away
under it was as secretly pleasing as when she used to wear her
best lingerie to section meetings.

Back when stupid things like that had mattered.

'I guess it's not so bad when you have supplies and transport,' he said, totally oblivious to her illicit train of thought,
'but it must have been a pretty treacherous environment for
early explorers. Especially if they were thirsty.'

She just blinked at him. What was he saying? What had
she asked?

He didn't bother with the rest of his clothes; he just slung
the jeans over his shoulder and followed her back up to camp
with his boots swinging in his left hand.

'Nice swim?' Yeah. Much easier to think with all that skin
and ink covered up.

'I've missed it. The water's so clean down here.'

'Isn't ocean always clean?'

'Not at all. It's so easy to imagine the Southern Ocean being
melt straight from Antarctica. Beautiful.'

'Maybe I'll take a dip tomorrow.' When Marshall was otherwise engaged.

They fell to silence as they approached the bus. Suddenly
the awkwardness of the situation amplified. One bus. Two people. One of them half-naked and the other fresh from a bout of
uncontrollable ogling. As though her-on-the-bed and him-on-
the-sofa was the only social nicety to be observed. There was a
bathroom and TV space and…air to consider. She was used to
having the bus entirely to herself, now she had to share it with
a man for twenty-four hours. And not just any man.

A hot man.

A really hot man.

'Um. You take the bus to change, I'll just—' she looked
around for inspiration and saw the quirky little public out-
house in the distance '—check out the facilities.'

Oh, good Lord…

'Thanks. I'll only be a few minutes.'

Her, too. Most definitely. There was a reason she'd held out until she found a live-in transport with a toilet built into it. Public toilets in remote Australia were not for the faint of heart.

As it turned out, this one was a cut above average. Well maintained and stocked. Some kind of eco-composting number. It was only when she caught herself checking out how the pipework operated that she knew just how badly she was stalling. As if toilets were anywhere near that fascinating.

Come on, Read, man up.

Returning revealed Marshall to have been as good as his word. He was changed, loosely groomed and waiting outside the bus already. *Outside.* Almost as though he was trying to minimise his impact on her space.

He held his new bike helmet out to her.

'Come on.' He smiled. 'I promised you a ride. While we still have light.'

It took approximately twenty-five seconds for Eve to get over her concern that Marshall only had one motorbike helmet and he was holding it out to her. After that, she was all about survival of the fittest.

'I don't remember agreeing to this—'

'You'll love it, Eve. I promise.'

She glared up at him. 'Just because you do?'

'Because it's brilliant. And fun.'

No. Not always fun. She'd lost one and nearly two people she loved to a not-so-fun motorbike. Though that could just as easily have been a car, her logical side whispered. Or a bus. Or a 747. Tragedies happened every single day.

Just that day it happened to them.

'Think of it like a theme park ride,' he cajoled. 'A roller coaster.'

'That's not really helping.'

'Come on, Eve. What else are we going to do until it's dark?'

Apart from sit in the bus in awkward silence obsessing on

who was going to sleep where…? She glanced sideways at the big orange bike.

'I'll keep you safe, I promise. We'll only go as fast as you're comfortable with.'

His siren voice chipped away at her resistance. And his vow—*I'll keep you safe*. For so long she'd been all about looking after her father and brother. When was the last time someone offered to look after *her*?

'Just slow?'

Of course there was small print, but it came delightfully packaged in a grin full of promise. 'Until you're ready for more.'

He seemed so incredibly confident that was going to happen. Her bottom lip wiggled its way between her teeth. She *had* always wondered what it would be like to ride something with a bit more power. If by *always* she meant after two hours of watching a leather-clad Marshall dominate the machine under him. And if by *ride* she meant pressing her thighs into his and her front to that broad, strong back, both of them hepped up on adrenaline. It was a seductive picture. The kind of picture that was best reserved for her and a quiet, deluded night in the bus. She hadn't imagined it would ever go from fantasy to opportunity.

He held the helmet out again.

'You'll slow the moment I ask?' she breathed.

'Cross my heart.'

Yeah, not really selling it. Everyone knew what came after that line…

But it was only when she was about to lower her hand away from the helmet that she realised she'd even raised it. What was she going to do, live in fear of motorbikes for the rest of her life? No one was even sure what had caused her mother's accident—even Trav, after he'd come out of the coma, couldn't shed much light. Tragic accident. Could have happened to anyone. That was the final verdict.

'You'll drive safely?'

Come on, Read, suck it up.

Sincerity blazed in his solemn grey gaze. 'I'll be a model of conservatism.'

How long had it been since she'd done something outside of the box? Or taken any kind of risk? She used to be edgy, back before life got so very serious and she took responsibility for Travis. And her risks had almost always paid off. That was part of the thrill.

Hadn't she once been known for that?

Here was a gorgeous man offering to wrap her around him for a little bit. And the price—a bit of reckless speed.

It had been years since she'd done something reckless. Maybe it would be good for her.

She took a deep breath and curled her fingers around the helmet's chin strap.

The KTM hit a breath-stealing speed in about the same time it took her to brave opening her eyes. The road whizzed below them in such a blur it was like riding on liquid mercury.

At least that was how it felt.

She immediately remembered the excitement of riding behind her mother, but her mother's bike had never purred like this one. And it had never glued itself to the road like the tyres on this one.

Maybe if it had, all their lives would have been very different now.

She pressed herself more fully into Marshall's hard back and practically punched her fingertips through his leather jacket from clenching it so hard.

'Is this top speed?' she yelled forward to him.

His hair whipped around above her face as he shook his head and shouted back. 'We're only doing seventy kilometres.'

'Don't go any faster,' she called.

She hated the vulnerable note in her voice, but she hated more the thought of hitting the dirt at this kind of speed. In

Travis's case it had been trees but she felt fairly certain that you didn't need trees to be pretty badly injured on a bike.

Marshall turned his face half back to her and smiled beneath his protective sunglasses, nodding once. She'd just have to trust those teeth.

The roads of the national park were long and straight and the bike sat atop them beautifully so, after a few tense minutes, Eve let her death grip on his jacket ease slightly and crept them back to rest on Marshall's hips instead. Still firm, but the blood was able to leach back into her knuckles.

For a death machine he handled it pretty well.

Ahead, the road bent around a monolithic chunk of rock and he eased off the gas to pass it carefully. The bike's lean felt extreme to her and her grasp on his leather jacket completely insufficient, so her fingers found their way under it and hooked onto the eyelets of his jeans.

A few paltry sweatshop stitches were the only thing between her and certain doom.

While the engine was eased, Marshall took the opportunity to call back to her, half turning, 'Doing okay?'

Eyes front, mister!

'Stop staring down,' he shouted. 'Look around you.'

She let her eyes flutter upwards as he turned his attention back to the oncoming road. The entire park was bathed in the golden glow of afternoon light, the many different textures changing the way the light reflected and creating the golden equivalent of the ocean. So many different shades.

And—bonus—the speed didn't seem anywhere near as scary as staring down at the asphalt.

It was almost like being in the Bedford. Sans life-saving steel exoskeleton.

She didn't want to look like a complete wuss, and so Eve did her best to ease herself back from where her body had practically fused with his. The problem with that was as soon as he changed up gears, she brushed, breasts first, against his back. And then again.

And again, as he shifted up into fourth.

Okay, now he was just messing with her. She was having a difficult enough reaction to all that leather without adding to the crisis by torturing her own flesh. Leaning into him might be more intimate, but it felt far less gratuitous and so she snuggled forward again, widening her legs to fit more snugly around his. Probably not how a passenger was supposed to ride—the fact her bottom had left the pillion seat in favour of sharing his leathery saddle proved that—but that was how it was going to be for her first ever big boy's motorcycle experience.

And if he didn't like it he could pull over.

Minutes whizzed by and she grew captivated by the long stretches of tufted grass to her left, the parched, salt-crusted trees and coastal heath to her right and the limestone outcrops that practically glowed in the late-afternoon light. So much so that, when Marshall finally pulled them to a halt at a lookout point, she realised she'd forgotten all about the speed. Her pulse was up, her exposed skin was flushed pink and her breath was pleasantly choppy.

But she hadn't died.

And she wasn't ready for it to be over.

'I can see why she—why *you* like this,' she puffed, lifting the visor on her helmet and leaning around him. 'It's a great way to see the country.'

'Are you comfortable?'

His innocuous words immediately reminded her of how close she was pressed against him—wrapped around him, really—and she immediately went to correct that.

'Stay put,' he cautioned. 'We're about to head back.'

She leaned with him as he turned the bike in a big arc on an old salt flat and then bumped back onto the tarmac. As if she'd been doing this forever. And, as he roared back up to speed, she realised how very much in the *now* she'd been. Just her, Marshall, the road, the wind and the national park.

No past. No future. No accidents. No inquests. No Travis.

And how nice that moment of psychological respite was.

The light was totally different heading back. Less golden. More orange. And fading fast. He accessed a fifth gear that he'd spared her on the first leg and even still, when he pulled back in near the bus, the sun was almost gone. She straightened cold-stiffened limbs and pulled off his helmet.

'How was that?' he asked, way more interest in his eyes than a courtesy question. He kicked the stand into position and leaned the bike into the solid embrace of the earth.

'Amazing.'

The word formed a tiny breath cloud in the cool evening air and it was only then she realised how cold she was. The sun's warmth sure departed fast in this part of the country.

He followed her back towards the bus. 'You took a bit to loosen up.'

'Considering how terrified I was, I don't think I did too badly.'

'Not badly at all. I felt the moment when the fear left your body.'

The thought that she'd been pressed closely enough to him to be telegraphing any kind of emotion caused a rush of heat that she was very glad it was too dim for him to see. But he stepped ahead of her and opened the back of the Bedford and caught the last vestiges of her flush.

'How are you feeling now about motorcycles?'

His body blocked the step up into the bus and so she had no choice but to brush past him as she pulled herself up.

'It's still a death trap,' she said, looking back down at him. 'But not entirely without redeeming qualities.'

Not unlike its owner, really.

CHAPTER FOUR

'I WAS THINKING of steak and salad for dinner,' Eve said, returning from her little bedroom newly clad in a sweater to take the edge off the cool coastal night.

Lord, how domestic. And utterly foreign.

'You don't need to cook for me, Eve. I ate up big at lunchtime in anticipation.'

'I was there, remember? And while it certainly was big you probably burned it all off with that epic swim earlier.'

And Lord knew, between the lusting and the fearing for her life, she'd just burnt all hers off, too.

Preparing food felt natural; she'd been doing it for Travis for so many years. Moreover, it gave her something constructive and normal to do for thirty minutes, but Marshall wasn't so lucky. He hovered, hopelessly. After the comparative intimacy of the bike ride, it seemed ludicrous to be uncomfortable about sharing a simple meal. But he was, a little.

And so was she. A lot.

'Here.' She slid him a bottle opener across the raw timber counter of the Bedford's compact little kitchen. 'Make yourself useful.'

She nodded to a small cabinet above the built-in television and, when he opened it, his eyebrows lifted at the contents. 'I thought you didn't drink?'

That rattled a chuckle from her tight chest.

'Not in bars—' with men she didn't know, and given her

familial history '—but I like to sample the local wines as I move around.'

She brought her solitary wineglass out from under the bench, then added a coffee mug next to it. The best she could do.

'You take the glass,' she offered.

He took both, in fact, poured two generous servings of red and slid the wineglass back her way. 'I guess you don't entertain much?'

'Not really out here for the social life,' she said. But then she relented. 'I did have a second glass once but I have no idea where it's gone. So it's the coffee mug or it's my toothbrush glass.'

And didn't that sound pathetic.

'You're going to need another storage cupboard,' he murmured, bringing the mug back from his lips and licking the final drops off, much to her sudden fascination. 'We're headed for serious wine country.'

'Maybe I just need to drink faster.'

He chuckled and saluted her with the mug. 'Amen to that.'

What was it about a communal glass of vino that instantly broke down the awkwardness barrier? He'd only had one sip and she'd had none, yet, so it wasn't the effects of the alcohol. Just something about popping a cork and swilling a good red around in your glass—or coffee mug—the great equaliser.

Maybe that was how her mother had begun. Social and pleasant. Until one day she woke up and it wasn't social any more. Or pleasant.

'So tell me,' Eve started, continuing with her food prep, 'did you have much competition for half a year in the bush checking on weather stations?'

He smiled and leaned across to relieve her of the chopping knife and vegetables from the fridge. 'I did not.'

It was too easy to respond to that gentle smile. To let her curiosity have wings. To tease. 'Can't imagine why not. Why did you accept it?'

'Travel the country, fully paid. What's not to love?'

'Being away from your friends and family?'

Being away from your girlfriend. She concentrated hard to keep her eyes from dropping to the bottom of the biceps dagger that peeked out from under his sleeve.

'Not all families benefit from being in each other's faces,' he said, a little tightly.

She stopped and regarded him. 'Speaking from experience?'

Grey eyes flicked to hers.

'Maybe. Don't tell me,' he nudged. 'You have the perfect parents.'

Oh…so far from the truth it was almost laughable. The steaks chuckled for her as she flipped them. 'Parent singular. Dad.'

He regarded her closely. 'You lost your mum?'

'Final year of school.'

'I'm sorry. New subject?'

'No. It's a long time ago now. It's okay.'

'Want to talk about it?'

Sometimes, desperately. Sometimes when she sat all alone in this little bus that felt so big she just wished she had someone sitting there with her that she could spill it all to. Someone to help her make sense of everything that had happened. Because she still barely understood it.

'Not much to talk about. She was in an accident. Travis was lucky to survive it.'

His fathomless gaze grew deeper. Full of sympathy. 'Car crash?'

Here it came…

'Motorbike, actually.'

His eyes flared and he spun more fully towards her. 'Why didn't you say, Eve?'

'I'm saying now.'

'Before I press-ganged you into taking a ride with me,' he gritted, leaning over the counter.

'I could have said no. At any time. I'm not made of jelly.'

Except when Marshall smiled at her a certain way. Then anyone would be forgiven for thinking so.

'I never would have—'

'It wasn't the bike's fault. It's good for me to remember that.'

He took a long, slow breath and Eve distracted herself poking the steaks.

'A 250cc, you said. Not your usual family wagon.'

'Oh, we had one of those, too. But she got her motorcycle licence not long after having Travis.' Like some kind of statement. 'She rode it whenever she didn't have us with her.'

Which was often in those last five years.

'I think it was her way of fighting suburbia,' she murmured.

Or reality, maybe.

'But she had your brother with her that day?' Then, 'Are you okay to talk about this?'

Surprisingly, she was. Maybe because Marshall was a fellow motorbike fanatic. It somehow felt okay for him to know.

'Yeah—' she sighed '—she did. Trav loved her bike. He couldn't wait to get his bike permit. I think she was going to give him the Kawasaki. He'd started to learn.'

'How old was he when it happened?'

'Fourteen.'

'Five years between you. That's a biggish gap.'

'Thank God for it. Not sure I could have handled any of it if I'd been younger.'

It was hard enough as it was.

It was only when Marshall's voice murmured, soft and low, over her shoulder and he reached past her to turn off the gas to the steaks that she realised how long she'd been standing there mute. Her skin tingled at his closeness.

'New subject?'

'No. I'm happy to talk about my family. I just forget sometimes…'

'Forget what?'

Sorrow washed through her. 'That my family's different now. That it's just me and Dad.'

'You say that like…'

Her eyes lifted. 'That's the reality. If Trav is missing by force, then he's not coming back. And if he's missing by choice…'

Then he's not coming back.

Either way, her already truncated family had shrunk by one more.

'You really believe he could be out here somewhere, just… lying low?'

'I have to believe that. That he's hurting. Confused. Off his meds. Maybe he doesn't think he'd be welcome back after leaving like he did. I want him to know we want him back no matter what.'

Marshall's head bobbed slowly. 'No case to answer? For the distress he's caused?'

Her hand fell still on the spatula. For the longest time, the only sound came from the low-burn frying pan. But, eventually, her thoughts collected into something coherent.

'I ask myself is there anything he could do that would make me not want to have him back with us and the answer is no. So giving him grief for what he did, or why he did it, or the manner in which he did it… It has no purpose. I just want him to walk back in that door and scuff the wall with his school bag and start demanding food. The *what*, *why* and *how* is just not relevant.'

Intelligent eyes glanced from her still fingers to her face. 'It's relevant to you.'

'But it's not important. In the scheme of things.'

Besides, she already had a fairly good idea of the *why*. Travis's escalating anxiety and depression seemed blazingly obvious in hindsight, even if she hadn't seen it at the time. Because she hadn't been paying attention. She'd been far too busy shrugging off her substitute mother apron.

Thinking about herself.

She poked at the steak again and delicious juices ran from it and added to the noise in the pan. She lifted her wineglass with her free hand and emptied a bit into the pan. Then she took a generous swig and changed the subject.

'So, who is Christine?'

No-man's-land the last time they spoke, but they weren't spending the night under the same roof then. They barely knew each other then.

We barely know each other now! a tiny voice reminded her.

But they did. Maybe not a heap of details, but they knew each other's names and interests and purpose. She'd seen him half naked striding out of the surf, and she'd pressed up against him a grand total of two times now and had a different kind of glimpse at the kind of man he was under all the leather and facial hair. He struck her as…safe.

And sometimes safe was enough.

But right now *safe* didn't look entirely happy at her words. Though he still answered.

'Was,' he clarified. 'Christine was my girlfriend.'

Clang. The pan hit the stovetop at his use of the past tense. There was the answer to a question she didn't know she'd been dying to ask. Unexpected butterflies took flight deep in her gut and she busied herself with a second go at moving the frying pan off the heat.

'Recent?'

His strong lips pursed briefly as he considered answering. Or not answering. 'Long time ago.'

Yeah, the ink didn't look new, come to think of it. Unlike the one she'd seen under his biceps.

Which meant he could still be someone else's hairy biker type. That she was having a quiet steak with. Under a gem-filled sky. Miles from anywhere. After a blood-thrilling and skin-tingling motorbike ride…

She shook the thoughts free. 'Childhood sweetheart?'

Tension pumped off him. 'Something like that.'

And suddenly she disliked Christine intensely. 'I'm sorry.'

He shrugged. 'Not your doing.'

She studied the tight lines at the corner of his mouth. The

mouth she'd not been able to stop looking at since he'd shaved and revealed it. Tonight was no different. 'So…there's no Christine now? I mean someone like Christine?'

His eyes found hers. 'You asking if I'm single?'

'Just making conversation. I figured not, since you were on a pilgrimage around the country.'

'It's my job, Eve. Not everyone out here is on some kind of odyssey.'

That stung as much as the sea salt she'd accidentally rubbed in her eye earlier. Because of the judgment those words contained. And the truth. And because they came from him.

But he looked contrite the moment they fell off his lips.

'You don't like talking about her, I take it?' she murmured.

He shook his head but it was no denial.

'Fair enough.' Then she nodded at his arm. 'You might want to get that altered though.'

The tension left his face and a couple of tiny smile lines peeked out the corners of his eyes. 'I couldn't have picked someone with a shorter name, huh? Like Ann. Or Lucy.'

Yep. Christine sure was a long word to tattoo over.

'It's pretty florid, too. A dagger?'

The smile turned into a laugh. 'We were seventeen and in love. And I fancied myself for a bit of a tough guy. What can I say?'

Eve threw some dressing on the salad and gave it a quick toss.

'She got a matching one I hope?'

'Hers just said *Amore*. Multi-purpose.'

'*Pfff*. Non-committal. That should have been your first warning.'

She added a steak to each of their plates.

'With good reason, it turns out.'

'Christine sucked?'

That earned her a chuckle. She loved the rich, warm sound because it came from so deep in his chest. 'No, she didn't. Or I wouldn't have fallen for her.'

'That's very charitable.'

He waved his coffee mug. 'I'm a generous guy.'

'So…I'm confused,' she started. 'You don't want to talk about her, but you don't hold it against her?'

'It's not really about Christine,' he hedged.

'What isn't?' And then, when he didn't respond, 'The awkward silence?'

'How many people end up with their first love, really?'

She wouldn't know. She hadn't had time for love while she was busy raising her family. Or since. More's the pity.

'So where did she end up?'

The look he gave her was enigmatic. But also appraising. And kind of stirring. 'Not important.'

'You're very complicated, Marshall Sullivan.'

His smile crept back. 'Thank you.'

Eve leaned across the counter and lifted the hem of his sleeve with two fingers to have a good look at the design. Her fingertips brushed the smooth strength of his warm biceps and tingled where they travelled.

She cleared her throat. 'Maybe you could change it to *pristine*, like the ocean? That way, you only have to rework the first two letters.'

Three creases formed across his brow as he looked down. 'That could actually work…'

'Or *Sistine*, like the chapel.'

'Or *intestine*, like the pain I get from smelling that steak and not eating it.'

They loaded their plates up with fresh salad and both tucked in.

'This is really good.'

'That surprises you?'

'I didn't pick you as a cook.'

She shrugged. 'I had a rapid apprenticeship after Mum died.'

She munched her way through half her plate before speaking again.

'Can I ask you something personal?'

'Didn't you already do that?'

'About travelling.'

His head tilted. 'Go ahead.'

'Do you…' Lord, how to start this question? 'You travel alone. Do you ever feel like you've forgotten how to be with somebody else? How to behave?'

'What do you mean?'

'I just…I used to be so social. Busy schedule, urban life-style, dinners out most evenings. Meeting new people and chatting to them.' Up until the accident, anyway. 'I feel like I've lost some of my social skills.'

'Honestly?'

She nodded.

'Yeah, you're missing a few of the niceties. But once you get past that, you're all right. We're conversing happily now, aren't we?'

Give or take a few tense undercurrents.

'Maybe you just got good at small talk,' he went on. 'And small talk doesn't take you far in places like this. Situations like this. It's no good at all in silence. It just screams. But we're doing okay, on the whole.'

She rushed to correct him. 'I didn't mean you, specifi-cally—'

'Yeah, you did.'

'What makes you say that?'

'Eve, this feels awkward because it *is* awkward. We don't know each other and yet I was forced into your world unnatu-rally. And now a virtual stranger is sitting ten feet from your bed, drinking your wine and getting personal. Of course it's uncomfortable.'

'I'm not…it's not uncomfortable, exactly. I just feel really rusty. And you don't deserve that. You've been very nice.'

The word *nice* hit him visibly. He actually winced.

'When was the last time you had someone in your bus?' he deviated.

Eve racked her brain… Months. Lots of months. 'Long

enough for that second wineglass to end up right at the back of some cupboard.'

'There you go, then. You're out of shape, socially, that's all.' She stared at him.

'Let's make a pledge. I promise to be my clunky self when you're around if you'll do the same.' He drew a big circle around the two of them and some tiny part of her quite liked being in that circle with him. 'This is a clunk-approved zone.'

'Clunk-approved?'

'Weird moments acknowledged, accepted and forgiven.'

Why was it so easy to smile, with him? 'You're giving me permission to be socially clumsy?'

'I'm saying I'll understand.'

It was so much easier to breathe all of a sudden. 'All right. Sounds good.'

And on that warm and toasty kindred-spirit moment…

'Are you done?' she checked.

He scooped the last of his steak into his mouth and nodded.

'Hop up, I'd like to show you something.'

As soon as he stood up and back, she pinched the tall stool out from under him and clambered onto it. That allowed her to pop the latch on what looked to anyone else like a sunroof. It folded back onto the bus with a thump. She boosted herself up and into the void, wriggling back until her bottom was thoroughly seated and her legs dangled down into the bus.

'Pass the wine up,' she asked.

He did, but not before adding a generous splash to both their vessels. Then he hoisted himself up opposite her—disgustingly effortlessly—and followed her gaze, left, up out into the endless, dark sky over the Southern Ocean.

'Nice view.'

Essentially the same view as when they'd stood up on the Bedford's back step, just a little higher, but somehow it was made all the more spectacular by the location, the wine and the darkness.

And the company.

'I like to do this when the weather's fine.' Though usually alone.

'I can see why.'

The sky was blanketed with light from a gazillion other solar systems. The full you'll-never-see-it-in-the-city cliché. Eve tipped her head back, stared up and sighed.

'Sometimes I feel like I might as well be looking for Trav out there.' She tossed her chin to the trillions of unseen worlds orbiting those million stars. 'It feels just as unachievable.'

He brought his eyes back down from the heavens. Back to hers.

'It was such a simple plan when I set off. Visit every town in Australia and put posters up. Check for myself. But all it's done is reinforce for me how vast this country is and how many ways there are for someone to disappear. Living or dead.'

'It's a good plan, Eve. Don't doubt yourself.'

She shrugged.

'Did you do it because you truly thought you'd find him? Or did you do it because you had to do something?'

Tears suddenly sprang up and she fought them. It took a moment to get the choke out of her words.

'He's so young. Still a kid, even if the law says otherwise. I was going crazy at home. Waiting. Hoping each day would be the day that the police freed up enough time to look into Trav's case a bit. Made some progress. My heart leaping every time the phone rang in case it was news.'

Fighting endlessly with her father, who wanted her to give up. To accept the truth.

His truth.

'So here you are,' he summarised, simply. 'Doing something constructive. Does it feel better?'

'Yeah. When it's not feeling totally futile.'

It was too dark for the colour of his eyes to penetrate, but his focus fairly blazed out from the shadows under his sockets. 'It's only futile when it stops achieving anything. Right now it's keeping you sane.'

How did this total stranger know her better than anyone else—better than she knew herself?

Maybe because it took one to know one.

She saluted him with her wine. 'Well, aren't we a pack of dysfunctional sad sacks.'

'I'm not sad,' Marshall said, pretty proudly.

What was his story? Curiosity burnt, bright and blazing. The intense desire to *know* him.

'Nothing to say about being dysfunctional?'

'Nope. Totally guilty on that charge.'

The wind had changed direction the moment the sun set, and its heat no longer affected the vast pockets of air blanketing the southern hemisphere. They were tickled by its kiss but no longer buffeted, and it brought with it a deep and comfortable silence.

'So,' Marshall started, 'if I want to use the bus's bathroom during the night I'm basically in your bedroom, right? How's that going to work?'

She just about gave herself whiplash glancing up at him.

'Uh…'

The bus's little en suite bathroom was on the other side of the door that separated it from the rest of the bus. And from Marshall.

Groan. Just another practicality she hadn't thought through thoroughly.

That's because you just about fell over yourself to travel with him for a bit.

'Or I can use the campsite toilet,' he suggested.

Yes! Thank the Lord for public services.

'It's not too bad, actually.' If you didn't mind rocks on your bare feet at three in the morning and spiders in the dark. 'What time do we need to be up?'

As soon as the words tumbled over her lips she regretted

them. Why was she ending the moment of connection so soon after it had begun?

'The boat's coming at eight.'

And dawn was at six. That was two hours of daylight for the two of them to enjoy sharing the clunk-approved zone together. 'Okay. I'll be ready.'

He passed her his mug, then swung himself down and in and took it and hers and placed them together on the bench below. Eve wiggled to the edge of the hatch and readied her arms to take her weight.

'You all right?'

'Yeah, I do it all the time.' Though she just half tumbled, half swung, usually. Gravity fed. Completely inelegant. 'I don't normally have an audience for this bit.'

His deep voice rumbled, 'Here, let me help...'

Suddenly two strong hands were around her waist, pressed sure and hot against her midriff, and she had no choice but to go with them through the roof and back inside the bus. Marshall eased her down in a far less dramatic manner than she was used to, but not without bunching her sweater up under her breasts and leaving her stomach totally exposed as she slid the length of his body. Fortunately, there were no bare hands on bare skin moments, but it was uncomfortable enough to feel the press of his cold jeans stud against her suddenly scorched tummy.

'Thanks,' she breathed.

He released her and stood back, his lashes lowered. 'No problem.'

Instantly, she wondered what the Japanese symbol for 'awkward' was and whether she'd find that tattooed anywhere on his body.

And instantly she was thinking about hidden parts of his body.

She shook the thought free. 'Well...I guess I'll see you in the morning. I'll try and be quiet if you're not up.'

'I'll be up,' he pledged.

Because he was an early riser or because he wasn't about to let her see him all tousled and vulnerable?

Or because all the touching and sliding was going to keep him awake all night, too.

CHAPTER FIVE

IT HAD BEEN a long time since Marshall had woken to the sounds of someone tiptoeing around a kitchen. In this particular case, it was extra soft because the kitchen was only two metres from his makeshift bed.

He'd heard Eve wake up, start moving around beyond that door that separated them all night, but then he'd fallen back into a light morning doze to the entirely feminine soundtrack. You had to live with someone to enjoy those moments. And you had to love them to live with them. And trust them to love them.

Unfortunately, trust and he were uneasy companions.

He'd been in one relationship post-Christine—a nice girl with lots of dreams—and that hadn't ended well. Him, of course. Just another reminder why going solo was easier on everyone concerned. Family included.

Thoughts of his brother robbed him of any further shut-eye. He pulled himself upright and forked fingers through his bed hair.

'Morning,' Eve murmured behind him. 'I hope I didn't wake you?'

'No. I was half awake, anyway. What time is it?'

'Just after six.'

Wow. Went to show what fresh air, hours of swimming and a good drop of red could do for a man's insomnia. He sure couldn't attribute it to the comfort of his bed. Every muscle creaked as he sat up, including the ones in his voice box.

'Not comfortable?'

'Better than my swag on the hard outback dirt.' Even though it really wasn't. There was something strangely comfortable about bedding down on the earth. It was very…honest. 'I'll be back in a tick.'

The morning sun was gentle but massively bright and he stumbled most of the way towards the campsite toilet. Even with her not in her room, the thought of wedging all of himself into that compact little en suite bathroom… It was just too personal.

And he didn't do personal.

'I have eggs or I have sausages,' she announced when he walked back in a little later. 'They won't keep much longer so I'm cooking them all up.'

'Nah. I'll be all right.'

'You have to eat something; we're going to be on the water all day.'

'That's exactly why I don't want something.'

She stopped and stared. 'Do you get seasick?'

'Doesn't really fit with the he-man image you have of me, does it?' He slid back onto his stool from the night before and she passed him a coffee. 'Not horribly. But bad enough.'

'How about some toast and jam, then?'

She was determined to play host. 'Yeah, that I could do.'

That wouldn't be too disgusting coming back up in front of an audience.

She added two pieces of frozen bread to the toaster and kept on with her fry-up. If nothing else, the seagulls would love the sausages.

'Is that okay?' she said when she finally slid the buttered toast towards him.

'Just trying to think when was the last time I had toast and jam.' Toast had been about all his mother stretched to when he was a kid. But there was seldom jam.

'Not a breakfast person?'

'In the city I'd grab something from a fast food place near work.'

'I'm sure your blood vessels were grateful.'

Yeah... Not.

'Mostly it was just coffee.' The liquid breakfast of champions.

'What about out here?'

'Depends. Some motels throw a cooked breakfast in with the room. That's not always a nice surprise.'

'Well, this is a full service b & b, so eat up.'

Eating with a woman at six o'clock in the morning should have felt wrong but it didn't. In fact, clunk-approved zone moments aside, he felt pretty relaxed around Eve most of the time. Maybe because she was uptight enough for the both of them.

'Marshall?'

'Sorry. What did you say?'

'I wondered how the boat would know where to come and get us?'

'They'll just putter along the coast until they see us waving.'

'You're kidding.'

'Well, me waving, really. They're not expecting two.'

'That's very casual,' she said. 'What if they don't come?'

'Then I'll call them and they'll come tomorrow.'

Dark eyebrows shot up. 'You're assuming I'd be happy to stay an extra night.'

'If not, we could just head back to Esperance and pick up the boat there,' he admitted. 'That's where it's moored.'

Her jaw gaped. 'Are you serious? Then why are we here?'

'Come on, Eve. Tell me you didn't enjoy the past twenty-four hours. Taking a break. Enjoying the scenery.'

Her pretty eyes narrowed. 'I feel like I've been conned.'

'You have—' he grinned around the crunch of toast smeared with strawberry jam '—by the best.'

She didn't want to laugh—her face struggled with it—but there was no mistaking the twisted smile she tried to hide by turning and plating up her eggs. Twisted and kind of gorgeous. But all she said was...

'So, talk to me about the island.'

The boat came. The *Vista II*'s two-man crew easily spotted the two of them standing on the rocks at the most obvious point of the whole beach. One of them manoeuvred a small inflatable dinghy down onto the stillest part of the early-morning beach to collect them.

The captain reached down for Eve's hands and pulled her up onto the fishing vessel and Marshall gave her a boost from below. Quite a personal boost—both of his hands starting on her waist but sliding onto her bum to do the actual shoving. Then he scrambled up without assistance and so did the old guy who had collected them in the dinghy that he hastily re-tethered to the boat.

'Thanks for that,' she murmured sideways to Marshall before smiling broadly at the captain and thanking him for real.

'Would you have preferred fish-scaly sea-dog hands on your butt?' Marshall murmured back.

Yeah. Maybe. Because she wouldn't have had to endure his heat still soaking into her. She already had enough of a fascination with his hands...

The next ten minutes were all business. Life vests secured, safety lecture given, seating allocated. Hers was an old square cray pot. Marshall perched on a box of safety gear.

'How long is the trip to Middle Island?' she asked the captain as soon as they were underway.

'Twenty minutes. We have to go around the long way to avoid the wrecks.'

'There are shipwrecks out here?' But as she turned and looked back along the one-hundred-strong shadowy islands of the Recherche Archipelago stretching out to the west, the question suddenly felt really foolish.

Of course there were. It was like a visible minefield of islands.

'Two right off Middle Island.'

As long as they didn't add the *Vista II* to that list, she'd be happy. 'So almost no one comes out here?'

'Not onto the islands, but there's plenty of fishing and small boating traffic.'

'And no one's living on Middle Island?'

Marshall's eyes glanced her way.

'Not since the eighteen-thirties, when Black Jack Anderson based himself and his pirating outfit there,' the captain volunteered.

Huh. So it *could* be lived on. Technically.

Eve turned her gaze towards the distant shadow that was becoming more and more defined as the boat ate up the miles and the captain chatted on about the island's resident pirate. Maybe Marshall's theory wasn't so far-fetched. Maybe Trav could be there. Or have been there in the past. Or—

And as she had the thought, she realised.

Travis.

She'd been awake two whole hours and not given her brother the slightest thought. Normally he was on her mind when her eyes fluttered open each day and the last thing she thought about at night. It kept her focused and on mission. It kept him alive in her heart.

But last night all she'd been able to think about was the man settling in just metres and a bit of flimsy timber away from her. How complicated he was. How easy he was to be around. How good he smelled.

She'd been pulled off mission by the first handsome, broad-shouldered distraction to come along. Nice. As if she wasn't already excelling at the Bad Sister of the Year award.

Well… No more.

Time to get back in the game.

'Eve?' Marshall's voice drifted to her over the sound of the outboard. 'Are you okay?'

She kept her eyes carefully averted, as though she was focusing on the approaching island, and lied.

'Just thinking about what it would be like to live there...'

They travelled in silence, but Eve could just about feel the moments when Marshall would let his eyes rest on her briefly. Assessing. Wondering. The captain chatted on with his sem-itour talk. About the islands. About the wildlife. About the wallabies and frogs and some special lizard that all lived in harmony on the predator-free island. About the southern rock lobster and abalone that he and his mate fished out of these perilous waters. About how many sharks there were lurking in the depths around them.

The promise of sharks made her pay extra attention as she slid back down the side of the *Vista II* into the inflatable and, before long, her feet were back on dry land. Dry, deserted land.

One glance around them at the remote, untouched, unin-habitable terrain told her Trav wasn't hiding out here.

As if there'd really been a chance.

'Watch where you step. The barking gecko is protected on this island.'

'Of course it is,' she muttered.

Marshall just glanced at her sideways. The fishermen left and promised to return for them in a couple of hours. A ner-vous anxiety filled her belly. If they didn't return, what would she do? How would she survive here with just a day's supply of water and snacks and no shelter? Just because Black Jack Whatsit got by for a decade didn't mean she'd last more than a day.

'So,' Marshall said after helping to push the inflatable back offshore, 'you want to explore on your own or come with me?'

Explore on my own—that was the right answer. But, at the same time, she didn't know anything about this strange little island and she was just as likely to break her ankle on the far-thest corner from Marshall and his little first-aid kit.

'Is it safe?' she asked, screening her eyes with her hands and scanning the horizon.

'If you don't count the death adders, yeah.'

She snapped her focus straight back to him. 'Are you kidding?'

'Nope. But if you're watching out for the geckos you'll almost certainly see the snakes before you tread on them.'

Almost certainly.

'I'm coming with you.'

'Good choice. Feel like a climb?' She turned and followed his gaze up to the highest point on the island. 'Flinders Peak is where the weather station would go.'

He assured her it was only one hundred and eighty-five metres above sea level but it felt like Everest when you were also watching every footfall for certain death—yours or a protected gecko's.

Marshall pointed out the highlights to the west, chatted about the nearest islands and their original names. Then he halted his climb and just looked at her.

'What?' she asked, puffing.

'I'm waiting for you to turn around.'

They'd ascended the easiest face of the peak but it had obscured most of the rest of the island from their view. She turned around now.

'Oh, my gosh!'

Pink. A crazy, wrong, enormous bubblegum-pink lake lay out on the eastern corner of the island. Somehow everyone had failed to mention a bright pink lake! 'What is it?'

'Lake Hillier.'

'It's so beautiful.' But so unnatural. It just went to show how little she knew about the natural world. 'Why is it pink?'

'Bacteria? The type of salt? Maybe something new to science. Does it matter?'

'I guess not.' It was just curiously beautiful. 'Can we go there?'

'We just got up here.'

'I know, but now I want to go there.'

So much! A bit like riding on his bike, little moments of

pleasure managed to cut through her miserable thoughts about Travis.

He smiled, but it was twisted with curiosity. And something else.

'What?' she queried.

'This is the first time I've seen you get really passionate about anything since I met you.'

'Some things are just worth getting your pulse up about.' And, speaking of which...

He stepped a little closer and her heartbeat responded immediately.

'Lakes and lizards do it for you?'

'*Pink* lakes and geckos that *bark*,' she stressed for the slow of comprehension. Right on cue, a crack of vocalisation issued from a tuft of scrubby foliage to their left. She laughed in delight. But then she caught his expression.

'Seriously, Marshall... *What?*' His focus had grown way too intense. And way too pointed. She struggled against the desire to match it.

'Passion suits you. You should go hiking more often.'

Her chest had grown so tight with the climb, his words worsened her breathlessness. She pushed off again for the final peak. And for the pure distraction of physical distress.

'I get how the birds get here,' she puffed, changing the subject, 'and the crustaceans. But how did the mammals arrive here? And the lizards?'

For a moment, she thought he wasn't going to let it go but he did, gracefully.

'They didn't arrive, they endured. Back from when the whole archipelago were peaks connected to the mainland. There used to be a lot more until explorers came along and virtually wiped them out.'

Eve looked up at a circling sea eagle. 'You can't tell me that the geckos didn't get picked off by hungry birds, before.'

'Yeah, but in balance. They live in *refugia* here, isolation from the world and its threats. Until the first cat overboard, anyway.'

Isolation from the world and its threats. She kind of liked the sound of that. Maybe that was what Trav was chasing when he walked out into the darkness a year ago. Emotional *refugia*.

She stumbled on a rock as she realised. Not a year ago…a year ago *tomorrow*. Not only had she failed to think about Travis for entire hours this morning but she'd almost forgotten tomorrow's depressing anniversary.

Her joy at their spectacular view drained away as surely as the water far below them dragged back across the shell-speckled beach where they'd come ashore.

Marshall extended his warm hand and took her suddenly cold one for the final haul up the granite top of Flinders Peak, and the entire south coast of Western Australia—complete with all hundred-plus islands—stretched out before them. The same sense of despair she'd felt when staring up at the stars the night before washed over Eve.

Australia was so incredibly vast and so incredibly empty.

So much freaking country to look in.

She stood, immobile, as he did what they'd come to do. Photographing. Measuring. Recording compass settings and GPS results. Taking copious notes and even some soil and vegetation samples. He threw a concerned glance at her a couple of times, until he finally closed up his pack again.

'Eve…'

'Are you done?'

'Come on, Eve—'

'I'm going to head down to the lake.' But there was no interest in her step, and no breathlessness in her words. Even she could hear the death in her voice.

'Stop.'

She did, and she turned.

'What just happened? What did I do?'

Truth sat like a stone in her gut. 'It wasn't you, Marshall. It was me.'

'What did *you* do?'

More what she didn't do.

'Eve?'

'I shouldn't be here.'

'We have a permit.'

'No, I mean I shouldn't be wasting time like this.'

'You're angry because you let yourself off the hook for a few hours?'

'I'm angry because I only have one thing to do out here. Prioritising Travis. And I didn't do that today.'

Or yesterday, if she was honest. She might have pinned up a bunch of posters, but her memories of yesterday were dominated by Marshall.

'Your life can't only be about your brother, Eve. It's not healthy.'

Health. A bit late now to be paying attention to anyone's health. Her own. Her brother's. Maybe if she'd been more alert a couple of years back...

She took a deep breath. 'Are you done up here?'

A dozen expressions ranged across his face before he answered. But, when he did, his face was carefully neutral. 'We have a couple of hours before the boat gets back. Might as well have a look around with me.'

Fine. He could make her stay...

But he couldn't make her enjoy it.

It took the best part of the remaining ninety minutes on the island but Marshall managed to work the worst of the stiffness from Eve's shoulders. He did it with easy, undemanding conversation and by tapping her natural curiosity, pointing out endless points of interest and intriguing her with imaginary tales of the pirate Anderson and his hidden treasure that had never been recovered.

'Maybe his crew took it when they killed him.' She shrugged, still half-numb.

Cynical, but after the sad silence of the first half-hour he'd take it. 'Seems a reasonable enough motive to kill someone. You know, if you were a bloodthirsty pirate.'

'Or maybe there never was any treasure,' she posed. 'Maybe Anderson only managed to steal and trade enough to keep him and his crew alive, not to accrue a fortune. Maybe they weren't very good pirates!'

'You've seen the island now. Where would you bury it if it did exist?'

She glanced around. 'I wouldn't. It's too open here. Hard to dig up without being seen by the crew.' Her eyes tracked outward and he followed them to the guano-blanketed, rocky outcrop just beyond the shores of Middle Island. 'Maybe over there? Some random little cave or hollow?'

'Want to go look?'

She turned wide eyes on him. 'I'm not about to swim fully clothed across a shark-infested channel to an outcrop covered in bird poo filled with God knows what bacteria to hunt for non-existent treasure.'

'You have no soul, Evelyn Read,' he scoffed.

'I do have one and I'd prefer to keep it firmly tethered to my body, thanks very much.'

He chuckled. 'Fair enough. Come on, let's see if the lake looks as impressive up close.'

It didn't. Of course it didn't. Wasn't there something about rose-coloured glasses? But it wasn't a total disappointment. Still officially pink, even once Eve filled her empty water bottle with it.

'You're not planning on drinking that?' he warned.

'Nope.' She emptied it all back into the lake and tucked the empty bottle into her backpack for later recycling. 'Just trying to catch it out being trickily clear.'

They strolled around the lake the long way, then headed back down to the only decent beach on the island. A tiny but sandy cove formed between two outcrops of rocky reef. The place the boat had left them. Marshall immediately tugged his shoes and socks off and tied them to his own pack, which he stashed on a nearby rock, then made his way out a half-dozen metres from where Eve stood discovering that the sand was actually comprised of teeny-tiny white shells.

'Water's fine…' he hinted. 'Not deep enough for predators.'

She crossed her arms grumpily from the shore. 'What about a stingray?'

He splashed a little forward in the waves that washed in from the current surging between the islands. 'Surfing stingrays?'

'Where lakes are pink and lizards bark? Why not?'

'Come on, Eve. Kick your shoes off.'

She glared at him, but eventually she sank onto one hip and toed her opposite runner and sock off, then she did the same on the other foot. Though she took her sweet time putting both carefully in her pack and placing the lot next to his backpack on the hot sand.

'Welcome to heaven,' he murmured as she joined him in the shallows. Her groan echoed his as her hot and parched feet drank up the cold water, too. They stood there like that, together, for minutes. Their hearts slowing to synchronise with the waves washing up and into their little minibay.

Just…being.

'Okay,' Eve breathed, her face turned to the sky. 'This was a good idea.'

He waded a little further from her. 'My ideas are always good.'

She didn't even bother looking at him. 'Is that right?'

'Sure is.'

He reached down and brushed his fingers through the crystal-clear water then flicked two of them in her general direction.

She stiffened—in body and in lip—as the droplets hit her. She turned her head back his way and let her eyes creak open. 'Thanks for that.'

'You had to know that was going to happen.'

'I should have. You with a mental age of twelve and all.'

He grinned. 'One of my many charms.'

She flipped her cap off her head, bent down and filled it with fresh, clean water and then replaced the lot on her head, drenching herself in salty water.

'Well, that killed my fun,' he murmured.

But not his view. The capful of water had the added benefit of making parts of her T-shirt and cargos cling to the curves of her body even more than they already were. And that killed any chance of him cooling down unless he took more serious measures. He lowered himself onto his butt in the shallows and lay back, fully, in the drink.

Pants, shirt and all.

'You know how uncomfortable you're going to be going back?' Her silhouette laughed from high above him, sea water still trickling off her jaw and chin.

He starfished in the two feet of water. 'Small price to pay for being so very comfortable now.'

Even with her eyes mostly shaded by the peak of her cap, he could tell when her glance drifted his way. She was trying not to look—hard—but essentially failing. He experimented by pushing his torso up out of the water and leaning back casually on his hands.

'Easy to say…'

But her words didn't sound easy at all. In fact, they were as tight as her body language all of a sudden.

Well, wasn't *that* interesting.

He pushed to his feet and moved towards her, grinning. Primarily so that he could see her eyes again. Her hands came up, fast, in front of her.

'Don't you dare…'

But he didn't stop until he stood just a centimetre from her upturned hands. And he grinned. 'Don't dare do this, you mean?'

'Come on, Marshall, I don't want to get wet.'

'I'm not the one with a soggy cap dripping down my face.'

'No, you're just soaked entirely through.'

And, with those words, her eyes finally fell where she'd been trying so hard not to look. At his chest, just a finger flex away from her upturned hands.

'I'm beginning to see what Anderson might have liked about this island,' he murmured.

She huffed out a slow breath. 'You imagine he and his crew took the time to roll around in the shallows like seals?'

The thought of rolling around anything with Eve hadn't occurred to him today, but now it was all he could do to squeeze some less charged words past the evocative image. 'Flattering analogy.'

The *pfff* she shot out would have been perfectly at home on a surfacing seal. Her speech was still tinged with a tight breathlessness.

'You know you look good. That was the point of the whole submerge thing, wasn't it? To see how I'd react?'

Actually, getting cool had been the point. Once. But suddenly that original point seemed like a very long time ago. He dropped his voice with his glance. Straight to her lips. 'And how will you react, Eve?'

Her feminine little voice box lurched a few times in her exposed throat. 'I won't. Why would I give you the satisfaction?'

'Of what?'

'Of touching you—'

If she could have bitten her tongue off she would have just then, he was sure. 'Is that what you want to do? I'll step forward. All you have to do is ask.'

Step forward into those still-raised hands that were trembling ever so slightly now.

But she was a tough one. Or stubborn. Or both.

'And why would I do that?'

'Because you really want to. Because we're all alone on a deserted island with time to kill. And because we'll both be going our separate ways after Esperance.'

Though the idea seemed laughable now.

She swallowed, mutely.

He nudged the peak of her cap upwards with his knuckle to better read her expression and murmured, 'And because this might be the only chance we'll have to answer the question.'

Her eyes left his lips and fluttered up to his. 'What question?'

He stared at her. 'No. You have to ask it.'

She didn't, though he'd have bet any body part she wanted to.

'Tell you what, Eve, I'll make it easier for you. You don't have to ask me to do it, you just have to ask me *not* to do it.'

'Not do what?' she croaked.

He looked down at her trembling fingers. So very, very close. 'Not to step forward.'

Beneath the crystal-clear water, his left foot crept forward. Then his right matched it. The whole time he kept his glance down at the place that her palms almost pressed on his wet chest.

'Just one word, Eve. Just tell me to stop.'

But though her lips fell open, nothing but a soft breath came out of them.

'No?' His body sang with elation. 'All righty, then.'

And with the slightest muscle tweak at the backs of his legs, he tipped his torso the tiny distance it needed to make contact with Eve's waiting fingers.

CHAPTER SIX

DEAR LORD...

How long had it been since she'd touched someone like this? More than just a casual brushing glance? All that hard flesh Eve had seen on the beach—*felt* on the bike—pressed back against her fingers as they splayed out across his chest. Across the shadowy eagle that she knew lived there beneath the saturated cotton shirt. Across Marshall's strongly beating heart.

Across the slight rumble of the half-caught groan in his chest.

One he'd not meant to make public, she was sure. Something that told her he wanted this as much as she secretly did.

Or, as her fingers trembled, not so secretly, now.

Marshall was right. They weren't going to see each other again. And this might be the only chance she had to know what it felt like to have the heat of him pressed against her. To know him. To taste him.

All she had to do was move one finger. Any finger.

She'd never meant to enter some kind of self-imposed physical exile when she'd set off on this odyssey. It had just happened. And, before she knew it, she'd gone without touching a single person in any way at all for...

She sucked in a tiny breath. All of it. Eight months.

Puppies and kittens got touch deprivation, but did grown women? Was that what was making her so ridiculously fluttery now? Her father's goodbye hug was the last time she'd had anyone's arms around her and his arms—no matter how strong they'd once been back when she was little—had never felt as sure and rooted in earth as Marshall's had as he'd lowered her from the bus's roof last night. And that had been fairly innocuous.

What kind of damage could they do if they had something other than *help* in mind?

How good—how *bad*—might they feel? Just once. Before he rode off into the sunset and she never got an answer.

Only one way to find out.

Eve inched her thumb down under the ridge of one well-defined pectoral muscle. Nervously jerky. Half expecting to feel the softness of the ink feathers that she could see shadowed through the saturated T-shirt. But there was no softness, only the silken sleeve of white cotton that contained all that hard, hot muscle.

God, he so didn't feel like a weatherman.

Marshall's blazing gaze roasted down on the top of her wet head, but he didn't move. Didn't interrupt. He certainly didn't step back.

Eve trailed her butterfly fingers lightly up along the line of the feathers, up to his collarbone. Beyond it to the rigid definition of his larynx, which lurched out of touch and then back in again like the scandalous tease it was.

Strong fingers lifted to frame her face—to lift it—and he brought her eyes to his. They simmered, as bottomless as the ocean around them as he lowered his mouth towards hers.

'Ahoy!'

Tortured lungs sucked in painfully further as both their gazes snapped out to sea, towards the voice that carried to them on the onshore breeze. Eve stumbled back from all the touching into the buffeting arms of the surf.

'Bugger all decent catch to be had,' the gruff captain shouted as he motored the *Vista II* more fully around the rocks, somehow oblivious to the charged moment he'd just interrupted. 'So we headed back early.'

Irritation mingled with regret in Marshall's storm-grey depths but he masked it quickly and well. It really wasn't the captain's fault that the two of them had chosen the end of a long, warm afternoon to finally decide to do something about the chemistry zinging between them.

'Hold that thought,' he murmured low and earnest as he turned to salute the approaching boat.

Not hard to do while her body screamed in frustration at the interruption, but give her fifteen minutes... Give her the slightest opportunity to think through what she was doing with half her senses and...

Marshall was right to look anxious.

But, despite what she expected, by the time the *Vista II*'s inflatable dinghy transferred them and their gear safely on deck, Eve's awareness hadn't diminished at all. And that was easily fifteen minutes. During the half-hour sea journey back to the campsite beach that followed—past seals sunning themselves and beneath ospreys bobbing on the high currents and over a swarm of small stingrays that passed underneath—still the finely tuned attention her body was paying to Marshall didn't ebb in the slightest.

She forced conversation with the two-man crew, she faked interest in their paltry fishy catch, she smiled and was delightful and totally over-compensated the whole way back.

She did whatever she needed to shake free of the relentless grey eyes that tracked her every move.

After an emotional aeon, her feet were back on mainland sand and the captain lightly tossed their last backpack out of the inflatable and farewelled her before exchanging a few business-related words with Marshall. Moments later, her hand was in the air in a farewell, her smile firmly plastered on and she readied herself for the inevitable.

Marshall turned and locked eyes with her.

'Don't know about you,' he said, 'but I'm famished. Something about boats...'

Really? He was thinking about his stomach while hers was twisted up in sensual knots?

'Have we got any of those sausages from breakfast still in the fridge?'

Um...

Not that he was waiting for her answer. Marshall lugged his backpack up over his shoulder and hoisted hers into his free hand and set off towards the track winding from the beach to the campsite. Eve blinked after him. Had she fantasised the entire moment in the cove? Or was he just exceptional at separating moments?

That was then, this was now. Island rules, mainland rules? What gave?

Warm beach sand collapsed under her tread as she followed him up the track, her glare giving his broody stare all the way back from Middle Island a decent run for its money.

They polished off the leftover sausages as soon as they got back to the bus. At least, Marshall ate most of them while she showered and then she nibbled restlessly on the last one while he did, trying very hard not to think about how much naked man was going on just feet from where she was sitting.

Soapy, wet, naked man.

Had the bus always been quite this warm?

'I think I would have been better off washing in the ocean,' he announced when he walked back in not long after, damp and clean and freshly clothed. Well, freshly clothed in the least used of three pairs of clothes he seemed to travel with. 'Lucky I didn't drop the soap because I wouldn't have been able to retrieve it.'

'I think the previous owners were hobbits,' Eve said, determined to match his lightness.

He slumped down next to her on the sofa. 'The hot water was fantastic while it lasted.'

Yeah. The water reservoir was pretty small. Even smaller as it ran through the onboard gas heater. 'Sorry about that. I guess Mr and Mrs Hobbit must have showered at different ends of the day.'

Not usually a problem for a woman travelling alone. The hot water was hers to use or abuse. And that had worked pretty well for her so far.

'So what's the plan for tonight?' Marshall said, glancing at her sideways.

Lord, if she wasn't fighting off visuals of him in the shower, she was hearing smut in every utterance. *Tonight.* It wasn't a very loaded word but somehow, in this tiny space with this über-present man, it took on piles of new meaning.

'Movie and bed—' She practically choked the word off.

But Marshall's full stomach and warm, fresh clothes had clearly put the damper on any lusty intentions. He didn't even blink. 'Sounds good. What have you got?'

Apparently an enormous case of the hormones, if her prickling flesh and fluttery tummy were any indication. But she nodded towards one of the drawers on the opposite side of the bus and left him to pick his way through the DVD choices. The mere act of him increasing the physical distance helped dilute the awareness that swirled around them.

He squatted and rifled through the box, revealing a stretch of brown, even skin at his lower back to taunt her. 'Got a preference?'

'No.'

Yeah. She'd have preferred never to have said yes to this excruciating co-habitation arrangement, to be honest. But done was done. She filled her one wineglass high for Marshall and then poured filtered water into her own mug where he couldn't tell what she was drinking. Maybe if he was sedated, that powerful, pulsing thrum coming off him would ease off a bit.

And maybe if she kept her wits about her she'd have the strength to resist it.

He held up a favourite. 'Speaking of hobbits...'

Yes! Something actiony and not at all romantic. He popped the disc at her enthusiastic nod, then settled back and jumped through the opening credits to get straight into the movie. Maybe he was as eager as she was to avoid conversation.

It took about ten minutes for her to remember that Middle Earth was definitely *not* without romance and then the whole movie became about the awkwardness of the longing-filled screen kiss that was swiftly approaching. Which only reminded her of how robbed she'd felt out in that cove to have the press of Marshall's lips snatched away by the approach of the *Vista II*.

Which was a ridiculous thing to be thinking when she should be watching the movie.

Hobbits quested. Wraiths hunted. Dramatic elven horse chase. Into the forests of Rivendell and then—

'Are we in the clunk zone, Eve?' Marshall suddenly queried. She flicked her eyes to her left and encountered his, all rust-flecked and serious and steady.

'What?'

Which was Eve-ish for *Yes...yes, we are.*

'Did I stuff things up this afternoon by kissing you?'

'You didn't kiss me,' she managed to squeeze out through her suddenly dry mouth.

But that gaze didn't waver. 'Not for want of trying.'

A waft of air managed to suck down into her lungs. 'Well, the moment has passed now so I think we're cool.'

'Passed?' he asked without smiling. 'Really?'

Yeah... She was a liar.

'That was hours ago,' she croaked.

'I wouldn't know,' he murmured. 'Time does weird things when you're around.'

Her brain wanted to laugh aloud, but the fluttering creatures inside her twittered girlishly with excitement. And they had the numbers.

'I think you're being adversely affected by the movie,' she said, to be safe.

'I'm definitely affected by something.'

'The wine?'

His smile was as gorgeous as it was slow. 'It is pretty good.'

'The company?'

'Yeah. 'Cos that's been terrific.'

She let her breath out in a long, apologetic hiss. 'I'm being weird.'

'You're weird so often it's starting to feel normal.'

'It's not awkward for you?'

His large hand slid up to brush a strand of hair from across her lips. 'What I'm feeling is not awkwardness.'

There went the whole dry mouth thing again. 'What are you feeling?'

'Anticipation.'

The fantastical world on-screen might as well have been an infomercial for all the attraction it suddenly held. Their already confined surroundings shrank even further.

'Maybe the moment's gone,' she said bravely.

He didn't move. He didn't have to. His body heat reached out and brushed her skin for him. 'Maybe you're in denial.'

'You think I'm that susceptible to low lighting and a romantic movie?'

Sure enough, there was a whole lot of elven-human longing going on on-screen. Longing and whispering against an intimate, beautiful soundtrack. Seriously, why hadn't she insisted on something with guns?

'I think the movie was an admirable attempt.'

'At what?' she whispered.

'At not doing this…'

Marshall twisted himself upright, his fingers finding a safe haven for his nearly empty wineglass. His other hand simultaneously relieved her of her mug and reached past her to place it on the sideboard. It legitimised the sudden, closer press of his body into hers.

'Now,' he breathed, 'what were you about to say?'

Heat and dizziness swilled around her and washed all sense out to sea. 'When?'

'Back in the cove. Was it no?' Grey promise rained down on her. 'Or was it yes?'

Truly? She had to find the courage to do this again? It had been hard enough the first time. Though, somehow, having already confessed her feelings made it easier now to admit the truth. She took the deepest of breaths, just in case it was also her last.

'It wasn't no.'

Those beautiful lips twisted in a confident, utterly masculine smile. 'Good.'

And then they found hers. Hot and hard and yet exquisitely soft. Pressing into her, bonding them together, challenging her to respond. She didn't at first because the sensation of being kissed after so very long with no touch at all threw her mind into a state of befuddlement. And she was drowning pleasantly in the sensation of hard male body pressed against hers. And sinking into the clean, delicious taste of him.

But she'd always been a sure adaptor and it only took moments for her feet to touch bottom and push off again for the bright, glittery surface. Her hands crept up around Marshall's shoulder and nape, fusing them closer. Her chin tilted to better fit the angle of his lips. The humid scorch of his breath teased and tormented and roused her, shamefully.

Revived her.

God, she'd missed hot breath mingling with hers. Someone else's saliva in her mouth, the chemical rush that came with that. Tangling tongues. Sliding teeth. And not just any tongue, breath and teeth but ones that belonged with all that hard flesh and ink and leather.

Marshall's.

'You taste of wine, Weatherman,' she breathed.

His eyes fixated on her tongue as she savoured the extra flavour on her lips. 'Maybe it's your own?'

'I had water.'

He lifted back slightly and squinted at her. 'Trying to get me drunk?'

'Trying to fight the inevitable.'

His chuckle rumbled against her chest. 'How's that working out for you?'

Gentle and easy and undemanding and just fine with something as casual as she needed. Wanted. All that she could offer.

And so she gave him access—tempting him with the touch of her tongue—and the very act was a kind of psychological capitulation. Her decision made. Even before she knew she was making it.

She trusted Marshall, even if she didn't know him all that well. He'd been careful and understanding and honest, and her body was *thrumming* its interest in having more access to his. With very little effort she could have his bare, hot skin against hers and her fingertips buried in the sexy curve of all that muscle.

He was gorgeous. He was intriguing. He was male and he was right here in front of her in living, breathing flesh and blood. And he was offering her what she suspected would be a really, really good time.

Did the rest really matter?

One large, hot hand slid up under her T-shirt and curled around her ribcage below her breast as they kissed, monitoring the heart rate that communicated in living braille onto his palm. Letting her get used to him being there. Doing to her exactly what she longed to do to him. Letting her stop him if she wanted. But no matter how many ways he twisted against her, the two of them couldn't get comfortable on the narrow little sofa. No wonder he'd struggled to sleep on it last night. And all the while she had an expansive bed littered with cloud-like pillows just metres away.

Eve levered herself off the sofa, not breaking contact with Marshall's lips or talented hands as he also rose, and she stretched as he straightened to his full height.

'Bed,' she murmured against his teeth.

His escalating kisses seemed to concur. One large foot bumped into hers and nudged it backwards, then another and the first one again. Like some kind of clunky slow dance, they worked their way back through the little kitchen, then through the en suite bathroom and toward unchartered territory. Her darkened bedroom. All the time, Marshall bonded them together either with his lips or his eyes or the hands speared into her hair and curled around her bottom.

There was something delightfully complicit about the way he used his body to steer her backwards into the bedroom while she practically tugged him after her. It said they were equals in this. That they were both accountable and that they both wanted it to happen.

Below her socked feet, the harder external floor of the en suite bathroom gave way to the plush carpet of the bedroom. Marshall's hands slid up to frame her face, holding it steady for the worship of his mouth. His tongue explored the welcome, warm place beyond her teeth just as much as she wanted him to explore this unchartered place beyond the doorway threshold.

A gentle fibrillation set up in the muscles of her legs, begging her to sink backwards onto her bed. The idea of him following her down onto it only weakened them further.

'Eve…' he murmured, but she ignored him, pulling back just slightly to keep the bedward momentum up. It took a moment for the cooler air of the gap she created to register.

Her eyes drifted open. They dropped to his feet, which had stopped, toes on the line between carpet and timber boards.

Hard on the line.

Confusion brought her gaze back up to his.

'I don't expect this,' he whispered, easing the words with a soft brush of his lips. And, when she just blinked at him, his eyes drifted briefly to the bed in case she was too passion-dazzled to comprehend him.

She pulled again.

But those feet didn't shift from the line and so all she achieved was more space between them. Such disappointing, chilly space. At least the hot grasp of his hand still linked them.

'Marshall…?'

'I just wanted to kiss you.'

Ditto! 'We can kiss in here. More comfortably.'

But the distance was official now and tugging any more reeked of desperation so she grudgingly let his hand drop.

'If I get on that bed with you we won't just be kissing,' he explained, visibly moderating his breathing.

'And that's a problem because…?'

'This isn't some roadhouse.'

Confusion swelled up around her numb brain. 'What?'

'You don't strike me as the sex-on-the-first-date type.'

Really? There was a type for these things? 'I don't believe in types. Only circumstances.'

'Are you saying you're just up for it because it's convenient?'

Up for it. Well, that sucked a little of the romance out of things. Then again, romance was not why she'd put her tongue in his mouth just minutes ago. What she wanted from Marshall was what he'd been unconsciously promising her from the moment they'd met.

No strings.

No rules.

No consequences.

'I'm tired of being alone, Marshall. I'm tired of not feeling anything but sadness. I need to feel something good.' A guarded wariness stole over his flushed face and she realised she needed to give him more than that. 'I have no illusions that it's going to go anywhere; in fact, I need it to be short. I don't want the distraction.'

He still didn't look convinced.

'I haven't so much as touched another human being in months, Marshall.'

'Any port in a storm, then?'

God knew it would be stormy between them. As wild and tempestuous as any sea squall. And just as brief.

'We've covered a lot of ground in our few days together and I trust you. I'm attracted to you. I need *you*, Marshall.'

All kinds of shapes seemed to flicker across the back of his intense gaze.

'But I'm not about to beg. Either you want me or you don't. I'll sleep comfortably tonight either way.' *Such lies!* 'Can you say the same?'

Of course he wanted her. It was written in the heave of his chest and the tightness of his muscles and the very careful way he wasn't making a single unplanned move. He wanted what she was offering, too, but there was something about it that he didn't want. Just…something.

And something was enough.

Eve went to push past him, back to the movie, making the disappointing decision for both of them.

But, as she did, his body blocked her path and his left foot crossed onto carpet. Then his right, backing her towards the bed. And then he closed the door on the sword fights of Middle Earth and plunged them into darkness, leaving only the smells and sounds and tastes of passion between them.

CHAPTER SEVEN

EVERY MUSCLE IN Eve's body twinged when she tried to move. Not that she could move particularly far with the heavy heat of Marshall's arm weighing her down. But in case she some-how managed to forget how the two of them had passed the long night, her body was there to remind her. In graphic detail.

Languid smugness glugged through her whole system.

She gave up trying to softly wiggle out of captivity and just accepted her fate. After all, there were much worse ways to go. And to wake up. Right now, her brain was still offering spon-taneous flashbacks to specific moments of greatness between them last night, and every memory came with a sensation echo.

Beside her, Marshall slept on in all his insensible glory. Buried face first in her pillows, relaxed, untroubled. It was very tempting just to lie here until lunchtime committing Sleeping Beauty to memory.

Although there was her bladder…

Ugh.

She took more decisive action and slid Marshall's arm off her chest, which roused him sufficiently to croak as she sprang to her feet. 'Morning.'

When was the last time she'd *sprung* anywhere? Usually she just hauled herself out of bed and gritted her teeth as she got on with the business of living.

'Morning yourself. Just give me a sec.'

Easing her bladder just a couple of metres and a very thin

en suite bathroom wall away from Marshall was an unexpectedly awkward moment. It seemed ridiculous after everything
they'd shared in the past twelve hours to have to concentrate
her way through a sudden case of bashful bladder. As soon as
she was done and washed, she scampered back into the toasty
warm and semi-occupied bed.

'You're better than an electric blanket,' she sighed, letting
the heat soak into her cold feet.

'Feel free to snuggle in.'

Don't mind if I do. She was going to milk this one-night
stand for every moment she could.

Marshall hauled her closer with the same strong arm that
had held her captive earlier, her back to his chest in a pretty
respectable spoon.

His voice rumbled down her spine. 'How are you feeling?'

Wow. Not an easy question to answer, and not one she'd expected him to ask. That was a very *not* one-night stand kind of
question. Thank goodness she wasn't facing him.

'I'm…' What was she? Elated? Reborn? She couldn't say
that aloud. 'I have no regrets. Last night was absolutely what
I expected and needed. And more. It was amazing, Marshall.'

It was only then that she realised how taut the body behind
her had become. Awkwardness saturated his words when they
eventually came.

'Actually, I meant because of today.'

She blinked. 'What's today?'

'One year?'

A bucket of icy Southern Ocean couldn't have been more
effective. The frigid wash chased all the warmth of Marshall's
hold away and left her aching and numb. And barely breathing.

Travis. Her poor, lost brother. Twelve months without a boy
she'd loved her whole life and she'd let herself be distracted by
a man she'd known mere moments by comparison.

She struggled for liberty and Marshall let her tumble out
of bed to her feet.

'I'm fine,' she said tightly. 'Just another day.'

He pushed onto his side, giving her a ringside seat for the giant raptor on his chest. She'd so badly wanted to see it last night but the room was too dark. And now she was too gutted to enjoy it.

'Okay…'

Mortification soaked in. What was wrong with her? How much worse to know that, for those first precious moments of consciousness, she hadn't even remembered she *had* a brother. She'd been all about Marshall.

What kind of a sister was she, anyway?

You wanted to forget, that little voice inside reminded her cruelly. *Just for one night. Wasn't that the point?*

Yes. But not like this. Not entirely.

She hadn't meant to *erase* Travis.

'It's a number,' she lied, rummaging in a drawer before dragging on panties and then leggings.

'A significant one,' Marshall corrected quietly.

She pulled a comfortable sweater on over the leggings. 'It's not like it took me by surprise. I've been anticipating it.'

Marshall sat up against the bed head and tucked the covers up around his waist ultra-carefully. 'I know.'

'So why are you making it into an issue?'

Ugh… Listen to herself…

Storm-grey eyes regarded her steadily. 'I just wanted to see how you were feeling this morning. Forget I mentioned it. You seem…great.'

The lie was as ridiculous as it was obvious.

'Okay.'

What was wrong with her? It wasn't Marshall's fault that she'd sought to use him for a bit of escapism. He'd fulfilled his purpose well.

Maybe too well.

'So, should we get going right after breakfast?' she asked brightly from the en suite bathroom as she brushed her hair. Hard to know whether all that heat in her cheeks was residual passion from last night, anger at herself for forgetting today or embarrassment at behaving like a neurotic teen.

Or all of the above.

A long pause from the bed followed and she slowed the drag of the bristles through her hair until it stilled in her hand.

'I've got to get back on the road,' she added, for something to fill the silence.

She should never have left it, really. She replaced the brush and then turned to stand in the bathroom doorway. Trying to be grown up about this. 'We both have jobs to do.'

What was going on behind that careful masculine expression? It was impossible to know. He even seemed to blink in slow motion. But his head eventually inclined—just.

'I'll convoy as far as the South Coast Highway,' he started. 'Then I'll head back to Kal. The road should be open by now.'

Right.

Was that disappointment washing through her midsection? Did she imagine that last night would have changed anything? She *wanted* them to go their separate ways. She'd practically shouted at him that this was a one-off thing. Yet bitterness still managed to fight its way through all her self-pity about Travis.

'Yeah. Okay.'

That was probably for the best. Definitely.

'Do you want me to take some posters for the Norseman to Kalgoorlie stretch? That'll save you doubling back down the track.'

It physically hurt that he could still be considerate when she was being a jerk. A twinge bit deep in her chest and she had to push words through it. Her shoulder met the doorframe.

'You're a nice man, Marshall Sullivan.'

His blankness didn't alter. And neither did he move. 'So I've been told.'

Then nothing. For ages. They just stared at each other warily.

Eventually he went to fling back the covers and Eve spun on the spot before having to face the visual temptation of everything she'd explored with her fingers and lips last night, and made the first excuse she could think of.

'I'll get some toast happening.'

Nice.

Just what every man wanted to hear from a woman he'd spent the night with. Not 'fantastic' or 'unforgettable'. Not 'awe-inspiring' or 'magnificent'.

Nice.

He'd heard that before, from the Sydney kids who had clambered over him in their quest to get closer to Rick and his chemical smorgasbord. From friends and girls and the occasional tragic teacher.

He'd always been the *nicer* brother.

But not the one everyone wanted access to.

Sticks and stones...

Problem was, Eve's lips might have been issuing polite compliments but the rest of her was screaming eviction orders and, though he'd only known her a couple of days, it was long enough for him to recognise the difference. He'd had enough one-off encounters with women to know *get out of my room* when he saw it. Despite all the brave talk last night, she was *not* comfortable with the aftermath of their exhausting night together.

And he was all too familiar with eyes that said something different from words. He'd had them all his life.

He'd been right in assuming Eve wasn't a woman who did this a lot; she was most definitely under-rehearsed in the fine art of the morning-after kiss-off. If he'd realised there'd be no lingering kisses this morning he would have taken greater care to kiss her again last night just before they fell into an exhausted slumber twisted up in each other.

Because Eve had just made it very clear that there would be no more kissing between them.

Ever.

He'd worked his butt off last night giving her the kind of

night she clearly needed from him. Making sure it was memorable. And, if he was honest, giving Eve something to think about. To regret. Maybe that was why it stung even more to see her giving it exactly zero thought this chilly morning.

Wham-bam, thank you, Marshall.

Somewhere, the universe chuckled to itself as the cosmic balance evened up. That was what he got for usually hotfooting it out the next morning the way Eve just had.

Only generally to fire up his motorcycle, not the toaster.

What did he expect? Days wrapped up in each other's arms here in this ridiculous little bus while his remaining weeks on the project ticked ever closer to an end and her bank balance slowly drained away? Neither of them had the luxury of indefinite leisure. He wasn't stupid.

Or maybe he was…because Evelyn Read was definitely not a one-off kind of woman and some deep part of him had definitely hoped for more than the single night they'd both agreed on between kisses. Which meant it was probably just as well that was all he was getting. Eve had no room for another man in her single-track life.

And he was done being a means to an end.

He pulled yesterday's T-shirt back on and rather enjoyed the rumples and creases. They were like little trophies. A reminder of how the shirt had been thoroughly trampled underfoot in their haste to get each other naked. A souvenir of the disturbingly good time he'd had with her beyond her bedroom door.

'Don't burn it,' he murmured, passing into the tiny kitchenette intentionally close to her, just to get one more feel of her soft skin. His body brushed the back of hers.

Her feet just about left the floor, she jumped that fast and high. Then a sweet heat coloured along her jawline and her lips parted and he had to curl his fingers to stop himself from taking her by the hand and dragging her back to that big, warm bed and reminding her what lips were made for.

It felt good to torture Eve, just a little bit. It sure felt good to surprise her into showing her hand like that. To shake the ambivalence loose. To watch the unsteadiness of her step. She might call a halt to this thing just getting going between them but he wasn't going to go easily.

He kept on moving past her, ignoring the sweet little catch in her breath, and he stopped at the back doors, flung them open and then stretched his hands high to hook them on the top of the bus, stretching out the kinks of the night, knowing how his back muscles would be flexing. Knowing how the ink there would flash from beneath his T-shirt. Knowing how that ink fascinated her.

If she was going to drive off into the horizon this morning, she sure wasn't going to do it with a steady brake foot.

Yup. He was a jerk.

He leapt down from the bus and turned to his KTM, and murmured to the bitter cold morning.

'*Nice*, my ass.'

The bus's brake lights lit up on the approach to the junction between the Coolgardie and South Coast Highways and Marshall realised he hadn't really thought this through. It was a big intersection but not built for pulling over and undertaking lingering farewells. It was built for turning off in any of the four points of the compass. His road went north, Eve's went further west.

But the uncertain blink of her brake lights meant she, too, was hesitating on the pedal.

She didn't know what to do either.

Marshall gave the KTM some juice and pulled up in the turn lane beside her instead, reassuring himself in the mirror that there was no one on the remote highway behind them. Eve dropped her window as he flipped his helmet visor.

'Good luck with the rest of your trip,' he called over the top of his thrumming engine and her rattling one.

'Thank you.' It was more mouthed than spoken.

God, this was a horrible way of doing this. 'I hope you get some news of your brother soon.'

Eve just nodded.

Then there was nothing much more to say. What could he say? So he just gave her a small salute and went to lower his visor. But, at the last moment, he found inspiration. 'Thank you for coming with me yesterday. I know you would have rather been back on the road.'

Which was code for *Thanks for last night, Eve*. If only he were the slightest bit emotionally mature.

She nodded again. 'I'm glad I did it.'

Middle Island, he told himself. Yesterday. That was all.

And then a car appeared on the highway in his mirror, way back in the distance, and he knew they were done.

He saluted again, slid his tinted visor with the obligatory squished bugs down between them and gave the bike some juice. It took only seconds to open up two hundred metres of highway between them and he kept Eve in his mirrors until the Bedford crossed the highway intersection and was gone from view, heading west.

Not the worst morning-after he'd ever participated in, but definitely not the best.

He was easily the flattest he could remember being.

He hadn't left his number. Or asked for hers. Neither of them had volunteered it and that was telling. And, without a contact, they'd never find each other again, even if they wanted to.

Eve Read would just have to be one of those memories he filed away deep inside. He added *The Crusader* to his list of badly handled flings.

Except she didn't feel like a fling. She felt like forever. Or what he imagined forever must feel like. Crazy. He'd known her all of five minutes. So the lingering sense that things weren't done between them was…

Ridiculous.

The shimmering haze of her exhaust as she couldn't speed away from him fast enough told a very different story.

Trees and wire fences and road signs whizzed by the KTM

in a one-hundred-and-ten-kilometre-per-hour blur. Plus a sheep or two.

Would he have stayed if she'd asked? If she'd crawled back into bed this morning and snuggled in instead of running an emotional mile? If he hadn't—like a freaking genius—brought up her most painful memory when she was half-asleep and vulnerable to his words?

Yeah. He would have stayed.

But it was the *why* that had him by the throat.

Eve was pretty but not beautiful, bright but not spectacular, prickly as a cactus and more than a little bit neurotic. She should have just been a charming puzzle. So what was with the whole curl-up-in-bed urge? He really wasn't the curl up type.

She's your damsel, man.

The words came burbling up from deep inside him, in his brother's voice. The kind of conversations they used to have way back when. Before they went down opposite off ramps of the values highway. Before Rick's thriving entrepreneurial phase. Certainly before Christine switched teams—and brothers. Back when Rick gave him stick for being a soft touch for girls in need of a knight on a white charger.

Orange charger, in his case.

Relief surfed his veins.

Yeah, this was about Eve's brother. That was all it was, this vague sense that leaving her was wrong. There was nothing more meaningful or complicated going on than that. He hated the helplessness he saw behind Eve's eyes and the flat nothing she carried around with her. It made him feel powerless—his least favourite emotion.

She's not yours to fix, Inner Rick nudged.

No, but was there really nothing more he could offer her than platitudes and some help with the posters and one night of sweaty distraction? He was a resourceful guy. He had connections.

And then it hit him…

Exactly why he'd chosen to place a woman he'd just met

and a man he hadn't seen in ten years next to each other at the dinner table of his subconscious.

His brain ticked over as fast as his tyres ate up the highway. If a person was going to go off grid, they might ditch their bank accounts in favour of cash, stop filing tax returns and opt out of claiming against Medicare. But what was Eve the most cut up about—? That Travis was struggling with his panic disorder, alone. And what did people who were being treated for disorders do? They took drugs. And who knew everything there was to know about drugs?

Rick did.

Enough to have driven his kid brother away years before. Enough to have made a thriving business out of supplying half of Sydney with their chemical needs. Enough to have a world of dodgy contacts inside the pharmaceutical industry—legal and otherwise.

Marshall eased off the throttle.

That meant he was just one uncomfortable phone call away from the kind of information that the cops would never think to access. Or be able to. Not ethical, probably not even legal, but since when did Rick let something as insignificant as the law stand between him and his goals?

Of course it would mean speaking to his brother, but maybe a decade was long enough with the silent treatment. Lord knew, Rick owed him.

Marshall down-geared and, as he did, his rapid pulse started to slow along with his bike. The pulse that had kicked up the moment parting from Eve was upon him. Back at the intersection. A kind of anxiety that he hadn't felt in a long, long time—since before he'd stopped letting himself care for people.

The descending thrum of his blood and the guttural throb of his bike colluded to soak him in a kind of certainty about this plan. As if it was somehow cosmically meant to be. As if maybe this was why he'd met Eve in the first place.

Because he could help her.

Because he could save her.

That was all this was. This…unsettling obsession. It was his Galahad tendency. Evelyn Read needed *help*, not *him*. And he was much more comfortable with the helping part.

He hit his indicator and looked for a safe place to pull over. He fished around in the depths of his wallet for a scrap of paper he'd almost forgotten he still carried. Ratty and brown edged, the writing half-faded. Rick's phone number. He punched the number into his phone but stopped short of pressing Dial.

This was Rick. The brother who'd made his teenage years a living hell. Who'd lured his girlfriend away from him just because he could. The brother who'd been the real reason that most of his friends craved his company and half the teachers gave him special treatment. They'd all wanted an in with *The Pharmacist*.

Rick was the reason he couldn't bring himself to trust a single soul, even now. Rick had taken the lessons they'd both learned from their mother about love and loyalty—or absences thereof—and turned the hurt into a thriving new industry where a lack of compassion for others was a corporate asset.

He'd made it work for him, while his little brother struggled in his shadow.

It had taken him years to fortify himself against those early lessons. His mother's. His brother's. And here he was, straddling his bike and contemplating leaping off the edge of his personal fortress of solitude to help someone he barely knew. He'd kicked the door of communication closed between every part of his old life and here he was, poised to take to that door with a crowbar and crack it open again.For a virtual stranger.

No…*for Eve*.

And Eve mattered.

He thumbed the dial button and listened as the number chirped its ominous melody. Took three deep breaths as it rang and rang. Took one more as a gruff voice picked up.

Marshall didn't waste time with niceties.

'You said to call if I ever needed you,' he reminded his brother. 'Did you mean it…?'

* * *

Rick had been at first surprised, then wary, when he recognised Marshall's serious tone after so very long. But—typical of the brother he remembered—Rick took the call at face value and accepted the subtext without comment. He listened to the request, grizzled about the dubiousness of what he'd been asked to do, but committed to help. And, despite anything else he'd done in his life, Rick Sullivan was the personification of tenacity. If he said he'd get this done, then, one way or another, some time Marshall's phone would be ringing again.

End of day, that was all that really mattered. Eve needed results more than he needed to maintain the moral high ground.

Rick even managed to go the entire phone call without getting personal.

The leathers of Marshall's jacket creaked as he exhaled. 'Thank you for your help, Rick. I swear it's not for anything too dodgy.'

'This whole thing is dodgy,' his brother muttered. 'But I'll do it because it's you. And because dodgy is where I do my best work. It might take a while, though.'

'No problem.'

Eve had been waiting twelve months. What was one more?

'I might find nothing.'

'Understood.'

'And one day maybe you can tell me what we're doing. And who for.'

He tensed up, mostly at the suggestion that there'd be a 'one day'. As if the door couldn't be closed once jemmied open.

'What makes you think there's a "who"?'

'Because you don't get invested in things, brother. Ever. You're Mr Arm's Length. But I can hear it in your voice. This matters.'

'Just let me know how you go,' he muttered. Eve was not someone he would trust his brother with, even mentally. He wasn't about to share any details.

'So…you want to know whether she's okay?' Rick asked, just before they ended the call.

'Christine?' Speaking of not trusting Rick… A few years ago, he would have felt the residual hurt deep in his gut. But now it just fluttered to earth like a burnt ember. Maybe the history really was history now.

'No, not Christine. I have no idea where she ended up.'

That bit. That Rick hadn't even kept his prize after working so very hard to take it from him.

'I meant Mum,' Rick clarified. 'Remember her?'

Everything locked up tight inside Marshall. He'd closed the door on Laura Sullivan the same day he'd locked Rick out of his life. The two of them were a package deal. The moment she'd realised her enterprising oldest son was going to be a far better provider than the Government, she'd made her allegiance—and her preference—totally clear.

That wasn't something you forgot in a hurry… Your own mother telling you to go.

'No. I'm good.'

There didn't seem much else to say after that.

It took just a moment to wind the call up and slip his phone back into his pocket. He'd get a new number just as soon as Rick gave him the info he needed. But he didn't hit the road again straight away. Instead, he sat there on the highway, bestride his KTM, breathing out the tension.

You don't get invested in things.

Well, that pretty much summed him up. Work. Life. He had a good ethic but he never let himself care. Because caring was a sure way of being disappointed. Or hurt. Life in his brother's shadow had taught him that. And as life lessons went, that one had served him well.

Until now.

As Rick had readily pointed out, he was invested now. With Eve—a woman he barely knew. He was more intrigued and conflicted and turned inside out for a woman he'd known just days than the people he'd grown up with. Maybe because she didn't want anything from him that she wasn't prepared to own. She had no agenda. And no ulterior motive.

Eve just…was.

And maybe he'd found a way to help her. Or maybe not. But he sure wasn't going to be able to do it from here.

He'd just sent her off down the highway with absolutely no way of locating her again. No email. No number. No forwarding address. How many Reads might there be in Melbourne? He couldn't shake the screaming thought that this was the only moment he had left. Right now, Eve was rattling down a long, straight road that only went to one place. After that, she could head off in any of five different routes into tourist country and his chances of finding her would evaporate. Tension coiled inside him like a spring…

And that was when he knew.

This wasn't just about helping Eve. If it was, he could just take whatever information his brother dug up straight to the authorities. Let them do the rest. This wasn't just about some cosmic interference to help her find her brother. That unfamiliar, breath-stealing tightness in his chest was panic. And he didn't do panic because that implied caring.

He'd no sooner let himself care for someone than void a ten-year stalemate with his criminal brother to get something that might ease Eve's pain. Eve—a complex, brittle, single-minded angel. The most intriguing woman he'd met in…more than years. The woman who'd barrelled through his defences and wedged herself there between his ribs. Just below his heart.

Oh, crap…

From where he sat, he could see the endless stretch of highway ahead—north to Kalgoorlie, where he could pick up his work trail where he'd left it a few days ago. But, in his mirror, he could see the long straight run behind him, back to the four-way turn-off. Back to a one hundred per cent chance of catching up with the bus before it turned off the western highway.

Back to the possibility he'd been too cowardly to explore.

Back to Eve.

He started his engine, dropped his visor and let his eyes lift to the northern horizon. Towards work and the conclusion of this trip and his safe, comfortable life.

But then they dropped again to the mirror, and the road he'd just travelled.

Sure, she might tell him to get lost. And if she did, he would.

But what if she didn't…?

In the end, his hands made the decision before his head did, and a leathered thumb hit his indicator before pulling the KTM's handlebars right, out across the empty highway and then back onto the opposite shoulder.

Before he could second-guess himself, he gunned the accelerator and roared off towards the south.

Towards the unknown.

CHAPTER EIGHT

It could be anyone—that speck in the distance behind her.

Car. Bike. Truck. It was too small for one of the massive road trains that liked to thunder past at breakneck speed, but a smaller truck, maybe.

Eve forced her eyes forward and ignored the impulse to check again. Plenty of people drove this road into Western Australia's tourist region. People who had far more legitimate reasons to be heading this way than *he* did.

Marshall was heading north. Back to his weather stations. Back to reality.

Which was exactly what she should be doing. Middle Island had been a nice couple of days of escapism—for both of them—but they both had jobs to be doing.

And Travis was her job.

He always had been.

If the past couple of days had taught her anything, it was that she couldn't take her eyes off the prize—or the map—for a moment. Look how fast she'd been swayed from her purpose. Besides, Marshall couldn't get out of there fast enough this morning. Not once he saw her in full neurotic mode. He was probably congratulating himself right now on a bullet well dodged.

The speck in her rear-vision mirror grew larger. But not large enough to be a truck. A car, then.

Or smaller, her subconscious more than whispered.

No.

Why would Marshall return? He hadn't left anything behind in her bus—she'd checked twice. And their parting had been as unequivocal as it was awkward. And definitely for the best. She was on a mission and didn't need the distraction. No matter how compelling.

And boy, was he ever. He'd been an intriguing curiosity while tattooed and hairy. Clean shorn and well educated, he was entrancing. Naked, he was positively hypnotic. All the better for being a long, long way from her.

She glanced helplessly back at the mirror and her pulse made itself known against the fragile skin of her throat.

Not a car.

Her gaze split its time between looking ahead and looking back, then the forward-looking part became a glance and then a mere flick to keep the bus on a straight and safe line.

Plenty of motorbikes in the sea. Impossible to even know what colour this one was yet.

Her gaze remained locked on her mirror.

If it was orange—if it was *him*—that didn't have to mean anything. Their one night together had probably been so good because it was a one-off. No past, no future. Just the very heated and very comfortable present. Even if Marshall was coming back for a second go at last night, there was nothing that said she had to oblige—no matter what her pulse recommended.

No matter how enticing the promise of a few more hours of mental *weightlessness* he brought.

A dull mass settled between her shoulder blades. She couldn't afford to be weightless. Not until her journey was complete and Travis was home.

Her own thought tripped her up. She'd never thought about this journey being over. What she would do. Would work have her back? She'd resigned with notice, so there were no burnt bridges there, but could she go back to meetings and minutes and deadlines? Would she have the patience? What would she be like after it was all over? Could she be *normal* now that she knew how secretly cruel the world really was?

As for weightless… Would she ever feel that way again?

Or was that just another disloyalty to Travis? To be worrying about any of it?

She'd put herself first once before and look how that had ended. Travis had melted down completely the moment she took her eyes off him.

She glanced up again, just in time to see a flash of black and orange changing into the inside lane and then roaring up beside her.

All the breath squeezed up tight in her suddenly constricted chest.

He was back.

Marshall whizzed by on her right, then changed lanes into the vanguard position and weaved in the lane in a kind of high-speed wave. She took several long, steadying breaths to bring the mad thump of her heart back into regular rhythm.

Should she stop? Hear what he had to say?

No. If he wanted her to pull over he'd be braking, slowing her. But he was pacing her, not slowing her. Guiding her onward. Besides, not far now until the turn-off to the Ravensthorpe poster drop. If he had something to say he could say it there.

And she'd listen politely and when it came to the time to part again she'd try and be a bit more erudite than her poor effort this morning.

Two vehicles whizzed by in the opposite direction, marking their entry into tourist country. *Tourism.* That was what she and Marshall were doing, right? Exploring the unchartered country that was each other. Enjoying the novelty. But how many tourists sold up and moved to the places they visited? How many stayed forever? No matter how idyllic.

Right. Because the real world eventually intruded.

And her reality was Travis.

Marshall wiggled his motorbike again and seemed to be

waiting for something. Did he seriously worry that she hadn't recognised him? She gave her headlights a quick flash of acknowledgement and his weaving ceased.

He placed himself squarely in the centre of their lane and let his bike eat up the highway.

And Eve did her best not to fixate on the strong breadth of his back and breathless imaginings about what it would be like to peel all that leather right off him.

The Bedford's front doors were as reluctant to open as Eve was to pass through them. But Marshall had made fast work of slinging the KTM onto its stand and pulling off his helmet. As he sauntered towards her on his thick-soled riding boots, he forked fingers through his thick helmet hair to ruffle it up.

Her first thought—on the clench of her stomach—was that finger-forking his hair was her job.

Her second thought—on the clench of her heart at the sound and smell of his creaking leathers as he stopped in front of her—was that she was completely screwed.

'Forget something?' she managed to squeeze out from the top of the Bedford's steps. More for something to say, really, because if he'd actually come back for his favourite socks she was going to be really crushed. She kept her body language as relaxed as was possible in a body ready to flee.

'Yeah,' he murmured, stepping up onto the bottom step, 'this.'

One gloved hand came up and lifted her chin as if he was holding a crystal flute and his lips brushed against hers. Then the brush got harder, closer. So...*so* much better. He turned his head and deepened the kiss, stroking his tongue into her mouth and against her own. Just when she'd thought no one would ever kiss her like that again.

She wavered there on the top step, the closest thing to a swoon she'd ever experienced.

'I didn't say goodbye properly,' he finally breathed against her astonished mouth. 'Now I don't want to say it at all.'

'You left,' she said between the head spins.

'But I'm back.'

'What about work?'

'What about it? There are plenty of weather stations still on my list. I'll just flex my route.'

What about my *work?* was what she really needed to be asking. Because how much of it was she going to get done with him around? If the past couple of days was any indication.

'You just assume I want to carry on where we left off?'

Just because she *did*... He wasn't to know that.

'I'm not assuming anything. If you send me away I've wasted...what...an hour of my time and a couple of bucks in fuel. Those are reasonable stakes.'

She pulled free. 'Charming.'

His grin managed to warm her right through, even as her heart screamed at her not to fall for it.

'Do you want me to go?'

She stared at him. Remembered how it felt to be with him. To be *with* him. And the thought of watching him drive off again was almost unbearable.

'I should,' she breathed.

'That's not a no.'

'No.' She stared at him. 'It's not.'

His puppy-dog grin graduated into a full, brilliant, blazing smile. 'Come on, then. Let's get some posters up. Time's a-wasting.'

He stepped down off the bus and held a hand out to help her. His eyes were screened by sunglasses but she could clearly see the trepidation still in the stiffness of his body. What she did next mattered to him. And that made her feel a whole lot better. She glanced at his outstretched hand. The unexpected chivalry excited and troubled her at the same time. She'd been jumping down off the Bedford's steps all by herself for eight months.

But just because she *could* didn't mean it wasn't a rare treat not to have to.

How would it feel to share this burden, just for a bit?

Would Travis understand?

After an age, she slid her bare fingers into his leathery ones and accepted his help.

But they both knew that taking his hand was saying yes to a whole lot more.

Marshall followed Eve as she chugged the Bedford into the biggest town in the Great Southern region behind the two-dozen cars that constituted peak hour in these parts. When she pulled up in a big open car park, Marshall stood the KTM and then jogged off to find something for them to eat. When he got back with it, she was set up and ready to go. Table and chair in place, bus sides up and covered in posters.

'I need to find the MP's office,' she announced. 'I'm getting low on posters.'

'Didn't you do that before?'

'Nope. Somebody distracted me.'

Yeah. He was probably supposed to feel bad about that. 'Too bad.' He winced.

'You don't look very sympathetic,' she admonished.

He just couldn't stop smiling. What was that about? 'MP's office was a few doors down from where I got lunch. I'll show you.'

Then it was her turn to smile. 'Thank you.'

She weighted down anything on her display that might blow away, grabbed a flash drive from her wallet and hurried alongside him. The door to the MP's office set off an audible alert as they entered.

'Hi there,' a friendly young woman said from behind the reception desk, addressing him. He looked straight at Eve, who slid the flash drive over the counter. 'Welcome to Albany.'

'Can you run off a hundred of these, please?'

The woman frowned and didn't touch the flash drive. 'What is it?'

'A missing-person poster,' Eve elucidated, but it didn't bring any hint of recognition. 'MP's offices are supposed to run off copies for free.'

A little explanation wasn't exactly an Open Sesame.

'Let me just check,' the woman said, stalling.

Eve looked as if she wanted to say more but his hand on her wrist forestalled it. A few moments later the woman came back, smiling, and chirped, 'Won't be long!'

Eve turned to the window and the port view beyond it and curled her arms around her torso.

Every day must have moments like these for her. When simple things like a bit of public bureaucracy suddenly reared up in front of her like a hurdle in her efforts to find her brother. No wonder she was so tired.

That kind of emotional ambush would be exhausting.

'Good morning,' a male voice said and Eve turned from her view.

An overly large, overly suited man with a politician's smile approached, hand outstretched. 'Gerald Harvey, MP.'

'Evelyn Read,' she murmured, sliding her fingers into his.

He followed suit. 'Marshall Sullivan.'

'You have a missing person?' the man asked and barrelled onwards before she could answer. 'I'm very sorry for your loss.'

'My loss?'

The statement seemed to stop Eve cold, and only the new colour in her face gave Gerald Harvey a hint that he might have put his finely shod foot in it. 'Your...uh...circumstances.'

Marshall stepped in closer behind her and placed his hand on Eve's lower back, stroking gently.

'Thank you,' she said to the man, more evenly than he would have expected based on her expression.

Harvey took the first poster that his assistant printed and read it aloud, rolling the name over his tongue like wine. 'Travis James Read.'

Just in case Eve didn't know who she'd been looking for the past year.

'Can't say I've seen him but someone might have. Are you circulating these in town?'

'All over the country.'

The man laughed. 'Not all over it, surely.'

Eve didn't waver. 'All over it. Every town. Every tourist stop.'

He stared as the poster in his hand fell limply over his substantial fist, and Marshall watched the interplay of disbelief and pity play over his ruddy face. Then it coalesced into kind condescension.

'That's a lot of posters.'

Brilliant. Of all the things he could have noted about Eve's extraordinary endeavour...

'Yes.'

'And fuel.'

Okay, enough was enough.

'Eve,' he interjected, 'how about we go back to the bus and I'll come back for the posters in fifteen minutes? You should get started. Don't want to miss anyone.'

Ironic, given her life was all about missing someone.

He thanked the MP and then bustled her out into the street, instantly feeling the absence of the tax payer–funded office heating. She didn't speak. Didn't confront him or rant. She'd turned inwards somewhere in that brief encounter and wasn't coming out any time soon.

He could endure the silence no longer than five minutes.

'Did I ever look at you like that?' he eventually asked as they walked back towards the main street. The mixture of pity and polite concern. As if she might not be all that mentally well herself.

His direct question dragged her focus back to him. Brown eyes reached into his soul like a fist and twisted. 'A little bit.'

Great. No wonder she'd taken a while to warm up to him. Maybe she still was.

'It's not crazy,' he insisted suddenly, stopping and turning her towards him. 'It's not common, sure, but what you're doing is…logical. Under the circumstances. I get it.'

'You do?'

He waved his hand towards her poster display of all *The Missing* as they approached. 'I imagine every one of their families would like to have the courage and commitment to do what you've done. To get out here and look, personally. To do something proactive. To know you've done as much as you possibly can.'

She tossed her head back in the direction of the MP's office. 'That reaction is pretty common.'

'People don't know what to say, I guess.'

She stared up at him. 'You didn't have that problem.'

Something bloomed deep inside on learning that she had forgiven him for whatever first impression he'd left her with. Enough to shrug and joke, 'I'm exceptional.'

The sadness cracked and her mouth tipped up. 'So you say.'

'Go,' he nudged. 'Get started. I'll go back and manage Mr Charm, and then I'll go find us a camping site after I've dropped your new posters to you.'

She seemed to do a full-body sigh. 'Thank you.'

'No problem. Back in a few.'

He turned back for the MP's office but only got a few steps before turning again. He was back beside her in moments.

'Wha—?'

It took no effort at all to pull her into his arms and tuck her safe and warm beneath his chin. To wrap his arms firmly around her so that nothing and no one could get between them.

How had it not occurred to him before now to hug Eve?

This was a woman who needed repeat and regular hugging. On prescription. And he was happy to be her spoonful of sugar. Her slim arms crept around his waist and hooked behind his back, and the rest of her pressed into his chest as she sagged into him. Stroking her hair seemed obvious.

Around them, the sounds of a busy coastal town clattered on. But inside their bubble there was only the two of them.

'That guy was a dick,' he announced against her ear.

'I know,' she muffled into his chest.

'I'm sorry that happened.'

She wriggled in closer. 'You get used to it.'

'You shouldn't have to.'

'Thank you.'

He curled her in closer, resting his chin on her head.

'Um…Marshall?' she eventually mumbled.

'Yeah?'

'Aren't you going to get us a site?'

'Yep. Leaving now.'

Around them traffic did its thing and somewhere a set of traffic lights rattled off their audible alert.

'Marshall?'

His fingers stroked her hair absently. 'Hmm?'

'We're making a scene.'

He opened one eye and, sure enough, a couple of locals walked by, glancing at them with amused smiles on their faces.

He closed the eye again and tucked her in even closer.

'Screw 'em.'

'Gotta say, you have a strange idea of what constitutes a "camping site".'

'I'm funded to stay in motels.' Marshall shrugged. 'You might as well benefit.'

'Are all your *motels* quite this flash?' She leaned on the word purposefully because the waterside complex was more of a resort than anything.

'Well, no. But you put me up the last two nights so I have some budget savings. And there's hardly anyone else here out of season so you can take as much car park room as you need for the bus.'

Because she'd be sleeping in the car park while he spread out in the suite's big bed all alone?

She glanced at him. Maybe she'd misunderstood what his return meant. But she wasn't brave enough to ask aloud. Or maybe that was actually a really good idea. A tempestuous one-night stand was one thing but a second night—that needed some managing.

'Come on. At least check it out since you're here.'

She followed him up to the second storey, where the suite's balcony looked out over a parkland walkway below to the turquoise, pine tree–lined swimming bay that curled left and right of them. The rest of the suite was pretty much made of either sofa or bed. Both enormous. A large flat-screen TV adorned the walls between local art and something tantalising and white peeked out at her, reflected, through the bathroom door.

Her breath sucked in. Was that a...?

'Spa?'

'Yeah, I think so,' he said a little sheepishly. Had it suddenly dawned on him that this was all starting to look a little *boom-chick-a-wah-wah*? 'It came with the room.'

How long had it been since she'd soaked her weary body? And having a spa, or lounging on the sofa, or sitting on the balcony with a glass of wine didn't have to mean she was staying the night here. Her own bed was pretty comfy, thanks very much.

She glanced at the crack in the bathroom door again and wondered how she could ask him for access without it sounding like a come-on. Or an invitation.

As usual, Marshall came to her rescue with the lift of one eloquent eyebrow and the careful and chivalrous choice of words.

'You want first crack?'

It took her about a nanosecond to answer in the positive and about two minutes to sprint back to the bus and get some clean clothes. It was only as she took the stairs back up two by two that she realised what the bundle of comfortable leggings and track top in her arms meant.

They weren't going back out again tonight.

So, that meant room service for dinner. Nice and cosy, just the two of them.

Wow. Her subconscious was really going to make this tough

for her. But the siren song of the bubbles was so strong she didn't care.

Bubbles. Heaven.

'It's a fast filler,' Marshall announced as she burst back into the room, more eager than she'd felt in a long time.

Oh, right…filling. Nature's brakes. Eve stood, a bit at a loss, shifting from foot to foot in the room's entryway.

'It has a shower, too,' he volunteered, bright light glinting in the grey of his eyes. 'You could get straight in and then just shower until the water level is high enough.'

She loved her bus, but its shower pressure was as weak as it was brief. The chance for a proper shower was overwhelming. 'Oh, my gosh, really?'

'Your face is priceless.' He grinned. 'You like a spa, I take it.'

'I used to have a jet bath,' Eve admitted to him. And then to herself, 'I miss it.'

Not that she'd given her big four-person bath much thought when she put her house on the market. Because brothers before bubbles, right? But—oh—how she missed the great soak at the end of a long, hard week. And out here where every week was long and hard…

'Go on,' he nudged. 'Get in there.'

Her thanks were practically a squeak as she slipped into the bathroom and closed the door behind her. She waited a moment too long to flip the lock—worrying how Marshall might read the click after such a long, silent pause—but decided to leave it. If he had something nefarious in mind, he'd had plenty of more isolated opportunities to perpetrate his crime. Not to mention the fact they'd already slept together.

Besides, sneaking into a woman's bathroom was beneath a man like Marshall.

He's a good man.

It took no time at all to get naked and under the thundering commercial shower as the water slowly rose up over her calves. Hot, hot water pounded down on her shoulders and back, then over her hair as she plunged fully under it.

Warm and reassuring and…home. The water brought with it a full-body rush of tingles.

Unexpected tears rushed to her support.

She'd been doing this so long. Being on the road. Was it okay to admit she was tired? That didn't have to mean she loved Travis any less, did it? The water thundered on and she lifted her face to let the fresh water wash away her guilty tears. Eventually, though, the spa reached a generous level of full- ness and she killed the overhead stream and slid down into the piping-hot pool. Her groan was inevitable and the long sigh that followed the perfect punctuation.

When was the last time she'd felt so…buoyant? When was the last time she'd just closed her eyes and floated? The wa- ter's heat did its job and immediately soaked into muscles she'd forgotten didn't always feel this way, including a few that had only been aching since the marathon of last night.

Was it only twenty-four hours ago that she and Marshall had twisted up in each other's arms? And legs. And tongues. Like some kind of fantasy. Had it even really happened? If it had really happened, wouldn't he be in here with her? Not respectfully waiting on the other side of a closed—but not locked—door.

She lifted one hand to better position it and the cascading tinkle echoed in the silent bathroom.

'Marshall…'

'Yeah?'

Water splashed slightly as she started in the bath at the speed and closeness with which he answered. The door was right next to her head but he sounded close enough to be in here with her. Her eyes went to the mirror reflection of the door instinctively, but she knew before they got there what they'd find.

Marshall wasn't really the Peeping Tom type. If he wanted to look, he'd just knock and enter and stare at her until she was as much a hot puddle as the spa water around her.

Because he's a good man, and he knows what he wants.

So what was he doing? Just lurking there? Or did the suite have some kind of weird acoustic thing going on?

She cleared her throat gently. 'Are you busy?'

'Nope. Just unwinding.' Pause. 'Why?'

'I just thought…maybe we could talk.'

'Didn't you want to relax?'

'It's a bit…quiet.'

'I thought you'd be used to that after eight months on the road.'

Yeah. He had a point. Astonishing what two days of company did for a girl.

'Normally I'd have music in my bathroom.' Classical. Mellow.

That deep voice was rich with humour. 'You want me to sing something?'

The very idea added to her hot-water tingles. 'Talking will be fine.'

'Okay.' Another pause. 'What do you want to talk about?'

'I don't know. Where you grew up? Your family? Anything, really.'

The door gave a muffled rattle and Eve wondered if he'd leaned on it. She took the complimentary sponge from its packet and filled it with warm water, then squeezed it down her arms.

Rinse. Repeat.

The slow splashes filled the long silence and the steam started working on her pores. And her soul.

'I'm not sure my history will be particularly conducive to relaxation.'

The tightness in his voice paused her sponge mid-swab. 'Really, why?'

'My family's about as functional as yours.'

Dead, drunken mother and AWOL brother was going to be tough to top. But her curiosity was piqued. 'Where are they now?'

'They're still in Sydney.'

'That doesn't sound so very dramatic.'

'Growing up had…its challenges.'

Her sponging resumed. Eve closed her eyes and let herself tune in to the low rumble of his voice. 'Like what?'

Was that a resigned sigh through the door?

'My family weren't all that well off, but we didn't starve. We were okay.'

Uh-huh…?

'But it was the nineties. The decade of excess and success, and all that.'

Eve lay her head against the back of the bath and just listened.

'I have a brother, too, Eve,' Marshall went on. 'And poverty wasn't really his thing. So he took matters into his own hands and got quite…creative. Before long, the whole neighbourhood knew he was the go-to for whatever soft-core drug they needed.'

She opened her eyes and stared at the bathroom ceiling. After a moment she murmured, 'Your brother was a dealer?'

'An entrepreneur, according to him.'

Right. 'How long did that last?'

'Until very recently I couldn't have answered that at all. But let's just say business is as good as ever for Rick. I don't really see him any more.'

No wonder Marshall could empathise about Travis. He knew exactly what it was like to lose a brother.

'Whose decision was that?'

The only sound in the long, long silence that followed was the dripping of the shower into the spa.

'It's complicated,' he finally said.

Yeah, wasn't it always?

'I struggled growing up with Rick for a brother.'

'Because he was a criminal?'

'Because he was a hero.' He snorted. 'This was the back suburbs, remember. Pretty rough area to grow up. People loved him, they loved what he sold and they scrambled to be part of his inner circle. And sometimes that meant scrambling over me.'

There was something so…suppressed in his voice.

Eve lifted her head. 'Are you talking about girls?'

'Girls. Friends. Even a teacher or two with insalubrious habits.'

Oh, poor teenage Marshall. 'You resented him.'

'No, I loved him.'

'But you hated that,' she guessed.

'It meant I was no different to them. The sycophants. I just wanted to despise him and be done with it.'

So, there were many ways to lose a brother, then.

'Do you miss him?' she whispered.

'I did. For a long while. It felt like he was all I had, growing up. But I just focused my attention on my work and suddenly a decade had passed and I hadn't really thought about him at all. Or my mother. Or Christine. Or what they were all doing together.'

She pushed herself up a little more. 'Christine is with your brother?'

'She was.'

The door rattled slightly again, but not the knob. Down lower. And that was when Eve realised how very close they were sitting to each other. Him sunk down onto the floor of the suite, leaning on the door. Her lying back in warm luxury.

And only a single thin wall between them.

No wonder Marshall was wary of people. And no wonder the tight pain in his voice. 'I'm sorry. I should have asked you about something else.'

'It's okay. I got myself out. It's history now.'

'How do you go from a bad neighbourhood to working for the Federal Government?'

He laughed and she realised how attached she'd become to that sexy little chuckle.

'It will shock you to learn that meteorology is not the sexiest of the sciences.'

Not sexy? Had any of them *seen* Marshall Sullivan?

'But that meant there were scholarships going wasting, and one of them came to me. And it came with on-campus residency.'

'The scholarship was your ticket out?'

'At first, but soon I came to love meteorology. It's predictive. Stats and signs and forecasting. You always know what's coming with weather.'

'No surprises?' she murmured.

'I guess I was just looking for a life where you could spot the truth of something before it found you.'

Yeah. Given he'd been used by his earlier friends, cast off by his mother and then betrayed by his brother, maybe that wasn't surprising.

'It suits you.'

'Being a weatherman?'

'Busting the stereotype.' And how. 'I'm sorry I called you Weatherman.'

'I don't mind it as a nickname. As long as it's coming from you.'

'Why?' She laughed. 'What makes me so special?'

His answer, when it came, was immediate. 'How long have you got?'

The same kind of warmth that was soaking into her from without started to spread out from within. But she wrestled it back down. She couldn't afford to be feeling warm and fuzzy about anyone right now.

She made much of sitting up straighter in the spa bath. The bathroom equivalent of shuffling papers. 'Speaking of specials…what's on the menu tonight?'

Subtle, Read, real subtle.

But he let it go after a breath-stealing moment of indecision. 'Give me a second, I'll check.'

Good man, knows what he wants and compassionate.

Marshall Sullivan was just getting harder and harder to not like.

CHAPTER NINE

THIS WASN'T GOING to end well for him…

It had dawned on Marshall, somewhere between sitting at the bathroom door with his head tipped back against the timber and watching Eve tuck so enthusiastically into a bowl of Italian soup, that not everyone was rewarded for goodness. Any more than they were rewarded for doing the right thing.

Hadn't he got that by now?

But done was done. He'd made his choice and he was here. Only time would tell whether it was a crazily fatalistic or brilliantly optimistic decision. But since he was here and since she hadn't driven him off the road, he could use the time practically. He could try and get to know Eve a bit more. Understand her.

Maybe that way he could get a sense of her truth before it hit him like a cyclone.

'Can I ask you what happened with Travis?' he asked, passing his empty plate into the long fingers she reached out and starting at the most obvious point. 'When he disappeared.'

Her bright, just-fed eyes dulled just a little.

'One day he was there—' she shrugged '—the next he was gone.'

'That simple?'

'It wasn't simple.'

'Losing someone never is.'

He fell to silence and waited her out. It had certainly worked well enough on him while she was in the bath. He'd offered up much more than he'd ever shared with anyone else.

'She was drunk,' Eve finally murmured and he didn't need to ask who. 'She'd passed the few hours of Travis's Under-Fifteens hockey at the nearest pub. As far as anyone could tell, she thought she was okay to drive.'

Oh. Crap. Drunk and in charge of the safety of a fourteen-year-old boy.

'Was she an alcoholic?' That certainly explained Eve's moderate approach to liquor.

Her dark head slowly nodded. 'And the whole neighbourhood got to hear about it.'

He let his hands fall between his splayed thighs. Stared at them. 'That's a lot for a girl to handle.'

'It was a lot for all of us to handle,' she defended. 'Travis watched Mum die, Dad endured her reputation being trashed and I...'

'What did you do?'

'I coped. I got on with things. Took over caring for them both.'

'A lot of pressure.'

'Actually, it was okay then.' *Then*... 'It gave me something to focus on. Purpose.

'Dad pulled Trav out of school for the last few months of the year and that might have been a mistake. It took him from his friends, his sport, his structure. He lost his way a bit. He got back into it the next year and got okay grades but he was never cheeky and joyous again. I think we all just got used to the new, flat Travis.' She took a big swallow of water. 'Maybe we got used to a new *us*, too.'

Yeah. Numbness crept up on a person...

'It wasn't easy, those first couple of years. At first it was all about getting him out of the hospital, but then life had to... We had to just get on with it, you know?'

Yep. He certainly did know all about just getting on... Story of his life. But not everyone could do it. There were times *he* really wanted to just opt out. In some ways maybe he had.

'What changed? To make him leave?'

Her beautiful face pinched up slightly. 'Um...'

Whatever it was, it was hurting her.

'There was an inquest the year he went, and there was all this media interest in the accident again.'

'Years later?'

'A legal queue, I guess.' Her slight shoulders shrugged and he'd never wanted to hold someone more in his life. But she looked so fragile he worried she'd shatter. 'So much pressure on all of us again.'

He shifted closer. Leaned into her. 'He couldn't take it?'

Her head came up but she didn't quite meet his eyes. 'I couldn't. I desperately wanted to understand what happened but I couldn't go through it all again. Supporting Dad, mothering Travis. Just as things were getting normal. I just couldn't do it while we relived the accident over and over again.'

Suddenly her blazing need to find her brother began to make more sense.

'What did you do?'

'I went back to my own place. Replaced the dead pot plants with new ones, cleaned the gutters, threw out years of junk mail, started easing back into my own life.'

'And what did Travis do?'

'I didn't abandon them,' she defended hotly. 'I still visited, did sisterly things. But they were both men. They needed to step up, too. They agreed.'

He said nothing, knowing the question was almost certainly in his eyes. *But...?*

'Trav was finding it harder than any of us realised. The inquest brought it all back just as he might have started to become stronger. He turned eighteen, and drifted further and further from us emotionally.' She shook her head. 'And then he just left. Right in the middle of the inquest. We thought he'd just taken off for a few days to avoid the pressure but then it was a week, and then two. We finally reported him missing when we hadn't heard anything for a month.'

'You blame yourself.'

Her slim shoulders lifted and then sagged again. 'I wasn't there for him.'

'Yeah, you were. For years.'

'But I withdrew.'

'You *survived*. Big difference.'

Her tortured eyes lifted. 'Why wouldn't he talk to me? If he was struggling.'

Yeah—she'd been carrying that around a while; he recognised the signs of soul baggage.

'Eighteen-year-old boys don't talk to anyone about their feelings, Eve. I've been that kid.'

Old agony changed her face. He pulled her into his arms. 'You aren't responsible for Travis being missing.'

'That's what people say, isn't it,' she said against his chest. 'In this kind of situation. But what if I am?'

Okay, so she'd heard this before and still not believed it. A rough kind of urgency came over him.

'What if it had nothing to do with you and everything to do with a young boy who watched his mother die? On top of the day-to-day trauma of having an alcoholic for a mother. My own mother was no prize,' he admitted, 'but she was at least present.'

He'd almost forgotten that she was Eve's mother, too. She seemed so disconnected from her past. 'What if you had turned up on his doorstep every single day and he had still done this?'

Tortured eyes glistened over. 'He's my brother.'

'He's a grown man, Eve.'

'Only just. Eighteen is still a kid. And with the anxiety disorder, and depression…'

'Which he was being treated for, right? He was on it.'

'Then why did he leave?'

It was always going to come back to that question, wasn't

it? And Eve was never going to be free of the big, looming question mark. 'Only Travis knows.'

She fell to an anguished kind of silence, picking at the fabric on the sofa beneath her. Marshall stacked up the rest of the dishes and put the lot outside his door on the tray left there by the staff and quietly turned back. He crossed to her and held out a hand.

'Come on.'

She peered up at him with wide, hurt eyes. 'Where are we going?'

'I'm walking you home. I think you need to be in your own place right now, surrounded by familiar things.'

She didn't argue for once. Instead, she slipped her fingers into his and let him pull her up and towards the suite's door.

'It's not really my place,' she murmured as they stepped out into the hall. 'And most of them aren't my things.'

How weird that such sorrowful words could bring him such a lurch of hope. If Eve wasn't all that attached to the Bedford or its contents maybe there was hope for him yet. Maybe he could wedge himself a place in her distracted, driven world.

He kicked off one of his shoes and left it wedged in the doorway so that he didn't lock himself out.

Down in the almost empty car park he opened the bus for her and followed her through to her bedroom. She didn't so much as glance at that presumption, and she didn't look the slightest bit anxious that he might stay. She just accepted it as though they'd been doing it for years.

He pressed his key-card into her hand. 'Breakfast on the balcony at eight?'

'Okay.'

He flipped back her bed covers and waited for her to crawl in, then he folded them back over her and tucked her so firmly in that she resembled something that had just tumbled out of a sarcophagus.

'It's not your fault, Eve.'

He was going to tell her that every day of their lives if he had to.

She nodded, but he wasn't foolish enough to think that she actually believed it. Maybe she just accepted that he didn't think so. Bending brought him dangerously close to her lips, but he veered up at the last moment and pressed his to her hot forehead instead.

'Breakfast. Eight o'clock.'

She didn't agree. She didn't even nod. But her eyes were filled with silent promise and so he killed the lights and backed out of the room and then the bus, giving the big back door a security rattle before leaving her snug and safe inside.

It went against everything in him to leave her in the car park, but Eve had been doing this a long time and she was a grown, competent woman. Just because she'd opened up a little and shown him some of her childhood vulnerability didn't mean he could treat her like the child she'd almost been when her mother killed herself and nearly her brother.

As hard as that was.

He limped along on one shoe and returned to the big, lonely suite.

A gentle kind of rocking roused Marshall out of a deep, comfortable sleep. The suite was as dark as an outback road but he knew, instantly, what was going on.

Except it wasn't eight o'clock. And this wasn't morning.

A warm, soft body slid in next to him, breathing carefully. He shunted over a bit to make room, but she only followed him, keeping their bodies close.

'Eve…?'

As if there was any question.

She snuggled up hard into his side. 'Shh. It's late.'

Or early, he suspected. But he wasn't about to argue with whatever God had sent her back to him, and he wasn't about to ruin a good thing by reading something into this. Instead, he took it—and Eve—at face value and just gathered her into him so that his sleepy heat could soak into her cold limbs.

But he wasn't so strong that he could resist pressing his lips to her hair and leaving them there.

And she wasn't of a mind to move away, apparently.

'I have no expectations,' he murmured against her scalp. 'If you tell me that going our separate ways yesterday felt okay to you then that's cool, I know where I stand. But it felt anything but okay to me and I came back so that we could just—'

'Finish things up more civilly?'

'—*not* finish things up,' he said into the dark. 'Maybe just explore this a little more. See where it goes.'

Her breathing filled his ears. His heart.

'I slept with you because you were riding off into the horizon the next day,' she whispered.

He turned a little more towards her, trying to make her out in the dark. 'And I slept with you knowing that. But then I discovered something about horizons.'

'What?' she mumbled.

'They're an awfully long way away.'

She pushed up onto one elbow, robbing him of her warmth. 'So…you're just going to ride shotgun for the next…what—days? Weeks?'

'Until we know.'

Her voice sounded tantalisingly close to his ear. 'Know what?'

'Whether we have potential.'

'You're in the middle of an epic road trip. It's a terrible time to be looking for potential.'

She was right. He should be aiming for fast, casual and uncomplicated. Like she had.

'That's the thing, Eve. I wasn't looking. It seems to have found me.'

She had nothing to say to that, but her steady breathing told him she was still awake.

Listening.

Thinking.

He bundled her back in close and fell with her—lips to hairline—into a deep slumberous heaven.

CHAPTER TEN

Waking the next morning was like an action replay of the morning before—but without all the action. This time, he didn't catch Eve creeping out of bed. This time, she was not freaking out and sucking all the warmth out of the room. This time, she was not back-pedalling madly from what they'd shared the night before.

Even though what they'd shared overnight was more intimate and meaningful than anything they'd done with each other back at the campsite.

Two bodies, pressed together in sleep. Wrapped around each other. Talking.

No sex.

But infinitely more loaded.

'Morning,' she murmured before her eyes even opened.

'How long have you been awake?'

'Long enough to feel you staring.'

'It's the novelty.' He chuckled.

Come on. Open them...

But she just smiled and squirrelled in closer, as if she was getting ready to go back to sleep.

'It's eight o'clock,' he pointed out.

And then her eyes opened—drugged, languorous, and he'd never seen anything quite so beautiful.

'No, it's not.'

'Yeah, it really is.'

And this was a workday for both of them. Technically.

Her eyes fluttered shut and she wiggled deeper into the covers. Okay, so he was going to have to be the brave one.

'So, look at you in my bed…' he hinted.

One eye half opened and he waited for the quip to follow. Something sharp and brilliant and completely protective. But he didn't get one. Her second eye opened and locked on him, clear and steady.

'I just woke up in the middle of the night,' she murmured, 'and knew this is where I wanted to be.'

Right. What could he say to that? This was what he'd come back for, wasn't it? To see what might grow between them. Wasn't that what he'd been murmuring at midnight about? Yet, now that he was faced with it, it suddenly seemed overwhelmingly real.

He cleared his throat. 'Breakfast?'

'In town, maybe? After I get set up.'

Right. Work.

'I have to do my thing today, too.' For the people paying him.

'Where's the weather station?'

He told her and she asked a question or two. More than enough to muddle his mind. He was in bed with a living, breathing, *radiating* woman and they were talking about the weather again. Literally. But somehow it didn't feel like small talk. It felt big.

And then it hit him why.

They were having a *couple* conversation. Comfortable. Easy. And they were having it in bed. Where all conversations should happen. And that was enough to scare him upright.

'I'm going to grab a shower, then I'll get us some food while you set up.'

She pushed up onto her elbows, blinking. 'Sorry if I made things weird.'

He forced a relaxed smile onto his face.

'Not weird. Just—' *dangerously appealing* '—new.'

He padded into the bathroom and put himself under the shower Eve had enjoyed so much the night before. Images filled his head—of Eve standing with the water streaming over her slight body, head tipped back, issuing those sounds he'd heard while he leaned on the doorframe out in the hall. How badly he'd wanted to step inside and join her. Shower with her until the end of time. And now, here he was freaking out that his dreams might be coming true.

In his world, dreams didn't come true.

They shattered.

It was so hard to trust the good feelings.

He nudged the taps and cut out half of the hot water feed and then made sure to keep his shave brief.

When he emerged, Eve was gone.

For half a heartbeat the old doubts lurched to the surface but then he remembered she had no clothes up here, only what she'd crept up the stairs in, and he opened the suite door a crack and peered down through the hallway window. Like a seasoned stalker. Long enough to see Eve heading back across the car park.

Come on, man. Pull it together. This is what you wanted.

He'd just learned the hard way not to want. It only led to disappointment.

So Eve had opted for more comfortable accommodation overnight. No biggie. That was hardly a declaration of passion. She'd snuggled in and enjoyed the heat coming off him, and today she was all about Travis again.

Eve was always about Travis.

It was part of what intrigued him about her. That fathomless compassion.

But it was part of what scared him, too. Because how could there be room for him with all that emotion already going on?

He quickly shrugged something decent on and ran a quick comb through his hair so that when she swiped the suite's door he was clothed and everything that needed brushing was brushed.

He threw her a neutral smile. 'Good to go?'

The pause before she answered was full of silent query. 'Yep. Meet you in front of the Town Hall?'

Wherever that was. 'Yup.'

The question mark shifted from her eyes to her soft smile but she simply turned and let him follow her back down to where his bike was parked. She headed for the bus.

'Egg and bacon burger?' he called.

'Sounds great.'

Great.

Okay, so it was officially his turn to be off. Most guys would be stoked to wake up to a warm, willing body but, instead of converting the opportunity to a goal, he'd let it get under his skin. Weird him out. Not the best start, true, but Eve didn't look too tragic about it. Her mind was back on her brother already.

As was always the way.

The bumbling MP yesterday was pretty normal, in Eve's experience. In fact, he'd been more tactful than many of the people she'd tried to explain herself to in the past.

Herself… Her choices.

But the only people who'd understood her odyssey the way Marshall had were the other family members in her missing-persons network. Which did, in fact, make him pretty darned exceptional.

Eve smiled and passed a poster to an older lady who stopped to peruse her display. The stranger took her time and looked at every single face before wandering off, which Eve particularly appreciated. Nothing worse than the glancers. Glancing was worse than not looking at all, in some ways. Eve knew it was a big ask to hope that people might remember one face, let alone dozens, but there was no chance of people remembering them from the wall displays in post offices that were half obscured by piles of post packs or pull-down passport photo screens most of the time.

Something inside her had shifted last night when Marshall

told her about his brother. As if he went from adversary to equal in her mind. He'd effectively lost a brother, too—to circumstance—so he knew what it was like to give up on a family member.

Except, in Marshall's case, he was the one who'd walked away.

And didn't that tear her up. Half of her wanted to hug him for the personal strength it must have taken to leave an intolerable family situation so young. The other half wanted to shake him and remind him he had a brother. A living, breathing brother.

And those weren't to be sneezed at.

She never would have picked him for the product of a rough neighbourhood, even with all the tattoos. He was just too *normal*. Beneath the 'keep your distance' leather smokescreen. But to find out that someone so close to him was neck-deep in criminal activity… That just made what he'd done with his life even more remarkable. Finished school, tackled university and then got himself the straightest and smartest of straight, smart jobs.

Meteorology.

A tiny smile crept, unbidden, to her lips. Who knew that she'd ever get quite so hot and bothered by a weatherman?

Yet here she was, very much bothered. And decidedly hot under the covers.

At least she had been last night.

Crawling in with him hadn't been quite the spontaneous exercise she'd confessed. The sprint across the car park had been as sobering as it was chilly and she had plenty of opportunity to think better of it. But she hadn't—because a big part of her had wanted him to roll over, see her and just keep on rolling. Up and over onto her. To make love to her like he had the first time—all breathless and uninhibited.

Another taste of lightness.

Her days were consumed by her brother—couldn't someone

else have her nights? When she'd normally be asleep? Wouldn't it be okay to let go just for those few short hours? To forget?

But Marshall hadn't taken advantage. He'd just tugged her close, murmured hot, lovely words in her ear and pulled her into unconsciousness behind him. And it was only as she'd fallen asleep that she'd realised how badly she wanted *not to* do the obvious thing. The easy thing.

Sleeping with Marshall was easy.

Falling for him would be treacherous.

But morning would always come. And it dragged reality with it.

Eve's reality was that she still had a monumental task ahead of her. Marshall had chased her up the highway to see what might form between them if they gave it a chance, but how could there be any kind of something between them while she had this dismal marathon to complete?

Good sex was one thing. A *happy families* future was quite another.

She had no room for anything beyond right now.

And both of them knew that *happy families* was just a myth. They knew it firsthand.

'Thank you,' she murmured belatedly to the man who took a poster as though from an unattended pile. She'd been so lost in thought, that might as well have been true.

Nope, she hadn't promised Marshall anything more than *right now* and he hadn't asked for it.

Two people could go a long way on *right now*.

The south-western corner of Western Australia was packed with small, wine-rich country towns, each with unique personality and spaced close enough for tourists to hop from one to another on their weekend trails.

Papering the two hundred square kilometres ahead with posters was going to be a much bigger job than the two thousand before it.

But they did a good job together, she and Marshall. When

he wasn't working, or they weren't curled up together in her bus or a motel room, he'd be with her, plastering Trav's face all over the towns they visited. Handing her the pins or the tape or the staple gun. Nothing she couldn't have done for herself but—boy—was it good not to have to.

Somehow, having someone to share all of this with made it more bearable. And she hadn't realised how unbearable it had become. How utterly soul-destroying. Until she felt her soul starting to scab over.

She glanced sideways at Marshall's handsome face. How fast she'd adapted to having him here by her side during her displays of *The Missing*. How willing she'd been to bring him into her journey.

A problem shared…

A man approached from the far end of the street, folded paper in his hands. He looked grim and twitchy.

'Movie tonight?'

Marshall's voice pulled her focus back to him. The two of them hadn't braved a movie since *that* night in her bus. As if the entire art form was now too loaded. The last time they'd settled in to watch a movie together they'd ended up sharing so much more.

'Maybe,' she said breathlessly. A girl couldn't live on spooning alone. And she was fairly sure neither could a man. They were well overdue for a rematch. The way Marshall's eyes locked on hers said maybe he thought so, too.

The stranger still hovered and it was only as he turned away, stuffing the paper in his pocket, that Eve's brain finally comprehended that he wanted to say something.

'I'm sorry,' she called, stretching taller in her seat. 'Can I help you?'

The man slowed. Turned.

'Do you know him?' he said, holding up the crumpled paper as he approached. It was one of her posters.

A tingle tickled between her shoulders and grew outwards

until gooseflesh puckered under her shirt. 'He's my brother. Why? Do you recognise him?'

The man stepped one pace closer. 'Not sure. He looks familiar.'

Eve shot to her feet. 'What do you mean?'

'Just that I feel like I've seen him before. But I don't want to get your hopes up if I'm wrong…'

'I don't need certainty,' she was quick to reassure, 'just leads.'

She felt Marshall's heat as he stood behind her and her heart began to hammer. God, she'd been so wrapped up in the promise in his eyes she'd nearly let this guy walk off. A guy who might know something.

'Where do you think you know him from?' Marshall asked.

The guy switched focus. 'I really can't say. Just…somewhere. And recently.'

'How recent? Two months? Six?' Eve could hear the urgency in her own voice but was incapable of easing it. A big hand fell on her shoulder as if to physically suppress her.

'Where do you live?' Marshall asked, much more casually.

The guy responded to his even tone. 'Here. In Augusta. But I don't think I know him from here.'

God, the idea of that. That Travis might be right here in this little seaside town…

'Somewhere else?'

'I run trucks. Maybe I saw him on one of those. In another—'

'What other town?' Eve pressed, and Marshall squeezed harder.

Are you freaking kidding me? The first reasonable lead she'd had in nearly nine months and Marshall wanted her to relax? Every nerve in her body was firing in a soup of adrenaline.

'Where do you do your runs?' Marshall asked calmly.

'Anywhere in the South West,' the man said, visibly uncomfortable at having started the conversation at all. He immediately started retreating from his earlier thoughts. 'Look, I'm probably wrong—'

Deep panic fisted in her gut.

'*No!* Please don't start second-guessing yourself,' Eve rushed on, critically aware that her urgency was pushing him further away. She fought to breathe more evenly. God, how close she'd come to just not calling out to him.

What was happening to her?

'The subconscious is a powerful thing,' she urged. 'It probably knows something your conscious mind can't quite grasp.'

The man's eyes filled with pity and, in that moment, she saw herself as others must. As Marshall must.

Obsessed. Desperate. Pathetic.

And she didn't like his view of her one little bit.

Lines appeared on the man's time-weathered brow. 'I'm just not sure…'

'How about just jotting down the routes you usually take?' Marshall grabbed another poster, flipped it over to the blank side and handed it and a pen to the man. 'We can take it from there.'

More lines formed in his weathered skin. 'I have two-dozen routes. That'll take time…'

They were losing him. And the best lead she'd had in an age…

Eve dashed to the front of the bus and rummaged in the glove box with clammy hands for the maps she carried detailing every region she was in. One was marked up with her own routes—to make sure she never missed a town or junction—but her spare was blank, a clean slate. She thrust the spare into the man's hands.

'On this then, just highlight the routes you take. I can do the rest.'

Possibility flickered over his face. 'Can I take this with me?'

The fist squeezed harder. Not because she risked losing a four-dollar map. But she risked losing a tangible link with Travis. 'Can't you do it here…?'

'Take it,' Marshall interrupted. 'Anything you can give us will be great.'

The stranger's eyes flicked between the two of them 'Hopefully, I can be clearer somewhere…away from here.'

Eve took two steps towards the man as he retreated with the map in his hand. She spun to Marshall. 'I should go with him.'

His strong hand clamped around her wrist. 'No. You should let him go somewhere quiet and do what he has to do. He's not going to be able to concentrate with you hovering over him.'

Hovering…! As if they were talking about her chaperoning a teenage date and not possibly finding her brother. 'I just want to—'

'I know exactly what you want, Eve, and how you're feeling right now. But stalking the guy won't get you what you need. Just leave him be. He'll come back.'

'But he's the first person that's seen Travis.'

'*Possibly* seen Travis, and if you push any harder he's going to decide he never actually saw a thing. Leave him to his process, Eve.'

She glanced up the street, hunting for the man's distinctive walk. Two blocks away she spotted him, turning into the local pub. She swung baleful eyes onto Marshall.

'Leave him to his process,' he articulated.

Deep inside she knew he was right, but everything in her screamed for action. Something. Anything.

'Easy for you to say!'

He took a long breath. 'There's nothing easy about watching you suffer, Eve.'

'Try feeling it some time,' she muttered.

She turned away roughly but he caught her. 'I do feel it. In you. Every day—'

'No, I mean try *feeling* it, Marshall. From this side of the fence.'

'It's not about sides—'

'Spoken like someone who's more used to cutting people out of their life than being cut out.'

For a moment she thought he was going to let that go, but he was a man, not a saint. Words blew warmly behind her ear as Marshall murmured in this public place, 'And what's that supposed to mean, exactly?'

'What you imagine it means, I'm sure,' she gritted.

'Eve, I know this is frustrating—'

She spun on him. 'Do you, Marshall? You've been travelling with me all of ten days. Multiply that by twenty-five and then tell me how you think I should be feeling as my only lead walks away from me and into a bar.'

His lips tightened but he took several controlled breaths. 'You need an outlet and I'm convenient.'

Spare me the psychoanalysis!

'How did this become about you?' she hissed. 'This is about me and Travis.'

She glanced at the pub again and twisted her hands together.

Warm fingers brought her chin around until her eyes met his. '*Everything* is about Travis with you, Eve. Everything.'

That truly seemed to pain him.

The judgment in his gaze certainly hurt her. 'Forgive me for trying to stay focused on my entire purpose out here.'

The words sounded awful coming off her lips, doubly so because, deep down, she knew he didn't deserve her cruelty. But did he truly not get the importance of this moment? How rare it was. How it felt to go nearly nine months without a single lead and then to finally get one?

A lead she'd almost missed because she was so off mission.

She dropped back into her seat.

All week she'd been going through the motions. Putting up posters, staffing her unhappy little table, answering questions about the faces in her display. But she hadn't actively promoted. She hadn't forced posters on anyone. She hadn't made a single real impression.

All she'd done was sit here looking at Marshall. Or thinking about him when he was gone. Letting herself buy into his hopeless fantasy.

She'd failed Travis. Again.

And she'd nearly missed her only lead.

Marshall sat back and considered her in silence. And when he spoke it was careful but firm.

'I think it might be time to stop, Eve.'

She did stop. All movement, all breath. And just stared.

'Maybe it's time to go home,' he continued. 'This isn't good for you.'

When she finally spoke it was with icy precision.

'How good for me do you imagine it is sitting around the house, wondering whether Travis is alive or dead and whether anyone will give him more than the occasional cursory check twice a year?'

'It's been a year—'

'I know. I've been living it every single day. But I'm nearly done.'

'You're not nearly done. You still have one third of the country to go.'

'But only ten per cent of the population,' she gritted.

'That's assuming that you haven't missed him already.' *And assuming he is still alive.* The words practically trembled on those perfect lips.

She glared. 'What happened to "What you're doing is logical"?'

'I meant that. I completely understand why you're doing it.'

'And so…?'

'I don't like what *it's doing to you*, Eve. This search is hurting you. I hate watching it.'

'Then leave. No one's forcing you to stay.'

'It's not that easy—'

But whatever logical, persuasive thing he was about to say choked as she ran over the top of him. 'Maybe you're just unhappy that I'm putting him ahead of you. Maybe your male ego can't handle taking second place.'

She'd never seen someone's eyes bruise before, but Marshall's did. And it dulled them irreparably.

'Actually, that's the one thing I'm more than used to.'

The fist inside tightened further. How could she do this? How could she choose between two men she cared so much about? Marshall was, at least, stable and healthy and capable of looking after himself. Travis was…

Well, who knew what Travis was? Or where.

But his need was unquestionably greater.

She ripped the emotional plaster off and pushed to her feet. 'I think it's time for us to go our separate ways.'

The bruising intensified. 'Do you?'

'It's been lovely—'

'But you're done now?'

'Come on, Marshall, how long would we have been able to keep this up, anyway? Your circuit's coming to an end.' And her funds were running out.

Her casual dismissal turned the vacuum behind his lids to permafrost. 'Is that right?'

'I don't have room for you, Marshall.'

'No, you really don't, do you.'

'I need to stay focused on Travis.'

'Why?'

'Because he needs me. Who else is going to look for him?' Or look *out* for him. Like she should have all along.

'Face facts, Eve,' he said, face gentle but words brutal. 'He's either gone or he's *choosing* to stay away. You said it yourself.'

Her breaths seemed to have no impact on the oxygen levels in her body. Dark spots began to populate the edges of her vision. 'I can't believe that.'

'People walk away all the time. For all kinds of reasons.'

'Maybe *you* do.'

His voice grew as cold as her fingers. 'Excuse me?'

She started to shake all over. 'I should have thought to seek your perspective before. I have an expert on cutting loose right here with me. You tell me why a perfectly healthy young man would just walk away from his family.'

Marshall's face almost contorted with the control he was trying to exert. 'You think I didn't struggle, leaving them?'

'As far as I can see, you crossed a line through them and walked away and you seem no worse for wear. That's quite a talent.'

'Are you truly that self-absorbed,' he whispered, 'that you can't appreciate what that was like for me?'

'Yet you chose it.'

Where were these words coming from? Just pouring like toxic lava over her lips. Uncontrollable. Unstoppable.

Awful.

'Sometimes, Eve, all your choices are equally bad and you just have to make one.'

'Just go and don't look back?' she gritted. 'Who does that?'

Something flared in his eyes. Realisation. 'You're angry at Travis. For leaving.'

I'm furious *at Travis for leaving*, she screamed inside. But outwardly she simply said, 'My brother left against his will.'

How many police counsellors had she had that argument with? Or fights with her father.

'What if he didn't?' Marshall urged. 'What if he left because he couldn't imagine staying?'

Pfff... 'Someone's been reading up on the missing-persons websites.'

'Don't mock me, Eve. I wanted to understand you better—'

'Those people were desperate or scared or sick. The Travis I know wouldn't do that.'

'Maybe he wasn't your Travis, have you thought about that? Maybe he's not the kid brother you raised any more.'

The trembles were full-body shudders now.

Marshall stepped closer. Lowered his voice. 'Do you see how much of your life he's consumed, Eve? This obsessive search. It's ruining you.'

'If I don't do it, who will?' she croaked.

'But at what cost?'

'My time. My money. All mine to spend.'

He took her hand. 'And how much of life are you missing while you're out here spending it? I'm right here, Eve. Living. Breathing. But any part of you that might enjoy that is completely occupied by someone who's—'

His teeth cracked shut.

Nausea practically washed over her. 'Go on. Say it.'

'Eve—'

'Say it! You think he's dead.'

'I fear he's a memory, one way or another. And I think that memory is stopping you from living your life just as much as when your mother died.'

'Says the man who hides out behind a face full of hair and leather armour to avoid facing his demons.'

Marshall took a long silent breath.

'This has become an unhealthy obsession for you, Eve. A great idea, practically, but devastating personally. You stripped yourself away from all your support structures. Your colleagues. Your friends. Your family. The people who could have kept you healthy and sane.'

'So we're back to me being crazy?'

'Eve, you're not—'

'You need to go, Marshall,' she urged. 'I can't do what I have to do with you here. That guy nearly walked off because I was off my game. I was busy mooning after you.'

'This is my fault?'

She wrapped her arms around her torso. 'I nearly let my only lead in a year walk off because I was distracted with you.'

'I guess I should at least be happy I'm a distraction.'

Misery soaked through her. 'You are much more than a distraction, but don't you get it? I don't have room for you—for us—in my life. In my heart.'

'You don't have room for happiness? Doesn't that tell you anything?'

'I don't get to be happy, Marshall,' she yelled, heedless of the passers-by. 'Not until Travis is back home where he belongs.'

Those dreadful words echoed out into the seaside air.

'Do you hear yourself, Eve? You're punishing yourself for failing Travis.'

The muscles around her ribs began to squeeze. Hard. 'Thank you for your concern but I'm not your responsibility.'

'So, I just walk away from you, knowing that you're slowly self-destructing?'

'I will be fine.'

'You won't be fine. You'll search the rest of the country and what will you do when you get back to your start point and you've found no sign of him? Start again from the top?'

The thought of walking away from this search without her brother was unimaginable.

'I will always look for him,' she vowed.

And that wasn't fair on someone as vibrant as Marshall. Hadn't he been sidelined enough in his life? She shook her head slowly.

'Find someone else, Marshall. Please.'

Someone who could offer him what he needed. Someone who wouldn't hurt him. Someone who could prioritise him.

'I don't want someone else, Eve,' he breathed. 'I want you.'

Those three simple words stole the oxygen from her cells. The words and the incredibly earnest glitter of Marshall's flecked grey eyes that watched her warily now.

Of all the times. Of all the places. Of all the men.

The seductive rush of just letting all of this go, curling herself into Marshall's arms and letting him look after her. Letting him carry half of all this weight. Of parking the bus for good somewhere and building a new life for herself with whatever she had left. With him. Of little grey-eyed kids running amuck in the sand dunes. Learning to fish. Hanging out with their dad.

But the kids of her imagination morphed, as she watched, into Travis when he was little. Scrabbling along the riverbank at the back of their house. Getting muddy. Just being a kid. A kid she loved so completely.

Eve took several long breaths. 'If you care for me as much

as you say you do, then what I need should matter to you. And what I need is my brother. Home. Safe. That's all I've got room for.'

'And then what?'

She lifted her eyes to his.

'After that, Eve. What's the plan then? You going to move in with him to make sure he stays safe? Takes his medication? Stays healthy? How far does this responsibility you feel go?'

The truth...? Just as there was nothing but black after not finding Travis, there was nothing but an opaque, uncertain mist after bringing him home. She'd just never let herself think about either outcome in real terms. She'd just focused on the ten kilometres in front of her at all times.

And the ten kilometres in front of her now needed to be solo.

She twisted her fingers into his. 'You're a fantastic guy, Marshall. Find someone to be happy with.'

'I thought I was working on that.'

It was time for some hard truths. 'You're asking me to choose between a man I've loved my whole life and a man I've—'

She caught herself before the word fell across her lips, but only just.

—*known ten days.*

No matter how long it felt.

Or how like love.

'Would I like to be important to you?' he urged. 'Yes. Would I like, two years from now, to live together in a timber cottage and get to make love to you twice a day in a forest pool beside our timber cabin? Yes. I'm not going to lie. But this is the real world. And in the real world I'm not asking you to choose *me*, Eve. I'm begging you to choose *life*. You cannot keep doing this to yourself.'

She stepped a foot closer to him, close enough to feel his warmth. She slid her unsteady hand up the side of his face and curled her fingers gently around his jaw.

'It's a beautiful image, Marshall,' she said past the ball of hurt in her chest. 'But if I'm going to indulge fantasies, it has to be the one where that guy with the map comes back and it leads me to finding Travis.'

The life drained right out of his face and his eyes dropped, but when they came back up they were filled with something worse than hurt.

Resignation.

This was a man who was used to coming last.

'You deserve to be someone's priority, Marshall,' she whispered. 'I'm so sorry.'

His eyes glittered dangerously with unshed truth and he struggled visibly to master his breathing, and then his larynx.

Finally he spoke.

'I'm scared what will happen to you if I can't be there with you to hold you—to help you—when you find him, or when you don't,' he enunciated. 'Promise me you'll go home to your father and start your life over and pick up where you left off.'

'Marshall—'

'Promise me, Eve. And I'll go. I'll leave you in peace.'

Peace. The very idea of that was almost laughable. Not knowing the true nature of the world, as she did now. Blissfully ignorant Eve was long gone.

And so she looked Marshall in the eye.

And she lied.

CHAPTER ELEVEN

DID EVE HAVE any idea how bad she was at deceit?

Or maybe she just saved her best lies for the ones she told herself. There was no way on earth that this driven, strong woman was going to go back to suburbia after this was all over.

She was too far gone.

And, try as he might, she was not letting him into her life long enough for him to have any kind of influence on what happened from here. His job was to walk away. To respect her decision.

To do what his brain said was right and not what his heart screamed was so very wrong.

I'm choosing Travis.

His gut twisted in hard on itself. Wasn't that the story of his life? Had he really expected the very fabric of the universe to have changed overnight? Eve needed to finish this, even if she had no true idea of what that might mean.

He needed her to be whole.

He just hadn't understood he was part of the rending apart.

He rested his hand over Eve's on his cheek, squeezed gently and then tugged hers down and over.

'I hope you find him,' he murmured against the soft skin of her palm.

What a ridiculously lame thing to say.

But it was definitely better than begging her to change her mind. Or condemning her to search, half-crazed, forever.

He stepped back. And then back again. And the cold air between them made it easier to take a very necessary third step. Within a few more, he was turning and crossing the road without a backward glance.

Which was how he generally did things.

You crossed a line through them and walked away.

Did she truly believe that he could cauterise entire sections of his life without any ill effect? That he was that cold? His issues arose from caring too much, not too little. But maybe she was also right about it being a life skill, because experience was sure going to help him now.

This was every bit as hard as walking away from his mother and brother.

Eve was not going to be okay. He could feel it in his bones. She had no idea how much she needed him. Someone. Anyone. And if he could feel that protective of her after just a few short weeks, how much must she burn with the need to find and protect the baby brother she'd loved all his life?

He kept walking up the main street through town but then turned down a side street as soon as he was out of her view and doubled back to slide in the side door of a café fronting onto the same road he'd just walked down. From his table he could see Eve, behind her display table, rocking back and forth in the cold air.

If that guy didn't come back soon, he was going to go and drag him out of that pub and frogmarch him back up the street. If Eve wasn't going to walk away from this whole crusade, and she wasn't going to have him by her side, then he was going to do everything he could to make sure that it all came out okay.

So that *she* came out okay.

The waitress delivered his coffee and he cupped his frigid hands around it and watched the woman who'd taken up residence in the heart he'd assumed was empty. The organ he thought had long since atrophied from lack of use.

She sat, hunched, surrounded by *The Missing*, curled forwards and eyes downcast. Crying in body if not in tears. Looking for all the world as bereft and miserable as he felt.

She wasn't trying to hurt him. She hadn't turned into a monster overnight. She was just overwhelmed with the pressure of this unachievable task she'd set herself.

She just had priorities. And he couldn't be one of them. It was that simple.

At least she'd been honest.

And if he was going to be, she'd never pretended it was otherwise. She'd never promised him more than right now. No matter what he'd hoped for.

So maybe he was making progress in life after all. At this rate he might be ready for a proper relationship by the time he was in his sixties.

Out on the street, Eve's body language changed. She pushed to her feet, as alert and rigid as the kangaroos they drove past regularly, her face turned towards the sea. A moment later, the guy from the pub shuffled back into view, handed her the folded map and spoke to her briefly, pointing a couple of times to places on the map.

Marshall's eyes ignored him, staying fixed on the small face he'd come to care so much about. Eve nodded, glanced at the map and said something brief before farewelling him. Then she sank back down onto her chair and pulled the map up against her chest, hard.

And then the tears flowed.

Every cell in his body wanted to dump his coffee and jog back across the road. To be there for her. To hold her. Impossible to know whether the guy had been unable to help, after all, and the tears were heartbreak. Or maybe they were joy at finally having a lead. Or maybe they were despair at a map criss-crossed with dozens of routes which really left her no further ahead than she'd started.

He'd never know.

And the not ever knowing might just kill him.

His fingers stilled with the coffee cup halfway to his mouth.

At last, he had some small hint of what hell every day was for Eve. Of why she couldn't just walk away from this, no matter how bad it was becoming for her. Of why she had no room for anything—or anyone—else in her heart. Adding to the emotional weight she carried around every day was not going to change the situation. Loving her, no matter how much, was not going to transform her. There was only one thing that would.

Someone needed to dig that brother of hers out from under whatever rock he'd found for himself. For better or worse.

A sudden buzzing in his pocket startled him enough to make him spill hot coffee over the edge of his mug and he scrambled to wipe the spillage with a napkin with one hand while fishing his phone out with the other.

He glanced at the screen and then swiped with suddenly nerveless fingers.

'Rick?'

'Hey,' his brother said. 'I've got something for you.'

Thank God for Rick's shady connections. And for health regulators. And maybe for Big Brother.

And thank God, for Eve's sake, that Travis Read was, apparently, still alive.

Rick had hammered home that the kid's name wouldn't have appeared anywhere on official records, if not for a quietly implemented piece of legislation at the start of the year. Even this was an *unofficial* record.

Accessing it certainly was—his brother had called in a number of very questionable favours getting something useful.

'The trouble with the Y-Gen is that they soon work out how to fly under the digital radar,' Rick had said over the phone. 'But he came undone by refilling his Alprazolam in his real name, even though he did it off the health scheme to stay hidden.

'As of February,' he'd continued, 'it became notifiable in order to reduce the amount of doc-shopping being done by addicts. Your guy wouldn't have known that because the GPs aren't required to advise their patients of its existence; in fact it's actively discouraged. And people call *me* dodgy…'

Marshall had ignored Rick's anti-government mutterings and scribbled the details down on the first thing at hand. The name of the drug. The town it was filled in. Ironic that prioritising his mental health had led to Travis's exposure. An obscure little register inside the Department of Health was pretty much the only official record in the entire country that had recent activity for Travis Read. Lucky for him, his brother knew someone who knew someone who knew some*thing* big about a guy in the Health Department's IT section. Something that guy was happy to have buried in return for a little casual database scrutiny.

Marshall's muttered thanks were beyond awkward. How did you thank someone for breaking innumerable laws on your behalf? Even if they did it every day.

'Whoever you're doing this for, Marsh…' Rick had said before hanging up '…I hope they know what this cost you. I sure do.'

That was the closest he'd come to acknowledging everything that went down between them in the past. He'd added just one more thing before disconnecting.

'Don't leave it so long next time.'

And then his brother was gone. After ten years. And Marshall had a few scribbled words on half a coffee-stained napkin. The pharmacy and town where Travis Read had shown his face a few months earlier.

Northam. A district centre five hours from where he was sitting.

Marshall pulled up his map app and stared at it. If Eve's intelligence was hereditary, then chances were her brother wouldn't be dumb enough to get his medical care in the town in which he was hiding out. So, he desktopped a wobbly fifty-kilometre radius around Northam and ruled out anything in the direction of the capital city. Way too public. It was also ninety-five per cent of the state's population and so that left him with only two-dozen country towns inside his circle.

If it was *him* trying to go underground, he'd find a town that was small enough to be under-resourced with government types, uninteresting enough to be off the tourist trail, but not so small that his arrival and settling in would draw attention. That meant tiny communities were out and so were any of the popular, pretty towns.

Agricultural towns were in because they'd be perfect for a man trying to find cash work off the books.

All of that filtering left him just a couple of strong candidates inside his circle. One was the state's earthquake capital and drew occasional media attention to itself that would be way too uncontrollable for a kid intent on hiding out.

That left only some towns on the southern boundary of his circle.

One was on a main route south—too much passing traffic and risk of exposure. Another too tiny.

The third was Beverley, the unofficial weekend headquarters for a biker gang and must regularly receive police attention.

He was about to cross that one through when he reconsidered. What better place to hide out than in a town filled with people with many more secrets to keep than Travis? People and activity that kept the tourists away and the authorities well and truly occupied. And where better for a newcomer to assimilate seamlessly than a town with a transient male population?

Beverley made it onto his top three. And he made a mental note to wear as much leather as he owned.

One day's drive away and he could spend a day each hunting in all three.

Then at least he would know.

It could be him.

Hard to say under the scrappy attempt at facial hair. The best of all the options he'd seen in the past couple of days, anyway. Marshall settled in at the bar and ordered something that he couldn't remember just five seconds later. Then he pulled out his phone and pretended to check his messages while covertly grabbing an image of the man that might be Eve's brother.

Evidence that Travis was alive and well.

If that even was him. Hard to tell from this far away.

There was an easy kind of camaraderie between the young man and his companions, as if an end-of-day beer was a very common thing amongst them. How nice that Travis got to sit here enjoying a beer with mates while his sister cried herself into an ulcer every night. Well-fed, reasonably groomed, clearly not here under any kind of duress, the kid seemed to have a pretty good gig going here in the small biker town.

Just before six, he pushed back from the table and his mates let him go easily, as if skipping out early was business as usual.

Out on the footpath, Marshall followed at a careful distance. How much better would the photo be if he could give the authorities an address to go with the covertly captured picture?

Authorities.

Not Eve.

This was about giving her back her brother, not getting back into her good books. Something he could do to help. Instead of hurt.

He was no better for Eve than she was for him. He'd finally accepted that.

The guy turned down a quiet street and then turned again almost immediately. Marshall jogged to catch up. The back of these old heritage streets were rabbit warrens of open backyards and skinny laneways. A hundred places for someone to disappear into their house. The guy turned again and Marshall turned his jog into a sprint, but as he took the corner into the quiet laneway he pulled up short.

The guy stood, facing him, dirty steel caps parted, ready to run, arms braced, ready for anything.

In a heartbeat, he recognised how badly he might have blown this for Eve. How easy it would be for Travis to just disappear again, deeper into Australia, where she'd never ever find him. And he realised, on a lurch of his stomach, that this cunning plan was maybe going to come completely unstuck.

And it would have his name all over it.

'Who sent you?' the guy challenged, dark eyes blazing in the dusk light.

Marshall took a single step forward. 'Travis?'

'Who sent you?' he repeated, stepping back. As he moved and the light shifted slightly, the facet of those blazing eyes changed and looked to him more like fear and less like threat.

And he'd know those eyes anywhere…

Marshall lifted both hands, palms outward, to show he came in peace.

'I'm a friend of your sister.'

CHAPTER TWELVE

'Hey…'

Marshall's voice was startling enough out of the silence without her also being so horribly unprepared for it. Eve's stomach twisted back on itself and washed through with queasiness.

She'd only just resigned herself to him being gone—truly gone—and now he was back? What the hell was he trying to do—snap her last remaining tendrils of emotional strength?

She managed to force some words up her tight throat. 'What are you doing here, Marshall?'

It felt as if she was forever asking him that.

Compassion from him was nearly unbearable, but it rained down on her from those grey eyes she'd thought never to see again.

'Sit down, Eve.'

Instantly her muscles tensed. Muscles that had heard a lot of bad news. 'Why?'

'I need to talk to you.'

'About…?'

'Eve. Will you just sit down?'

No. No… He was looking at her like her father had the day Travis was officially declared a missing person.

'I don't think I want to.'

As if what she wanted would, in any way, delay what she feared was to come.

'Okay, we'll do this upright, then.'

His mouth opened to suck in a deep breath but then snapped shut again in surprise. 'I don't know where to start. Despite all the trial runs I've had in my mind on the way back here...'

That threw her. Was he back to make another petition for something between them? She moved to head that off before he could begin. Hurting him once had been bad enough...

'Marshall—'

'I have news.'

News. The tightness became a strangle in her throat. Somehow she knew he wouldn't use that word lightly.

'You're freaking me out, Marshall,' she squeezed out.

The words practically blurted themselves onto his lips. 'I've found Travis.'

The rush of blood vacating her face left her suddenly nauseous and her legs started to go.

'He's alive, Eve,' he rushed to add.

That extra piece of information knocked the final support from under her and her buckling legs deposited her onto the bus's sofa.

'Eve...' Marshall dropped down next to her and enveloped her frigid hand between both of his. 'He's okay. He's not hurt. Not sick.'

Eve's lips trembled open but nothing came out and it distantly occurred to her that she might be in shock. He rubbed her frigid fingers and scanned her face, so maybe he thought so, too.

'He's living and working in a small town here in Western Australia. He has a job. A roof over his head. He's okay.'

Okay. He kept saying that, but her muddled mind refused to process it. 'If he was okay he'd have been in touch...'

And then his meaning hit her. New job and new house meant new life. They meant *voluntary.* Her heart began to hammer against her ribs. Everything around her took on an other-worldly gleam and it was only then she realised how many tears wobbled right on the edges of her lashes.

'Where is he?' she whispered.

It was then Marshall's anger finally registered and confusion battled through the chaos in her mind. Anger at her? Why? But colour was unquestionably high in his jaw and his eyes were stony.

'I can't tell you, Eve.'

Okay, her brain was seriously losing it. She waited for the actual meaning to sink in but all she was left with was his refusal to tell her where her long-lost brother was.

'But you found him…?'

'He asked me not to say.'

'What? No.' Disbelief stabbed low in her gut. And betrayal. And hurt. 'But I love him.'

'I know. *He* knows,' he hurried to add, though the anger on his face wasn't diminishing. 'He told me that he would disappear again if I exposed him. So that you'd never find him. He made me give him my word.'

Pain sliced across her midsection. 'But you don't even know him. You know me.'

You love *me.*

She might as well have said it. They both knew it to be true. Not that it changed anything.

'Eve, he's alive and safe and living a life. He's on his meds and is getting healthy. Every day. He just can't do that at home.'

The thump against her eardrums intensified. 'Okay, he doesn't have to come back to Melbourne. We could move—'

'It's not about Melbourne, Eve. He doesn't want to go *home.*'

Realisation sunk in and she whispered through the devastation, 'He doesn't want to be with his family?'

God, did she look as young and fragile as her disbelief sounded? Maybe, because Marshall looked positively sick to be having this conversation.

'He wants to be healthy, Eve. And he needed to start over for that to happen.'

Start over…

'He doesn't have to come back, I can go to him. If he likes where he is—'

'I'm so sorry.' He squeezed both his hands around both of hers and held on. And, after an endless pause, he spoke, leaning forward to hold her stinging eyes with his. 'He doesn't want you to come, Eve. Particularly you.'

Particularly you.

Anguish stacked up on top of pain on top of misery. And all of it was wrapped in razor blades.

'But I love him.'

His skin blanched. 'I know. I'm so sorry.'

'I need to see him,' she whispered. 'I've been searching for so long—'

'He wants a fresh start.'

A fissure opened up in her heart and began to tug wider. Her voice, when it came, was low and croaky. 'From me?'

'From everything.'

'Is this…' The fissure stretched painfully. 'Is this about *me*?'

Pity was like a cancer in his gaze. 'He can't be with you any more. Or your dad.'

'Why?' Her cry bounced off the Bedford's timber-lined walls.

Words seemed to fail him. He studied his feet for the barest of moments and then found her gaze again.

'Because of your mother, Eve.'

She stared at him, lost. Confused. But then something surfaced in the muddle of pain and thought. 'The accident?'

His expression confirmed it.

God, she could barely breathe, let alone carry on a conversation. 'But that was years ago.'

'Not for him, Eve. He carries it every day. The trauma. The anxiety. The depression. The guilt.'

Guilt? 'But Mum wasn't his fault.'

His fingers tightened around hers again and his gaze remained steady. 'It was, Eve. I'm so sorry.'

She shook the confusion away, annoyed to have to go back

over such old ground. But being angry at him helped. It gave all the pain somewhere to go.

'No. He was with her, but… She was driving drunk.'

But she could read Marshall like a book—even after just a few weeks together—and his book said something else was going on here. Something big. She blinked. Repeatedly.

'Wasn't she?'

'Didn't you say they were both thrown from the bike?'

She was almost too dizzy for words. So she just nodded.

'And the police determined that she was in control?'

'Travis was the only other person there. And he couldn't ride properly then. He was underage.'

Marshall crouched over further and peered right into her face. Lending her his strength. 'No. He couldn't.'

But it was all starting to be horribly, horribly clear.

Oh, God…

'Trav was driving?' she choked. Marshall just nodded. 'Because Mum had been drinking?'

No nod this time, just the pitying, horrible creasing of his eyes.

No… Not little Travis… 'And he never told anyone?'

'Imagine how terrified he must have been.'

A fourteen-year-old boy driving his drunk mother home to keep her safe and ending up killing her.

'He wouldn't have lied to protect himself.' Her certainty sounded fierce even to her.

'But what if he thought you'd all blame him? Hate him. That's a lot for someone to carry. Young or old. He can't face you.'

She sagged against the sofa back, this new pain having nowhere to go.

'He carried that all alone? All this time?' she whispered. 'Poor Trav. Poor baby…'

'No. Don't you take that on, too. He's getting treatment now. He's got support and he's getting stronger. He's doing pretty bloody well, all things considered.'

So why was Marshall still so very tense?

'But he knows what he wants. And needs. And he isn't going back to your world. And he doesn't want that world coming to him either.' He cursed silently. 'Ever.'

A tiny bit of heat bubbled up beneath her collar and she'd never been so grateful for anger. It cut like a hot knife through the butter of her numb disbelief and reminded her she could still feel something. And not a small something. The feelings she'd been suppressing for twelve months started to simmer and then boil up through the cracks of Marshall's revelation.

Ever.

'So…that's it?' she wheezed. 'I gave up a year of my life to find him—I broke my heart searching for him—and all this time he's been living comfortably across the country *starting over*?'

Marshall's lips pressed together. 'He's made his choice.'

'And you've made yours, apparently. You've taken his side pretty darned quick for a man you don't know.'

'Eve, I'm on your side—'

It was as if someone was puffing her with invisible bellows filled with hot air…making this worse and worse.

'Don't! How do I know you're not just making this all up to further your cause?'

'You can't be serious.'

'How would I know? The only evidence I have that any of this is true is your word. You might not have found him at all. You might just want me to think that. You might say anything to get me to stay with you.'

The words poured out uncontrollably.

'What the hell have I done to make you believe that of me?' But he rummaged in his pocket, pulled out his phone and opened his photo app. 'Believe this, then.'

Seeing Travis just about broke her heart.

Her baby brother. Alive. Healthy. Enjoying a beer. Even laughing. *Laughing!* She hadn't seen that in years.

She certainly hadn't done it in as long.

Tears tumbled.

'Eve—'

'What would happen, Marshall?' she asked desperately. 'If you told me where he is. How would he even know?'

She was flying through the stages of grief. At bargaining already.

'I know you, Eve…'

'So you're just going to take the choice away from me? Like some child?'

'You wouldn't be able to stay away. You know it.'

'I'm not about to *stalk him*, Marshall.'

'You already are, Eve! You're scouring the country systematically, hunting him down.'

Her gasp pinged around the little bus. 'Is that how you see it?'

'Why else would you want to know where he is? Unless you were going to keep tabs on him.'

'Because I *love* him. You have no right to keep this from me.'

'I'm not doing this to be a bastard, Eve. I don't want you in any more pain.'

'You think this doesn't hurt? Knowing he's alive and I can't get to him? Can't hold him? Or help him? You think that's kinder than letting me hear from his own lips that he doesn't want to come home?'

Just saying the words was horrible.

He took her chin in his fingers and forced her to look at him and, despite everything, her skin still thrilled at his simple touch. It had been days…

'Hear me, Eve,' he urged. 'If you go there he will disappear again. He knows what to do now, he'll be better at it and he might go off his meds to keep himself hidden. You will never see or hear from your brother again. Is that what you want?'

In all her wildest, worst dreams she'd never imagined she'd be sitting here, across from Marshall—of all people—fighting him for her brother's whereabouts.

But, dear Lord, fight she would.

'How is that any different to what I have now?'

'Because I know where he is and he's agreed to check in with me from time to time.'

The grief and hurt surged up right below her skin, preparing to boil over.

'So…what? You get to be some kind of gatekeeper to my family? Who the hell gave you that authority?'

'He has a legal right to go missing. He wasn't hurt, or forced, or under any kind of duress. He decided to leave.'

'He was sick!'

'And managing his condition.'

He had an answer for every single argument. 'Then he must have been desperate.'

'Maybe, but he's not now. He's doing okay, I swear.' He caught her eyes again and brought everything back to the simple truth. 'You've found him, Eve.'

'No, *you* found him. I have as little as I had before.' Less, really. 'And, whatever he's going through, he clearly needs some kind of psychological help. People don't just walk out on perfectly good families.'

'They do, Eve. For all kinds of reasons. He couldn't stay, not knowing what he'd done. Fearing you'd discover it. Knowing how much you'd sacrificed—'

The inquest. The random timing of his disappearance suddenly came into crystal focus. 'I can help him.'

'You're still protecting him from responsibility? He's an adult, Eve. He doesn't want your help.'

'He needs it.'

'Does he, Eve? Or do you just need to believe that?'

She stiffened where she sat.

'You were his big sister. You looked after him and your father after the accident. That became your role. And for the last twelve months you've been about nothing but him. You chucked in your job. You sold your house. What do you have if you don't have him?'

'I have…plenty, thanks very much. I'll go back to my career, reignite my friendships. Get a new place.'

Oh, such lies. There was no going back. She didn't even know how to be normal now.

'And then what? What are you if you're not all about your brother, Eve? You've been doing this since you were barely out of school.'

Furious heat sped up the back of her neck and she surged to her feet. 'Don't put this on me. You're choosing to protect him instead of me. How about we talk about that for a bit?'

He shot up right behind her and angry fists caught her upper arms. But he didn't shake her. It was more desperate and gentle than that.

'I would *never* protect him, Eve. I hate what he's done to you. I hate that I found him sitting in a pub having a relaxed beer with friends while your soul was haemorrhaging hope *every single day*. I hate that he's got himself a new life when he was gifted with *you* in his old one.'

He said 'you' as if that was something pretty darned special. The stress faults in her heart strained that tiny bit more.

'I hate that he ditched you and your father rather than find the strength to work through it and that he didn't believe in your strength and integrity more.' He sucked in a breath. 'I would never put him ahead of you. I'm choosing *you*. This is all about you.'

'Then tell me where—'

'I can't!' he cried. 'He will disappear, Eve. The first sign of someone else looking for him. The first poster he sees in a neighbouring town. The first time his phone makes a weird noise. The next stranger who looks at him sideways in the street. He's dead serious about this,' he urged. 'Please. Just let it go.'

'How can I possibly do that?' she snarled.

'You once told me that all you wanted was to know he was all right. To have an answer. And nothing else mattered. Well, now you know. He's fine. But you're shifting the goalposts.'

'So, knowing is not enough! Maybe I do want him home, safe, with us. What's wrong with that?'

'Nothing. Except it's not achievable. And you need to accept that. It will be easier.'

'On who?'

'While your head and heart are full of your brother, then no one and nothing else can get through.'

'Are we back to that, Marshall? You and me?'

'No. You've been painfully clear on that front. I just wanted…'

He couldn't finish, so she finished for him. 'To save the day? To be the hero? Guess you weren't expecting to have to come back and be the bad guy, huh?'

'I didn't *have* to be anything.'

'You preferred to have me despise you?'

His eyes flared as if her words hit him like an axe. But he let her go and she stumbled at the sudden loss of his strength.

'You bang on about your great enduring love for your brother,' he grated. 'But you don't recognise it when it's staring you in the face. I chose *you* here today, Eve. Not myself and certainly not Travis. I am critically aware that the end of your suffering means the end of any chance for you and me. Yet here I am. Begging you to come back to the real world. Before it's too late.'

'Reality?' she whispered. 'Life doesn't get much realer than having someone you love ripped from you and held away, just out of reach.'

His eyes bled grey streaks. 'Finally. Something we agree on.'

He pushed away and walked to the bus's back door. But he caught himself there with a clenched fist on each side of the doorframe. His head sagged forward and his back arched.

Everything about his posture screamed pain.

Well, that made two of them.

But he didn't step forward. Instead, he turned back.

'You know what? Yes. Maybe I did want to be the man who

took your pain away. Who ended all your suffering. Maybe I did want to see you look at me with something more heartfelt than curiosity or amusement or plain old lust.'

Haunted eyes bled.

'You're halfway to being missing yourself, emotionally speaking. And if Travis was found, then you'd have no choice but to return to the real, functional, living world. And I wanted to be the man that helped get you there.'

'Why?'

Frustrated hands flew up. 'Why do you think, Eve? Why do any of us do anything, ultimately?'

She blinked her stinging eyes, afraid to answer.

'*Love*, Eve.' So tired. So very weary. Almost a joke on himself. He made the word sound like a terminal condition. 'I love you. And I wanted to *give* you your heart's desire if I couldn't be it.'

'You barely know me,' she breathed.

'You're wrong.' He stepped up closer to her. Towered above her. 'You spend so much time stopping yourself from feeling emotion that you've forgotten to control how much of it you show. You're an open book, Eve.

'I know you're heartbroken about Travis betraying you like this,' he went on, 'and confused about loving him yet hating this thing he's done. I know you're desperate for somewhere to send all that pain, and you don't really want to throw it at me but you can't deal with it all yourself because you've closed down, emotionally, to cope with the past year. Maybe even longer. And it's easier to hate me than him.'

Tears sprang back into her eyes.

'I know it particularly hurts you that it's *me* that's withholding Travis from you because deep down you thought we had a connection even if you didn't have the heart to pursue it. You trusted me, and I've betrayed you. Maybe that's the price I had to pay for trying to rescue you.'

She curled her trembling fingers into a fist.

'I could have told you nothing, Eve. I could have simply kept driving after letting him know that you were all looking for him. Left you thinking well of me. And maybe I could have come back into your life in the future and had a chance. But here I am instead, destroying any chance of us being together by telling you the hard truth about your brother. So you hear it from me rather than from him.'

Her voice was barely more than a croak. 'What do you mean?'

'I've seen your route maps, Eve.' He sighed. 'You would have reached his town before Christmas. And *you* would have found him drinking in that pub, and *you* would have had to stand there, struggling to be strong as he told you how he'd traded up to a better new life rather than the tough old one he'd left, and as he threw everything you've sacrificed and been through back in your face.'

She reached out for something solid to hold on to and found nothing. Because he wasn't there for her any more.

'And you would have knocked on his door the next morning with takeaway coffee, only to find he'd cleared out, with not a single clue. And you would have spent the rest of your life hunting for him.

'And so, even though it hurts like death to do this to you, I would take this pain one hundred times over to spare you from it.'

She stared at him through glistening eyes—wordless—as he stepped up closer.

'I'm not fool enough to think there's a place for me here now, even if you did have some capacity in your heart. I wouldn't expect—or even want—to just slide into the emotional vacancy left by your brother. Or your mother. Or anyone else you've ever loved.

'I deserve my *own* piece of you, Eve. Just mine. I think that's all I've ever really wanted in my sorry excuse for a life. The tiniest patch of your heart to cultivate with beautiful flowering vines and tend and spoil until they can spread up your walls and through your cracks and over your trellises. Until you've forgotten what it was like to *not* have me there. In the garden of your heart.'

He leaned down and kissed her, careless of the puffy, slimy, tear-ravaged parts of her. Long, hard and deep. A farewell. Eve practically clung to the strong heat of his lips.

'But I can't do anything with the rocky, parched earth you'll have left after all this is over. Nothing will ever grow there.'

He tucked a strand of damp hair behind her ears and murmured, 'Go home, Eve. Put him behind you. Put me behind you. Just…heal.'

This time, he didn't pause at the door, he just pushed through, jumped down to the ground and strode off, leaving Eve numb, trembling and destroyed in the little bus that had become her cage.

CHAPTER THIRTEEN

Five months later

MARSHALL SPRINTED UP the valley side to the cottage, sweaty from a morning of post-hole-digging and dusting the rich dirt off his hands as he went. He snatched the phone up just before his voicemail kicked in.

Landline. Not many people called that any more.

'Hello?'

'Marshall?'

A voice familiar yet…not. Courtesy of the long-distance crackle.

'Yeah. Who's this?'

'Travis Read.'

His heart missed a beat. 'Has something happened?'

That was their agreement. Marshall would call twice a year to check in and, apart from that, Travis would only call if something was up. It had only been five months since they'd last spoken. He wasn't yet due.

'No, I'm…uh…I'm in town this afternoon and wondered if I could come and see you.'

Since Travis only had his new Victorian phone number, not his new home address, 'in town' had to mean Melbourne. That was all the area code would have told him. But what could Eve's brother possibly have to say? And why did he sound so tense? Unless it was recriminations. It occurred to him to question why he would have caught a plane anywhere since that would flag him on the Federal Police's radar and risk exposure. Unless he used a fake name. Or drove. Or maybe his family had taken him off the missing-persons register so that scarce resources weren't wasted on a man who wasn't really missing.

He'd given Travis one more go all those months ago for Eve's sake. Pointlessly tried to get him to change his mind, told him the damage it had done to his own life—in the long-term—to walk away from his family, as imperfect as they were. How it hadn't solved any of his problems at all—he'd just learned to function around them.

Or not, as the case may be.

But Travis hadn't budged. He was as stubborn as his sister, it seemed. And now he wanted to meet.

Irritation bubbled just below Marshall's surface. He was already keeping Travis's secret at the expense of his own happiness. Hadn't he done enough?

But then he remembered how important this kid was to the woman he was still struggling to get over and he reluctantly shared his new address and gave Travis a time later in the day before trundling back down the hill to the Zen meditation of punching three-dozen fenceposts into the unsuspecting earth.

About fifteen minutes before Travis was due, Marshall threw some water on his face and washed his filthy hands. The rest… Travis would have to take him as he found him.

About six minutes after their appointed time Marshall heard a knock at his front door and spied a small hire car out of one of the windows as he reached the door.

'Trav—?'

He stopped dead. Not Travis.

Eve.

In the flesh and smiling nervously on his doorstep.

His first urge was to wrap her up in his arms and never, ever let her go again. But he fought that and let himself frown instead. His quick brain ran through the facts and decided that she was obviously here in Travis's place. Which suggested Eve and Travis were in communication.

Which meant—his sinking heart realised—that everything he'd done, everything he'd given up, counted for absolutely nothing.

'How did you find him?'

'Good to see you, too,' she joked. Pretty wanly. But he wasn't in any mood for levity. Not while he was feeling this ambushed.

'I didn't find him,' she finally offered. 'He found me.'

So Travis had finally found the personal courage to pick up the phone. Good for him.

And—yeah—he'd be a hypocrite if not for the fact that he'd since taken his own advice and done the same with Rick. His brother hadn't commented on the new mobile number but Marshall felt certain he'd tried to use the old one. That was why he'd yanked out the SIM and tossed it somewhere along the Bussell Highway the same awful night he'd last seen Eve.

The whole world could just go screw itself. Travis. Eve. Rick.

Everyone.

'I was heading home,' Eve said now. 'Backtracking through Esperance. My phone rang and I thought it might be you, but… it was him.'

The flatness of her tone belied the enormity of what that moment must have meant for Eve.

'Why would you think it was me?' Hadn't they been pretty clear with each other when they'd parted?

She shrugged lightly. 'I'd tried your number several times and it was disconnected, but—you know—hope springs eternal.'

On that cryptic remark, she shuffled from left foot to right on his doorstep.

Ugh, idiot. He stepped aside. 'Sorry, come on in.'

There was something about her being here. Here, where he'd had to force himself finally to stop imagining what the cottage would be like with her in it. It felt as if he'd sprinted up the valley side and into an alternate dimension where his dreams had finally turned material.

Inside, she glanced around her and then crossed straight to the full wall window that looked out over the picturesque valley.

'Gorgeous,' she muttered almost to herself.

While she was otherwise occupied with the view, he took the opportunity to look at her. She'd changed, but he couldn't quite put his finger on how. Her hair was shorter and glossier but not that different. Her eyes at the front door had been bright but still essentially held the same wary gaze he remembered. She turned from the window and started to comment further on his view when it hit him. It was the way she carried herself; she seemed…taller. No, not taller—straighter. As if a great burden she'd been carrying around was now gone.

And maybe it was.

But having her here—in his sanctuary—wasn't good for him. It physically hurt to see her in his space, so he cut to the chase and stopped her before she offered some view-related platitude.

'What are you doing here, Eve?'

Maybe she deserved his scepticism. The way they'd left things… Certainly, Eve had known she wouldn't be walking into open arms.

'I'm sorry for the deception,' she began. 'I wasn't sure you'd see me. We didn't really leave things…open…for future contact. Your phone was dead and your infuriating Government privacy procedures meant no one in your department would give me your new one. And you moved, too.'

She caught herself before she revealed even more ways she'd tried to reach out to him. It wasn't as if she'd been short of time.

'Yet here you are.'

'I guilted Travis into hooking this up,' she confessed. 'He

wasn't very happy about betraying you when you've kept his secret in good faith.'

Which explained the tension on the phone earlier. And the long-distance hum. 'To absolutely no purpose, it seems, since you two are now talking.'

'"Talking" is probably an overstatement,' she said. 'We speak. Now and again. Just him and me at this stage but maybe Dad in the future. Trav reached out a few months ago. Said you'd called him again.'

'I did.' Though it had never occurred to him that the contents of that call might some day end up in Eve's ear.

'Talking about everything that happened is pretty hard for him,' she said flatly. 'You were right about that. And you were right that he would have bolted if I'd pushed. He was very close to it.'

'That's partly why I called him again. To make sure he hadn't already done a runner.'

But not the only reason. 'Whatever you talked about, Travis got a lot out of it. It was a real turning point for him.'

Silence fell between them and Eve struggled to know how to continue. His nerves only infected her more.

'So, you went home?' Marshall nudged.

'I was paralysed for a few days,' she admitted. 'Terrified of any forward move in case I accidentally ended up in his town and triggered another disappearance. You could hardly tell me which town not to visit, could you?'

She fought the twist of her lips so that it felt more like a grimace. Great—finally tracked him down and she was grinning like the Joker.

'So I backtracked the way I'd come,' she finished. 'That seemed safe.'

'I wondered if you might still be in Western Australia,' he murmured.

So far away. 'There wasn't anything to stay for.'

Travis in lockdown. Marshall gone. Her journey suspended. She'd never felt so lonely and lost.

'So, here you are.'

'Here I am.' She glanced around. 'And here *you* are.'

All these months he'd been here, within a single day's mountain drive of her family home. God, if only she'd known. She would have come much sooner.

'Do you know where we are?' he asked.

Not exactly warm, but not quite hostile. Just very…restrained.

'The satnav says we're near MacKenzie Falls.' A place they'd both enjoyed so much on their separate trips around the country. 'That's quite a coincidence.'

'Not really. It was somewhere I wanted to come back to.'

Okay. Not giving an inch. She supposed she deserved that.

'You gave up meteorology?'

'No. I consult now. From here, mostly. The wonder of remote technology.'

She glanced out at the carnage in his bottom paddock. 'When you're not building fences?'

'Who knew I'd be so suited to farming.'

'I think you could do pretty much anything you turned your hand to.'

'Thanks for the vote of confidence. Now why are we having this conversation, Eve?'

She sighed and crossed closer to him.

'I wanted to… I *need to* thank you.'

'For what?'

Her fingers were frozen despite the warm day. She rubbed the nerves against her jeans. 'The wake-up call.'

He crossed his arms and leaned on his kitchen island. Okay, he wasn't going to make this any easier.

'When you love a missing person,' she started, 'you can't grieve, you can't move on. You can't plan or make life decisions. So it just becomes easier to…not. It hurts less if you just shut down. And when one system goes down, they all do.

'In my case,' she went on, 'I coped by having a clear, single purpose.'

Find Travis.

'And that was all I could deal with. All I could hold in my head and my heart. I developed tunnel vision.'

Marshall studied the tips of his work boots.

'I once told you that if Travis walked in the door, healthy and alive, nothing he'd done would matter.'

He nodded. Just once.

'Me dealing with it so maturely was every bit as much a fantasy as him walking in the door unannounced. Turns out, I'm not so stoic under pressure.' She lifted her eyes. 'It matters, Marshall. It matters a lot. Even as I argued with people who warned me that he might not be alive, I secretly wanted them to be right. Rather than accept he might torture his family like this, deliberately. Leave us wondering forever. And then I hated myself for allowing those thoughts.'

Realisation dawned on his face. 'So when it turned out to be true…'

She shook her head. 'I'm very sorry for the things I said. The way I said them. I thought you were putting Travis ahead of me and that clawed at my heart. I'm sorry to say it took me days to realise that was what I did to you every single day. Put you second. The truth is, you sacrificed yourself—and any chance of us being together—for me. To help spare me pain.'

'So you came to apologise?'

Could a heart swell under pressure? Because hers felt twice its usual size. Heavy and pendulous and thumpy. And it was getting in the way of her breathing.

'You put yourself second.' After a lifetime of coming second. 'For me. Not many men would have done that.'

His voice, when it came, was not quite steady. But still a fortress wall. 'So you came to say thanks?'

She took a breath. Inside her long sleeves she twisted her fingers. Over and over. 'I came to see if I'm too late.'

Marshall didn't move. 'Too late for what?'

'For that vision you had,' she said on a sad, weak laugh.

'The timber cabin in the forest with the clear pools…and me. And you,' she finished on a rush.

And the making love twice a day part. She'd clung to that image for the many lonely nights since he'd left.

Marshall gave nothing away, simply pushed from the island bench and moved to stare out of his window.

'You stuck with me, Eve,' he admitted. 'I finished my audit and returned to Sydney, assuming that a little time was all I needed to get you out of my system. But months passed and you were still there. Under my skin like ink. I couldn't shake you. You were wedged in here.'

He tapped his chest with a closed fist.

'But it doesn't really matter what my heart thinks because my head knows better. And if my life has taught me anything, it's to listen to my head.' He turned back to her. 'I've walked away from much longer relationships than ours when they weren't good for me, Eve. Why would I set myself up to be the second most important person in your life?'

'That's not—'

'So, yes, Eve. I got the cottage in the forest surrounded by pools and, yes, I hope to be happy here. Very happy.' He expelled a long, sad breath. 'But no…there's no *you* in that plan any more.'

A rock of pain lodged in her stomach.

'At all?' she whispered.

'You don't have room for me, Eve. I'd convinced myself that you'd cast me as some kind of substitute for your brother but I no longer think that's true. I just don't think you have any emotional capacity left. And I deserve better than sorry seconds.'

She struggled to steady her breath. But it was touch and go. Every instinct she had told her to go, to flee back home. Except that when she'd come here she'd really hoped that *this* might turn out to be home.

And no home worth having came without risk. It was time to be brave.

'I wasn't out there to find Travis,' she whispered, taking

the chance. 'I think I was out there trying to find a way to let him go.'

She shuddered in a breath. 'But that was terrifying. What if I had nothing but a massive, gaping hole inside where my love and worry and pain for him used to be? What if I could never fill it? Or heal it. Who was I without him? So much of *me* was gone.'

His strong arms wrapped across his chest and all she could think about was wanting them around her.

'And what little was left around the outside was just numb.' She stepped closer to him. 'But then you came in with your ridiculous orange motorbike and your hairy face and your tattoos and you were like…an icebreaker. Shoving your stubborn way through the frost. Inch by inch.'

A tragic kind of light flickered weakly behind his eyes and it sickened her that she'd been the one to extinguish it before. The memory of him standing in her bus, appealing from the heart, in visible, tangible pain. And she'd not been able to feel a thing.

But his body language was giving nothing away now.

'I'm not a plug, Eve. I'm a person. You'll have to find someone else to fill the void.'

'I don't want you to fill it. I want you to bridge it.'

His eyes came up.

Eve picked up a cushion off his sofa and hugged it close. 'When you left, it was horrible. You gone. Travis gone. Mum gone. Dad on the other side of the country. I'd never felt so alone. Which is ridiculous, I realise, given I'd been travelling solo all year.'

His brow twitched with half a frown, so quick she almost missed it. His posture shifted. Straightened. 'What changed?'

'I couldn't stay frozen.' She shrugged. 'I tried to do what I'd done before, just…deal. But all these emotions started bubbling up out of nowhere and I realised that I'd been harbouring the same feelings Travis must have had since Mum died. Despair. Anxiety. I'd been suppressing them, just like he must have.'

'So you developed some empathy for your brother. That's great.'

'I wasn't thinking about him, Marshall,' she rushed to correct. 'God knows, I should have been, and it took me a while to notice, but eventually I thought how strange it was that I should feel such despair about my brother being *alive*. Anger, sure. Resentment, maybe. But despair…?

'Travis has been absent in my life since Mum died. Even back when he was still physically present. I'd learned how to compensate for his absence and not fall apart. But there I was, trundling up the highway, completely unable to manage my feelings about the absence of someone I'd known less than a fortnight.'

His face lifted. His eyes blazed. But he didn't say a word.

'I wasn't thinking about Travis. I wasn't weeping about Travis. I was thinking about you. Missing…you.'

He had nothing to say to that.

'Nothing felt right without you there,' she whispered.

Agony blazed from his tired eyes. 'Do you understand how hard this is to hear? Now?'

It was too late.

Something grasped at her organs and fisted deep in her gut.

She gathered up her handbag. 'I don't want you thinking badly of me, Marshall. I don't want you remembering me as the outback psycho in a bus. I have years' worth of coping mechanisms that I need to unlearn. I barely know where to start. It's going to be a long work in progress.'

She stepped up to him. Determined to get one thing right in their relationship, even if that was goodbye.

'But I'm on my way. Thanks to you. I just didn't want you never knowing how much you helped me. What a difference you made. I'm just sorry I couldn't return the favour. I'm sorry I hurt you.'

She pushed up onto her toes and pressed a kiss to his face, over the corner of his mouth, and then whispered into it, 'Thank you.'

Then she dropped back onto her soles and turned for the door.

'Eve.'

His voice came just as she slid her hand onto the heritage doorknob. But she didn't turn, she only paused.

'What about that bridge?'

The one over the void where her love for Travis used to be?

'I guess I won't be needing it,' she murmured past the ache in her chest. 'It doesn't go anywhere now.'

He stepped up behind her and turned her to face him. 'Where did it go? Before?'

As she spoke, her eyes moistened and threatened to shame her. But she didn't shy away from it. She was done hiding her emotions.

'Someone once told me about a garden,' she breathed, smiling through the gathering tears. 'One which used to be barren rubble. With old stone walls and handmade trellises, and where someone had planted a beautiful, fragrant vine. That's where it went.'

He swallowed hard. 'How will you visit it with no bridge?'

'I won't,' she choked. 'But I'll imagine it. Every day. And it will grow without me—up and over the trellis, through the cracks in the wall. And eventually it will cover up all the rocky and exposed places where nothing could thrive.'

And then she'd be whole again.

Marshall glanced away, visibly composing himself. And then he spoke. 'There's something you need to see.'

He slid his fingers through hers and led her out through the front door and down the paving stones to the rear of the house where a large timber door blocked the path. He moved her in front of him and reached around her to open the door.

It swung inwards.

And Eve burst into tears.

She stepped through into the garden of her imagination. Complete with trellis, flowering vines, stone wall and even a small fishpond. All of it blurred by the tears streaming down her face.

All so much prettier than she could ever have imagined.

'Don't cry, Eve,' Marshall murmured right behind her. Closer than she'd allowed herself even to dream.

Which only escalated the sobs that racked her uncontrollably.

'It's so perfect,' she squeezed out between gasped breaths.

'I made it for you,' he confessed. 'It was the first thing I started when I came here.'

Her body jerked with weeping. 'Why?'

'Because it's yours—' he shrugged, stroking her hair '—it was always yours.'

He turned her into the circle of his arms. Warm. Hard. Sweaty from a day of work. Heartbreakingly close. One arm pulled her tighter, the other curled up behind her head so that he could press his lips there.

'You are not some outback psycho,' he soothed into her hair. 'You're passionate and warm and you feel things intensely.'

Maybe she could now that the ice inside her was starting to thaw.

'I wanted all that love you kept in reserve for your brother,' he breathed. 'I hated that Travis was hoarding it. That he'd just walked away from it as though it wasn't the most precious commodity on earth.'

She pulled back and gave him a watery smile. 'He doesn't want it.'

'Someone else does, Eve. Every single bit of it.' Grey eyes blazed down on her. 'I don't care where it comes from, or where it's been. I just care that it's here, in your garden. With me.'

She curled her hands in his shirt. 'You don't hate me?'

'I never hated you,' he soothed. 'I hated myself. I hated the world and everything in my past that stopped me from being able to just love you. And I was angry at myself for trying to be your champion and fix everything, when all I did was make things worse for you.'

'If you hadn't found Travis, I'd still be driving around the country, heartbroken.'

'If I hadn't found Travis, I'd still be driving around with you,' he avowed. 'I would never have left that easily. I would have just given you some breathing space. I was trying to protect you, not control you.'

'I couldn't face the road without you,' she admitted. 'That's why I went home.'

'I have a confession to make,' he murmured. 'This farm wasn't just about MacKenzie Falls. I picked it so that your father wouldn't have to lose you twice.'

She peered up at him and he tackled her tears with his smudged flannel shirt. 'Lose me where?'

'Lose you to here,' he said, kissing one swollen eyelid and then the other. 'To me.'

Breathless tension coiled in her belly. 'You wanted me to come here?'

'I wanted you with me.'

'Five minutes ago you said it was too late.'

'Eve…if I've learned anything from you it's that surviving is not enough. I survived by leaving my mother and brother behind but it didn't change anything—it didn't change me. I've been on emotional hold since then, just like you. And that can work to a point but it's no good forever. At some point I had to take a risk and start believing in people again. In you.'

'I let you down so badly.'

'I was expecting it. I would have found it no matter what.'

Confused joy tripped and fell over its own feet in her mind. 'You believe in me now?'

'Better, Eve. I believe in myself.'

'And you want me to stay here?'

His lips, hot and heavy, grazed hers, and it wasn't nearly enough contact after so long. She chased his touch with her own.

'I want you to *live* here,' he pledged. And then, in case her addled mind really wasn't keeping up, he added, 'With me.

And the forest. Somewhere we can retreat to when our crazy all-consuming families get too much. Somewhere we can just be us.'

A joyous blooming began somewhere just behind her heart.

'I'll always worry about him,' she warned. She wasn't simply going to be able to excise Travis from her life the way he'd done to her. Once a big sister, always a big sister.

'I know. And I'll always have the family felon to help keep tabs on him.' Then, at her quizzical expression, he added, 'Long story.'

'Everything I said—'

'*Everything* is in the past, Eve. I'm asking you to choose the future. I'm asking you to choose me.'

The last time he'd asked that of her, she'd chosen her brother. And broken Marshall's soul.

She slid her arms around his gorgeous, hard middle and peered up at him from the heart of their fantasy garden.

'No,' she said breathlessly, and then squeezed him reassuringly as he flinched. 'This time *I choose us.*'

* * * * *

ONE BABY STEP
AT A TIME

MEREDITH WEBBER

CHAPTER ONE

HE HADN'T EXPECTED it to feel so strange, walking into the ER at Willowby Hospital. After all, he'd been here often enough as a child—broken arm, a badly sprained ankle and, on one memorable occasion, suffering hypothermia after he'd been trapped down a well. Bill's fault, that! Bill crying pitiably at the top because her cat had fallen in—Bill going all girlie on him!

Whillimina Florence de Groote—his friend Bill!

Finally producing a daughter after six sons, Bill's mother had named her after both grandmothers, thinking it a nice feminine name, but from before she could talk, Bill had decided she was one of the boys and early on had insisted her name was Bill.

So Bill she'd stayed.

Lost in the past, he was startled when the woman who'd met him at the door—Lesley?—spoke.

'I'll introduce you to our senior nursing staff, and you'll meet the rest as you move around.'

But once again he was distracted, for there she was!

The wild, vivid, red hair, ruthlessly tamed for her work shift, burst like tendrils of flame from beneath her white cap, bringing smudges of colour to the sterility of the room.

'Bill!'

His delighted cry echoed around the still-quiet space and as he strode towards her, Lesley—he was sure it was Lesley—bleating, 'Oh, you know Bill?' as she followed him.

He watched as disbelief chased surprise across Bill's face, then delight dawned in a smile that made the brightly lit room seem even brighter.

'No one told me!' she said, abandoning the patient she'd been shepherding towards a cubicle to give him an all-enveloping hug. 'You didn't tell me you were coming,' she added, with a punch on his shoulder. 'But I'm so glad! Gran will be so happy. But what are you doing here? I'm working. Did you just call in to say hello?'

He grinned at her, the pleasure of seeing her again, from hearing the rush of words that was pure Bill, warming him right through.

'I'm working too,' he said, and saw shock dawn on her face.

'Working?'

He nodded.

'Here?'

He nodded again, still smiling broadly because he'd never seen Bill flabbergasted before, but flabbergasted she truly was.

'You've got a patient, I'll explain later,' he said, delighted that he could keep her guessing a while longer.

That drew a scowl but she did return to her patient, fully focussed on work once again, leaving Nick with a strange sense of... Well, he wasn't sure what it was—surely not *rightness* about returning home?

No, he was being fanciful. It was probably nothing more than the pleasure of seeing Bill again.

'You know Bill?' Lesley had been hovering behind him during the exchange.

'You could say that,' he replied, still smiling because somehow seeing Bill had made this decision to come home seem comfortable—even inevitable—for all he'd been thrown into work before he'd had time to settle in because of some emergency in the senior ER registrar's family.

Four hours later he'd had plenty of opportunities to see his old friend in action, her seniority evident in the way she designated duties and handled patients, always busy yet always calm and smiling.

Always attracting his attention whenever she was in sight, but that was nothing more than his natural delight in seeing her again. That she felt the same he had no doubt, for she'd flash a smile at him as their paths crossed.

Until now, when she was coming towards him with determination in her easy, long-legged stride, another scowl on her face.

'Tearoom *now*, Dr Grant!' she ordered, and he fell in obediently behind her, knowing he'd have a lot of explaining to do but pleased to have an opportunity to sit and talk to her in this small lull.

Had she ordered everyone out, that the area was empty? he wondered, as he followed her into the messy room. He wouldn't have put it past her, but right now he didn't care. All he wanted to do was give her a proper hug, to reaffirm he really *was* home again.

He caught her in his arms and swung her round, not easily as she was nearly as tall as he was—and only for a moment as she pushed away and glared at him.

'And what's all this about?' she demanded. 'Creeping into town without a word to anyone? And don't tell me Gran knows because I saw her yesterday and you know she can't keep a secret.'

He grinned at the red-headed termagant who'd bossed him around all his young life.

'Neither can you,' he reminded her, 'and I wanted it all settled before I told Gran. In the end, the job came up sooner than I expected so there was no time to tell anyone.'

Gold-brown eyes narrowed suspiciously.

'*What* is all settled?'

'The contract—twelve months with an option to extend.'

And now Bill was hugging him!

'Oh, Nick, Gran will be so happy. She never says anything but since that fall a month ago she's been feeling fragile and I think that makes her miss you more than ever. I can hear it in her voice when she talks about you.'

And you? Nick found himself wanting to ask, although why he wasn't sure. He and Bill had kept in close touch over the years, with regular emails and infrequent phone calls, very occasionally catching up in person when they'd both happened to be in the same city at the same time. It was what friends did so, yes, he did want her to be happy he was home…

'Sit, I'll make coffee,' Bill was saying, so he set the thought aside and sat, happy to watch her move around the little room, totally at home, composed—beautiful really, his Bill, although he'd probably always been too close to her to see it.

* * *

Bill shook her head as she set the kettle to boil, disbelief that Nick was actually here still rattling her thoughts. Her first glimpse of him had made her heart thud in her chest—just one big, heavy thud as she'd taken in the sight of the tall, lean man with a few threads of grey in the softly curling brown hair that had been the bane of his younger life. The black-rimmed glasses hid eyes she knew were grey-blue and gave him a serious look.

Her Nick, all grown up and devastatingly handsome now, she realised as she stepped back from their friendship and looked at him as a man.

They'd met in kindergarten class at Willowby West Primary School, a friendship begun when she had punched the boy who'd called Nick Four-Eyes. She'd dragged him home with her that afternoon, made him phone his gran to say where he was, then ordered a couple of her brothers to teach him how to fight.

And so the bond had been forged—a bond that had survived years of separation, though they'd always kept in touch and shared with each other what was happening in their lives.

Was there any tougher glue than friendship?

She found the tin of biscuits and put it on the table in front of him then brought their coffees over, setting them both down before plopping into the battered lounge chair opposite him, unable to stop staring at him and slightly embarrassed that he seemed to be equally focussed on her.

'Well?' she finally asked, mainly to break a silence that was becoming uncomfortable.

'It's been too long since we've seen each other,' he said. 'You've changed somehow.'

'It's been five years and then only for an hour at Sydney airport. Anyway, I never change, you should know that,' she teased. 'I was a skinny kid with wild red hair who grew into a skinny adult with wild red hair. But you, who knew you'd get so handsome?'

It was a weird conversation to be having with Nick—strained somehow. Although they'd gone in different directions after high school, he to Sydney to study medicine, she choosing Townsville for her nursing training, on other occasions when they'd caught up with each other, even briefly, they'd fallen back into their old patterns of friendship as if they'd never been parted.

Yet tonight was different.

'Will you stay with Gran?'

Gran was Nick's relation, not hers, but Bill was in the habit of calling in a couple of times a week, taking Gran shopping or getting library books for her.

With Nick here, Gran wouldn't need her...

'No, I spoke to Bob when the idea of the contract first came up. He offered me one of the penthouses at the new marina development he's just completed.'

'The sod!' Bill muttered, thinking of her eldest brother, the developer in the family. 'So *he* knew you were coming and said not a word to me! What's more, all I've got is a one-bedroomed apartment on the sixth floor in that building, and I bet he's giving you family discount as well.'

Nick smiled.

'But I am family, aren't I?' he retorted. 'I'm your seventh brother. Isn't that what you've always said?'

It was, of course, but it wasn't their relationship that was disturbing Bill right now, though what it was she couldn't pinpoint.

'It'll be a bit weird working with you,' she said, fairly hesitantly because that didn't seem to be what it was either.

Nick smiled and her heart gave another of those strange thuds.

'You only think that because you're used to being the one bossing me around and in the ER a doctor trumps a nurse.'

She rose to the challenge in his words.

'Oh, yeah? Says who?'

He didn't answer, just picked up his coffee, his smile still lingering about his lips, showing in fine lines down his cheeks and a crinkle at the corner of his eyes.

It was because she hadn't seen him for so long she had to keep staring at him, she was telling herself when the smile turned into a grimace.

'Aaargh! You call this coffee? You haven't heard of coffee machines? How backward *is* this place?'

Bill laughed.

'Not too backward these days but budget cuts are everywhere. You want fancy coffee you'll have to provide the machine and the beans, and everyone will use both and one night a junkie will steal the machine and you'll be back to instant.'

'I'll get a small one and lock it in my locker and it will be for my exclusive use,' Nick growled, sounding so like the old Nick of her childhood that Bill felt warmth spread through her.

This was going to be all right—wasn't it?

Bill was pondering this when Lesley burst through the door.

'Critical emergency on the way in, Dr Grant. Can you take the call from the ambulance?'

* * *

Forty minutes later Nick was ready—well, as ready as he would ever be. Although the town had grown, Willowby Hospital was still little more than a large country health centre. No specialist resuscitation area here, no emergency trauma surgeon on standby, just him and whatever nurses could be spared from the usual stream of patients on a Sunday night.

Him and Bill!

Right now she was setting up a series of trays on trolleys, IV and blood-drawing supplies, chest tubes, ventilator, defibrillator, medications, and was checking the supply of oxygen, the suction tubes, not fussing but moving with swift confidence and precision. Just watching her gave him added confidence about whatever lay ahead.

'The baler they spoke of—it's one of those things that rolls hay into huge round bales?' he asked, and she looked up from what she was doing to nod.

'Though what the lad was doing, putting his arm anywhere near the machine, is beyond me,' she said, before adding thoughtfully, 'I suppose if the string got caught you might think you could pull it loose and give it a tug. I've always thought night-harvesting had an element of danger because, unless you're used to night shifts, your mind might not be as sharp as it should be.'

Images of the damage such a machine could do to a human arm and shoulder flashed through Nick's mind, and he had to agree with Bill's opinion, but further speculation was brought to an end by the arrival of the ambulance and their patient, unstable from blood loss, his right arm loosely wrapped in now-bloody dressings, a tourniquet having been unable to stop the bleeding completely.

Nick listened as the paramedic explained what had been done so far—the patient intubated, fluid running into him, morphine to ease the pain, conscious but not really with them, so shocked it was clear the first-response team doubted he could be saved.

Hypovolaemic shock from loss of blood. The young man's heart would be racing, his hands and feet cold and clammy, his pulse weak—

'All we need to do is stabilise him enough for him to be airlifted down to Brisbane,' Bill reminded Nick, as if she'd heard the same thing in the paramedic's tone and had the same symptoms racing through *her* head.

So it began, the flurry of activity to keep the young man alive long enough for surgeons down south to save him. The paramedics had fluid flowing into him through his radial artery but he needed more.

While Bill hooked the patient up to the hospital's oxygen supply and monitors, taking blood to send to the lab for typing, Nick prepared to put a catheter into the left subclavian vein, anaesthetising the site, then advancing a needle carefully down beneath the clavicle, a guide wire following it when blood flowed freely into the needle's syringe.

Removing the needle, he made a small incision, his hands working mechanically while his mind raced ahead. Once the catheter, guided by the wire, was in place and more fluid was flowing in, he could examine the torn arm and shoulder in order to find the source of the blood loss.

'The tourniquet is holding back blood loss from the brachial artery,' Bill said, making Nick wonder if their childhood ability to follow each other's thoughts was still alive and well.

He looked across to where she was gently probing the damaged arm, flushing debris and carefully tweezing out bits of dirt and straw—the work a surgical assistant would be doing in a major trauma centre.

'I've been releasing the tourniquet and can see where the artery is damaged but he's so shocked I doubt that's the only source of blood loss.'

They were definitely following each other's thoughts!

He moved round the table, leaving another nurse to control the fluid while a third watched the monitors. He'd have liked to have an anaesthetist present, but that, too, was for city trauma centres, so he used a nerve block to anaesthetise the arm before examining it.

'There,' Bill said, passing him a loupe so he could see the torn artery more clearly.

Two tiny sutures and the tear was closed, but the nurse watching the monitors reported falling blood pressure.

Drastically falling blood pressure…

'V-tach,' the nurse said quietly.

The words were barely spoken before Bill had the defibrillator pushed up against the trolley and was already attaching leads to the paddles. Nick set the voltage, gave the order to clear, placed the paddles above and below the heart and watched as the patient's body jerked on the table.

He looked at the monitor and saw the nurse shake her head.

He upped the voltage, cleared again and felt the tension in the room as the body jerked and stilled, then the green line on the monitor showed the heartbeat had stabilised.

A release of held breath, nothing more than a sigh, but he knew everyone had been willing the lad to live.

For now!

'He's had three litres of fluid—he's definitely losing blood somewhere else,' he muttered, then turned to Bill. 'We need full blood—has he been cross-matched?'

'It's on its way,' she said quietly, then nodded towards the door where a young man in a white coat had appeared, stethoscope around his neck and, thank heavens, two blood packs in his hands.

'Rob Darwin, I'm one of two doctors on duty upstairs but Bill said you needed help down here, and when Bill calls, I obey. Her slightest wish is my command.'

He was joking, teasing Bill, but Nick had no time for jokes.

'Get that blood into him—it's warmed?'

Rob nodded and took up a position at the head of the table, fiddling with the fluid lines as he prepared to give the patient the transfusion.

'The bleeding has to be internal, but how? Where?'

Nick was talking to himself as he looked at the swollen, badly dislocated shoulder, picturing how the machine must have caught the arm and twisted it, trying to imagine where internal damage would have occurred.

'A tear to the axillary artery?' Bill suggested quietly, looking up from where she was putting clean dressings on the damaged arm.

'That or the subclavian,' Nick agreed. 'I'm going to have to go in and have a look.'

He glanced up at Rob.

'You okay with anaesthesia?'

Rob grinned.

'I haven't been here long but as Bill told me soon after I arrived, country doctors do the lot,' he said. 'How long would you want him out to it?'

'Hopefully twenty minutes, but double it—make it forty to be on the safe side. He's due to be flown out if we can get him stable.'

'The plane will wait,' Rob assured him, already checking the available drugs and drawing up what he'd need.

Bill prepared the area beneath where the young man's shoulder should be, quickly shaving the hair and swabbing antiseptic all around then stepping back as Nick made the incision.

'We know it's in the armpit—it should be right there,' Nick grumbled, but the muscle had been torn so badly it was hard to see where the armpit should have been.

A fresh flush of blood as Bill moved the lad's scapula revealed the tear, blood pulsing from it into the surrounding tissues.

'The pressure must have been enormous,' he murmured. 'It looks as if it's been ripped apart. I'll have to cut off the torn ends and sew it back together. The vascular surgeons in Brisbane can do the fancy stuff.'

Bill watched in utter amazement as the man she'd known so well as a boy—her first best friend—calmly performed life-saving microscopic surgery on their patient. But the whole shift had been one surprise after another, beginning with Nick walking into the ER as if he belonged there.

'Another suture!'

He snapped the order, making her realise he'd already asked while she'd been reliving the shock of his arrival. Her mind back in gear, she worked with him, actually thrilled to be seeing him in action—seeing just how good an emergency doctor he'd turned out to be.

Not that she'd ever doubted it. Nick had always been able to do anything, and even excel at it, once he'd set his mind to it.

Her friend Nick…

CHAPTER TWO

THE PATIENT WAS finally wheeled away, heading for an airlift to Brisbane and the experts who might or might not save his life and, with even more luck, his arm. Bill slid down the wall and slumped to the floor of the trauma room, oblivious to the mess of packaging, blood, swabs and tubing that littered the floor.

'Not bad for a first night on duty?' she said to Nick, smiling up at the man who leant against the wall across from her. 'Think you'll enjoy work back in the old home town?'

His face was drawn, the stress of the two-hour fight to keep the youngster alive imprinted clearly on his features, yet he found the shadow of a smile.

'Anything you can do I can do better,' he teased, using a phrase that had been bandied back and forth between them a thousand times in their youth.

A young nurse poked her head into the room.

'Want me to clean up?' she asked.

Bill shook her head.

'I'm off duty, I'll do it in a minute.'

She turned back to Nick to find him studying her, a strange expression on his face.

'What?' she asked, disturbed not by him looking at her but by her reaction to it—to him, the new him.

'Rob Darwin? Love interest?' he asked.

'As if!' Bill snorted. 'Not that he's not a nice young man, and not that he wouldn't like there to be something, but…'

She hesitated, finding her reluctance to date hard to put into words.

'No spark?'

Nick had found the words for her.

'None at all,' she said, 'and it seems a waste of my time and unfair to him just to date for the sake of dating.'

'Very noble of you,' he teased, then he smiled again.

This smile was better than the first one, and her reaction more intense.

Weird when this was Nick, but she didn't have time to consider it as he was speaking again and, anyway, maybe the reactions were nothing more than tiredness and the aftermath of stress.

'There must have been a spark with Nigel,' he was saying. 'What really happened there? You could have married him, the Great God of Surgery, and been taken away from all this. You could be down in the city, doing social stuff, running fundraising balls, lunching for good causes, decked out in designer gear instead of bloody scrubs.'

'Now, there would be a fate worse than death!'

The words were lightly spoken but pain pierced her heart as she remembered it had been that same 'Great God' who'd ordered her to have an abortion a month before their wedding because he didn't want people thinking they'd got married because she was pregnant.

She breathed deeply, aware that too much bitterness still leaked into her veins when she thought of that disastrous time.

The realisation that the man she'd loved had been nothing more than a shallow, social-climbing pretender had rocked her self-confidence and made Bill question her judgement about people, particularly men. The miscarriage two months later had exacerbated her loss of self-worth and it had taken years, back here in Willowby with her family and friends, to rebuild it.

Although now she'd grown a thicker skin and heavier armour to shield her fragile heart...

Nick heard the change in her voice and wondered how much damage her broken engagement had done to her trust—to Bill herself, given she was the most trusting person he had ever known. It worried him that he didn't know the background to the break-up—didn't know a lot of things about his friend.

His best friend!

What did the kids call it these days? BFF? Best friends for ever?

'Anyway,' she was saying, while his mind had drifted back to the past, 'if we're going to talk of what *might* have happened in our lives, *you* could have married Seraphina or whatever she called herself when *she* fell pregnant, and gone swanning off to New York to live off her earnings as a top supermodel.'

That was better, more like old times, Bill taking the fight to him!

'Serena,' Nick corrected. 'You're muddling her up with Delphina, who was the one before, and, anyway, I did offer to marry Serena but she wanted none of it, not me, not a child and definitely not marriage.'

Silence fell, the ghosts of dead children lying between them among the empty packaging and blood.

Bill reacted first, pushing herself up off the floor, stripping off her soiled apron and flinging it into a bin, then bending to begin collecting the rubbish off the floor.

'I'll do that.'

The young wardsman who appeared, mop and bucket in hand, waved her away and although she picked up a few more bits of rubbish, she was happy to leave him to it, following Nick out of the trauma room to find the big open area of the ER eerily quiet at six on a Monday morning.

'Everyone's sleeping in,' Andy, the duty ER manager, told them. Newly arrived on shift, he was spic and span, his face alert, his smile bright. 'Go home, both of you.'

'Got to dictate some notes on that last case,' Nick said.

'And I'm having a shower then heading for beach,' Bill told them. 'I need some sea air to clear my head before I can think about sleeping.'

Would she go to Woodchoppers? Nick wondered, not wanting to ask in front of Andy but aware he'd like to join Bill at the beach. Weird name for a beach, but it had been their favourite swimming beach growing up, Bill and her six brothers declaring it their personal fiefdom, keeping it free of any less desirable elements, particularly those pushing drugs to impressionable teenagers.

Whillimina de Groote and her brothers! They'd become the family he'd never had. Bill dragging him to her home after his first day at school, insisting her brothers teach the five-year-old Nick how to defend himself.

They'd taught him a lot after that...

* * *

Bill stood under the shower, the water so hot that steam was fogging the cubicle, but no amount of heat or water could wash away the uneasiness that lingered over her reaction to Nick.

To Nick as a *man*!

How pathetic!

She'd known him for close to thirty years, considered him her best friend in all the world, so why, now, would she be reacting to him as a man?

Maybe it was nothing more than the stress and tiredness engendered by their battle to save the teenager's life.

She could only hope...

Accepting that the hot water wasn't helping, she turned off the taps, dried herself hurriedly, rubbed at the tangled mess of red curls that topped her head and fell down past her shoulders, then pulled on an old bikini she kept in her locker, covered it with a voluminous T-shirt, grabbed her handbag and hurried out the staff exit, not wanting to bump into Nick before she'd had a good run on the beach and a swim in the limpid, tropical waters to clear her head.

Not before she happened to be on duty with him again, in fact, and if she spoke to the ER secretary who drew up the rosters, total avoidance might be possible.

Well, not total. He was back to see his gran, so they'd undoubtedly run into each other at Gran's house...

But at least he'd come home.

She pulled up in the small parking area at Woodchoppers Beach and slogged across the sand dunes, glad the effort of crossing them made the beach the least used of the beaches around Willowby. Pulling off her T-shirt and dropping it on the sand, she began to run, slowly at first then, as her muscles warmed, sprinting faster and faster—short sprints then slow jogs, alternating the two, feeling the blood surge through her body, bringing it to life in a most satisfactory manner.

Two more lengths of the beach and then she'd swim.

'You shouldn't come here on your own—you never know who might be around.'

Nick's appearance startled her.

'Obviously!' she snapped at him.

But as he ignored her comment and fell into stride beside her, she knew all the good of her run had vanished, and with it her peace of mind.

It's only Nick, she told herself, but that didn't seem to stop the awareness that prickled in her skin all down one side—the side closest to her jogging companion.

Veering away from him, she headed for the water and dived from ankle depth into the clear, green-blue sea, surfacing to breathe then diving again to porpoise along parallel to the beach, relishing the silken kiss of the water against her skin.

Had she always been this gorgeous?

Long, lean, and tanned in a way redheads weren't supposed to tan?

Nick watched as she dived and surfaced in the water, only to dive again, her limbs flashing in the sunlight, her hair trailing behind her—a mermaid at play.

Was it because she'd always been a friend that he'd never seen her as a woman? Not that he could afford to see her that way now—they were friends! There'd be plenty of interesting and intelligent, even beautiful, women here in Willowby. It was only a matter of connecting up with some of them, and the thoughts he found himself having about Bill would disappear.

For all she joked about having escaped a fate worse than death when she'd dumped Nigel, she was the kind of woman who should be married—married with a tribe of red-headed kids clustered around her—because she'd always been a mother hen, adopting not only him but any fellow pupil in danger of being bullied or excluded from one of the childhood gangs.

He stripped down to his jocks and dived into the water, surfacing a little distance from her, uncertain enough about the strange reactions of the night to not want to be too close.

'Race you to the rocks,' she challenged, and started immediately, but his longer strokes and stronger kick soon had him catching up, so they swam together towards the smooth, rounded rocks that jutted into the water at the end of the bay until they were close enough for him to swim away, beating her by a body length.

Strange reactions or not, he wasn't going to let her beat him!

'Oh, that was good,' she said, coming up out of the water, her hair streaming down her back. 'I find it's so much easier to sleep during the day if I have a run and a swim before I go home.'

She looked at him for a moment, her golden-brown eyes assessing.

'*And* a hearty breakfast at the surf club back at the main beach. You up for that, or has your body become a temple so you can't eat delicious crispy bacon, and beef sausages, and fried tomatoes, and all the other things that are loaded with cholesterol and fat?'

Nick shook his head in disbelief.

'So you still eat like a navvy and stay as slim as a whip. Some metabolism you de Grootes inherited.'

'Not all of us,' Bill told him, smiling as she waded in front of him back to the beach. 'Bob's developed a most unsightly paunch, and Joel's heading in the same direction. Too many business lunches and not enough exercise, that's the problem with those two.'

Nick watched the way her butt moved as she walked in front of him and tried to think of Bill's brothers rather than how those twin globes would fit into his hands.

'Have you already moved into the apartment?'

She threw the question over her shoulder but it brushed right past him, his attention snaffled by the way the woman in front of him moved, and how her breasts hung low as she bent to retrieve her T-shirt from the sand, the bikini she wore barely covering her nipples.

'Nick?'

Had she caught him watching her as she turned, her eyebrows raised as she waited for a reply?

What had she asked?

Had he moved in…?

'If you call dumping a couple of suitcases in the bedroom and unpacking my wash bag as moving in, then yes,' he responded, hoping the gap between the question and the answer hadn't been too long. 'It's fully furnished so all I had to bring were clothes and personal stuff. I'd hardly begun to unpack when the hospital phoned to ask if I could work last night.'

Bill didn't respond, so disturbed was she by the sight of Nick's lean, toned body that casual conversation was beyond her. He'd shrugged as he'd mentioned unpacking, an unfortunate movement as it had drawn her attention back to his chest, with its flat wedges of pectoral muscles and clearly defined six-pack.

She wanted to ask if he'd been working out, but that would give away the fact she'd noticed and the way she was feeling it was better if the question went unasked.

She climbed the first dune and raced down the other side then up the next, aware he was pacing himself to stay beside her—aware of *him*!

It was bad enough that he was living in the same building, so now she'd have to avoid seeing him out of work hours as well as at work, without him suspecting she might see him as other than a friend.

A passing fancy, surely?

But her reactions to him were forgotten as she topped the last dune.

'What is *that*?'

The words burst from her lips as she saw the racing-green sports car, hood down, cream leather seats, sleek lines shouting speed and, yes, seduction.

'My car?' His voice was quiet but she heard the pride in it.

'Well, *that* will get you noticed in Willowby,' she muttered, aware of just who would notice it first—the constant stream of beautiful women who used Willowby as a jumping-off place for reef adventures. True, they worked, if you could call hostessing on luxury yachts or on the six-star island resorts working, but since the mining boom had led to the town becoming one of the wealthiest per capita in the country, the place had been swamped by women, and men if she was honest, looking to separate some of that money from those who had it.

'Gets me noticed most places,' Nick replied, and the smile on his face made her stomach clench.

That's why he'd bought it! She knew that much immediately, remembering the email he'd sent her many years ago when he'd returned from his first stint with the army reserve, serving overseas. He'd helped to put back together young men blown apart by bombs in wars that ordinary people didn't understand.

He'd come home, he'd said, with one aim—to live for the day. He'd promised himself a beautiful car, the best of clothes and as many beautiful women as cared to play with him. 'I'm honest with them, Bill,' he'd said in the email. 'I tell them all it's not for ever, that marriage isn't in my long-term plans. You'd be surprised how many women are happy with that—even agreeing that it's not for them either. Things are different now.'

Were they? Bill hadn't been able to answer that question then and couldn't now. For herself, she knew she wanted marriage, and children too, but not without love and so far, apart from that one disastrous experience, love hadn't come along.

'Ride with me,' Nick suggested. 'I'll drop you back at your old bomb after breakfast.'

'Ride in that thing? The town might have grown, Nick, but at heart it's still the same old Willowby. I only need to be spotted by one of the local gossips and my reputation would be ruined. Did you see the de Groote girl, they'd be saying, running around in a fast car with a fast man? You, of course, will be forgiven. About you they'll say, hasn't he done well for himself, that grandson of old Mrs Grant? And such a kind boy, coming home to be with his gran now she's getting on.'

Nick laughed and headed for his car.

'Okay, but I won't offer to race you to the surf club,' he teased. 'Too unfair.'

Bill climbed into her battered old four-wheel drive, the vehicle her father had bought her new when she'd passed her driving test. She patted the dash to reassure the car she wasn't put off by its shabby appearance, or influenced by the shining beauty of Nick's vehicle, but it was she who needed reassurance as her folly in suggesting he breakfast with her finally struck home. Even with her sea-drenched curls, and the tatty old T-shirt, she'd always felt quite at home at the surf club, but these days many of the beautiful people breakfasted there as well—

Whoa! Surely she wasn't concerned that Nick would compare her to some of the other women and find her wanting?

Of course she wasn't!

Then why was she wondering if there might not be a long shift somewhere in the mess of clothes, books and papers in the back seat of the car—wondering if there might be a slightly melted tube of lip gloss in the glove box?

Hopeless, that's what she was.

He'd selected a table that looked out from a covered deck over the town's main beach and the placid tropical waters. Bill slipped into a chair beside him, so she, too, could look out to sea. Far out on the horizon they could see the shapes of the islands that dotted the coastline—tourist havens on Australia's biggest natural wonder, the Great Barrier Reef.

'I've ordered the big breakfast for both of us,' Nick

informed her. 'Anything you don't want, I'll eat. And coffee—double-shot latte still your drug of choice?'

'It is, and thanks,' Bill replied, telling herself at the same time that a nice normal breakfast with Nick should banish all the silly stuff that had been going on in her head.

Especially as Nick was wasting no time checking out the talent, with his eyes on a group of three long-haired blondes, laughing and joking on the other side of the wide deck.

'The town's scenery's improved,' he joked.

'It's the money that's being splashed around,' Bill reminded him, deciding to take his comment seriously. 'Money attracts money but it also attracts the kind of people who like to have it—like to spend it. The problem is that while the miners and the people who work in mining support services are all earning big money, the price of housing goes up, rents go up, and the ordinary people of the town, especially those who don't own their own houses, are stuck with costs they can't afford.'

Nick smiled.

'Still a worry-wart,' he teased.

'Well, someone has to worry about it. Nurses at the hospital don't get paid more than their counterparts in other places in the state, yet accommodation costs in town are enormous. Fortunately the hospital has realised it has a problem and has built some small rental apartments in the grounds, but you spread that problem out across the town—the check-out staff at supermarkets, the workers in government offices, the council truck drivers—all the locals suffer.'

She stopped, partly because she was aware she'd mounted her soap-box and really shouldn't be boring

Nick with the problem but also because the blondes appeared to have noticed him—new talent in town?—and were sending welcoming smiles his way.

'Maybe they saw the car when you drove in,' Bill muttered.

'Ouch! And anyway the car park's out the back. No, it's my good looks that have got their attention—see, one of them is coming over.'

One of them *was* coming over. The leggiest one, with the longest, shiniest, blondest, dead-straight hair!

'Aren't you Nick Grant?' she asked, and as Nick nodded, she held out her hand.

'I told the girls it was you. You used to go out with Serena Snow, didn't you?'

Again Nick had to agree, and the leggy blonde introduced herself.

'I'm Amy Wentworth. I met you a couple of times at parties back then. What are you doing up in this neck of the woods? Holidaying? Off to the reef for a few days' R and R?'

So far she'd totally ignored Bill—not that it mattered, Bill told herself.

She studied the woman while Nick explained he was working here, living in the new apartment building at the marina but with no elaboration on why. Amy raised her eyebrows.

'Can't imagine you in a hick town like this. Oh, I know there's a lot of money around, but what do you *do* when you're not working?'

Nick grinned at her.

'I'll be doing pretty much what I did when I wasn't working in Sydney.'

Amy drifted away but Bill wasn't going to let him get away with that tantalising reply.

'Which was?' she asked.

'What which was?'

'The "pretty much what you did in Sydney" bit of that conversation.'

'Ah, but I told you years ago,' he reminded her. 'I had a good time and I intend to do just that up here. You don't need nightclubs and friends with yachts on the harbour to have a good time.'

'We've got a nightclub and a two of my brothers have yachts, or big motor launches,' Bill said defensively, and Nick laughed.

'Exactly, although I think the nightclub crowd are a bit young for me, but you can have a good time wherever you are. In fact, I'm off for three days next week and think I might pop across to one of the island resorts—do a bit of diving and fishing and...'

'Meeting beautiful women,' Bill finished for him.

Again Nick smiled, although this time it was a little forced because in the back of his mind he'd had another reason for returning to Willowby, one that was becoming important to him.

'That too, of course,' he answered glibly. 'Want to come?'

CHAPTER THREE

SHE DIDN'T REPLY, studying him intently for a moment instead, and he knew that look. Undoubtedly she'd picked up something from his tone.

'Did it hurt you?' she asked.

Yep, he'd been right about the look and although he knew full well what she meant by the question, he wasn't going to cede ground to her by admitting it.

'Did what hurt me?'

'You know full well what I mean,' she said crossly. 'Serena saying no to your proposal.'

His turn to study her. The problem with friendship— a strong and enduring friendship like the one they shared—was that you couldn't lie to the other party. Oh, you could fudge around a bit and dodge answering, but you couldn't right out lie.

He turned his gaze from Bill's too-perceptive eyes and looked out over the beach and island-strewn sea.

The truth!

'More than I could have imagined,' he admitted, and turned back so, now it was out, he could meet the gold-brown eyes fastened so steadfastly on his face. 'I don't think it was Serena's rejection so much. I liked her well enough. For all her self-focus she was fun to be with

and happy that we more or less lived separate lives—
both of us working long hours at different times—so I
can't see why it wouldn't have worked.'

Bill's small, rather shocked 'Oh' broke into his
thoughts but now he'd started he wanted to finish what
he'd been saying.

'You know how I feel about the "l" word, Bill, so I
can't say I loved her, but what had…not excited but certainly intrigued me was the idea of having a family—
a wife and child—people who belonged, not to me but
with me, if you know what I mean.'

The disbelief on Bill's face was so easy to read he
had to laugh.

'Yes, yes, I know I said it would never happen,
but finding out Serena was pregnant, well, it kind of
changed something inside me, as if a wire that had
been shorted out was suddenly reconnected and family
stopped being in front of going down mines, abduction
by aliens and the bogeyman in my fears.'

He paused, marshalling his thoughts.

'In part, it's why I came home—came back to the
only family I've ever known: Gran and you de Grootes.'

'Looking for a family of your own?' Bill asked.

Again he paused, but honesty won out.

'Yes, I think so—I think it's what I need, Bill. What
I really want.'

'Oh, Nick,' Bill said softly, and she covered his hand
with hers as she had so often in the past. Though he'd reciprocated often enough, when some fool of a youth had
hurt her in some way or when her pet hamster had died.

The strange thing was that this time it felt different.
Nice, but different.

'I also need to sleep,' he said, regaining control over

some erratic emotions and reclaiming his hand at the same time. 'Then this afternoon I must go over and see Gran. You want to come?'

Fool! Wasn't he going for distance here until he'd sorted out his reactions to his old friend?

'No, I saw her yesterday—well, the day before now—although,' Bill said firmly, 'that brings me to another issue. I had an email from you only last week—you answered the one I sent to say she was looking a whole lot better—and there wasn't a word about coming here to work. And if you were talking to Bob and pinching the best apartment in his building then you must have been fairly certain then.'

Nick laughed again—the disjointed sentence was sheer Bill, words tumbling over each other to get said, especially when she was angry with him.

'One,' he said, holding up his hand and pointing to his first finger, 'I wanted to surprise Gran and if I told you…'

He let the sentence hang but had the satisfaction of seeing a faint blush colour her cheeks. As honest as the day was long, Bill would be the first to admit she found it almost impossible to keep a secret.

'And two…' he pointed to his next finger '…I wasn't sure you were even here. In that email you'd said you had time off and were going to Townsville to talk to someone about some course.'

She nodded.

'The mine rescue people, about a new course. It *was* to be this week and next, but was cancelled. Pity really because it was going to be on flooded underground rescues and I haven't done that yet.'

'Mine rescue—flooded underground mines?' He

could hear his voice rising but couldn't stop it. 'What do you mean, you haven't done that yet? What on earth are you doing, getting involved with mine rescue, and what are your brothers doing, letting you do it?'

Her laugh made the sun seem brighter.

'Oh, Nick, you sound just like Bob, but Danny and Pete are already in the elite mine rescue squad and they've encouraged me to get involved. I'm not up to their standard yet—not flying off to foreign parts to help out—but I can hold my own as part of the local team when the experts are away, especially with my nursing and paramedic experience.'

Nick didn't know why he was surprised, but just the thought of mine rescue made him shudder. Danny, the second of the de Groote boys, had taken him and Bill down a mine when they'd been in their early teens, and though Bill had revelled in the darkness and gloom, he had hated every minute of the musty smell and the idea of being over a mile beneath the mountain.

Had been afraid every minute of it, to be honest, but he hadn't mentioned that part to his fearless friend.

Though Bill was terrified of snakes, so—

'I'm heading home to bed,' she said, cutting into his thoughts and sounding so casually at ease she obviously wasn't feeling any of the strangeness he was. 'I guess I'll be seeing you around.'

She stood up, paused, then dropped a light kiss on the top of his head.

'Nice to have you back, curly,' she added lightly, before weaving her way between the tables and disappearing round the corner of the deck.

He couldn't help but turn and watch her go.

* * *

Bill pondered Nick's startling revelation that he'd discovered he wanted a family. Was that why he'd come
home? Did he see Willowby as the place to raise this
family?

They were unanswerable questions so she moved on
to considering the uneasiness the subject had caused in
her insides when it was nothing at all to do with her.

Although hadn't that been *her* dream? The memory
of her delight in finding she was pregnant made her
stomach tighten.

Enough!

No melancholy!

And anyway, wasn't there enough to occupy her
brain with Nick's sudden reappearance?

She drove home slowly and carefully, aware she was
tired, but her mind now snagged on the unexpectedness
of the situation—on Nick.

But thinking about it, she could see it was only natural that Nick *would* want a family for all he'd spent
his youth mocking the institution. She'd always known
his mockery was to cover the hurt of his own parents'
behaviour, jaunting around the world, crewing on luxury yachts, visiting exotic places, their son left with his
grandmother not, as they'd said, so he'd have stability
but because it had made it easier for them to continue
to enjoy their lifestyle.

They'd eventually drowned at sea when their own,
much smaller yacht was caught up in a typhoon, but
their deaths had had little effect on Nick because Gran
had given him more than stability, she'd given him
love—unquestioning and all-encompassing love.

So, while Nick's admission was surprising, it was

her own reaction to it that needed more consideration. As did her reaction to the sight of his bare chest, and the way his muscled thighs had matched her strides on the beach, or the strange feelings seeing him had produced, not in her heart where their friendship lived, but along her nerves and—

No, she wasn't going there!

Surprise—that's what had caused the weird reactions.

She stopped at the control panel to the underground parking area to press in the security code then drove in as the big door opened. She parked and made her way to the lift, the exhaustion that followed a busy night on duty fast catching up with her.

Exiting on the sixth floor, she headed down the corridor to her apartment, an end one with a view out to sea, a really special place to live for all she'd complained about its size. Two floors above her the two penthouses spread across the top level—big four-bedroom homes, each with three bathrooms, wide decks taking in the view out over the Coral Sea, and a smaller deck on the western side, looking back towards the green-clad mountains.

Bill smiled to herself, pleased that even in choosing accommodation that might only be for a year, Nick was following his avowed intention to have nothing but the best!

It had to be tiredness, Nick decided as he drove home, that had weakened him to the extent he'd admitted his disappointment over Serena and the baby to Bill. Normally he'd have teased her about being nosy, or asked a question about her own love life to divert her attention from the fact he hadn't answered, but, no, he'd heard himself bleating out his pathetic reaction, even feeling remembered pain for the loss of a dream—a family of his own.

But he *hadn't* lost the dream, he reminded himself. Wasn't that why he was here? He'd been drawn back by Gran, of course, but also by the feeling that in Willowby he might find the woman who would help the dream come true. A family woman and, yes, his thinking had been that Bill would know someone who'd be just right for him—Bill or someone in *her* family. They were into family in a big way, the de Grootes.

And hadn't he always turned to Bill when he had a problem, or needed help?

Letting himself into the penthouse, he set aside his tumbling thoughts and sighed with pleasure. The familiar view out across the island-dotted sea still took his breath away. And tired though he was, a part of him wanting nothing more than to slip into bed, he had to walk out onto the balcony and breathe in the fresh sea air.

He was home.

Second night on duty. No life-threatening emergencies and he'd heard from the hospital in Brisbane that his patient from the previous night was doing well.

'It has to be the night for the bizarre,' Bill said, slumping down beside him in the tea room during a lull in proceedings. 'I suppose dog bites are common enough, but the bite usually doesn't come with a couple of dog teeth in the wounds. The dog must have been a hundred and five for its teeth to have come out so easily.'

Nick shook his head.

'I can't believe I nearly missed the second one. It was weird enough discovering one tooth in a puncture wound, but it was only when you were putting on the dressing that I realised I hadn't probed the second hole and, sure enough, another tooth.'

'Perhaps someone wrenched the dog off and that's why it lost the teeth.'

Nick considered this for a moment.

'No, there'd have been tearing around the wounds and there was no sign of that—just bite holes and teeth.'

'From an ancient dog or one with a gum problem.'

'And the kid with his head stuck in the bars of his cot,' Nick recalled. 'You'd have thought his father would have had a hacksaw to cut through a bar and release him instead of taking the cot to pieces to bring it in for us to do it.'

'It did look funny.' Bill smiled at the memory of the two parents arriving with the side of the cot held between them, and the grandmother carrying the perfectly contented baby, which had been looking around with wide-eyed curiosity and doubtless wondering about all the fuss.

'Cute baby, though,' Bill added, although she knew she should dodge baby conversations altogether because even after more than a year it hurt to see other people's babies.

'Very cute,' Nick agreed, rising to his feet as his pager buzzed.

'Drunk in cubicle three,' the duty manager told Bill as she returned to work. 'There's a nurse in there with Nick but they might need more help.'

Bill closed her eyes for a moment. Babies were upsetting enough, but if there was one thing she hated, it was handling drunks. They came in all shapes and sizes, and varied from angry and abusive, through straight obstreperous, to wildly happy, laughing hilariously as they threw up on your uniform and shoes.

'Obstreperous,' Nick said under his breath as Bill entered the cubicle. 'He's had a fall, I'd say into a bougainvillea as he has multiple abrasions, a dislocated finger and some very nasty thorns sticking out of his legs.'

The man in question was insisting he was perfectly all right, if Bill was translating his drunk speech correctly, but whenever he moved on the examination table the thorns dug in and he'd yelp with pain.

'I'm going to give him a local anaesthetic then fix the finger,' Nick continued. 'If you two can hold him still for a minute, I'd be grateful.'

The finger joint went back into place, and the young nurse cleaned and bandaged the man's hand so the finger would be supported while the joint healed.

'We'll start on the thorns,' Nick told Bill, but it was easier said than done when the man kept insisting he was fine and trying to climb off the table.

'Who brought him in?' Nick asked the young nurse.

'His wife. She's out in the waiting area.'

'Could you ask her to come in?' Nick smiled as he made the request and Bill couldn't help but notice the nurse's blush.

Still winning women over wherever he goes, she thought, but though she'd thought it a thousand times before, this time it didn't prompt a smile.

'Being a nuisance, is he?' the woman who entered demanded, before turning to her husband. 'Now, listen, you, sit still and let the doctor do his job or I'll take you home and throw you back into the bougainvillea my-self, and don't think I wouldn't do it.'

The man on the table quietened immediately and looking from him, a bulky six-footer, to the small slim wife, Bill had to smile.

'Thank you, madam.' Nick gave the wife a small bow. 'It's good to know who's the boss in the house-hold.'

She smiled at Nick.

'It probably wouldn't work if he was a habitual drunk, but as it is, he can't hold his grog so mostly he doesn't drink, but we've just had our first grandchild and he went out with his mates to wet the baby's head—they insisted, and now look at him. Fine example for the kid he'll be!'

She spoke fondly and even smiled at her husband, settling into a chair beside the wall to make sure he behaved.

Bill worked beside Nick, swabbing each scratch and wound as he pulled out the thorns.

'I can do this,' she said to him, but he shrugged away her offer and continued working until they had the now sleeping drunk patched up and able to be released to his wife.

'Just watch the wounds in case they begin to fester. There's no point starting antibiotics if he doesn't need them, but come back or go to see your own GP if they worry him,' Nick told her as he helped her take the man out to the waiting room where an aide would help her out to the car.

'Babies do keep cropping up,' he said to Bill as she came out of the cubicle, a bag of debris in her hand.

I'm glad he said that, Bill decided, setting aside her

own feelings and thinking just of Nick. It must mean he's over or getting over the loss of what he'd thought would be his very own family.

'Some nights are like that,' she reminded him. 'I'd far prefer a run of babies, as long as they're not too sick, to a run of drunks.'

'Hear, hear!'

This from the nurse who had followed Bill out of the cubicle, although she'd spoken to Nick rather than Bill. The nurse was from an agency—distinctive in the agency uniform—someone Bill didn't know. But studying her now, as the nurse continued to chat to Nick, Bill realised she was exactly his type—tall, curvy, blonde.

And, no, that wasn't a stab of jealousy. Her and Nick's friendship had survived a long stream of blondes, some, like Serena, Bill had seen in photos, and some she'd only heard about through emails and texts.

The agency nurse was now suggesting she and Nick have a coffee and as the ER was virtually deserted, it was only natural he should accept, although he did turn his head to ask, 'Want another coffee, Bill?'

Bill shook her head and headed off to dispose of the rubbish, hearing the agency nurse question the name Bill and Nick explaining.

This had to stop! she told herself as she hurled the bag of rubbish down the chute. Her friendship with Nick had survived because neither of them had ever had the slightest interest in the other in a romantic way. Growing up, she'd have as soon considered falling in love with one of her brothers.

It had to be that she hadn't seen him for so long that she was suddenly seeing him as a man.

Reacting to him as a man!

When *had* she last seen him?

He'd been in New York, proposing to Serena, when she'd broken off her engagement to Nigel, and although Nick had promised faithfully he'd be home for her wedding, once that was off, he'd headed for foreign parts, doing his bit for the army once again.

Oh!

It all fell into place now. There'd been no mention of a second deployment overseas prior to all that happening, but obviously he'd been sufficiently upset to want to get as far away as possible from everyone and everything.

Poor Nick!

Nick chatted to the nurse—Amanda—and wondered why Bill hadn't joined them.

Not that it mattered. Amanda was amusing and obviously happy to keep both sides of the conversation going so he could brood a little over the reactions he was feeling towards Bill.

Physical reactions!

Disturbing, because at the same time it felt a little like incest—this was Bill, his friend...

'So, you'll come?' he heard Amanda ask.

Unwilling to admit he had no idea what she was talking about, he said, 'Of course!'

'Great. The boat will leave from the City Marina, gangway four, at ten.'

'Ten today?' Dead giveaway, that question, but it had just burst out.

'No, Saturday, silly,' Amanda said, giggling and cuffing him lightly on the arm, moving close enough

on the settee for him to know he should have been following the conversation.

Oh, well, some time between now and Saturday he'd
have to sort out an excuse. Except going out on a boat
with Amanda, and presumably her friends, might get
his mind off Bill.

And wasn't he here to meet women—maybe the one
woman with whom he could plan his family?

The shift ended and he was pleased to see Bill's ageing car still in the car park. He wouldn't be tempted to
follow her to the beach, which was good as he didn't
think his libido could handle the sight of her in a bikini
again. Not just yet, anyway.

Perhaps after Saturday…

Tired enough to sleep without the swim and run on
the beach, he drove to his apartment, pulling up at the
security panel at the entrance to the building's basement, staring in shock at what looked like a derelict's
collection of junk on the footpath beside the big doors.

Except it wasn't a derelict but Serena rising from
the pile of belongings. Serena with a doll in her arms.

Obviously he was losing his mind—hallucinating…

What drugs had he handled during the night?

Shock had him riveted to his seat as the mirage that
possibly *was* Serena walked towards the car. Now he
could hear the words she was saying clearly enough,
he just couldn't make sense of them.

'Came in on an early flight, no one answering the
bell, thought you'd be home eventually, and as you'd
never walk if you can drive, I thought this was the best
place to catch you, but now you're here I really need
to hand Steffi and all her gear over, and I'm terribly
sorry to do this, Nick, I really am, and I know you're

going to be mad as hell, and I'll explain when we get to your apartment, but we'll have to hurry because I'm booked to fly out again at midday to catch the evening flight to New York.'

New York!

It was in New York he'd last seen Serena, heard her tell him she didn't want a baby, yet here she was, not with a doll but a baby in her arms...

He leapt out of the car, straight over the door, looming over her.

'What will you explain?' he roared.

Then a voice behind him said, 'Hush, Nick, you'll upset the baby.'

Bill!

Unable to get into the car park with him blocking the road, she must have pulled up behind him and got out to see what was happening.

'You must be Serena,' she added politely, and he remembered sending Bill a glamour shot of Serena some years before. 'You don't know me but I'm Nick's friend Bill. We grew up together and now we both live in this apartment block my brother built. And as our cars are blocking the entrance, what if we put all the gear into my car and you and the baby get in with Nick and we'll get the stuff up to his apartment and the two of you can take it from there?'

Nick watched in total bemusement as Bill efficiently loaded what looked like a truckload of baby paraphernalia into her car and Serena, plus baby, slid into his.

'Drive through!' Bill ordered, and he recovered sufficient composure to do as she told him, sliding the car into his parking space and watching as Bill stopped beside the lift and unloaded Serena's belongings.

But Serena was flying to New York this evening—so why had she flown a couple of thousand miles north to leave the stuff here?

And the baby?

No, he couldn't think about the baby.

By now Serena had joined Bill at the lift and together they were stacking the gear inside, Bill's voice echoed around the basement—Bill's voice finally bringing him out of his daze.

'You're saying this little girl is Nick's baby?' Bill's outrage was clear and the words sank through his bewildered brain.

This is where you get out of the car and demand an explanation, Nick told himself, but his legs had turned to jelly.

He had a child.

A daughter!

Nick saw Bill take the baby and turn his way. She obviously felt it was time he emerged from his car and took control of the situation.

Would his legs work?

Of course they would.

He had a child—

He leapt out of the car.

'This is *my* baby?' he demanded, coming close to Serena and echoing Bill's words. 'You didn't have an abortion and you didn't bother telling me? Why would you do that? And now what? You've decided kids are more trouble than they're worth and you want to hand her over, as if she's a bit of furniture you no longer need?'

Bill had moved a little away, cradling the little head

protectively against her chest, one hand over the baby's other ear so it couldn't hear him yelling at its mother.

'Look,' Serena muttered, holding up her hand as if she needed to ward off further attack. 'I know this is inconvenient, Nick. When I had the baby Mum looked after her, with nannies to help out, but Mum's just got married again and I've got this huge offer for a special show in New York and Mum had a nanny lined up—Mum always vetted the nannies—but the nanny walked out and so I thought, well, it's not as if you haven't got family up there—with Gran and all those de Grootes you talk about all the time—you'll find someone to take care of her.

'She's a good little thing and she's used to strangers minding her and she's been to day care as well. I've brought all her things and the last nanny wrote down her schedule so I'm sure with a bit of help you can sort things out.'

At least Serena was right about family. At last count Bill had about twenty-two nieces and nephews, so someone in the family would be happy to take care of one more baby.

The thought brought anger in its train—a hot, deep, burning fury!

'I can't believe that even you—' he began, before Bill arrived and put her hand on his chest, pushing him back a step.

'You cannot murder her here—not in front of Steffi,' she said firmly. 'Besides, don't you think it's time you met your family?'

Bill's smile was forced but it worked, dousing his anger just a little, and when she put the little curly-haired girl into his arms it disappeared altogether.

Bill said, 'Steffi, meet your daddy.'

And Nick understood that love wasn't something you could explain or analyse, it was something you felt…

CHAPTER FOUR

NOW HE TOOK control of the situation, ordering—yes, it definitely was an order—the two women to take the stuff up to his apartment.

'And you'll be?' Serena demanded huffily.

'Coming in the next lift—I'm certainly not going to overload it with a baby in my arms.'

And with that he turned his back on them and looked down at the warm scrap of humanity snuggled against his chest.

He had a baby!

Or did he?

Serena had been adamant about the abortion, so was this little girl really his?

He held her out and had to smile. A fluff of soft brown curls, wide blue eyes—Gran's eyes—and a dimple, now she smiled at him, in her left cheek, just where his annoying dimple was.

His heart jolted in his chest then hammered furiously and he held the baby close again because he knew he was shaking with the sheer enormity of this revelation.

He pressed kisses on her head and murmured nothings until his heart resumed its normal beat and he felt confident enough to hold her out again and look into her face.

'Hi, there,' he said softly. 'I'm your dad!'

Serious eyes studied him, taking him in.

Judging him?

No smile, but who could blame her?

'We'll be all right,' he assured her, and hugged her closer.

The lift returned and he got in, taking it to the top floor and striding out, ready to face whatever lay ahead, but knowing, already, that the baby was here to stay.

Bill had heard the word 'besotted', and probably even used it herself to describe a teenager's crush, but she'd never seen besotting happen—not as quickly and completely as it must have happened for Nick to walk into the apartment looking as he did.

Oh, dear, she thought, absolutely thrilled for Nick but worried over what might lie ahead.

She'd helped Serena take all Steffi's belongings up to Nick's penthouse, mentally listing all the things he'd need if he intended keeping the baby here—a cot to begin with and probably a playpen so she'd be safe if he was called to the phone.

Baby bath?

'Bill?'

Nick's voice brought her out of her mental listing.

'I asked if you'd mind taking Steffi down to your place for half an hour while I have a talk to Serena?'

Bill smiled as she took the baby, although the smile was forced.

But this was for Nick and she was pleased he didn't want the little one to hear her parents yelling at each other, because some yelling was sure to happen, although as ever when she held a baby she had very mixed emotions—reminders of what might have been.

Could babies feel doubt and uncertainty churning in the breast that held them?

Just in case they could, she pulled herself together and made a special effort, smiling at the little girl and talking gently.

'So, Steffi,' she said as they went down to her apartment, 'you're, what? Nearly a year old? Ten months? You're gorgeous, do you know that?'

The little girl smiled and that was it for Bill as well—besotted!

Oh, dear.

Falling in love with this particular baby would *not* be a good idea. This was Nick's family, not hers.

She'd expected Nick to phone so the knock on the door when she'd just got Steffi to sleep on cushions on the floor surprised her.

'I had to phone Bob to find out where you lived,' Nick said, running his hand distractedly through his hair. 'You've no idea, Bill, you just won't believe it. Where is she? Steffi?'

Bill led him inside, pointed to the sleeping child, then took him through to the kitchen for coffee.

'Sit,' she ordered, 'and drink this before we start.'

She handed him a fresh coffee, made one for herself, then sat opposite him at the breakfast bar.

'So?'

Nick was still shaking his head, and she understood the depth of his disbelief when he began.

'Having told me she'd have the abortion, she goes

to stay with Alex, the Russian photographer who worships the ground she walks on, and he throws up his hands in horror, not at her destroying a human life but because this is the photographic opportunity of a lifetime, something he's always dreamt of doing, and here's his favourite subject, his muse, presenting him with the opportunity!'

'What is?' Bill asked, totally bewildered.

'Well you might ask,' Nick growled. 'A coffee-table book detailing nine months of pregnancy—well, seven and a half months, in actual fact. Nude photos of Serena in all poses, in all lights, the bulge growing ever larger. Imagine how Steffi's going to feel about *that* when she's growing up.'

Bill had to laugh.

'Right now I think you have more to worry about than what Steffi's going to think as a teenager. Why didn't Serena tell you she'd changed her mind and was going ahead? You'd offered to marry her—you wanted a family.'

Nick groaned.

'Yes, I had and, yes, I did, but she really didn't want to be married, and apparently my talk of family had frightened her because it was the last thing *she* wanted. A family would tie her down and she needed to be free to pursue her career. I know that makes hers sound cold and uncaring, but she isn't really, she's just got the most total self-focus of anyone I've ever met.'

'So what was she thinking, going ahead with the pregnancy?' Bill demanded, wondering where uncaring finished and self-focus began.

'Oh, that's easy. You have to remember that Serena thinks differently to ninety-nine per cent of the human race and it turned out she knew this wonderful couple in New York who wanted to adopt so she knew the child would go to a good home, and she could keep in touch as a kind of surrogate aunt.

'*Only* Serena could think something like that was okay. The woman has a warped mind—I always knew that, even when I was going out with her. Her career is the be-all and end-all of her life, and everything else, even romance, is incidental. I blame her mother, who had Serena appearing in ads from the time she was born, but as an adult Serena's had choices and the number-one choice has always been her career.'

The disbelief and despair in Nick's voice shocked Bill so much she came round to give him a hug.

'It's okay. For whatever reason, she did keep the child, and Steffi's here.'

'It's not okay!' Nick roared, then turned quickly to see if he'd woken his daughter, and quietened his voice when he added, 'The only reason she didn't give *my* daughter up for adoption—apparently that old goat Alex had intended putting his name down as the father for adoption purposes—was that he suddenly decided he could document the child's life as well, but, you know what, once she grew from a swaddled bundle to a chubby six-month-old, she *wasn't photogenic*!'

Nick was right, the behaviour of two so-called adults defied belief, and he had every right to the anger she could feel in the tight muscles and sinews of his body.

'So, Steffi's now surplus to requirements,' Bill muttered, as a murderous rage began to build inside *her*.

'Well, not entirely. I think Serena, in her own way, probably loves her, and Serena's mother was always around, but who knows what would have happened to

Steffi if that Amy woman hadn't seen us at breakfast yesterday and phoned Serena, whose pea-brain immediately came up with a solution to the dilemma of this offer in New York right when her mother's off on a honeymoon, and whatever nanny she had decided to leave at a moment's notice. Give Steffi to her daddy for a while!'

'For a while?' Bill repeated.

Nick looked at her and shook his head.

'Apparently we can "talk"—Serena waggled her fingers in that silly way to make the inverted commas—when she comes home. *I'll* say we'll talk!'

'Let's worry about that later,' Bill suggested, hearing the exhaustion beneath the anger in Nick's voice and hugging him again. 'Now, at least, Steffi's landed in a proper family, with you to love her, and Gran, and me, and twenty-two kind-of cousins, and a plethora of aunts and uncles. All we have to do is sort out how to manage.'

'Manage?' Nick repeated, looking up at her as she went back round the bar and resumed her stool, aware that hugging Nick was *not* a good idea, no matter how badly he had needed to be hugged.

'Nick, you have a baby and you work and the ER at the local hospital isn't the kind of place where you can take your baby to work.'

He turned to look at his sleeping child and the expression in his eyes caused a stab of pain in Bill's chest.

'I work nights,' he said softly. 'I don't suppose there's such a thing as night care.'

Bill saw the complexity—the enormity—of the situation dawn on his face so wasn't surprised when he turned to her, anguish in his voice.

'What will I do, Bill? How can I manage?'

With a great deal of difficulty, Bill thought, but she didn't say it. The poor man was bamboozled enough as it was.

'*We'll* manage,' she said firmly. 'Serena was right about one thing. While Gran might be a bit beyond minding a baby full time, you've a whole herd of de Grootes out there who'll be only too willing to help. But first you have to decide just what help you want.

'Full time, part time? I know you've just started a new job, but there's such a thing as paternity leave. We can make some temporary caring arrangements until the hospital replaces you, if you want to be a full-time dad for a while so you and Steffi can get to know each other. Then there are well-trained nannies you can get, even in Willowby, again either full time or part time, live-in or daily, and they can be contracted short or long term.'

He stared at her and she knew he hadn't taken in much of what she'd said, his mind still reeling from shock and disbelief.

'You're exhausted. Give me your keys then go into my bedroom and go to sleep. When Steffi wakes I'll take her back upstairs and get things set up for her there.'

Oh!

'You do intend she lives with you?'

That woke him out of his daze.

'Where else would she live?' he demanded.

'Good! Now go to bed?'

It had to be a measure of his shocked state that he obediently handed over his keys and went into her bedroom, shutting the door behind him, no doubt so she wouldn't see him slump onto the bed and bury his head in his hands as he tried to come to grips with this massive change in his life.

A measure of his state that he didn't argue that she, too, needed to sleep, but Bill knew it would be easier for the hospital to find another nurse to take her night shift tonight than it would be to find another doctor.

Bill looked towards the closed door. In her heart she knew she should be getting less involved with this child, not more, but Nick was in trouble and she'd reacted automatically—helping out in times of trouble was what they'd always done for each other.

Nick sat on Bill's bed, head bowed, his fingers running through his hair as if rubbing at his scalp might stimulate his thinking.

What thinking?

His brain was numb!

He had a daughter?

What was he going to do?

How could he look after her even for a short time?

What did he know about bringing up children?

He didn't even know her birthday...

He gave a despairing groan and slumped back on the bed, surprised to find that he might actually go to sleep.

His body handling stress by shutting down his mind, the doctor in him suggested as he drifted off.

He woke mid-afternoon to find a note from Bill beside the bed.

We're at your place, here's a key.

'We're at your place...' he read again, this time aloud, and felt dread and panic surging in his stomach.

What should he do?

What *could* he do?

But even as he asked himself the question he remembered the feel of that little body against his chest and he headed into Bill's bathroom, took a shower, used her far-from-adequate razor to scrape stubble from his cheeks, then, clad in a rather ragged towelling robe he found behind the bathroom door, he grabbed his dirty clothes, and the key, and headed up to his apartment.

Except it wasn't his apartment, it was a nursery school. Colourful toys and strange objects were strewn around the place, and in the midst of this chaos a small person stood, holding onto his glass-topped coffee table—he'd have to get rid of that—and waving a chubby hand in his direction.

'Hey,' he said quietly, squatting down—not easy to do decently in the robe—and moving carefully towards her. 'How are you, Steffi? How are you, little girl?'

Wide-set eyes studied him intently, the little face serious as she took in the stranger talking to her. Then one chubby hand reached out for his and as he took it he felt his heart breaking right in two. Suddenly she let go of the coffee table and with grin as wide as the universe she toddled towards him, her delight in her forward progress bringing a gurgle of laughter as well as the smile.

He caught her as she toppled, and sat on the floor with her in his arms, picking up a floppy doll and making it dance in front of her.

But she was more interested in him, probing at his glasses, studying his face again, touching his hair, his ear, his lips until he felt his chest would burst with the love blossoming inside it, and he knew tears were forming in his eyes.

Bill must have been watching from a distance because as Steffi's crawled off his knee to stand up at the glass table again to practise her walking, Bill came in and sat down on the sofa, waving her hand at the chaos around them.

'I'm sorry about all this,' she said, 'but you know the de Grootes, competitive to a man—or woman in this case. I phoned Bob's wife to ask about a cot and a high chair and next thing I knew every one of the sisters-in-law had turned up, all bringing something for Steffi. You should see the bedroom. As well as the cot you have chests of drawers, colourful mobiles, pictures on the wall, a change table and some kind of bin that wraps up dirty nappies. That is, of course, if you're going to use disposables, which are a lot more eco-friendly now.'

For about the fortieth time today Nick was dumbfounded.

'Disposable nappies? I have to make decisions about things like that?'

Bill laughed.

'About a lot of things, Daddio!' she teased. 'There's home-cooked or scientifically balanced bottled food, there are about ten different kinds of baby formula and you have to choose one, there's how early to start swimming lessons, there's day care or a nanny, which kindy to put her name down for, which school will she go to, how young's too young to have boyfriends—'

'Okay!' Nick said, and as he held his hand up to stop Bill's teasing, Steffi grabbed it as support and again walked towards him, collapsing happily into a giggling heap on his lap.

He was in love!

'From a purely practical point of view,' Bill continued, 'I've told the hospital I won't be in for a week and can mind her while you're at work and when you're sleeping during the day. She's so good about going down for a nap—on the cushions at my place and in a totally strange cot—I think she's used to being passed around to different carers—but I think it would be best if she gets settled into her bedroom so, if it's okay with you, I'll sleep over here until you're sorted.'

'Okay with me? Until I'm sorted?'

Nick rested his chin on his daughter's curly hair and looked up at his friend, and smiled.

'You realise that might be never,' he warned, 'the sorted bit. And when did we ever have to ask about staying over at each other's places?'

He looked around at all she'd achieved while he'd slept, and added, 'Thank you, Bill, from the bottom of my heart. I was in such a blind panic I had no idea where to turn or what to do, and you've calmly worked everything out—made it easy for me. I owe you, big time!'

Bill smiled at him, but he thought he saw a hint of sadness in the smile.

The broken engagement? Had *she* been looking forward to a baby of her own?

In which case was this fair, relying so much on her to be Steffi's carer while he worked things out?

'Well, now you're up and about, I'll introduce you to your new belongings—the physical ones.' Bill's voice was carefully neutral, nothing to read there, so maybe he'd imagined the sadness. 'You can bring Steffi,' Bill

continued, 'because learning to do things with her on
one arm is all part of fatherhood training.'

Which was all very well but how did he stand up
with a baby in his arms? What if he fell?

He solved this dilemma by putting Steffi on the floor,
standing up then lifting her, although he knew full well
he *could* have performed the feat with her still in his
arms. In the kitchen he was introduced to bottles, formula, baby food in small jars, yoghurt in the refrigerator, a sterilising machine that would have held its own in
a hospital, bibs, baby bowls, baby spoons, baby cereal.

He took it all in, realising it was far less complicated
than it had seemed at first glance, but it was Bill's attitude that was bothering him. Nothing overt, nothing
he could put a name to, but it seemed as if she was distancing herself from him.

From him or from Steffi?

The Bill he remembered had been passionate about
small children, babysitting all through their teenage
years, so while he wasn't actually doing her a favour
by letting her mind Steffi while he got sorted, he'd have
thought she wouldn't mind. And, after all, she'd suggested it!

But there was something off—something too matter-
of-fact in all this—

'Are you listening?' the person he was worrying
about demanded.

'Boiled water,' he repeated diligently, then had to
admit, 'No, I wasn't. What do I do with boiled water?'

Bill frowned at him.

'According to the notes, you still have to boil the
water to mix with her formula for her bottles and she
has three a day, one before each nap and one before bed.

She's got to be, what, eleven months old, so I would have thought maybe by now ordinary water would do, but I've written Kirsten's number on the notes, she's Andre's wife and the most sensible of my sisters-in-law and won't talk on for ever if you ring to ask her something.'

Nick looked at the notes, then back at Bill, thinking of the expression he thought he'd seen on her face—thinking too that, with the other strange stuff happening when he was around Bill, he should be seeing less, not more of her.

'Are you sure you want to take this on?' he asked. 'After all, I *could* just tell the hospital I can't work for a while, they'd battle on, and once I've read the notes, how hard can it be?'

She shook her head.

'You'll soon find out. I'm going to have a sleep, but I'll be up before you go to work. You can organise whatever you like with the hospital once you've thought it through.'

She tapped the notes to remind him to read them, and departed, leaving his bunch of keys and taking the single spare he'd used when he'd come up from her apartment.

And, despite the warm body he held in his arms, the place felt cold now Bill had gone...

Exhaustion hit Bill as she left the apartment, tiredness so strong it sapped her energy and she barely made it home, throwing off her clothes and climbing into bed, unfortunately conscious enough to pick up the scent of Nick on her sheets.

Damn it all. She *had* to sleep!

But emotion churned inside her—an emotion she'd never felt holding one of her nieces or nephews. This was a new emotion—a heart-rending sorrow that Steffi's mother hadn't really wanted her, while she, Bill, had so longed for the baby she'd conceived, her arms had ached for a year.

And were aching again…

Go to sleep, she ordered herself, and training held true. She fell asleep but dreamt of empty cots and abandoned babies and Nick with his daughter in his arms.

She woke, barely refreshed, at six, and knew she'd better get upstairs so Nick could go to work. Showering, she told herself that if anyone in the world deserved to have his own family it was Nick, and she should be glad for him—*was* glad for him!

Kind of.

'How do mothers know to do all this?' he demanded as she walked into his apartment. 'The notes say she has dinner at five-thirty, a little meat cut up fine with mashed vegetables. It doesn't say what kind of meat or how you can cook a piece of steak while holding a crying baby in your arms and not burn the child, and is she crying because she's hungry or she needs her mother or what? How do I know?'

'You don't,' Bill told him, taking Steffi in her arms and rocking her back and forth until the crying stopped. 'You have to guess, but didn't she have a nap?'

'Of course she had a nap. Bottle and a nap at three, the notes said, and we did that, although I had to put the bottle in the freezer to cool the boiled water before I could give it to her. I can see I'll have to boil water ahead.'

'So you read the notes?' Bill persisted, watching as Nick turned a very large piece of steak on a griddle pan.

'Of course!'

He was cranky and she had to hide a smile so she didn't make things worse.

'The bit that said when she had dinner and what she ate?'

'Of course!' Really cranky now.

'And it didn't occur to you to get it ready while she slept?'

He looked up from the steak, frowning, growling.

'I was busy on the computer.'

'Oh, yes?'

'Well, I obviously can't put a baby seat in my car, can I, so I had to do some research on the safest vehicles for kids to travel in. You've no idea.'

Bill grinned at him, reminded him to turn the steak, then went to the cupboard where one of her sisters-in-law had stacked bottles of additive- and colouring-free baby food. She set Steffi in the highchair, strapped her in, gave her a small plastic spoon to play with, and opened the jar.

'Here,' she said to Nick when she'd warmed the jar in some hot water. 'Feed her this. It won't hurt not to have fresh cooked every now and then, and later, when it's cooled, she can gnaw on a bit of that steak.'

Knowing she would definitely laugh if she watched him feed an infant for the first time, she left him to it, going into the bathroom to run a bath, which Steffi would certainly need.

She'd just set a small plastic duck floating in the water when Nick appeared, both he and Steffi liberally smeared with food.

'I'll get the hang of this!' he muttered as he handed her over, and he was halfway out the door before he added, 'I have to shower. Did I thank you?'

He came back in, embraced them both, then to Bill's astonishment he kissed her, not on the cheek or forehead or even the top of her head, as he was wont to do, but on the lips—*full* on the lips!

'Beyond the call of duty, this, friend Bill,' he said, his voice husky with what couldn't possibly be tears.

Except he hadn't had much sleep, and he'd certainly had the most emotional day of his life, so perhaps…

CHAPTER FIVE

HE'D KISSED BILL on the lips—Bill, his friend, on the lips!

Nick stood under the shower, wondering why this one small incident from an unbelievably momentous day should be occupying his attention to the exclusion of all else.

Including the fact he had a daughter...

Because Bill's lips had felt so soft?

Tasted so sweet?

Or because when he'd tasted that sweetness, felt the softness, he'd also felt a stirring somewhere else?

No, it was because he was shocked and tired—not to mention emotionally exhausted—that kissing Bill had suddenly taken over his mind.

Or he was thinking of it to stop himself worrying over what would become of him and Steffi.

So why was a voice in the back of his head suggesting he kiss Bill again? Perhaps when he left for work, although what the voice was really suggesting was a proper kiss—an in-the-arms kiss, Bill's slim body pressed to his, her lips parting to his invading tongue—

'Out now!'

He spoke the order aloud, hoping to rein in his rampaging thoughts. Far better to think of Steffi and all the problems her arrival was going to cause in his life.

'She'll need some new clothes—just lightweight cotton tops and pants to suit this climate,' Bill said when he walked into the room she'd prepared for Steffi. The little girl was dressed in a long-sleeved pink and white striped suit that covered her from ankles to neck. 'Most of her clothes will be too heavy up here. We'll shop tomorrow, she and I.'

Bill handed him the baby and wandered off, muttering something about getting the bottle ready.

He wanted to follow her, to have a good look at her, although he knew *her* reaction to the kiss wouldn't be written on her face.

In fact, she probably hadn't reacted at all, thinking, if anything, that he'd just happened to miss her cheek.

Deciding to follow her to the kitchen anyway— maybe looking at her would sort out why he'd kissed her lips—he wandered out of the bedroom and stood in the hall, looking into the kitchen where Bill was shaking a bottle to mix the formula.

Her back was to him so he was able to study her— slim legs encased in black leggings, a loose white T-shirt hanging to her thighs, tangled red hair falling below her shoulders, the front bit of it bunched up on the top of her head.

Bill, as he'd seen her thousands of times—so how could he possibly have become attracted to her now?

And why?

Because he hadn't had a regular lover lately?

Lover?

How could he possibly even think that word about Bill?

Was it that insidious longing for a family that had started when Serena had first been pregnant that was making him look at Bill differently?

No, far too convenient an excuse.

Steffi made a gurgling noise and Bill turned, apparently startled to see him there as faint colour spread across her cheeks.

'Have you got time to give Steffi the bottle?' she asked, handing it to him, then, without waiting for a reply, adding, 'I'll get a bib.'

Bill fled, heading for Steffi's room, unable to believe Nick had caught her as she'd been staring vacantly out the kitchen window, thinking about a kiss.

Not just any kiss, but his, Nick's, kiss!

A lip-kiss of all things. Of course, he'd probably aimed for her cheek and she'd moved her head at just the wrong moment.

And although she knew full well he'd have only seen her back view when he'd come into the kitchen, she'd actually blushed—her cheeks burning—at being caught out.

But the kiss had affected her so strangely she hadn't been able to *not* think about it.

Which was crazy as his lips had barely brushed hers, yet she'd felt fire travel from that touch, right through her body, heating her flesh and sending her nerves into a quiver of excitement.

Tiredness, she told herself, and grabbed a bib from where she'd put them in a drawer, intending to hurry back to Nick despite legs heavy with reluctance.

This is totally insane—that was the next bit of information she offered her disordered brain and twitchy body. This is Nick we're talking about.

Nick!

'Bib!'

She handed it to him as he sat on the couch, showing the bottle to Steffi while he tried to work out how best to hold her.

'Like this,' she said, settling the infant in his arms and fixing the bib herself.

Now walk away.

She knew this last bit of advice offered by her few still-functioning brain cells was extremely sensible—even compelling—but how could she walk away from the sight in front of her? Steffi totally absorbed in sucking down her milk, but one hand clutching Nick's little finger and her eyes never moving from his face.

As for Nick, he simply sat, looking down at his daughter, the love he felt for her already written so clearly on his face it hurt Bill's heart to see it.

Rationally she knew that finding he had a daughter was the best thing that had ever happened to Nick, but what lay ahead? Could Steffi be the start of the family he wanted or would he grow to love her more and more then have her snatched away?

Knowing the pain of that kind of loss, Bill could only feel for him—worry for him—yet that was better, surely, than worrying about kisses?

No, one kiss, singular.

One kiss didn't count...

Nick arrived home after a distracted night on duty to a silent home. Tiptoeing, he made his way to Steffi's room but the cot was empty. He assumed Bill was sleeping in the next bedroom, although they hadn't discussed any arrangements—anything at all, really.

The door was open and tucked under a sheet was Bill, making little snuffling noises as she slept, and nestled in beside her was his daughter, also asleep, although an empty bottle on the bedside table suggested that at some time during the night she'd woken up hungry and had needed to be fed again.

Nick stood in the doorway and looked at the pair of them, and felt again an overwhelming surge of love.

For Steffi, of course…

He walked away quietly, into the kitchen, but he'd barely reached the door when he heard a gurgle of laughter. His daughter was awake.

Thinking he'd pick her up and let Bill sleep, he hurried back to the room, but the gurgle had woken Bill as well, and she was smiling tiredly as Steffi played peek-a-boo in the wild red hair.

'Bad night?' Nick asked, moving into the room to scoop Steffi into his arms.

'Not really,' Bill said, sitting up so he couldn't help but notice the minimal nightdress she was wearing, a fine cotton shift that barely covered her small but shapely breasts and clearly showed her body curving down to a tiny waist. 'She woke at three and didn't settle so in the end I gave her another bottle and brought her in with me. So much change and strangeness for the wee mite, I thought she probably needed cuddling, lots of cuddling.'

She grinned and added, 'Then, of course, I was so worried about rolling over and squashing her that I took ages to fall asleep myself. She'll need changing and you'll find clean clothes in the second drawer down in the dresser. I'll be out when I've woken up properly.'

'And put some clothes on,' he muttered to himself as he walked away.

Steffi looked up enquiringly at him and he gave her a reassuring smile, then his nose told him that she really did need changing and that fatherhood wasn't going to be all smiles and gurgling laughter.

Bill was in the kitchen when he'd undressed, cleaned and dressed his daughter again.

'Have you any idea how much excrement a child this size can produce?' he demanded, handing Steffi to Bill so he could have a proper wash himself.

'It's what they're good at, at this age,' Bill told him, as she settled Steffi in the high chair and started asking what she'd like for breakfast.

'Cereal and fruit?' Bill suggested.

Steffi banged her spoon on the tray and Bill grinned at her.

'I thought so,' she said, pulling the box of baby cereal and a small jar of puréed fruit from the cupboard. 'Now your dad's clean, he can feed you.'

'Oh, no!' Nick retorted. 'I did it last night. I'll make our breakfast—coffee and toast do you? I haven't shopped but Bob made sure there were some essentials here.'

Bill agreed that coffee and toast would be fine. She lifted the highchair close to the breakfast bar and perched on a stool so she could feed Steffi while they had breakfast.

Nick tried to focus on what he was doing, but making coffee and toast demanded little in the way of concentration so the domesticity of the situation attracted most of his attention. He watched Bill, noticed the way her lips parted slightly as she spooned food into Steffi's mouth, saw the concentration on Bill's face, but something else...

Concern?

Something more he couldn't understand?

'I know Serena said she was used to being cared for by strangers, but you'd think she must be missing if not her mother at least her grandmother.'

Bill's statement cut into his thoughts.

Had she been worrying about Steffi's well-being while he tried to guess at something deeper?

'You'd think so,' he agreed. 'So, what can we do?'

Bill frowned at him but he knew the frown was for her thoughts, not for him—at least, he hoped so.

'I think all we can do is give her lots and lots of physical love—cuddles, talking, kisses, songs—using her name and telling her we love her. I've no idea how much infants understand at different ages, but I don't know what else we can do.'

Nick felt his chest squeeze. Hadn't love always been Bill's answer to everything? Love for her friends, her pets, her family. The arguments they'd had over love— he claiming it was something poets and musicians made up to write about, she firm in her belief it made the world go round.

But now he'd felt this thing called love—for what else could the emotion he felt towards his daughter be?—he realised that while it might not make the world go round, it was probably all they could do to help Steffi feel secure—give her lots and lots of love.

Show her love with talk and cuddles.

But was it wrong of him to expect Bill to be doing this when Steffi wasn't Bill's child?

Was it something to do with *her* relationship to Steffi that was causing the shadows he kept catching on Bill's face?

'Write a list of what you need at the supermarket and Steffi and I will go there after we've bought her some tropical clothes,' the woman he was worrying about said as she scraped the last of the cereal out of the bowl and spooned it into Steffi's mouth, neatly wiping off the excess with a small facecloth she'd had the foresight to have nearby.

He'd show her love and he'd learn to do all these things, Nick told himself, and concentrating on learning all he could about caring for his daughter would distract him from the wayward thoughts he was having about Bill.

'I could shop later when I've had a sleep,' he said, knowing he needed to start right now because his wayward thoughts were increasing despite the fact he and Bill must have breakfasted together like this—yes, a thousand times...

Except he hadn't felt his gut clench when she smiled at him—not once in those thousand times.

'I think for a few days at least your spare time should be spent with Steffi, so you learn the rhythms of her life and you get to know each other better. Write a list and we'll shop while you sleep, then this afternoon she'll be all yours.'

It made sense so he wrote a list—a good distraction—although if Bill was staying here he needed to consult her on what she liked to eat.

'Same as you, remember, steak and salad, lamb cutlets and salad, roast lamb—basic food. Put what you want in the way of snacks and drinks on the list, I'll do the rest. If I'm to be lolling around here for the week I might as well do the evening meal. We can gradually shift Steffi's evening meal a little later, and with you working nights you need to eat early so we can all eat together, which, the sensible Kirsten tells me, is a good habit to get into.'

Except it makes us seem like a family—the thing I wanted—but we're not, Nick thought as he left the room to find a pen and notepad, really leaving the room because the distraction of Bill's long, tanned legs tucked up on the stool was stronger than the distraction of learning to look after his daughter.

One week, that's all it would be, Bill promised herself as Nick left the room. Within a week she'd have settled Steffi into her new, if temporary home, found a decent, reliable nanny to give Nick back-up care when he was working and she could leave him to get to know his daughter on his own.

The 'if temporary' part worried her. It was all very well for Serena to tell Nick they'd 'talk' when she returned, but knowing Nick there was no way, now he knew about her, that he would give up his daughter.

No way he could, Bill suspected, remembering the besotted look on Nick's face.

She sighed and reminded herself that she needed to be careful too. Even more careful than Nick, for Steffi wasn't and never would be her daughter, so falling in love with the wee mite was just not on.

Detached—that's how she had to be. She could love Steffi as she loved her nieces and nephews, but stay detached...

She'd sent Nick off to have a sleep and was clearing

up the kitchen when he reappeared, clad only in long-ish boxer shorts that he must wear as pyjamas. Her eyes were drawn inexorably towards his chest and were so focussed there she hadn't a clue what he was saying.

'I missed that,' she said, cursing inwardly because her voice came out all breathy.

'I was saying you can't take Steffi to the shops—no car seat.'

Desperate to distract herself from that chest, Bill lifted Steffi out of the highchair and set her on the floor, handing her a couple of wooden spoons and a sauce-pan to bang.

'I've got a car seat,' she responded, 'and whichever sister-in-law brought it insisted on installing it so she knew it was secure. She even adjusted the straps to fit Steffi. And there's a stroller in the car as well, so we're all set,' she said, skipping out of Steffi's reach as the toddler decided hitting legs was more fun than hitting a saucepan.

'You've thought of everything,' Nick grumbled as he turned back towards his bedroom, although he did relent, swinging back to smile and say, 'I have thanked you, haven't I?'

To Bill's dismay she felt a blush rising up her neck towards her cheeks as she remembered just how he'd thanked her. Thinking quickly, she bent down to lift Steffi in her arms to shield her so-transparent reaction from Nick.

'Of course you have,' she mumbled against Steffi's fluff of hair.

Now he'd never sleep because *now* he was remembering the kiss. Nick headed for his bedroom, muttering under his breath. Bad enough he'd had to fight the impulse to touch Bill—on the shoulder, knee, neck, cheek—all through breakfast, but by reminding him that he *had* thanked her, she'd reminded him of the kiss.

He couldn't do it—couldn't have her living here while this peculiar reaction to her was going on in his body.

Not that he could manage without her.

Although…?

Running through his roster in his head, he remembered he had three days off coming up soon.

When?

Five nights on then three off, wasn't that the system here at Willowby?

So two more nights on duty, and by the end of his three days off, the hospital human resources department should have found a locum to fill in for him. Two weeks, that's all he'd asked for.

He'd need to sleep for some time on the first of his days off, but he could sleep when Steffi slept. He'd show Bill over the next two afternoons how well he could manage his daughter so his friend wouldn't be worried when he told her he could cope without her.

And on that cheery note he fell asleep, only to dream of a long-legged, red-haired siren running through his life, always just ahead of him, taunting and tantalising him but never within reach.

Something really good was cooking when he woke up, and the aroma permeating the house was more than enough to tempt him out of bed.

'What *are* you cooking?' he demanded as he came into the kitchen, starving because he'd slept through lunch.

'Casserole for dinner,' Bill replied, 'but there's ham in the fridge if you want to make a sandwich for a late lunch. I'm doing a big casserole of meat and veggies in the slow cooker so you can freeze it in meal-sized portions and always have something you can shove in the microwave when it's been a bad day.'

Nick was pulling butter and ham from the refrigerator as she finished talking and from where he was the words had an ominous sound.

'What kind of bad day?'

Bill turned from where she was adjusting knobs on the steriliser and smiled at him.

It had to be hunger that was making his heart miss a beat while a desire stronger than he'd ever felt before surged through his body.

Sure the state of his arousal would be obvious, he dumped the makings of his lunch on the table, mumbled, 'Tell me later—I should shower before I eat,' and fled the kitchen.

It had to be the dream, he decided as he stood under the shower that was not quite cold but definitely cool.

And if it wasn't the dream—if he was going to get an erection of mammoth proportions every time Bill smiled at him—then one of them had to go.

Now.

A not unhappy wail from Steffi's bedroom made him amend that to *soon*.

Very soon.

He dried himself, pulled on clothes then, thinking Bill would still be busy in the kitchen, went to retrieve his daughter from her cot.

She'd pulled herself up and was peering at him over the top, smilingly delighted with her achievement.

'Yes, you are a clever girl,' he assured her, lifting her and holding her close, feeling again the somersault of love this small mortal had brought into his life.

And because, for at least the next few days, they both needed Bill, she would have to stay.

'So I'll have to keep my mind on you and the problems you're causing in my life, young lady,' he told Steffi as he put her on the change table and began the process of nappy-changing.

'Yuck!' he said, as he undid her nappy.

The word brought a crow of delight from his daughter, but as he cleaned up the little bottom he noticed redness.

Nappy rash.

He knew the words, but treatment?

With one hand on Steffi's tummy he surveyed the array of tubes and jars of cream on hand beside the change table.

'This thick stuff?' he wondered, waving the jar in front of the little girl.

Steffi gurgled her approval, but it was the 'Well done!' from the doorway that confirmed he'd chosen the correct remedy.

'I need to read the notes again,' he said as he smeared the white cream liberally all over Steffi's little bottom, but only part of his mind was on the job, the rest of it thinking about Bill—wondering why on earth, after all these years, he should suddenly be attracted to her.

He finished changing Steffi and, remembering she usually had a drink of water after her sleep, carried her into the kitchen where Bill had a covered container of boiled water ready for any occasion.

'I'll get the cup,' Bill offered, and she filled the little

cup and screwed the lid on, handing it not to Nick but to Steffi, who grasped one of the handles and tried to manoeuvre the sipping part into her mouth.

'Can't quite manage it, kid?' Bill teased, and she held the cup so Steffi could suck from it.

They were close, so close, Nick holding the baby, Bill with one hand on Steffi's back, helping her to drink, then gold-brown eyes lifted and met his, and a heaviness in Nick's chest stopped his breathing.

It seemed their gazes held for minutes, although seconds seemed more likely, the spell broken when Bill smiled and said, rather breathlessly, 'Well, isn't this the silliest thing ever?'

And without waiting for an answer, she took Steffi from his arms, said, 'Get your lunch,' and disappeared with his daughter into the living room.

He made his sandwich and considered staying right there in the kitchen to eat it, but that would be even sillier than whatever was happening between them. Bill's statement had confirmed she, too, was feeling the attraction, so surely the best way to deal with it would be to talk about it.

Calmly and sensibly discuss it—maybe work out some rational reason why this should be happening between them now.

He took his sandwich into the living room, where Bill was lying on the floor, Steffi bouncing up and down on her stomach.

Nick sank into an armchair, took a bite of his sandwich, a sip of tea, then decided there was no time like the present to get it out into the open.

It?

Could something like the desire he was feeling for this woman be encompassed in a simple 'it'?

'It must be that we haven't seen much of each other over the last few years,' he said, then worried that perhaps she hadn't been talking about attraction earlier and he'd gone and made a fool of himself.

She peered at him around Steffi's head.

'You think?'

'Well, something's happened, hasn't it?' he grumbled. 'Come on, it's not like you not to be offering an opinion—several opinions, in fact.'

'About what?' she asked, all innocence, shifting so Steffi was now on the floor but remaining close to her so Steffi could play with her hair.

'You know damn well what.'

He was growling now, certain the woman was taunting him, stretched out so languidly on his floor, legs, hips, waist, breasts offered up to him, while the lips that had tasted so soft and sweet quivered with a little smile that was driving him to distraction.

He finished his sandwich, refusing to play her game, but when Steffi's attention was fully absorbed with a toy that made the most extraordinary noises when she pushed buttons and pulled on levers, Bill sat up, moving closer to him but stopping just short of resting her head on his knees, as she'd done countless times in the past when they had been no more than friends.

Which they were now, weren't they?

'Remember us sitting like this while we sorted out one or other of our love lives?' she asked, following his thoughts with such precision it was scary.

'Or sorting out the problems of the world,' he reminded her.

She nodded, then put her hand on his knee.

It was nothing more than a friendly gesture, yet his skin beneath that hand burned as if she'd branded him. He wanted to lift it off so the pain would go away, and he wanted it to stay there—for ever...

Silence fell between them, although the bells and whistles continued to rattle around the room from Steffi's toy, and her giggles of delight distracted Nick so when Bill spoke he didn't catch what she was saying until she was well into her statement.

'—because your life is complicated enough as it is right now, what with Steffi, and Serena coming back to talk. We don't need to make it more complicated by having an affair.'

'Who mentioned an affair?' he demanded.

She grinned at him.

'Are you saying that isn't what your body wants?'

'Of course it is—no, of course it isn't. Why an affair anyway?'

'Well, I hardly think it could turn into a for-ever-and-ever thing, could it?'

She ran her finger over his lips, freezing his thoughts, although he'd have liked to ask why it couldn't be for ever and ever...

'Nick, the attraction is there,' she continued gently. 'It's inconvenient, nothing more than that. I'm saying I think we have to live with the inconvenience of it. We'll both be busy enough with work and caring for Steffi, and once you're sorted with a nanny I won't need to be living here so it will be easier. But your world has been turned upside down—mine too, to a lesser extent—so it's only natural that our bodies should be turning to each other for support.'

'It's not support my body wants from yours,' Nick growled, taking that tantalising finger and sucking gently on it.

'Or mine from yours, to tell the truth,' Bill admitted, shivering a little as she removed her finger and leaned against his legs, resting her head on his knees, licking at his skin to get a taste of Nick—the kind of taste she'd never considered she could ever want.

'And you can stop that,' he told her, easing her away from his legs and settling on the floor to play with Steffi. 'Go and do whatever you have to do—we'll be right until dinner and bathtime. See you around five?'

So, that was it for the attraction conversation, Bill realised. She hauled herself off the floor, bent to kiss the top of Steffi's head as she said goodbye, and left the apartment.

But she couldn't shut the door on thoughts of Nick.

Nick as a man.

Nick as a desirable, sexy man who was stirring her body into an agony of wanting.

She pulled her mobile out of her pocket and phoned him.

'I suppose the alternative would be for us to have a quick, passionate fling and get it out of our systems then we could go back to where we were,' she said as soon as he answered.

'And just when could we conduct this fling?' he demanded. 'I can't even answer the phone without my daughter trying to wrestle it from me, and we'd no sooner get to the interesting part than she'd be yelling from her cot. *Coitus interruptus* at its best.'

'At least I wouldn't get pregnant,' Bill told him,

chuckling at the image he'd described. 'But you're right, best we just ignore the whole thing and hope it will go away.'

'Like a really, really bad cold,' Nick grumped, then he disconnected the call.

CHAPTER SIX

BILL DID BUSY stuff to distract herself, washing, vacuuming, putting fresh sheets on the bed, and clearing debris from the refrigerator as she'd be eating at Nick's for this week at least.

Food, refrigerator, Nick's—

She grabbed her phone again and hit Nick's speeddial number.

'Not another suggestion about our sex lives?' he muttered as he answered.

'Of course not,' Bill told him. 'Something far more important than sex. I don't know why I didn't think of it earlier but, Nick, we haven't told Gran about Steffi, and if we don't someone else is sure to now all the de Grootes know, but what do we say?'

She heard Nick groan.

'Damn and blast—I should have gone over yesterday but yesterday was a disaster from start to finish. Can I borrow your car? I'll take her now. We'll have time before dinner—but then there's her nap.'

'She'll sleep in the car and, yes, we'll go in my car. I'll drive.'

'You'll come?'

Nick sounded so surprised Bill had to laugh.

'Didn't we always face Gran, or my parents for that matter, together when we were in trouble?'

'I'm not sure trouble quite covers this situation,' Nick replied, sounding so uneasy Bill felt a pang of sympathy for him.

Better that than lust, she realised as she told him to pull himself together, grab a brightly coloured bag off the chest of drawers—'It's got spare nappies, cream, clothes and baby wipes in it'—and meet her in the car park.

She brought her car close to the lift and had the back door open when Nick and Steffi emerged. Taking Steffi from him, she strapped her in, aware Nick was watching every move, learning all the time.

Aware too of Nick as a man—the impossible dream...

'I wondered when I was going to meet my great-granddaughter. Whillimina's family have been phoning all day,' Gran greeted them, then she lifted Steffi into her arms and smiled down at her. 'And don't bother telling me what it's all about,' she said, addressing both Nick and Bill. 'I'm too old to be bothered with details. I just need to know the little girl is being properly looked after, and that I get to see her at least once a week and mind her from time to time.'

'Oh, Gran,' Nick said, his voice so husky the words barely came out, then he hugged the woman who'd brought him up, his arms easily encompassing both her and his daughter. 'I'm sorry I didn't let you know about her earlier but it's all come as such a shock.'

Gran led them into the living room and waved for them to sit down. Steffi was playing with the glass beads around Gran's neck, apparently quite comfortable on the older woman's knee.

'I'm glad you're back, of course,' Gran said, 'but when you made the arrangements to return you didn't know about young Steffi here. Things will change, you know.'

'And how,' Nick told her, but Gran wasn't finished.

'Not just in adjusting to having a child, but now you know about Steffi you will have different priorities and I don't want you to feel you have to honour your contract in Willowby because of me. You were a good boy and you've grown into a fine man, and you keep in touch with me more than most young men would with their parents or grandparents, but you have to live your own life, remember.'

What was she saying?

Nick ran her words through his head, thinking he could ask Bill later what she'd thought of them, but Bill had excused herself to make some tea.

'Once I've sorted out the care arrangements, Steffi won't make too much difference in my life,' he told Gran, who smiled and raised her eyebrows.

'We'll see,' she said gently. 'We'll see.'

Bored with the beads, Steffi was trying to climb off Gran's knee so Nick rescued her and put her on the floor, pulling a stacking toy out of the bag Bill had obviously prepared for outings such as this.

'And Whillimina?' Gran asked, nodding her head towards the kitchen. 'I hear she's helping you take care of Steffi.'

'Only until the hospital can give me some time off and we get a nanny to look after her when I go back to work.'

It sounded like an excuse and he knew Gran would pick up on it.

'Is it fair on her, considering all that happened to her in the past?' Gran asked, right on cue.

All that's happened in the past?

Nick wanted to ask Gran what she meant, but Bill came through the door at that moment, carrying a tray with teapot, milk and sugar, cups and saucers and a plate of biscuits on it.

'Set it down on the sideboard where Steffi won't be able to reach it,' Gran said, removing a Dresden figurine from her great-granddaughter's hands.

Bill poured the tea and the rest of the visit was taken up with local gossip and general conversation.

'Do you think someone's told her about Serena and what happened that she was so incurious about how a baby lobbed into my life?' Nick asked Bill as they drove back towards the apartment.

Bill considered the matter for a while then shook her head.

'I doubt it. I didn't tell my lot much—just that you had a small child and needed stuff for her. Some of my sisters-in-law are probably dying to know, but most people would just shrug and accept it. I think with Gran she knows you'll talk about it when you're ready and she's willing to wait until then.'

'Talk about it when I'm ready?'

Nick's voice was so loud Steffi gave a little whimper then settled back into sleep.

'How can I ever be ready when I haven't a clue what's really going on?' Nick asked in a more subdued but still panicked tone. 'So I know about Steffi and she's here with me now, but what of the future? What will Serena's "talk" entail? I want to stay here, Bill, to work here, for at least for a year and probably longer. I'd actually been thinking for ever...'

His voice tailed off and he was silent for a moment, before he asked, 'Can we drive to the beach? Not Wood-choppers but Sunrise, where we can sit in the car and look out at the water.'

Bill understood exactly what he was asking—understood why as well. As teenagers they'd often sat on the headland at Sunrise Beach, looking out at the sea while they'd solved the problems of the world.

Or their love lives...

Bill parked the car in a corner of the car park and they sat in silence, Steffi asleep in her car seat.

'I came here to see Gran and be with her,' Nick finally said, 'but, in truth, the life I'd decided to lead was palling. You can have too much fun, you know.'

He sounded so serious Bill had to fight an urge to laugh, but instead turned towards him and took his hand.

'It was the family thing, I imagine,' she told him. 'Once you'd had that thought—seen the image of yourself as a family man in your head—it would have been hard to shift, and Willowby would have been a natural place for you to settle.'

He lifted her hand and dropped a light kiss on her fingers.

'I guess so, although at the time I didn't dwell on the family thing for long. Serena had squashed the idea so quickly and completely I thought I'd put it out of my head until quite recently when coming up here mainly for Gran made me think of it again.'

'You could never have put it out of your heart,' Bill

murmured. 'Not having had a real family of your own. Once the idea sneaked in it would have been hard to dislodge.'

He squeezed her fingers.

'I suppose you're right, but what next, Bill? What do I do? What do we do?'

Bill retrieved her hand before he could excite it—and her—further, though a light kiss and a hand squeeze was hardly erotic foreplay.

'*We* do nothing,' she said, 'not as a "we". But you look after Steffi with me or a nanny to help and you go to work and visit Gran and do all the things you intended doing when you came up here.'

'Except,' she added, remembering the leggy blondes at breakfast, 'the rushing out to the islands to have a wild old time on your days off. Later, when Steffi gets to know you and feels at home, you can have a social life again, though judging from my family's experiences late nights are severely limited by their children's habit of getting up at an unreasonably early hour in the morning.'

Thinking she'd handled the conversation quite well, for all the churning in her stomach as she'd denied the 'we', Bill sat back in her seat and looked out towards the islands, noticing how calm and clear the water was, thinking a swim might clear her head.

'So, that's me done,' Nick said. 'What about you?'

She turned towards him.

'Me?'

His eyes were shadowed, his mouth serious, and she wondered what on earth could be coming next.

'Gran asked if it was fair to you to have you minding Steffi. To quote Gran, "considering all that happened".'

He touched Bill's cheek and she felt the shiver of re-action—or possibly despair—rattle through her body.

'What happened? Is this to do with Nigel? With you calling off the wedding?'

His voice was deep with understanding, with sym-pathy—with love, the friendship-love they'd shared for ever—and Bill felt something crack inside her.

The lump in her throat was too big to swallow so she made do with a nod.

'Tell me.'

It wasn't an order, more a whispered plea, but sud-denly the lump disappeared and she found she could talk about that time, about discovering she was preg-nant a month before the wedding, Nigel's horrified re-action—'people will think that's why we married, we can't have that'. His demand she have an abortion, her realisation that he was a shallow, selfish, social-climb-ing toadie and calling off the wedding. Then—

'But what happened?' Nick asked, obviously enough as she certainly didn't have a baby now.

'I miscarried,' she said, and felt his arms close around her, drawing her to his chest, holding her tightly as he told her how sorry he was, how stupid she was not to have told him, how he'd have come to her, she should have known that.

When the hug turned from sympathy to something else she afterwards wasn't sure, but somehow they shifted their positions and Nick was kissing her full on the lips.

The sun was shining, the sea was calm, Steffi was asleep...

Bill kissed him back.

The world didn't come to an end.

Anything but!

In fact, as Bill responded, meeting the demands of Nick's lips with demands of her own, her body came to life in a way she'd never felt before. Heat surged through her, her blood on fire, while her breasts grew heavy with desire and the ache between her thighs made her twist in her seat as she tried to ease the longing.

'This is stupid.' she managed to mutter as Nick's hand left her cheek and roved across the skin on her neck, sliding down to cup one heavy breast. 'Idiocy!'

'I know,' he mumbled back, nuzzling now at the base of her neck and causing goose-bumps all down her spine.

But the kissing didn't stop, the desperation in it suggestive of a starving man needing to eat his fill in case the meal should be his last.

Bill's head tried to rationalise the situation—this was Nick, he was in trouble at the moment, shocked by the discovery he had a daughter, he needed comforting.

And she'd just told him what had happened—she was entitled to a little comfort herself.

But as the intensity of her response to Nick's kisses grew, she lost track of the excuses and gave herself up to the pleasure of kissing Nick and being kissed by him.

It wasn't Steffi waking up that stopped them but the arrival of another vehicle, a battered four-wheel drive, pulling up not at the other side of the car park, in spite of it being empty, but right beside them.

They broke apart, and seeing Nick's flushed face Bill knew she'd be fiery red herself. To hide her telltale cheeks, she turned in her seat, pretending she was checking Steffi, who still slept on, blithely unaware of the behaviour of her father and his best friend.

'And what are you doing here, Whillimina Florence? Not necking with some worthless boy, surely?'

Dirk, the youngest of her six brothers, a mad keen fisherman no doubt heading for the rocks below where they were parked.

'We're actually enjoying a few moments' peace and quiet while Steffi sleeps,' Nick responded, getting out of the car and coming around the hood to shake Dirk's hand—shielding Bill from him at the same time.

'Or we were until you arrived,' Nick added.

'Heard about the kid,' Dirk said, grinning at Nick and peering into the back of the vehicle to check his information was correct. 'Bet that's put a dampener on your social life.'

'Maybe it needed one,' Nick replied, and Bill knew he meant it, though she wondered, apart from his sudden longing for a family, if something more had happened to her friend.

Perhaps he'd really loved Serena and had been hurt by her refusal to marry him?

Oh, damn and blast. Surely not?

Although it would explain the passion of his kiss.

Rejected by the woman he adored, he'd taken off for overseas and now, back in Australia, had turned to the next one that came along, who just happened to be her, Bill...

She wanted to wail in protest and bang her head against the steering-wheel, then bang Nick's head against anything handy.

How stupid could one woman be? Kissing him back when she knew nothing could happen between them— knew, whatever had happened in the past between him and Serena, Serena would be back...

'Sorry, but I have to feed the kid then get to work,' Nick was saying to Dirk, 'but if I can organise Gran to sit with her for a few hours later in the week, I'd love to join you on the rocks. I'll give you a call.'

Organise Gran to sit with Steffi?

So Nick, too, had realised just how stupid the kiss had been, and he was already working out how to get *her* out of his life—well, possibly not right out but he was definitely figuring how to put distance between the two of them.

'Fishing with Dirk?' Bill asked when she'd said goodbye to her brother and Nick was back in the car.

He turned and smiled.

'Simple pleasures,' he said. That fitted with all the other stuff he'd said, but it also wiped away any memory of the kiss—drew a line under it without it being mentioned while telling her in no uncertain terms that there *was* a line, and it would not be crossed again.

Driving back to the apartment block, she wasn't sure whether to be glad or sorry. Common sense, of which she'd once had plenty, told her she was glad. She could count it as an aberration and tuck it away deep in her memory and with any luck forget it altogether.

That's likely, an errant voice in her head piped up, but she knew she had to ignore it.

Somehow he had to ease himself out of this situation without hurting Bill, Nick decided as she drove him towards the apartments. The hurt she'd already endured—hurt he'd known nothing about—was more than enough and Gran was right—how fair was it to expect Bill to take care of his child now he knew what she'd suffered?

As for that Nigel…

No, Nick told himself as he felt anger against the man building in his gut, forget the past and work out how to get through the next little while.

He had to get over the attraction business and definitely avoid physical contact because kissing her had made the situation worse. He had to forget the hunger he'd tasted on her lips, a hunger that had met and matched his own.

His future was too uncertain.

Well, not uncertain in one way. Steffi was his future and if he could just concentrate on that and ease Bill out of his life—or at least out of his apartment—as quickly as possible, then everything should be okay.

He glanced at her, and saw the little frown puckering the clear skin of her forehead and wanted more than anything to touch her, to assure her everything would be all right, but the kiss had made it impossible for him to touch her—possibly ever again. The kiss had shifted their relationship into a place where it couldn't be...

'If you cook a potato and mash it with some peas and a little gravy and carrot from the casserole in the slow cooker, I think Steffi will eat that for her dinner.'

Nick's turn to frown.

Was that all Bill had been frowning about?

Steffi's dinner?

Could she have shoved her emotional confession back into some box in her mind and switched back to practical Bill?

Could she have dismissed the *kiss* so easily?

They'd reached the entrance to the car park and she was leaning out to press the code that opened the big doors so he couldn't see her face, but even if he could see it, would he be able to read it?

The Bill he'd kissed, and who'd kissed him back with mind-blowing enthusiasm, was a Bill he didn't know at all.

'I'll drop you both off and be back in time for you to go to work,' she added as she pulled up next to the lift. 'I need to pop over and see Kirsten to ask her about nannies—she had one when she went back to work after her kids started school—just part time, some kind of share arrangement with another mother. I know there are a couple of agencies in town but she'll know which one is best.'

Nick took in the information, aware as he did so that Bill was intent on distancing herself from him, just as he'd intended doing from her. Yet somehow it aggravated him that she'd moved first.

Pathetic.

That's what he was.

'Well, go on, out you get, and don't forget your daughter,' Bill told him, back to her old bossy self, which aggravated Nick even more.

But he got out, unstrapped Steffi from her car seat—a feat in itself—and carried her and the colourful bag into the elevator, refusing to wave as Bill took off, tyres squealing on the concrete floor.

CHAPTER SEVEN

'HA! YOU WEAKENED,' Nick said to Bill when she turned up an hour before he was due to go to work. 'Bet you thought I couldn't do the bath myself.'

This, he'd decided as he'd fed and bathed his daughter, was how he was going to play things. As if nothing had ever happened between them.

The tightening of his body suggested it hadn't totally accepted this idea but he soldiered on.

'Nothing to it,' he said, pointing to where a pyjama-clad Steffi was playing with toys on the living-room floor.

'Until you need to shower yourself,' Bill said, smiling as Steffi noticed her and began to crawl towards her, gurgling a welcome.

'I did wonder about that and decided that's why you had the playpen thing. Pop her in there with some toys and shower quickly.'

'Well done, you,' Bill said, swinging Steffi up into her arms so Nick wasn't sure if her praise was for him or his daughter. 'But now I'm here I'll read her a story while you do whatever you have to do to get ready for work, okay?'

Bill turned back to face him as she added the last word, and he knew she was asking something else.

Like were things okay between them?

Or, dread thought, was it okay if they never mentioned the kiss?

'The casserole was fantastic,' he said by way of reply, 'but Bob didn't include containers for freezing things when he furnished this place so I've left it all in the pot.'

He decided that had answered the first possible question—a normal Nick-Bill conversation. The second question was unanswerable.

He showered, shaved and dressed for work, returning to the living room to find Steffi already asleep in Bill's arms.

'You want to pop her into bed?' Bill asked, and he bent and lifted his daughter, smelling the baby smell of her and feeling his heart swell again with love and pride.

Knowing that, whatever happened in the future, Steffi's welfare would come first.

He carried her into the bedroom and laid her down gently in her cot. Bill had followed him, carrying a small ornamental angel. She fiddled with it for a moment, plugging a lead from it into a power point then pressing one of the angel's wings.

'Intercom,' she explained. 'I put the receiver near my bed so I can hear her if she wakes in the night. Kirsten gave it to me this afternoon, along with some info about nannies. We can talk about that tomorrow.'

And with that she slipped away, leaving him watching his sleeping daughter, trying to take in the enormous changes that had happened in his life in three short days.

'Not that I regret them,' he told the sleeping Steffi, reaching down to pull a light sheet over her.

He called goodbye to Bill, who'd disappeared into the bedroom she was using, and left for work, hoping it would be a busy night so he didn't have time to think about Bill or bedrooms or anything other than work really.

Bill heard the door close behind him and came out of the bedroom, telling herself how pathetic she was, hiding away like that. Although she'd had a valid excuse, putting new batteries into the receiver of the intercom and setting it up on the table next to her bed.

In the kitchen she peered into the slow cooker, cursing herself for not slipping back down to her apartment before Nick left, to get some containers to freeze the leftovers.

Tomorrow would do.

Helping herself to a plateful, she sat down to eat it, wondering how long it would take to find a nanny and wondering if *not* living here with Nick would make things better or worse as far as the attraction went.

She'd barely finished her meal when her mobile trilled.

The hospital!

Nick?

Answer the damn thing, she told herself, and did so.

'Mass panic,' Angie, the triage sister, told her. 'I know you've got time off for some reason or other but we need anyone we can get. A backpackers' minibus overturned on the bypass, fourteen passengers and driver all with various injuries. The first admissions will be at the hospital in fifteen minutes. Can you come?'

Thank heaven she'd seen Kirsten just that afternoon was Bill's first thought.

'I'll be there, possibly not within fifteen minutes but as soon as I can get there,' she told Angie, then she phoned Kirsten, who'd offered to babysit any time, explaining, as she'd said it, that her two were off at her mother's place for a few days and being school holidays she was free herself.

She could also ask Kirsten to bring freezer containers...

'Kirsten's minding Steffi,' Bill said, finding Nick as soon as she walked into the ER, knowing if he saw her there before she explained, he'd panic.

He was bent over a stretcher, listening to the ambo explain the treatment that had already been given to the patient, but he nodded to show he'd heard Bill's words then smiled.

'Glad you're here,' he said briefly but with such genuine gratitude that Bill knew the situation was dire.

'Second ambulance two minutes out,' Angie said, when Bill approached the triage desk. 'I've more doctors coming in but no one to take this patient yet. Will you meet and assess? Nick can join you when and if he stabilises the young woman he's with now.'

Bill nodded, and grabbed a trolley, knowing the ambulance would have to turn around to return to the accident. They'd move the patient onto it, quickly transferring her to hospital monitoring equipment so the ambulance equipment would be free.

The patient was another young girl, blunt chest

trauma, intubated and with fluid flowing into her, but Bill could hear a wheezing noise and wondered if the oxygen she was getting was flowing out as quickly as it flowed in.

'Open pneumothorax,' the ambo said after they'd settled her on the trolley. He lifted the sheet that covered the young woman and pointed to a large sterile dressing on the left-hand side of her chest. 'Freak accident. She must have been holding her backpack on her knee when the bus tipped over and a weird silver thing went into her chest. We had to remove it to put the patch on her, but it's there near her legs somewhere in case the docs need to see what it is.'

He handed Bill the paperwork and took the empty stretcher back to his ambulance.

The 'weird silver thing' was of no importance to Bill or the young woman right now. The patch was acting as a flutter valve, one side open to allow air to escape, but the wound would have to be closed, and quickly. Were there surgeons coming in? Another nurse arrived and together they assessed the patient, knowing everything they did, even in an emergency, had to be checked and rechecked.

The young woman's breathing was slow and shallow and oxygen levels in her blood were veering towards dangerously low.

Thoracostomy!

Did every nurse's head have words rarely thought of just sitting there waiting to be thrown up when necessary?

'See if there's a doctor free,' Bill said to her assistant. 'She needs a drainage tube put into her chest to get rid of any fluid collecting in there, then the wound closed as soon as possible. But if we can get the drainage going she'll be more comfortable and hopefully her blood gases will improve.'

The nurse returned, almost inevitably, with Nick, but this was work and in a work situation personal issues were forgotten.

Bill explained while he examined the patient, then, taking care to keep away from the wound, anaesthetised a small area of her chest. Bill had the thoracostomy needle and drainage tube ready for him and within minutes the drain was in, fluid and blood flowing from it.

Lifting the sterile dressing, Nick examined the wound.

'She needs it closed,' he said, and turned to the young nurse. 'Can you find out how soon a surgeon will be here and where this lass is on the triage list? I can close it if no one else is available.'

Of course you could, Bill thought, again realising just how competent an ER doctor Nick was, but it was the realisation of why he was so good—his time with the army—that made her heart ache. That time must also have deepened his desire for a family. Well, now he had one—or part of one. With Serena's return he'd have the real thing, which was why she herself had to butt out right now.

Rob Darwin arrived before she had time to become melancholy over this decision—one, in fact, she'd already made.

'Two surgeons up in OR with the bus driver who looks like losing his leg, but if you're happy to do this, I'll assist,' he said to Nick.

Around them they could hear the noise of other nurses and doctors shouting for this or that, the chaos of a multiple casualty accident continuing, but within the cubicle everyone's concentration was on the patient, on closing the young woman's chest so her heart and lungs could function properly.

Nick worked with such precision, cutting more skin around the wound, cleaning the flap he'd need later to close the hole, clearing blood clots from deep inside, Rob holding back the skin while Bill irrigated the flesh beneath. Whatever had driven in had gone between ribs but had torn the cartilage connecting them.

Carefully Nick put the muscles and tissue back together again, stitching and stapling until finally the wound was sealed by the young woman's own skin, drawn tightly across her ribs.

'What did it?' he asked as he straightened up, leaving Bill to apply the dressing.

'Something silver—it should be by her legs,' Bill told him. 'The ambos think it was in her backpack, which she was holding on her knees.'

Nick felt beneath the sheet and found the small silver statue of a cat with its right paw raised.

'If it's a good luck charm, it didn't work, did it?' he said, returning it to its place beside the girl. 'That paw must have gone straight through her chest when the accident happened. Perhaps she had it in her hand at the time, showing it to someone.'

'Well, she's had some good luck landing in a hospital where an ER doctor can close her chest with a minimum of fuss,' Rob said, then he turned to Bill. 'Can I grab you a coffee?'

As soon as the words were out he must have realised his mistake and offered to get one for Nick as well, but as an approaching siren told them another patient was on the way, they both refused, and Rob went off to refresh himself before heading back into the fray.

'He's still hopeful of getting a date,' Nick said, his voice strained but that could be stress. 'Perhaps if you went out with him you'd find the spark.'

And put a distance between you and me, Bill thought, but didn't say it, knowing it was exactly what Nick was thinking.

'I think that's called using people and I'll deal with the stupid situation between us in my own way,' she snapped, then headed for the entrance to prepare for the next arrival, although as she watched the ambos unload the patient, she wondered if going out with Rob might not be a good idea.

Not all romances began with instant attraction.

And Rob was relatively new in town and lonely, and by going out with him she could introduce him to some other women and maybe he'd find someone who *did* feel a spark.

So, rather than using him, she'd be doing him a good turn and at the same time distancing herself from Nick .

By midnight all the patients had been stabilised, some flown south for further treatment, some hospitalised and the lucky few with minor injuries had been packed off to their hostel. Not wanting to keep Kirsten up later than necessary, Bill signed off and headed home.

'No trouble at all,' Kirsten said. 'She's a gorgeous little thing, isn't she? I've been watching her sleep. What's the story?'

Bill sighed.

'Who knows really? The bits I do know are so unbelievable I don't like to think about them. Briefly, Nick thought his girlfriend was having an abortion but she didn't and now there's Steffi, and right now her mother is in New York, which is why the baby's here with Nick, and after that—who knows?'

'Nick won't let her go,' Kirsten said, 'Steffi, I mean. Never having had a family, she must seem like a miracle for Nick.'

'Exactly,' Bill said, and must have sounded bleak for Kirsten put an arm around her shoulders.

'It *is* good, isn't it—for Nick, I mean?' she probed, and Bill assured her it was.

'I'm just overtired,' she said. 'How you manage kids and work I'll never know.'

She thought she'd sounded okay but the wondering look on Kirsten's face told her she'd failed.

'Well, look after yourself,' Kirsten said, giving Bill a hug. 'And if you need to talk to anyone, remember I'm not the family gossip.'

Bill had to smile for it was Bob's wife Jackie who claimed that title. Kirsten was the last person in the family to repeat anything told to her in confidence.

Nick found himself scowling at Rob Darwin every time they crossed paths that evening, but as the flow of ambulances was reduced to a trickle and the patients he was treating only had minor injuries, he had time to consider the situation more rationally. He knew he should be glad the man was interested in Bill because he himself certainly had no proprietorial rights on her, no claim at all, in fact.

And he definitely shouldn't be kissing her, for all his mind *and* body were obsessed by her.

Perhaps obsessed wasn't the word. Surely he couldn't

be *obsessed*? Obsessed drew pictures of stalkers and serial killers in most people's minds—

'You all right?' his patient asked, and he knew he must have groaned.

'Fine, just a long night. And you'll be fine too. Just remember to check the coverings on the wounds every day and if you start getting some yellowish seepage, come back here or see a GP.'

'I'll definitely come back here,' the patient said, and for the first time Nick registered that she was a very attractive young woman. English, from her accent, and though her long blonde hair was matted with blood and her face streaked with grime, he knew she'd clean up into something special.

He smiled at her, hearing Bill's voice whispering *Cradle-snatcher* in his head.

'You do that if you need to,' he said in his most professional voice, knowing it was highly unlikely she'd be back while he was on duty. One more night then he could take some time off and sort out a workable arrangement for himself and Steffi.

The thought of her brought a half-smile to his face and he realised again that, whatever lay ahead, giving Steffi a stable, happy life had to be his number-one priority.

Once Bill shifted out, it would be easier to work out what to do next. Easier to stop thinking about her as well.

It had to be.

He looked around the ER. The place had gone from chaotic to all but empty, only one sad drunk sitting on a bench and Nick had been told the man was homeless and often spent the night in the ER.

Had *he* ever had a family?

Surely not, for wouldn't a family have kept him sane and safe and off the streets?

Although not all families worked…

'Mine will,' he muttered.

And was startled when a passing nurse said, 'Your what will what?'

He grinned at her.

'Sign of advancing age, talking out loud,' he said, then realised the nurse in question was Amanda, the woman who'd asked him to join her and her friends on a trip to the islands. 'Oh, by the way, I won't be able to make it at the weekend—unexpected complications.'

'Old friend Bill more than just an old friend?' Amanda asked, surprising Nick so much he had no time to retort before she added, 'Hospital gossip machines work just as well in the country as in the city, and everyone in the ER has seen the way you look at her.'

He had to quash this right now! More for Bill's sake than for his.

'I've known Bill since we started school together in the kindergarten class, what's more—' like some pathetic loser about to tell a lie, he found himself crossing his fingers behind his back '—the gossip I've heard links her with a certain other doctor—one who was in here earlier.'

He walked away before he got himself deeper into the mire, sorry he'd had to implicate Bill in a relationship that didn't exist but not wanting to explain his current situation.

Not that he could explain it because he had no idea exactly what it was—apart from a disaster.

Although Steffi wasn't a disaster and if he concentrated on getting life right for her, then everything else should fall into place.

Or so he hoped.

He arrived home to find his friend and his daughter both dressed for the beach.

'She loves the bath so much I thought I'd try her in the pool—there's a paddling pool beside the big pool and the water in it is quite warm. But I thought it best to go early before the sun gets too hot. Here, you can have a little play with her before you head to bed and I'll put the washing on.'

Bill handed Steffi to him and walked away, and though he wanted to watch, he didn't, turning his full attention on his daughter, who was gurgling with delight, hopefully because she was pleased to see him.

'We'll manage on our own, won't we?' he said, lifting her high into the air. 'Just one more night with Bill then it's you and me against the world, kid,' he added, while she laughed down into his face.

He hugged her close, reaffirming the fact that she was more important than anything else in the world right now, and getting their lives together sorted out had to be his first priority.

So why the hell, when Bill returned, did he suggest he grab a coffee and some toast and join them at the pool?

Because he wanted to see with his own eyes how his daughter took to the water?

Or he wanted to see Bill in a bikini again?

Ridiculous—that was tempting fate and the look Bill gave him told him she thought so too, but he excused himself by deciding he didn't want to miss Steffi's first dip in a pool and hurried to fix some breakfast so he could join them.

Hell! She could do without seeing Nick with no shirt on. Didn't he realise they had to be seeing less of each other, not more?

Bill brooded on this as she and Steffi went down in the lift, exiting on the ground floor and walking out the back of the foyer to a beautifully landscaped recreation area. The two pools, formed so they looked like natural rock pools, were set in lush tropical vegetation. To one side was an outdoor barbeque and picnic space, tables and chairs set up beneath palm-fronded shelters.

On the other side was a long, narrow lap pool for serious swimmers, but for now all she and Steffi needed was the paddling pool.

Steffi saw the water and began to clap, making Bill realise she wasn't new to pools. Of course, her mother's New York apartment building could be modern enough to have one on site, probably on the roof.

Her mother.

Serena.

Just keep the beautiful blonde in the forefront of your mind when those abs come into view, Bill told herself, dropping their towels on a nearby chair, putting a little more sunscreen on Steffi's face then carrying her towards where the pool sloped from ankle depth to probably shoulder depth on Steffi.

The little girl paddled happily on the edge, splashing water up at Bill and chortling her delight.

'The notes said she's had swimming lessons.'

The abs had arrived, although right now they were decently covered by a T-shirt.

'I must have missed that part but lessons or not, you can't take your eyes off them for a minute around water,' Bill replied, then felt foolish and added, 'But of course you'd know that. I think child drownings are among the cruellest things we see in the ER.'

'Well, that's put a dampener on the fun, hasn't it, Steff?' Nick sat down in the water with his daughter and squirted water in his fists to make fountains.

She squealed with delight and once again he felt his heart fill with happiness. Whatever he had to sacrifice to give her the best possible life, he would. Not that resisting his attraction to Bill could be regarded as a sacrifice when they hadn't got past the kissing stage!

'One kiss does not a relationship make,' Bill said quietly, and he knew that once again their ability to follow each other's thoughts was in play.

'You are so right,' he told her. 'Now, how about you take over here while I swim about a hundred laps to convince my body of that?'

Bill laughed, which suggested that everything would be okay between them, but he knew it wouldn't—not unless they saw as little as possible of each other between now and when Serena returned. And, no, he told himself, he wasn't going to question the ethics of going back to Serena for the sake of his daughter—it was the right thing to do and he would do it.

Swim first, then sleep then one more night on duty, after which he'd get his new life organised…

How could so much have been organised while he slept?

Nick woke at two in the afternoon to find a note that

informed him his daughter was at playgroup, whatever that might be, and would be home at two-thirty. Two nannies were coming for interviews, Anna at four-thirty and Dolores at five-thirty.

Dolores? Who was called Dolores these days?

It had to be a measure of his overall confusion that he was spending precious brain power, limited right now, on an unknown person's name.

He showered, glanced around the apartment to make sure it was tidy then phoned Bob, who put him onto the right car dealer for the vehicle he'd decided would be safest for Steffi.

CHAPTER EIGHT

'AND JUST WHERE have you been?'

Bill was obviously angry when she greeted him just inside the door of the apartment when he returned at four twenty-five.

'I'm not late for the appointment,' he pointed out.

'No, but nervous would-be employees are usually early. Anna's sitting out on the deck with Steffi.'

Nick took in the faint flush of colour in Bill's cheeks and guessed the anger in her voice was more that of relief, the release of tension when someone had been worrying.

Over him, or the fact that he might miss the interview?

'I'd have phoned if I'd thought I'd be late,' he said, touching her gently on the forearm.

She stiffened immediately, then turned away, obviously not interested in the answer to her earlier question.

So he didn't tell her...

Why she'd let herself get all uptight over Nick being late, Bill didn't know. All she *did* know was that her relief at seeing him had prompted a surge of anger.

Stupidity, that's what it was!

She closed her eyes and prayed he'd like one of the

nannies enough to employ her and *she* could fade quietly into the background of his life.

This idea should have brought pleasure, but her visit to the playgroup with Steffi, seeing the other mothers and their children, watching Steffi's delight as she'd taken in the noise and colour, had brought back all the pain she'd suffered with the miscarriage, in her arms *and* in her heart.

'Plenty of small children around for you to play with,' she reminded herself, only to realise that since she'd come home after the miscarriage she'd deliberately avoided spending too much time with her smaller nieces and nephews. The older ones, yes, she regularly took them to the beach or went to watch their sporting fixtures.

But the infants—the toddlers…

'Would you two like tea or coffee?'

She called through the open door out to the deck, not venturing out because she didn't want to get involved.

Steffi looked up at her voice and left her hold on Nick's knee to stagger a couple of steps towards her, but Bill resolutely turned away.

Losing one child had been bad enough. To have this one worm her way any further into her heart then be lost to her—that would be too much.

She made the coffees, as requested, set the mugs on a tray, added biscuits and a fruit strap for Steffi and took the lot out on to the terrace.

'Aren't you joining us?' Nick asked.

Bill forced a smile as she replied.

'No, Anna and I had a good chat earlier.'

She fastened a bib around Steffi's neck and handed

her the treat, sitting her down on the tiled deck so she could eat it without smearing it all over the furniture.

'She seems a very placid child,' Anna said, and Bill found a better smile.

'She's the best,' she said, glad to be able to answer honestly. 'I suppose she's been used to so many different carers, she takes change for granted.'

Bill slipped away. While she'd been talking, Nick had leaned down and lifted Steffi onto his lap and the adoration on the little girl's face as she looked up at her father had nearly broken Bill's already badly damaged heart.

It's right they stay together, she told herself. It's how things should be.

But accepting the rightness of it did nothing to alleviate her pain.

Nick liked Anna and having read her references— all excellent—and seen her interacting with Steffi, he was certain she'd be the perfect nanny for his daughter. Because Bill had arranged another interviewee he would see her, too, but he felt more relaxed now he had at least one carer available.

'How do you see the hours working?' Anna asked. 'The agency explained you're a doctor who mainly does night duty, so would it be a live-in job?'

He studied the young woman, attractive enough, with a bright smile and a pleasant personality, then tried to picture her living with them—with him and Steffi—in the room Bill was using now—

'Look,' he said, feeling his way as another solution took vague form in his head. 'Originally, yes, I was employed to work in the ER and I told the hospital management that I'd be happy to do night shifts. Night shifts give you more time off—five nights on then three days

off. In point of fact, it turns into four days off as they
don't count the first day when you're supposed to catch
up on the sleep you missed the previous night.'

Anna nodded but looked vaguely puzzled about
where the conversation might be going.

'I should explain that I came back to Willowby
largely to see more of my elderly grandmother, and
the night shifts offered more opportunity to do things
with her during the day. But now...'

Anna smiled.

'You're confused because you have to consider Steffi's needs as well, but in my opinion you'd still be better
off doing night shifts. You get to see her in the morning
when you come home, and in the afternoon. Depending on your timetable you could even eat dinner with
her and put her to bed. Then on those days off you're
all hers—or all hers and your grandmother's.'

'You're right,' Nick agreed, although in his gut he
was still uncomfortable about the young woman sleeping here.

'How would you arrange your working hours if I
stick to night duty?' he asked, throwing the onus of the
decision back on her.

She considered it for a while, absentmindedly picking up another biscuit and eating it.

'I could start on the evening you begin duty and stay
over for the five nights and days so you can sleep on
your first day off. I'll be getting a meal for myself and
Steffi so will do dinner for you each night, then when
you're off duty I leave you in charge.'

It sounded okay but Nick still had misgivings.

'Is this the way nannying works? Do you not worry
about living in a house with a man you barely know?

And doesn't if affect your social life? I mean, do you live at home or do you rent and if you rent, do you still have to pay rent if you're not there five nights a week?'

Anna smiled at him.

'Most employers don't give a damn about their nanny's social or financial life. In my case, I live with my partner—we've been together four years now. How I see it working is once Steffi's in bed and all my duties are done, with your permission and after you've met him, I'm sure my partner would be happy to visit.'

Uh-oh! Nick thought, imagining the two in the bedroom while Steffi screamed blue murder. Although wasn't there an intercom…?

'Not every night,' Anna continued, 'because he has his own interests, but occasionally he might bring over a DVD we can watch together. But that would only be with your permission. If you have any doubts, that's okay. You say the job's only temporary—that Steffi's mother is coming back—so I can survive a few weeks of not seeing my partner for five nights of the week.'

Nick felt reassured—mostly reassured. His sticking point still seemed to be the bedroom, which he now considered Bill's…

'You sound like a very sensible young woman and, being one, you probably realise the agency has sent two people for me to interview. I'll try to make up my mind by tomorrow morning and will be in touch either way.'

To Nick's surprise, because he'd been very impressed by Anna, Dolores won the nanny stakes hands down. An older woman, perhaps fifty, she was bright and vivacious and Steffi sank into her ample bosom and grabbed the chunky beads around her neck, obviously enamoured.

'No worry about the times you go or come, Doctor,' Dolores told him when he tried to explain the hours. 'I will be here for the little one. If you are here, I make myself scarce but can still make meals for you and her so you can spend more good time with her. She and I we do shopping, you write down what you like to eat. Money you pay for five nights I stay is more than enough for the week if you don't mind my living here even when not working. That way I can work a little bit—like a housekeeper as well as nanny. Nothing extra to pay.'

Nick knew he had to delve further and discovered Dolores's permanent home was with her son and his wife and family.

'This kind of job a nice holiday for me,' she told Nick. 'My grandchildren, five of them, and so wild, but being mother-in-law not my place to tell them how to behave so I have to keep mouth shut. I love them all, and they are good for me, but whew!'

She waved her hand in front of her face to indicate how tiring her grandchildren were.

Nick laughed, even more certain this woman would be the best possible nanny for his daughter.

He made arrangements about time and pay, aware he had to pay her through the agency. She played with Steffi for a while then carried her to the door, kissing both her cheeks before handing her back to Nick.

'I teach her a little Spanish,' she said. *'Adios, mi angelita.'*

Steffi waved a chubby hand, her gaze following Dolores as she headed for the lift.

'Well, kid?' Nick said to her, and Steffi crowed with delight.

Bill was in the kitchen, chopping vegetables, apparently for Steffi's dinner as the pile was varied but rather small.

'I thought we'd have grilled salmon and salad,' she said, without looking up. 'I'll do a lamb cutlet for Steffi but she can try the fish as well because she should be eating fish and it's not mentioned in the notes about what she eats and doesn't eat.'

Bill glanced up long enough to hand Steffi a piece of broccoli then turned her attention back to what must have been a really difficult carrot.

'So, she doesn't want to know about your new nanny,' Nick said to Steffi, who was munching on the broccoli.

Bill glanced up again, anxiety and something he couldn't read in her eyes.

'You've decided on one of those two?' she asked. 'There was one that will suit?'

Steffi slid out of his arms and crawled over to where her saucepan and wooden spoons were left on the floor, so Nick could turn his full attention on Bill, who sounded even more anxious than she looked.

'They were both great but Dolores wins hands down. She's older, which appeals to me, and she's obviously very used to children, and there was something motherly—or grandmotherly, I suppose—about her that won Steffi over from the start.'

'That's good,' Bill muttered, and turned her attention back to the carrot, though she did glance up to ask, 'Do you want to eat early with Steffi? If so, it might be an idea to turn on the barbeque to heat the grill plate. It's always better to cook fishy things outside because of the smell.'

Thus dismissed, Nick headed for the balcony, where the beauty of the view struck him afresh. He walked back inside, picked up his daughter, took Bill by the hand and led her outside.

'Isn't it great?' he said. 'And smell the sea.'

The sun was setting behind the building so the water was washed with pink and streaked with gold, the islands nothing more than purple lumps along the far horizon.

He put his arm around Bill's shoulders, as he must have done a thousand times in the past, and although she stiffened, he left it there.

'I thought you'd be pleased to be free of looking after me and Steffi,' he said quietly to his friend, resolutely ignoring the cries of his body that it wanted more than friendship.

'I would never want to be free of our friendship and I would hate to not be some small part of Steffi's life,' Bill said carefully, after a silence that had stretched too long.

Nick hugged her close, a friend hug.

'Daft woman!' he said. 'As if you'd ever be free of the two of us. You're our best friend, remember?'

Bill eased away from him, kissed Steffi's cheek and headed back indoors.

'Unfortunately, I do,' she said as she disappeared.

Nick set Steffi down with some toys Bill had left on the deck, and turned on the grill plate on the barbeque. He knew Bill was hurting, but why, he wasn't sure. There was the sudden eruption of attraction between them. It was mind-bogglingly strange, and with the advent of Steffi, definitely inconvenient, but they were both mature adults, they could resist attraction.

Couldn't they?

Of course they could, Bill probably better than him for she was a strong woman.

But there was something more, some pain he—Steffi!

He'd been in New York when Bill had let him know the wedding was off. So Steffi must be much the same age as her child would have been and here he was, accepting her help, relying on her to look after Steffi when every time she looked at the child she must feel pain stabbing into her heart.

How stupid could one man be?

Not that there was much he could do about it now, but Dolores was starting work in a couple of days...

They ate their early dinner on the deck, Steffi finding salmon very tasty.

'I'll clean up while you bath her and yourself,' Bill said, and though Nick longed to talk to her, to say he understood and to apologise for the pain he must unwittingly have caused her, he knew now wasn't the time. He'd be too rushed and, anyway, how could he put his thoughts and emotions into words?

Bill watched the pair depart for the bathroom and sighed. She stared at the after-dinner debris and sighed again.

'Get a grip!' she finally muttered to herself, and she stood up and began to stack the dishes on a tray.

It was great that Nick had found a good nanny, even better that she could get out of his apartment. Then this—surely you couldn't call it love-sickness—would pass and her life would return to normal.

Or something approaching normal anyway...

She stacked the dishwasher, cleaned up the kitchen, put away all Steffi's toys and seriously considered getting into bed and pulling the covers over her head, possibly for a year.

Although it would be better to do that in her own apartment, rather than Nick's.

And she certainly shouldn't be thinking bed and Nick in conjunction like that because it reminded her of all that could never be...

Giving up on the bed idea she went back out onto the deck. The lights from the marina at the base of the building lit up the neighbouring area, but the sea was a deep, dark navy and the distant islands nothing more than black shadows.

The familiar view, even seen from this height, soothed her troubled mind and eased the ever-present ache in her heart. She could almost smile at her stupidity because being attracted to one's unavailable best friend had to top the stupidity list.

'Steffi's asleep and I've set the baby monitor.'

Nick's voice came from behind her and she didn't turn, although when he slid his arms around her waist and held her lightly, she leaned back against him—yes, stupidity again but didn't she deserve *something*?

'I've been totally insensitive, letting you take over Steffi's care,' Nick said, his voice gruff as if this weird conversation he'd just begun was affecting him deeply. 'I didn't know what you'd been through but that's no excuse. I just let you step in without even considering how it would affect your life.'

Bill turned to face him, distancing herself by putting her hands on his shoulders and stepping back so she could look into his face.

'*What* are you talking about? I was happy to step in—in fact, I took it all on myself. You didn't have much say in it. So why are you wallowing in guilt?'

Nick studied her for a moment, as if trying to read

something in her face, and just standing there, looking at him looking at her, Bill knew it was more than attraction she was feeling for this man.

It was love.

'Steffi must be the same age as your baby would have been,' Nick said, pulling her close again into a warm hug—a *friendly* hug! 'It must hurt you just looking at her.'

Bill pushed away again and shook her head.

'And this is worrying you now when I'm about to be replaced?' she teased, then she became the hugger and Nick the huggee. 'Of course I look at Steffi and wonder what if, but having her to play with, to care for has been sheer joy, so enough of the guilt trip. Just get yourself off to work so you can afford to pay the nanny, not to mention kindergarten fees, swimming lessons, school fees…'

Nick stopped her teasing with his hand across her mouth and the kiss she pressed against his palm was as automatic as breathing.

The hand stayed there for an instant, then Nick turned and walked away, saying, over his shoulder, 'And that's a whole other problem, isn't it?' in a voice edged with what sounded like anger, although it could just as easily have been frustration.

Isn't it just, Bill sighed to herself.

CHAPTER NINE

DOLORES HAD FITTED so well into his and Steffi's life that Nick found himself, as his next days off drew close, wondering if he should consider some social activities. Amanda had mentioned a party and Bob had invited him to some big do at the yacht club. Bill, who hated boats because they moved so much, was unlikely to be there.

Bill.

She'd moved the few things she'd had with her out of his apartment on the day Dolores had moved in, and although Dolores obviously saw her—Miss Bill says this, Miss Bill says that, she would report to Nick in the evenings—Nick hadn't set eyes on her.

He knew from an occasional scribbled note on a patient chart that she must be working the day shift in the ER, but their paths hadn't crossed.

Should he call her?

He knew he should, if only to say thank you for all she'd done, but if he called, he couldn't trust himself not to ask to see her, and as she was obviously distancing herself from him, that would be unfair.

Although he *really* would like to know if she was finding this separation as difficult as he was. Did she think about him all the time, catch glimpses of someone she thought was him in the distance, only to be disappointed? Did she think about the kiss and find her body heating as she remembered?

Sitting at his desk in the little alcove he'd set up as a home office, he leaned his elbows on the desk and clasped his head in his hands.

And groaned!

'Dinner, Dr Nick,' Dolores called, and he pulled himself together and went through to the kitchen, where Steffi was already in her high chair, a lolly-pink bib around her neck, her chubby hands banging spoons on the tray.

'Nice bib, kid,' Nick said, and she crowed with delight.

'Miss Bill gave it to her.' Dolores straightened the bib, showing the giraffe appliquéd on it, then brushed her hand on Steffi's hair. 'Didn't she, sweetie?'

Dolores set a plate of meat and vegetables in front of Nick then sat down to feed Steffi. He'd learned by now that Dolores preferred to eat later but always made sure he and Steffi ate together.

The meal was delicious—all Dolores's meals were delicious—but this evening it failed to distract him from thoughts of Bill—Miss Bill, as Dolores insisted on calling her.

He'd thought, once their cohabitation had stopped, that the ache of desire that had been there in her presence would disappear, but, no, it simply grew stronger.

Work and Steffi, all he had to do was concentrate on those two things and surely, eventually, the attraction would die a natural death. People talked about unrequited love, but this was simply unfulfilled desire, a completely different animal.

'And we were at the mall so I didn't get the mail today.'

Dolores had finished feeding Steffi and was stacking dirty dishes in the dishwasher when Nick caught up with her conversation.

'If you don't want to collect it on your way to work,' Dolores continued, 'I will get it tomorrow.'

How could anyone be thinking of mail?

Nick smiled to himself at this totally inappropriate thought. He simply *had* to get his mind off Bill.

'I'll get it on my way out,' he assured Dolores, although it would mean stopping in the foyer on his way down to the basement car park.

It also meant he just happened to run into Rob Darwin, who was stepping into the lift as Nick exited.

They exchanged nothing more than courteous good evenings, but Nick knew someone in the building must have let Rob in and what were the chances that three people living here knew him?

Nick opened his mail box, emptied it, and tucked all the mail under his arm while he relocked the box. Given his mood, it was probably inevitable that the one piece of mail that slid to the floor was a postcard with a picture of the Statue of Liberty on it.

Refusing even to read it, Nick thrust it back in with the rest and went down to the basement.

Work didn't help. For a start he kept picturing Bill there, buzzing around with her quiet efficiency, always anticipating his needs when he had a tricky patient.

And when he wasn't picturing her there he was picturing her out with Rob Darwin, dining across a candlelit table from him, her hand touching his, just casually at first.

Would they park by Sunrise Beach on the way home?

His gut churned at the thought and by the end of his shift it took all his strength of mind to not knock on Bill's door when he got back to the apartment building the next morning, just to see how she looked…

And check whether Rob Darwin was there?

No!

He went directly to his apartment, showered, played with Steffi, ate the French toast Dolores cooked for him, and went to bed, certain that in sleep he'd lose the torment of his mind and body.

They were at Woodchoppers, Bill in a lime-green bikini, a colour that seemed incongruous until she slid into the water and the bikini apparently disappeared, melding in with the colour of the water so her sleek, slim body, rolling slowly over in the tiny waves, appeared naked.

Then he was in the water with her, both of them naked, swimming together in some way, bodies touching, arms pulling in unison through the water, Bill's body fitting into his, made to fit into his, her back moulded to his chest, the water cool, his blood on fire.

She turned and lay before him, offering herself up to him, but he didn't take her, simply looked, drinking in the riotous red hair, the pale pink of her lips, the tips of her breasts, as pink as her lips. He leaned closer to lick them, first one then the other, while she smiled to hide the trembling of her body.

Slim waist and flaring hips, more red curls, a nest that tempted his fingers, but he needed to know her better, to trace the contours of her body, feel the satin texture of her skin, kiss the little freckle just there at the base of her neck and now, a desire prolonged too long, taste again the sweetness of her lips.

Honeyed sweetness, moist warmth within, Bill no longer passive, stirring beneath him, raising her hips so her body slid against his—slid into place—to where it was made to be.

Drifting now, entwined, their bodies one, but the water failed to cool the fire that raced through his blood and burned along his nerves—the fire of need, of want—the urgency of desire.

He'd take her, she was his after all, part of him, the better part. They'd reached the rocks, soft rocks, and there he rolled her so she lay along his body, her breasts crushed against his chest, kissing him with a passion that told him the fire was in *her* blood as well, burning along *her* nerves...

He rolled her beneath him, touched her face, brushed back the burnished hair, smoothed his fingers over the lightly tanned skin that stretched across her cheekbones. Kissed her eyelids, kissed her nose, kissed the indentation beneath her pink ear, then lost himself once more as her lips parted, begging for a kiss.

For more than a kiss?

Of course for more. She was his, he was hers, it had to be—

Had he groaned aloud that he woke to the agonised sound reverberating around his bedroom?

That he woke up and sat, sweating, shivering, cursing now that he'd regressed to adolescence and the steamy dreams of youth, though Bill had never been part of those?

He clambered out of bed, aware he was alone from

the silence in the apartment, and headed for the shower, letting the water cascade over him, trusting it to wash away the memory.

Dreams faded, didn't they? Disappeared soon after waking, leaving nothing but ephemeral fragments too fine for memory to grasp?

Not this dream.

CHAPTER TEN

'You look fantastic!' Rob said when Bill collected him from his apartment near the hospital.

'Thank you,' she said, enjoying the compliment—stupidly pleased because, guessing her brother had also asked Nick, she'd made an extra effort, even straightening her hair so it hung like a shining dark red curtain down past her shoulders. 'But just remember I'm taking you there so you can meet some people outside the hospital circle. This is not a date.'

'Yes, ma'am.' Rob saluted as he said it, adding, with a wry smile, 'And I'll try to hide my broken heart.'

'Piffle,' Bill retorted, 'I bet you're so used to women falling at your feet, I'm nothing more than a novelty because I haven't.'

'Not *that* many women have fallen at my feet,' Rob argued, but he grinned as he said it and Bill had to hide a rueful sigh.

How simple it would have been to have fallen at Rob's feet—or even fallen just a little in love with him. How easy and uncomplicated. He was attractive, attentive, intelligent and had a good sense of humour—what more could a woman want?

But, no, she had to do the unthinkable, and for some

perverse reason fall in love with her totally unavailable best friend.

This time the sigh must have escaped for Rob, who'd been opening the car door for her, said, 'You're not regretting asking me to this do, are you? Do you not usually mix with the local social crowd?'

Bill slid in behind the wheel.

'As a lot of the local social crowd are related to me I can't avoid mixing with them, but as family, not at things like this. But, no, I don't regret asking you, it will be fun, beginning with the shock on my various sisters-in-laws' faces when I walk in with a handsome man who absolutely none of them know.'

Rob came round the car and sat beside her.

'Good,' he said. 'Let's both have fun!'

'Fun?' she muttered to herself ten minutes later.

Had she been out of her mind?

She didn't even have time to register her family's reactions to her presence, because the first person she sighted was Nick.

Nick, looking superb, in light-coloured slacks, a white open-necked shirt and a grey jacket that would probably exactly match his eyes.

Nick, talking to the leggy blonde they'd seen at breakfast that first morning—

Amy someone?

Nick, raising an eyebrow, nothing more, as he took in Rob by her side.

Glad she'd spent a fortnight's salary on the slinky white dress that showed off her curves as well as her tan, Bill led Rob into the throng, introducing him to friends and relations, assuring him he didn't need to remember names, finally finding Kirsten's sister, Sally, a stunning brunette, who was currently single, having recently discovered the man she'd thought she loved was married.

'Sally, this is Rob, a friend from the hospital. He's new in town so would you be a darling and look after him for me while I do the rounds of the brothers who are here? If I talk to one and not another, they get all precious.'

Sally whisked Rob off to get a drink, and Bill, aware she had to drive home—with or without Rob—took a glass of sparkling mineral water from a passing waiter and slid towards one of the open doors that led onto a narrow deck overlooking the boats in the yacht club marina.

Straight hair and a slinky dress hadn't cut it when it came to armour against Nick. Just seeing him had made her stomach somersault, leaving her so shaken it had taken all her strength to smile and nod and talk until she'd found an opportunity to hand Rob to someone else and escape while she collected her emotions.

She breathed deeply, taking in the salt-laden air, listening to the clinking of the ropes and fastenings on the boats as they moved in their moorings, gazing upwards at the star-filled sky.

Now think!

Obviously if she was going to have this kind of physical reaction every time she saw Nick, she had to take steps to *not* see him. They'd remained friends through long separations so if one or other of them left town, surely they could revert back to their platonic relationship?

She could get a job anywhere and maybe it was time to move on. She'd come home to lick her wounds after the Nigel debacle and the loss of the baby she'd never had, but she was fine and fit and strong once again.

Apart from a little heart-sickness, love-sickness, whatever—but work could cure that. Challenging work—something different, a foreign country, somewhere she'd be needed—

'I think your boyfriend's fallen hard for Sally— surely there was a less attractive woman you could have left him with?'

Nick was right behind her, so close she could feel the heat of him, smell his aftershave.

'He's just what Sally needs,' Bill answered, refusing to turn round because if hearing Nick's voice made her feel so uptight, then seeing him would probably paralyse her completely. 'He's nice and uncomplicated and funny and definitely not married.'

'I'm not married,' Nick said, his voice tight, strained, husky with emotion.

'No, but you have a family you can't betray so it's the same thing.'

Bill had done her best to keep *her* voice light and even, but the words had come out in a pathetic, wimpy kind of wail.

It was because he was so close—so close and yet not touching. Her nerve endings were reaching out towards him, straining against her skin so it was tight and hot— wanting to feel him, to be held, to lose herself in—

She stepped closer to the railing, hoping to break the bond that wasn't there.

Refocussed on her thoughts.

Maybe—

'Will you go back to live in Sydney?'

The 'when Serena returns' hung, unspoken, in the air.

Nick didn't reply, the silence stretching so long Bill wondered if he would, but when he did speak she knew it was something he'd been considering already.

'I want to stay here, Bill. I owe it to Gran, and also, now there's Steffi, I think I'd like her to grow up here. Serena has always worked out of Sydney, but these days she's in demand all over the world so I can't see why she couldn't be based here as well. She's Steffi's mother, Bill, for all her bizarre behaviour, and I'm sure, in her own way, Serena must love her daughter. Mother, father, child—that's a family, isn't it?'

'Exactly what you wanted,' Bill reminded him. 'But you should at least *try* to sound pleased about it.'

'How can I?' came the anguished cry, then his arms looped around her waist and he pulled her back so she was held against him, her body fitting his as neatly as two matching pieces of a puzzle. 'Damn it, Bill, how could this have happened? And why now, when it's impossible? Was life meant to be this way? One disaster after another?'

Bill rested her head against his shoulder and looked up at the sky.

Play it lightly, she told herself, although she knew the rapid beating of her heart beneath his hands would have already given her away.

'Melodrama, Dr Grant?' she teased. 'You can hardly label Steffi a disaster. More a miracle, and a delightful, gorgeous miracle at that. As for us, well, that would probably never have worked, even if we'd given in to the attraction. We know each other too well—there'd have been no mystery to keep the buzz alive.'

She was doing really well, she thought, until he lifted her hair and kissed the nape of her neck, sending a violent shudder of desire right through her body. And if her heart had been racing earlier, it now went into overdrive, hammering against her chest, while she could feel the moisture of her need between her thighs.

'Say that again—the bit about it not working,' Nick murmured against her skin, but Bill was beyond speech, beyond thought or voluntary movement. She let Nick hold her, let him kiss his way along her shoulder, let his hands roam across her breasts, thumbs teasing at her traitorously peaking nipples.

She grabbed the railing, no longer trusting her legs to hold her up as her bones melted under the onslaught of Nick's touch.

A sudden gust of wind, a louder rattle in the rigging of the yachts and she came thudding down to earth.

'For heaven's sake, Nick, we're practically in public!' she growled, trying to twist out of his grasp but only succeeding in turning to face him.

'So, where can we be private? Your place?'

Now she pushed away, shaking her head, hoping like hell she wasn't going to cry.

'You don't mean that, Nick, I'm sure you don't. Mother, father, child—family, remember? If you were to betray that then you're not the man I've always thought you, and certainly not the man I love.'

She spun away, heading not back inside but down the steps at the end of the balcony towards the marina itself. The 'l' word had come out without censorship but hopefully he'd take it as friend love not lover kind of love. Rob would have to fend for himself because there was no way she could go back inside and face family and friends with any kind of composure.

The tears she refused to shed were banked up behind

her eyes and she knew from the heat in her cheeks that they'd be fiery red.

With anger, frustration or pain?

She had no idea. All she knew was that her feelings for Nick had strayed so far beyond the realms of friendship that she would *have* to get away.

Nick wanted to follow her but knew he couldn't. Knew also he'd have to stay out on the balcony a little longer while the raging desire in his body cooled and he could face the crowd with some semblance of control.

She was right, of course. Even thinking about the things he'd like to do with Bill was a betrayal of sorts, but how could he face Serena with the suggestion of family if he'd physically betrayed her?

He thumped his fist against the railing, which did nothing more than hurt his hand, and was relieved when he heard a voice behind him—Amy joining him on the balcony.

'I thought I'd lost you,' she said. 'Boy, it's a crush in there. You didn't say if you're interested in a trip to Hayman Island on your next days off. I'm working as a boat hostess out there now and can get you a good deal on accommodation, and there's a huge party for the launch of some new perfume going on all week.'

'Thanks, but, no, thanks,' Nick said, but inside his gloom lifted just a little as he realised how much one small person had changed his life. A couple of days on a tropical paradise had no appeal whatsoever when set against a couple of days playing with Steffi.

Perhaps he wouldn't always feel like this, but right now the more he got to know his daughter, the more fascinating he found her.

So fascinating he found himself explaining his refusal.

'Steffi's going to walk on her own any day now, and I'd hate to miss seeing her take off.'

Amy laughed and shook her head.

'I gathered when you were talking about her earlier that she'd won you over, but to hear Playboy Nick refusing a gala party to see a baby take her first steps, that beats everything.'

She studied him for a few moments before adding, 'So it means you and Serena will get back together?'

'I'm assuming so,' Nick replied, ignoring the cold lump that formed in his stomach as he spoke.

'Well, that *will* be interesting,' Amy said with a smile he couldn't quite fathom. He hadn't liked the emphasis on the 'will' either but she disappeared back into the party before he could ask what she meant.

But at least now he could leave without worrying he'd run into Bill either in the marina car park or the building basement. The less he saw of Bill the better.

'Oh, Doctor Nick, I was going to phone you but Miss Bill arrived with the spade just in time. The little one, she was making an awful noise with breathing but Miss Bill has her in the en suite and she's okay now.'

Bill arrived with a spade?

Nick was striding towards his bedroom but that bit of the garbled conversation kept repeating itself in his head.

He opened the door to a fog of steam, a bedraggled-looking Bill sitting on the lavatory seat with Steffi asleep on her knee.

No spade.

'Croup!' Bill said as Nick bent over his daughter, automatically feeling for a pulse, listening to her breathing. 'Dolores said she opened the air-conditioning vent in Steffi's room because she was restless when she went to bed. If she has a bit of a cold, the cool, dry air could have caused the croup.'

Bill was talking sense, he knew that, but his medical brain was telling him that sudden stridor in a child's breathing could be caused by an inhaled foreign object.

'She's breathing normally now.' Bill answered his doubts as he lifted Steffi into his arms and held her tightly against him. 'I think she can go back to bed. I asked Dolores to turn off the air-conditioning earlier and although humidifiers are rarely needed up here in the tropics, it might be advisable to have one on hand for those hot nights when Steffi might need air-conditioning in her room.'

Nick looked down at Bill, at the hair beginning to regain its curl, at the damp dress clinging to her figure...

No, he wouldn't look there.

'We never had it, did we?'

Bill met the question with a puzzled frown.

'Had what?'

'Air-conditioning, you dope.'

That won an almost normal Bill smile.

'Never knew it existed outside of supermarkets and shopping malls. Remember how packed the malls were on really hot days?'

'Malls, hospitals and court houses,' Nick recalled, while relief flooded through him that he and Bill hadn't lost their easy, casual friend-type conversation.

Relief that vanished when she stood up and he remembered his dream when the lime-green bikini had apparently disappeared. The white slinky dress was in danger of doing the same thing and in his mind he saw her standing there naked in front of him.

His heart stopped beating, his breathing arrested, the world stood still and silent as he simply gazed at the woman he couldn't have.

'Put Steffi to bed—or maybe into your bed,' she said, breaking the spell so his organs resumed their normal function. 'That way you'll hear her if her breathing becomes hoarse.'

She smiled at him then—a lovely, cheeky Bill grin—and added, 'I bet that's one you haven't thought about yet. Is the kid allowed to sleep in your bed from time to time?'

He hadn't, but neither had he ever thought he'd feel anything other than the love of friendship for Bill, although right now, in this steamy bathroom, he began to suspect that was exactly what had happened.

Escaping was the obvious thing to do and he had the perfect excuse—putting Steffi to bed. The steam had made her clothes damp and she'd need a dry nappy. He'd do that—change her—now...

'I can't get out with you blocking the doorway,' Bill complained, but a tremor in her voice suggested that she, too, was feeling the tug of desire that had come from nowhere to confuse them.

The tug of love?

Had she said 'love' earlier?

'Move!' she ordered, remaining where she was, not coming close enough to push him out the door.

Not wanting to touch him for fear of where it might lead?

He moved, carrying Steffi through to her bedroom,

assuring Dolores the little girl was all right, reassuring himself at the same time.

A small red plastic spade was lying on the floor beside Steffi's cot. Having dug with it himself when he'd taken his daughter to the beach, he now understood the earlier conversation.

Dolores, who followed him in, picked it up and set it in the box of toys.

'Miss Bill found it in the lift and knew it was Steffi's,' she explained, then she burst into tears, falling over herself as she apologised again and again.

'Dolores, I would have turned on the air-conditioning,' Nick said very firmly. 'No one is blaming you. Now, go and have a cup of tea or a drink of whatever you need. I'm home and I'll take care of her tonight so shift the monitor into my room and get a good night's sleep yourself.'

But Dolores didn't move, repeating all she'd said, apologising tearfully over and over again until Bill appeared, put her arm around the older woman's shoulder and led her away.

Steffi, woken by the noise or by having her clothes changed, looked up at Nick and smiled sleepily. His heart filled with joy and as he bent and kissed her belly button he knew she had to come first in his life, her welfare, her physical and emotional development the most important things in his life.

The thought brought pain but better he suffer than she grow up with parents fighting for her. Mother, father, child—a family...

Bill sat in the kitchen, pouring a little rum into the cup of hot chocolate she'd made for Dolores, pleased the woman was finally calming down. But much as she,

Bill, wanted to leave—to escape before she had to face Nick again—she couldn't leave an even half-hysterical woman on his hands.

His attention had to be focussed on Steffi.

'It was a natural thing to do and of course Nick isn't going to fire you. You're the best thing that's ever happened to him and his daughter,' Bill repeated for about the eleventh time.

Dolores looked at her, her eyes red from weeping, her normally olive skin blotchy with emotion.

'You think so, Miss Bill?'

'I know so,' Bill said, and she leaned over and kissed the older woman on the cheek. 'Nick and Steffi couldn't do without you.'

'And when his wife comes back? He showed me postcard from New York.'

'Heaven only knows what will happen,' Bill told her, 'but I can't imagine you won't be part of their lives.'

Dolores smiled and Bill knew she could finally escape. Nick would stay with Steffi wherever she was sleeping.

Nick…

CHAPTER ELEVEN

TEN DAYS LATER Nick flew to Sydney with Steffi, Dolores and all the baby paraphernalia he now counted as normal baggage. Much as he hoped he and Serena could make a life in Willowby, he knew it would be easier to talk to her in her own apartment.

She'd had two days to get over any jet-lag she might be suffering, and although she hadn't sounded delighted when he'd told her they were coming, she hadn't objected.

Surely that had to be a good sign.

And she wasn't stupid, so she'd understand his argument that she could really be based anywhere...

'You worried, Dr Nick?' Dolores asked, as he drove the hire car he'd organised from the airport to Double Bay.

'No, Dolores,' he replied, although his gut was churning and every imaginable disastrous scenario was racing through his head.

The only scenario he hadn't imagined was finding Alex at the apartment—Alex cooing over Steffi, who obviously remembered him, while Serena barely acknowledged her child.

'Alex is here because he wants to photograph Australia,' Serena explained, and while Nick thought that might be a tall order, he refrained from comment. 'I didn't know you'd bring your nanny, she'll have to share with Steffi. I think the building manager has roll-out beds available.'

Nick had already fitted five people into three bedrooms in his head and realised Serena was assuming he would share her bed.

But wasn't that why he'd come?

To build the family that he wanted?

Mothers and fathers did share beds...

'I can sleep on the couch,' he heard himself say, when Alex, carrying Steffi, had led Dolores off to show her the bedroom they would use.

Serena studied him, eyebrows raised.

'Do you hate me so much, Nick?'

He shrugged, feeling awkward and uneasy because he didn't fully understand the situation himself.

'I don't hate you at all,' he said—at least that much was true. 'Yes, I was angry and upset over your deception but how could I hate you when you've given me Steffi? However, we're virtually strangers to each other. Not counting your brief visit to Willowby it's been eighteen months since we've seen each other—longer than that since we've been together.'

She smiled now.

'I doubt we've forgotten how to make love,' she murmured, moving closer so he knew he should take hold of her, feel her body against his—feel excitement, even.

Except he couldn't.

'I think we need to talk first, to work out where we're going.'

The smile faded from her face and it was her turn

to shrug. With all the elegance of her trade she moved away, over to the marble coffee table in the centre of the living room, bending to pick up a packet of cigarettes.

'You're not going to smoke with Steffi in the apartment!'

The words burst from his lips and he knew he must have spoken far too loudly because Serena spun towards him, more shock than surprise on her face.

'So now you're the smoking police,' she said, her voice tight. 'I remember *you* used to have a cigarette from time to time.'

The sly smile that crept across her face told him she knew her words had struck home, because occasionally, when she'd had a cigarette after sex, he'd had a puff or two—sharing hers, thinking of it as another kind of shared act...

He forced himself to remain calm.

'I'm sorry I reacted badly but Steffi's had a bad attack of croup and I've been worried about her lungs. Can we sit outside while you smoke?'

Serena nodded and led the way out onto the balcony. From here he could see glimpses of the harbour, the sun glinting off the water.

'The view from my apartment in Willowby has more water, but the harbour view is always magnificent,' he conceded.

'So, you could get used to it again?' Serena asked. 'We'd need to move to a bigger apartment because the nanny should have her own room and we'll always need a spare for visitors.'

This was it! This was where he had to say something.

But what?

And how?

How!

The word appealed to him. He knew her life, he'd work into it that way.

'How are your bookings looking? Where do you go next? Will you be mainly overseas?'

Serena squinted through a trail of smoke that curled up from her lips—lips that would kiss Steffi tasting of tobacco.

If she ever kissed Steffi...

'And you're asking why?'

Yes, Serena wasn't stupid. Self-focussed but not stupid.

He'd come to talk, Nick reminded himself. So talk.

'I think, ideally, Steffi needs both her parents. I realise your career is very important to you and I think she'd learn to live with the fact that you're often away, as long as she has stability in the rest of her life, like myself and Dolores—or whatever nanny we might employ.'

That sounded good so far, he congratulated himself while he waited for a comment from Serena.

'And?'

That was it? A one-word prompt, giving no indication of what she was thinking or feeling?

'As you know, I returned to Willowby to be close to Gran, to whom I owe so much. I think it would be a great place to raise a child, or children, and I wondered whether it mattered to you where you were based. If you're mostly flying out to assignments around the world, you could just as easily fly from there, not right away as you've obviously got this Australian trip planned, but after that?'

He'd made a mess of it, he could feel it in his bones, although Serena's face showed no emotion whatsoever.

Neither did she respond, simply putting out one cigarette and taking another one out of the packet, holding it distractedly between her fingers.

'Well?' he finally asked, and hoped it hadn't sounded like a demand.

'You've obviously been thinking about this for some time,' she said, 'this fantasy of family. Yet you're not willing to share my bed.'

So that was what had upset her!

You could fix that by agreeing—would it be so hard? a voice in his head demanded.

The shiver that ran through his body—not distaste but definitely uneasiness—gave him the answer.

'I think we should look at where we're going before we leap into bed together,' he said. 'Sex rarely solves anything—in fact, it probably makes situations more complicated.'

'You've changed,' she said, and although he knew a lot of the change was to do not with Steffi but with his feelings for Bill, he had an easier answer.

'I think having a child changes everyone.'

'Maybe.'

Nick had to be satisfied with that enigmatic response because Alex joined them on the balcony, still carrying Steffi, who was playing with his beard.

'We could photograph the child in all the places we spoke of,' he said to Serena. 'Ayers Rock and White-haven Beach and in the snow.'

'No!'

Nick and Serena spoke together, Nick adding, 'Well, at least we agree on something,' although he guessed Serena's 'no' was for a different reason. She didn't want Steffi stealing her limelight.

'Okay,' Alex said, accepting the judgement and setting Steffi down on the floor. 'And don't you dare light that cigarette and breathe smoke all over the child,' he added to Serena, who, to Nick's surprise, obediently put the offending object back into its box.

'So, the Australian photography, that's one project you've got lined up?' he said to Serena, grasping Steffi's hand as she pulled herself up on a chair and stumbled towards him. 'What's next?'

But Serena didn't answer. Standing up, she stepped carefully over Steffi and headed inside, the slamming of a door suggesting she'd taken refuge in her bedroom.

'I keep telling her not to smoke at all,' Alex complained, 'but she says it's all that keeps her from eating and that way she stays slim.'

He shook his head and followed Serena indoors, knocking cautiously on her bedroom door.

Nick swung Steffi onto his knee.

'Not going too well, is it, kid?' he said, then he kissed her neck and delighted in her baby smell and her warm chuckles.

But not for long!

He had four days to work something out with Serena, and although his head told him Willowby was the ideal place for his family, his heart suggested that staying in Sydney might be easier for a whole lot of reasons—not because it was definitely Serena's preference but because of the distance from Bill.

Bill tried not to think about what was going on in Sydney. She told herself she hoped Nick could work it out, but in her heart of hearts she hoped he'd work it out so they stayed in Sydney. He could fly up to visit Gran...

So life went on—going to work, coming home, doing everything she could to not think about Nick, although memories were everywhere, especially when she visited Gran, who talked so excitedly about Nick bringing Serena home to Willowby, about weddings and more babies, every word a drop of acid etching pain into Bill's heart.

Work provided, if not solace, a least a release from constantly thinking about Nick. It was impossible to let your thoughts drift in a busy ER.

'Bill, you're on the mine rescue team, aren't you?'

Angie had slid into the cubicle where Bill was dressing an elderly man's leg ulcer.

'Yes,' Bill replied, her mind on the job, thinking Angie might be asking because she was interested in joining the team.

'Then I'll take over there,' Angie said. 'There's an alert. An accident at Macaw.'

Bill's heart, which had stopped beating at the word 'alert', resumed when she heard Macaw mentioned. It was an underground mine and both her brothers now worked in open cuts.

As she left the cubicle the phone she carried in one pocket began to vibrate and she knew this would be the call asking her to report to Rescue Headquarters.

Her stomach clenched as she thought of what might have happened. All the mines had their own safety officers and trained rescue personnel, but the mine rescue team was called in for serious accidents—a roof collapse, miners trapped...

'It's what we've all trained for,' the team leader reminded the group as they kitted themselves out in overalls, breathing apparatus, hard hats with attached lights, and lethal-looking tools that could cut, or lever; with ropes and whistles and walkie talkies.

Emergency equipment was already being moved to the mine, including the huge jet engine that would pump inert gas in to smother explosive gases. She knew enough about underground mining to be aware of the safe-refuge chambers, where trapped miners could gather, and escape shafts equipped with ladders for them to escape. Gas was the big problem, gas that could explode into fire or poison people trapped beneath the earth.

'It's a rock fall, not a fire,' the team leader told them. 'And Macaw's got the latest in monitoring and communication equipment so by the time we get there they will know just how many and where the men are trapped.'

Bill thought of other mine disasters she'd read about or seen on TV and was glad about the communication because at least the men could talk to the outside world.

When the team arrived at the mine, the management had their rescue protocols under way and could tell them fourteen men were trapped, eleven in a safe-refuge chamber, only one miner that they knew of quite seriously injured.

'We've one team working on access to the chamber now, and another drilling a new ventilation shaft down to it. We think the other three men are further down that stope and we've men trying to get to them from an escape shaft.'

Knowing no one would have been allowed into the mine, even for a rescue mission, unless the air readings were good and the shafts secure, Bill felt a surge of hope that all the men would be rescued alive.

Maybe not today, but before too long.

* * *

In Sydney, Nick had renewed his conversation with Serena. Steffi was having a sleep and Alex had apparently calmed Serena down so she was willing to listen to him.

'We got on well before,' he reminded her. 'We really only broke up because your work took you away so often. I'm not asking you to stop work, only asking if you don't think, for Steffi's sake, we could make it work again.'

'In Willowby?' Serena demanded. 'I think not. I was only there for a few hours and the heat nearly killed me. Besides that, there's my social life. It's all right for you, you've friends up there, but all my friends are here or overseas.'

Nick wanted to point out that people's social lives changed as they grew older and had more responsibilities but knew that wouldn't cut any ice with Serena. They'd suited each other before because they'd matched—playboy and playgirl.

And he'd thought that life was fun?

'And Steffi?' he asked, as he'd yet to see any indication that Serena cared one jot for her child.

'She's my daughter.'

The shrug Serena gave as she answered made Nick want to shake her. She might not love her child but she was obviously willing to use her as a bargaining chip.

Or was she?

Was he just assuming that her blood tie was as strong as his?

'Do you want her?' he asked, and now Serena turned to face him.

'Why wouldn't I?' she demanded, and Nick threw up his hands in despair.

'I've no idea,' he said. 'Not about this, or you, or anything! According to what you told me earlier, you were willing to have her adopted as soon as she was born, then last month, when you had to fly to the States for work, you were apparently quite happy about dumping her on me, so what am I supposed to think?'

'You're supposed to understand I'm her mother,' Serena said, and Nick, his heart sinking, knew she saw Steffi as nothing more than a pawn in whatever game she was currently playing.

'And?' he prompted, not wanting to say too much, not wanting to let the anger building inside him loose anywhere near his daughter.

'That's all. You must realise that in family law disputes the judge almost always gives custody to the mother.'

'You're saying you want her?' Nick demanded, his stomach in knots at the thought of having a legal fight for his daughter. 'You want to be part of her life? Always, or just until she gets in the way of your career?'

Serena lit another cigarette from the stub of the one she'd just finished, and blew a lazy plume of smoke into the air.

'What do *you* want, Nick?' she asked, and Nick, although now he was wondering about it himself, answered her.

'I want us to be a family,' he said. 'I think that's the least we can do for Steffi. She didn't ask to be here, but now she is, let's see if we can give her the best possible life, which, to me, means two parents.'

'I only ever had my mother, and you had no one but your grandmother,' Serena reminded him.

'And look at the mess we both made of things,' Nick

snapped. 'Why do you think I want two parents for Steffi?'

'I won't accept such nonsense. I'm successful, you're successful, but I get your point, I just don't get living in that God-awful place up north. If you want to play happy families with me and Steffi, you'll have to play here.'

It would be best to be here, Nick conceded in his heart. Far away from Bill and the threat to his equilibrium that she now represented.

'There's Gran...' he muttered, but so tentatively Serena had no trouble laughing off his feeble objection.

'You could fly up twice a month to visit her,' she said. 'Even take the child.'

The child?

Was he wrong to be thinking of Serena as the mother figure in his family if she didn't love Steffi?

'Do you love her?'

The question erupted out of him—far too loud and far too abrupt.

Serena smiled the serene smile he knew she practised so it matched her name.

'I'm her mother, aren't I?' she responded, telling him absolutely nothing.

He slept on the couch, took Steffi for walks around traffic-busy streets, talked to Alex and Dolores, his life in limbo.

Because he wouldn't share Serena's bed?

He'd asked himself the question, suggested perhaps everything would fall into place once he did, but something held him back—something more than a few errant kisses up in Willowby. It came down, he decided, to Serena's attitude towards Steffi. She showed no interest in her child, never stopping to play with her, to touch her, to hold her in her arms and cuddle her.

And slowly it began to seep into his family-obsessed brain that perhaps the mother, father, child scenario wasn't all that it was cracked up to be. Well, he'd always known that, known the divorce statistics and the prevalence of single-parent families, so why had it seemed so important to him?

'I've booked a table at Fiorenze for tonight,' Serena announced, coming out onto the deck where he was watching Alex and Steffi build a tower of blocks. 'Alex and I are off tomorrow, so this will be our last chance to talk.'

'Tomorrow?' Nick repeated, looking from Serena to Alex, who simply shrugged.

'Tomorrow!' Serena repeated.

Nick knew he must look as stunned as he felt. The previous talk had been of a departure ten days away.

'You mean we've got one whole day in which to work out the rest of our lives?' he demanded.

'And one night,' Serena added, smiling in such a way he knew she'd planned this carefully. A candlelit dinner at a place where they'd eaten often in the past, then home, slightly tipsy, to fall into bed together.

Maybe it would work…

He'd barely had the thought when she added, 'You're more than welcome to stay on here—it would give you time to find us a bigger apartment.'

Nick closed his eyes and counted to ten, determined not to explode in front of Steffi. He realised now that Serena's mind had been made up from the start, which was why she'd cut off any discussion about their future.

For some obscure reason—just to have a man around?—
she wanted him back and was happy to have 'the child',
as she called her daughter, included in the package. Tonight, in Serena's mind, he'd fall back into her bed and
the matter would be settled.

She'd disappeared before he'd regained enough control to follow her and insist they talk—off to buy a new
dress for tonight, according to Dolores.

He slumped down on the couch, knowing he'd been
too weak, too tentative, trying to do what was best for
everyone without upsetting any of the parties.

Well, maybe not best for everyone but best for Steffi.

Sick of the chaos in his head he flicked on the television and stared blankly at the screen, only slowly coming to the realisation that every channel was showing
the same thing—a mine, miners trapped, mine rescue
teams already on site. The disaster was here in Australia—Macaw.

Macaw was near Willowby...

CHAPTER TWELVE

'DOLORES, PACK UP all Steffi's things, we're going home,' he yelled, beginning to stuff his own gear into his bag then realising he'd need to book a flight.

Impossible. Every journalist in Australia was trying to get to Willowby—

'Dolores, can you drive? Have you got a licence?'

'Of course, Dr Nick, you know that, but why, what is wrong?'

'We'll have to drive, no chance of a flight. We'll take turns and stop overnight somewhere on the way—we have to think of Steffi.'

Serena arrived home as he was stacking all their gear in the hall.

'What's this?'

'I'm going home—there's trouble—I'm needed there.'

She looked at him for a long moment then said, 'It's that woman Bill, isn't it? It's always been Bill!'

And on that note she stormed away, slamming the bedroom door for must have been the twentieth time since his arrival.

It wasn't until he was out of the city, on the freeway, heading north, that he had time to consider what Serena has said.

It's always been Bill!

Had it?

No, he was certain that wasn't the case. Until he'd come back to Willowby he'd never thought of Bill as other than a friend.

So why had the attraction flared so quickly?

'I don't know,' he muttered, waking Dolores up from a light doze then being unable to explain exactly what it was he didn't know.

Because Bill had done some of her training at Macaw and knew it well, and possibly because, in the stressed situation, the recue organiser didn't realise she was a woman, she was one of the two chosen to go down the escape shaft to follow the miners through to where the three missing men might be trapped.

Excitement and trepidation churned inside her as she followed her partner down the ladder. Her brother Dan had told her that the ladders were checked every day so although this one seemed to move away from the wall a little, she kept faith in it.

'Two more levels to go,' the miner at the bottom of the shaft told her, and Bill touched him on the shoulder in thanks and sympathy, knowing how much he must want to be doing more to help his mates but sticking to his job in the whole operation right there at the bottom of the ladder.

The next shaft was darker and they turned on their lights so it glowed like a vertical tunnel with a train coming through. One more shaft and they were on the level of the fall, bright lights ahead showing them where the men were working.

'We've opened up a small passage over the top of

this fall,' one of the miners explained, 'but we can't get the communication probe through.'

He looked at Bill, the least bulky of the four people in the shaft.

'Reckon you can crawl up there and push it through.'

'I'll just drop this gear,' she said, and ignored the 'Crikey, it's a woman' comment from the second miner, leaving her partner to explain she was one of the top members of the mine rescue team. Clad just in her over-alls and with a tiny mike attached to her shirt just below the collar, she was ready.

One of the men hoisted her up and she clambered into the small space the men had cleared, slowly edging her way forward, following the fine metal tube that was the probe, glad to see bolts in the stone above her that told her the roof of this part of the tunnel was safe.

The going was so slow she sometimes wondered if she was moving at all, but eventually she could see the end of the thin wire.

The probe had stuck on a rock that projected from the wall and she had to manoeuvre the tube around it, and keep feeding it forward. The opening she was in grew narrower and she knew she wouldn't be able to follow the probe, but a shout as she pushed it further and fur-ther told her it had reached the trapped men.

Berating himself all the way, Nick drove north. How stupid had be been to think a family could work with-out love? How stupid had Bill been, too, now he came to think about it!

Berating Bill for her stupidity was easier than think-ing of her endangering herself in a mine accident, or trapped underground, or—

He'd think of numbers. He could reach Brisbane in ten hours, twelve allowing time to stop and rest and eat and let Steffi have a run around. Another ten—or twelve—and he'd be home.

He pressed the speed dial on his phone for the fortieth time and got the out-of-range message from Bill's mobile. He thought of phoning Bob but common sense told him it was better he didn't know what Bill was doing—not while he was driving.

Dolores drove as calmly and competently as she did everything else so he could sleep while she was at the wheel.

It was tempting to keep driving but, no, working in the ER he knew too well the risk of an accident when driving for too long. They'd stop, eat, sleep and go on refreshed. Tomorrow they'd be home.

Home!

He didn't dare dwell on Bill, on where she was or what she might be doing, he just knew he had to be there, to be close to wherever she was…

Bill could hear the excitement in the voices ahead of her, but although their words would be clear to those at the other end of the communication probe, they were jumbled coming through the rock to her.

She tried to work out differences in the voices, certain there were two, but three? She wasn't so sure.

'I'm coming out,' she said into her mike and, carefully, she began to edge backwards, knowing there would probably be other things she'd have to shove through to the men. Squirming backwards over stones wasn't fun, and it took far longer than she'd taken going in. Time ceased to exist but in the end she managed, knowing she was almost out when someone caught hold of her boots then guided her feet to footholds on the rocks.

'All three safe,' one of the miners told her. 'You did good,' adding, 'for a girl,' but smiling as he said it—the smile a bigger thank you than words could ever express.

She sat now, knowing the rule to rest when you could, while the men listened to the probe and began to plan the next move.

'How big is the gap, do you think?'

Her rescue partner came to sit beside her and Bill replayed her journey in her head.

'There's a rock jutting out from the wall that had stopped the probe and from what I could feel with my hand in that area, there's maybe a gap the size of a small water pipe. Once I got the probe through there, it wasn't impeded in any way. It reached the men about a metre past that small gap.'

'Small water pipe?'

He shaped his fingers to show her the circumference he was imagining and she agreed he'd got it right.

'Could it be widened?'

Bill closed her eyes and looked at a mental image of the rock jutting out in the light from her helmet, at the rocks around it, one exceedingly large one right at the top.

'Not without a great deal of trouble,' she replied.

'Well, we'll make do with what we've got,' her partner said. 'You willing to go back in?'

'Of course, but if you're getting pipe sent down, get that flexible stuff that will bend a bit around obstacles. I can use a guide wire to push it through, like the one the probe had.'

Technicalities kept them busy, messages going back and forth for hours until it was time for Bill to crawl back into the narrow space again, this time pushing the pipe in front of her, the pipe that might prove a lifeline for the miners if they were trapped there for much longer.

He *had* to know!

Having spent the night in a motel just north of Brisbane, they were on the road again at dawn, and Nick finally cracked and turned on the radio. He knew Dolores would have watched the drama on the television in her room at times during the night, but he'd been resolute in not watching anything that might stop him sleeping.

'It is bad, Dr Nick,' Dolores said. 'It is why we're going home?'

'Yes.'

One word was all he could manage, the news that rescuers had reached the eleven men in the safe refuge should have cheered him, but it had been followed by the information that members of the mine rescue squad were three levels underground, still trying to get to the other three men, and that had dried the saliva in his mouth, certain Bill was there—three levels underground...

Drive carefully and steadily, he told himself as he switched off the radio and turned Steffi's nursery rhymes back on, singing along to 'One little, two little, three little ogres' and wondering why nursery rhymes, like most fairy-tales, were unnecessarily grim.

Steffi, however, loved it, and after they'd done monsters and goblins he had to turn off the next song and keep singing, coming up with other creatures like bunyips and yetis that they could include in the song.

'Miss Bill, she sings this song too,' Dolores said, and Nick felt his stomach clench.

How stupid had he been to even consider Serena might want to be a mother to their child! Serena, who hadn't once cuddled her daughter, let alone sung her a song.

They stopped by a park and got out to let Steffi play awhile, Dolores buying sandwiches and fresh bottles of water, heating Steffi's bottle in a café across the road, promising Steffi a proper cooked meal once they reached home.

'No more of this bottled stuff,' she told the little girl, who didn't seem to mind what she ate any more than she objected to a two-thousand-kilometre car ride.

Dolores drove and he tried to sleep, but the closer they got to Willowby the more anxious he became. In the end he phoned Bob.

The tube was harder. It caught on things and bent the way she didn't want it to go, not that she could see where she *did* want it to go. She reached one arm as far forward as she could, scraping it, even through her overalls, against the jutting rock but needing to find the obstacle that lay ahead.

Loose dirt.

Dirt was easy.

Dig it out.

Glad she was wearing gloves, she dug and scraped, pulling the dirt back towards her body, tucking it under herself then digging and scraping again.

Behind her she could hear the anxiety building,

someone trying to push the tube further into her tunnel, although she wasn't ready for it.

She tried to explain the problem to the men back at the rock fall but as she had no earpiece she didn't know if she'd been heard. So she continued, digging, scraping, pulling back the dirt until finally the tube advanced, very slowly, guided by the wire and now her hand, which might be stuck in the hole for ever the way she was feeling now.

They were within four hours of home, late on the second day of their mammoth journey, when they heard that the eleven men, one seriously injured, would shortly be brought to the surface of the mine.

In an unemotional tone the reporter announced that rescue attempts were continuing for the three other miners.

'And that's all?' Nick demanded of the radio, because by now he knew, from Bob, that Bill was down that mine.

'She will be safe,' Dolores assured him. 'The one thing Bill is is sensible so she won't take any risks.'

'Oh, no?' Nick muttered, and drove on.

The tube went through.

Bill heard the shout of delight then felt it move beneath her as they tugged it further into their small area of dubious safety.

Now to get out so things could be fed through the tube. Water and eventually food going in, information about the situation in the tunnel coming out. The probe was good for communication but if the engineers in charge of the rescue needed a diagram of the area and some indication of the placement of the rock fall, the men could supply it.

She began to edge backwards, harder to do now because of the tube *and* the dirt she'd shifted back.

Harder to do because she was tired.

Nonsense! You've been a lot tireder than this on night duty and still kept focussed on your work.

She edged a little further, inching backwards, body cramped and aching, praying that any moment someone would grasp her boot and she'd know she'd made it.

Nick dropped Dolores at the apartment, carried up all their baggage, then, not bothering to return the hire car, drove straight to the mine.

Growing up in Willowby, with mines on the doorstep of the town, he knew exactly where Macaw was, and if he hadn't, the mass of emergency and private vehicles parked nearby would have told him. Daylight was fading as he pulled up outside the high wire fence but bright arc lights lit up the scene so it was like something out of a movie.

Or a nightmare.

Certain they wouldn't let him in, he stood by the gate and scoured the grim faces of the men by the site office for one he knew.

Dan de Groote!

He yelled the name and Dan turned, saw him waving from behind the fence and came towards him.

'Word was you were back in Sydney,' Dan said, looking none too happy to see him.

'I'm not, I'm here. Bill's down there, isn't she? Can I come in and wait?'

Dan waved his hand towards the crowds of people gathered outside the fence.

'I should let you in and not all of them—other relatives?'

'I *am* a doctor,' Nick reminded him. 'I could be helpful.'

Dan's glance towards the ambulances already within the perimeter fence told Nick what he was thinking, but in the end he nodded.

'Just wait there while I get you a tag and once you're in keep out of everyone's way, okay?'

Nick almost smiled because just so had Dan, the eldest of the boys, always treated him and Bill, letting them join in some wild game the 'big boys' were playing, as long as they kept out of the way.

She couldn't move.

The tube had somehow changed the dynamics of the little tunnel. The tube and the probe and the dirt.

Well, she had to move, to wiggle and wriggle and ease herself just a little, forget inches, they were old measurements, go for millimetres. A millimetre at a time—she could do it.

Tag hanging around his neck, Nick waited on the periphery of the crowd of sober, worried men near the mine office. Something had gone wrong, he could tell from their voices.

And now arrangements were being made for more men to go down below, Dan saying very loudly he was going, Nick, without thinking, stepping forward.

'I'll go with you.'

Dan threw him a hard look.

'You're claustrophobic, remember?' he said, 'besides not being trained. But you can make yourself useful as a doctor. We brought up the badly injured man first and the doctor we had here has gone with him to hospital. The rest of the eleven men we've rescued are coming up now. Go check them out.'

He pointed to where a large tent had been set up, close to where the ambulances were parked, and Nick, knowing Dan was right—an untrained person in this situation could bring risk to all the rescuers—went across to make himself useful.

'Someone else is trapped, one of the mine rescue people.'

He heard the whisper as he waited for his patients to arrive and knew, with cold certainty in his gut, that it was Bill.

And he hadn't told her he loved her.

Where that thought came from he had no idea, but he knew it was true. The mad dash from Sydney had been for love.

CHAPTER THIRTEEN

FINALLY ALL ELEVEN men were up, checked and reunited with their anxious families before being ferried to hospital for more comprehensive examinations and treatment.

Night had fallen, and an eerie silence hung over the complex. Nick edged his way back towards the site office where, he knew, the rescue was being co-ordinated, and found not Dan but Pete.

Nick heard an echo of Bill's voice—Dan and Pete, both members of the elite rescue team—the best of the best.

'I'm going down,' Pete said. 'Dan let me know you were here. You want to come?'

One look at Pete's face was enough to confirm that the rescuer in trouble was the boys' adored little sister, Bill.

And in bad trouble if Pete was here, too.

Nick didn't hesitate, taking the overalls Pete was holding and clambering into them as he followed the miner to an area behind the main buildings.

'You won't go soft on me?' Pete demanded as he handed Nick a helmet with a light attached. 'We're going down three levels.'

'I won't go soft on you,' Nick promised, and they started carefully down the ladder that led into what, to Nick, was like the very centre of the earth.

One shaft, another, then another, until finally voices and bright lights led them to where the fall blocked the three men from escape. In the bright lights three miners, stripped down to underwear, sweat gleaming from their skins, were carefully levering and shifting rocks from the base of the fall. A rescuer in full gear talked quietly to the trapped men through a communication probe, and a thinish, flexible tube that led up and over the rock fall told Nick exactly where Bill was trapped.

He couldn't think of how far underground he was, all he could do was concentrate on Bill, willing her free from her prison. Pete had joined the men digging while Dan and the second rescue team member talked about tubes and probes and the possibility that there'd been a slight movement in the rocks that had been enough to trap Bill in her narrow tunnel.

'Can you remove the tube?' Nick asked Dan, and they all stared at the dark hole above their heads, seeking inspiration. 'Would that help?'

'Who knows? The danger is that in moving it we might do more damage. She's okay, she's only about a metre from the trapped men, and although she must have lost her mike while she was wiggling around, she is talking to them and they're relaying information back to us. Apparently she had to dig away some dirt to get the tube through and she pushed it back underneath her as she dug. Now she's using her free hand to dig it out from underneath her and trying to edge backwards that way.'

Nick closed his eyes, trying to picture the situation,

shutting down the panic in his chest when he considered just who was stuck in that unbearable situation.

'Suction? Like a vacuum cleaner?' he said to Dan. 'Would it alter the dynamics and make things worse if we sucked some loose dirt and rubble away from up there?'

Dan considered the idea for a moment then walked away to talk to the men.

'We can't use the mine's ventilation suction,' Pete said, 'it'd be far too strong and could bring down more rock, but Nick's idea is worth a go—some kind of industrial vacuum cleaner that'll suck up dirt.'

The second rescuer sent a message to the operations room and within ten minutes a very clumsy-looking barrel vacuum cleaner was in Nick's hands.

But not for long!

'Sorry, mate,' Dan said, 'but you have to take a back seat on this one. We can't risk a further fall.'

The valiant little machine sucked, was emptied, sucked again, emptied again, until a yell of triumph went up from the man currently manning it—Bill's boots were in sight, edging gradually towards them.

He shouldn't be here.

He didn't belong.

But how could he be anywhere else?

Pete reached up as the boots came closer, talking to Bill now, easing her feet down onto footholds in the rocks, talking all the time. But it was Nick who pushed both Dan and Pete aside to catch her as she fell the last few feet to the ground, catch her and hold her, just hold her.

'You're the doc, you're supposed to be checking her

out,' Dan reminded him, but Nick's arms wouldn't un-
clamp from around the woman he'd so nearly lost.

Eventually he climbed behind her up the first shaft,
Bill recovering enough to tease him all the way about
how at any moment the earth could come crashing down
on them.

'Don't worry, when I heard about Macaw I thought
it had,' he told her. 'I thought I'd lost you for ever without ever telling you I love you.'

'Telling me you love me?'

Bill's startled reply echoed down the shaft but hopefully they were far enough up for it not to have been
heard by the men still working below.

'Of course I love you. According to Serena I always
have, I just hadn't realised it.'

Bill had reached the next level and waited until he
emerged when, ignoring the miner standing guard there,
she turned to hug him hard.

'Serena?' she asked.

'We'll work it out,' he assured her.

'Steffi?'

'We'll work that out too.'

Nick eased his arms from around her and looked into
her dirt- and blood-streaked face.

'Preferably above ground,' he reminded her, and she
led him to the next shaft and began to climb.

'When did you get here?' she asked, and it took most
of that climb to explain their mad drive north.

The third shaft was easier, the light from above reassuring Nick that the real world still existed. But Bill
was tiring fast, so he climbed closer to her, trying to
take some of her weight off her arms and legs, half carrying her when they finally reached the top and anxious

helpers hauled out first Bill then helped him clamber up and stand upright.

Paramedics had already put Bill onto a stretcher and as they wheeled her to the makeshift emergency room, he walked beside her, holding her hand, not caring what anyone thought.

Apart from a multitude of scratches, torn nails and fingers from her digging, and red patches that would eventually be bruises, she was fine.

'Nothing a good hot shower won't cure,' he told her, when he'd finished what he'd tried to make a professional examination, although his heart went into overdrive when he remembered the danger she'd been in.

'Take me home,' she said quietly, and Nick was only too happy to oblige.

She was quiet in the car, sitting with one hand on his knee, and he knew the stress of her entrapment must be catching up with her.

Except that when she spoke, it was to ask what she'd asked earlier.

'Serena?'

He shrugged.

'I don't know,' he said, 'I really don't. All I know is that I'd be living a lie if I settled with her, loving you as I do. I had thought it was the right thing to do for Steffi, but now I realise it would be unfair to everyone. Somehow we've got to come to some agreement over Steffi without her becoming the rope in a tug-of-war. But all that can wait. You're safe and you probably need some sleep and I definitely need some sleep, and tomorrow, as the wise men say, is another day.'

'I think we might be at tomorrow already,' Bill reminded him, and she moved the hand that lay on his knee, giving him a little squeeze that brought him more joy, right then, than a kiss.

He took her back to her own apartment, where he helped her out of her clothes, showered her gently, applied antiseptic lotion to the scratches and put dressings on her hands, then slid a big T-shirt over her head and tucked her into bed.

'I'll take your spare key so Dolores can bring you some food,' he told her, bending to kiss her on the lips.

She slid her arms around his neck.

'You're not staying?' she whispered. 'I thought you'd wanted us to be here alone? That night at the yacht club?'

'No, I'm not staying and, yes, I do want us to be alone, but not now, not like this, my love,' he responded, kissing her again, but gently still. 'You need to sleep and then you need to think about where *you* want to go in this situation. It might be hard, Bill, if I have to fight Serena because there's no way I'm giving up Steffi. If that happens, you'll be caught in the crossfire.'

She cupped his face in her palms.

'And if I said I didn't care—that however bad things get they couldn't be worse than life without you?' she asked him. 'If I said I loved you?'

His heart was behaving badly again and it was only with a mammoth effort of will that he eased away from her, tucked the sheet around her and kissed her one more time, this time a goodnight kiss but not goodbye...

Bill woke, stiff and more than a little sore but with a sense of well-being in spite of her physical state. She examined her surroundings as she considered this state and slowly memory returned—Nick had kissed her goodnight—and she had to smile.

Although…

Might have to fight Serena—you'll be caught in the crossfire—Steffi rope in tug-of-war…

Memories of before the kiss dampened the sense of well-being.

It was all very well being gung-ho about fighting side by side with Nick so he could keep Steffi, but what if they lost?

What would it do to Nick?

Thinking of that was bad enough, but she knew she was only throwing that around in her head to stop herself thinking of the big one.

What would it do to her?

Okay, so she already loved Steffi, but at a distance— a little closer than her nephews and nieces but still as an outsider in her heart. But if she married Nick—and that had seemed to be the gist of things last night—and having mother 'rights' so to speak, Bill knew damn well her love for the little girl would send its roots deep into her heart.

And *then* to lose her?

From being ready to leap out of bed, shower, and rush up to see Nick and Steffi, Bill indulged in a tiny whimper of self-pity and stuck her head under the pillow.

Two minutes later she realised just how pathetic her behaviour was. She didn't do the leap-from-bed thing but she did drag her body up and out into the shower, where all her scrapes were red and sore and her bruises coming out nicely.

She stood under the steaming water until it started to

get cold—Bob must have put in cheap water heaters—
then she dried her herself, rubbed at her hair, carefully
dressed herself—whimpering occasionally at the pain of
movement or when she dragged clothing over an extra
sore spot—then made her way up to Nick's apartment.

It was Nick she had to consider in this business—
Nick her friend, Nick the man she loved and, if memory
served correctly, Nick who loved her back.

Nick who'd overcome his very real claustrophobia
to come down a mine to help rescue her.

And she was going to leave him to battle Serena on
his own?

Not stand beside him because of some wimpish fear
of being hurt?

She rang the bell of his apartment but when he appeared, Steffi in his arms, she felt again that dreaded
fear of loss.

Nick looped his arm around her and drew her inside,
scolding quietly all the time.

'You should have stayed in bed. Dolores is making some chicken soup for you. Have you had enough
sleep? How are your cuts and scratches? I'll have to have
a look, put something on them. Come and sit down.'

The words flowed over Bill like balm, but although
they soothed it was the way Steffi's fingers caught at
her hair that hurt more than scratches.

Bill eased away and sank down into an armchair,
staring at a mess of Steffi's toys on the living-room
floor. Nick set the little girl down and she toddled off
into the kitchen.

'She's walking properly now,' Bill said, and the mix
of happiness and dread made her voice crack.

Nick came and sat on the arm of her chair, tangling

his fingers in her still-damp hair the way his daughter had.

'Tell me,' he commanded, and somehow Bill did, pouring out her doubts and fears.

'It hurt so much, losing the baby, Nick,' she said, doing pathetic again, 'that now, twelve months later, I'm only barely over it. I just don't know if I could go through that again—if I'd find the courage a second time around.'

Nick lifted her out of the chair, and sat down in it with her on his knee.

'I can't pretend there's not a chance,' he told her, his lips pressing kisses on her neck by way of punctuation. 'But do we throw away the joy and happiness we could have now—right now—because of what might happen in the future?

'By some miracle we've found each other in a way we never expected to—we've loved each other for so long, but this love is different, special and all the more powerful because of the love that was already there. So it might not move mountains, but with you by my side—and now I've been down to Level Three in a mine—I'd give it a damn good try.'

He turned her enough to kiss her properly now and Bill felt all his conviction—and all his love, *their* love—in that long, deep, probing kiss.

Eventually, she kissed him back, telling him without words that she agreed.

Or thought she did.

A long time later he lifted his head and looked down into her face.

'I would understand if you decided to run for your

life—to head off to deepest, darkest somewhere to get away from this.'

The slight tremor in his voice told her he meant every word, and it was that tremor that restored her courage.

'When you've gone down to Level Three for me?' she teased softly, then *she* kissed *him*.

CHAPTER FOURTEEN

'So, WHAT HAPPENED in Sydney?'

Such a simple question, Nick thought as Bill clambered off his lap and settled on the floor close to his legs, looking up at him with such trust and love and hope he found it hard to talk.

Let alone explain.

'I've no idea,' he admitted honestly. 'Well, to a certain extent I can describe the visit, but the underlying currents are beyond me.'

He hesitated.

How could he tell Bill about Serena's attitude without being disloyal to his daughter's mother or portraying her as cold and heartless, which he knew for a fact she wasn't?

'Start when you arrived,' Bill suggested, resting her head on his knee so she was no longer looking up at him.

Which somehow made it easier...

'It was weird, Bill. For a start, she barely acknowledged Steffi's existence. Alex was there and he was delighted to see Stef and she was obviously just as pleased to see him, but Serena...'

Another pause as he tried to recall their arrival, but

the days had blended into each other and the bit he had to get out wasn't getting any easier.

'I don't know why,' he said, still hesitant, 'but for some reason she had taken if for granted we'd get back together—physically. I think I might have told you that. It didn't make sense, especially when she didn't seem to care about Steffi at all and got downright angry when Alex suggested he photograph Steffi again.'

Having got that out, he lapsed into silence because he couldn't think of any more words to say.

Bill, resting against his legs, reached up one hand to grasp one of his and they sat in silence for a while until finally she stood up and perched on the arm of the chair.

'If you think back to when she was persuaded by Alex to keep the baby so he could photograph her, at that stage she was determined to give Steffi up for adoption as soon as she was born, so I would imagine, during her pregnancy, she was determined not to get emotionally attached to the child she was carrying.'

'Hmm,' was all Nick could add to that suggestion, although it did make a kind of sense. 'But after that, when she *did* keep Steffi?'

'Again it was for Alex. She's been his favourite model for ever, his muse, as you called her, and suddenly here's this interloper capturing his attention. You said she got angry when he wanted to photograph Steffi here—maybe it's nothing more than Serena's own insecurity. Maybe that's why she wanted you back again, so she'd have the security of someone special in her life. From what I've read of Alex, he's getting old, and a model's working life doesn't last for ever, so...'

Nick reached up so he could pull Bill's head down to his and kiss her.

'You realise you're making excuses for a woman you barely know, and what you do know about her must make your teeth itch.'

Bill grinned at him and he felt his heart swoop around his chest in a great burst of love.

'I'm not really. I've never understood other people's relationships and I don't try, but I would imagine there's huge insecurity in any model's life—are my looks going, am I getting fat, will I get the top jobs this year? Possibly having Steffi around only added to it. If you think about Serena's childhood, she barely stopped working to *be* a child, so she's probably at a loss as to what to do with one.'

'You're probably right,' he told her, and kissed her again, because not only was she beautiful, and bright, and a wonderful woman, but she was kind, and compassionate, and understanding—and he wanted to kiss her anyway.

'Do you think she'll fight for Steffi?'

So they were back there again—back in doubtful land, with Bill remembering the pain of loss.

'I can't promise that she won't,' he said.

Now, Bill thought to herself. Now's the time to commit to Nick.

'Of course you can't,' she said, 'but I can promise that, whatever happens, I'll be with you every step of the way—with both of you.'

Nick stood up and pulled her into his arms again, holding her close, not kissing her, just holding her, and Bill knew that everything would be all right. Somehow they would get through whatever the future might hold because their love was strong enough to—

Well, to move mountains!

'Marry me,' he whispered in her ear, just as Steffi came toddling back, her high-pitched 'Beee!' making them spring fairly guiltily apart.

The day, which had begun underground about a million years ago, was finally drawing to a close. With Steffi in bed, and Dolores visiting her family for the last few days of the leave Nick had taken, he and Bill were alone on the deck, lights out, looking out to sea, sipping hot chocolate with marshmallows in it because it had been that kind of day.

'You didn't answer my proposal,' Nick complained when, his drink finished, he set the cup down and took Bill's hand in both of his.

'What proposal?' she demanded, turning to face him. In the dim light reflecting up from the marina her hair was a dark cloud around her pale face, her eyes nothing more than deep shadows.

'My proposal in the living room'

'In the living room?'

He could practically hear the gears turning in her head and wondered how far he could push her before she exploded into anger.

'I asked you something,' he reminded her, telling himself that teasing her was only getting a little of his own back for his panicked agony of the rescue mission.

'You *did* not!'

Good, she was angry now and he loved an angry Bill. Once she'd let fly at him he could take her in his arms and feel the tension in her body then feel it ease as he held and kissed her, eventually feeling it turn to a different kind of tension...

And why the hell was he wasting time teasing her like this when he could be holding her, kissing her right now?

He stood up and pulled her out of the chair, wrapping his arms around her just as he'd known he would.

'I said, marry me, remember?' he whispered as he brushed the hair back from her ear to kiss her in the hollow just below it. 'Steffi came in and you didn't answer and now it's too late because I'm taking no answer as a yes and I'm going to kiss the breath out of you.'

'Starting here,' he added, his mouth taking possession of hers.

'Like this,' he murmured, sliding his tongue between her lips...

Random questions flashed through Bill's head. Was this okay? Hadn't it been too sudden? Was it just Steffi that had brought them together? This was Nick, but was this love?

She heard a faint moan and thought it might have been hers, then her mind went blank and she gave in to sensation—to the warmth in her blood, the fire along her nerves, the prickly expectation on her skin and the ache of desire deep within her body.

All this from a kiss?

All this and more because kissing Nick was like nothing she'd ever experienced before, like nothing anyone in the universe could possibly have experienced because otherwise they'd all be doing it right now...

'Bed?'

She heard the word but was still grasping for its meaning, too lost in sensation to be thinking straight.

Had she hesitated too long that Nick released his hold on her, just slightly, so he could look down into her face.

'Too soon?'

She smiled, and shrugged, and felt the heat that told her she was blushing like a schoolgirl.

'No—yes—oh, I don't know.'

'I do,' he whispered, and kissed her once again, so gently, so thoroughly, so beautifully she had an urge to cry—again! 'It's been a very long and enormously emotional day, one way and another, so for tonight we shall be abstinent. In fact, how soon can you organise a wedding? We could stay abstinent till then, get a few days off somewhere, with Dolores minding Steffi, and stay in bed the entire time, room service providing enough in the way of food to keep up our strength.'

Bill smiled at him—at her friend Nick, trying, as always, to do the right thing. She rested her hand on his cheek and said, 'Or we could go to bed tomorrow night…'

EPILOGUE

GIVEN THE SIZE of Bill's family, they'd decided to hold Steffi's second birthday party in a park. Balloons hung from trees, a marquee festooned with ribbons provided shade and shelter should it be necessary, and twenty-three small boys and girls, all dressed, more or less, as bears were rioting on the grass.

'Do we have to do this party thing every birthday?' Nick demanded, coming to sit beside his wife, who was settled on a folding chair in the shade of a tree, watching three of her brothers trying to organise a pin-the-tail-on-the-donkey game with very little success.

Katie, the eldest of the de Groote grandchildren, had adopted Steffi from their first meeting, and she was organising some of the smaller ones in some game that involved standing up then falling over, the little ones screaming with glee.

'I think every second year will be enough,' Bill told him, 'but then on the off years this one will probably need a party, so get used to it.'

Nick reached over to pat the very large bulge of his wife's stomach.

'If you got this guy out today or tomorrow then we

could combine the parties, considering Steffi's real birthday isn't until tomorrow.'

'Yes, but would it be fair?'

She was actually frowning over the fairness of combined birthday parties for her children and Nick felt again a gust of love so strong it nearly struck him down. He had thought that after a year of marriage this might stop happening, but although he loved Bill all the time—well ninety-nine point nine per cent of the time as she could still be aggravating—these gusts of love still came out of nowhere, leaving him shaken at the thought that this might never have happened—that they might never have got together in this way, just gone on being friends and lost the magical, rewarding, cosmic wonder that was their love.

Steffi, with Katie's help, was blowing out the candles on the bear birthday cake when Bill felt the first contraction.

Hmm, the doctor had said any day now, although she still had a fortnight to go.

Ignoring it, she helped cut the bear into small sections and handed around plates of gooey chocolate cake.

The second contraction suggested things might be getting serious. Could she really have the baby on Steffi's birthday?

This time last year she'd been preparing to get married—they'd decided their daughter's birthday was as good a day as any.

Preparing to marry Nick—her BFF.

It still seemed surreal, yet sometimes when she caught an unexpected glimpse of him and her insides turned upside down, she knew that it was real—somehow they'd moved from friends to lovers, from friend-

ship to passion so hard and hot she could feel herself
blushing right now as she thought about it.

She'd read somewhere once that love was all-encompassing, and as the third contraction tightened her belly,
Bill looked around at all her family, at Gran, wearing bear ears on her head, various de Grootes in fancy
dress, Steffi the cutest bear of all, theirs now Serena had
agreed they have custody, Dolores, on standby for when
Bill went into hospital. Yes, love *was* all-encompassing!

Nick came and stood beside her, his arm coming to
rest around her shoulders.

'Not to worry you,' she said quietly, 'but you might
drop me off at the hospital on your way back to the
apartment.'

He turned to look at her, his face going pale under
his tan.

'You're serious?'

She smiled and with difficulty got close enough to
kiss him on the lips.

'Of course! I'm a nurse, remember, I know these
things.'

'But shouldn't you be sitting—or lying down—or
doing *something*?'

'I am, I'm counting the minutes between contractions
and you've been to all the pre-natal classes, you know
I can stand up and move around as much as I like all
through the birth if I want to. Right now I want to watch
everyone enjoying themselves, but you might speak to
Dolores and tell her we'll need her to move in tonight.'

Nick stared at her.

'You're for real?'

She had to laugh.

'Nick, you knew this was coming. You said yourself

today or tomorrow would be good. Surely you're not going to go to pieces on me now?'

He wasn't, of course!

He was a doctor, he knew about this stuff, it was just that his brain had stopped working and his legs were none too steady, and he wasn't sure that he could handle having two children—could he love them equally, could he ever love another child as much as he loved Steffi?—and then there was Bill, and he didn't know that he could go through seeing her in pain like he'd seen other women during labour, and—

'Nick!'

Bill's voice brought him out of his funk.

Well, almost.

'Go and talk to Dolores, ask Kirsten if she'd mind organising the clean-up here at the park, then we'll put Steffi and all the presents in the car, you can drop me at the hospital, then when Dolores gets to the apartment you can come back to the hospital.'

He stared at her.

'And bring my bag—the one that's packed. We've been through this.'

Nick stared at her some more, saw her smile and knew she knew exactly what he was thinking.

She kissed him once again, although he felt the wince of pain she gave as another contraction grabbed her body.

'We'll be fine,' she promised him. 'You'll love this baby differently from Steffi but still love him just as much. Love is the one thing we've got plenty of. And I won't die in childbirth and you won't faint, watching it.'

She looked at him again and added, 'Now, was there anything else?'

He shook his head and took her in his arms.

'Except to tell you that I love you, Mrs Grant,' he said, his voice so husky he wondered if she'd heard the words.

'That's good,' Bill told him. 'Now go and talk to Kirsten and Dolores and find Steffi and the presents and—'

Nick cut off the instructions with another kiss and when Bill kissed him back he knew she was right, and that this new baby he and Bill had made would be every bit as special as Steffi, and—

Well, he couldn't really remember all the other things he'd been worrying about.

Stuart Alexander Grant, weighing in at a splendid three point eight kilos, arrived on his sister's birthday, much to everyone's delight. Holding him in his arms, looking down into his red, downy face, Nick felt again that rush of pure, unadulterated love he'd felt when he'd first held Steffi.

'We'll be right, mate,' he said to his son, then looked up into the radiance of Bill's smile, at Steffi cuddled up to Bill on the bed, her little fist holding tightly to Bill's curls, and he knew they'd all be right—his family!

* * * * *

LET'S TALK
Romance

For exclusive extracts, competitions
and special offers, find us online:

f facebook.com/millsandboon

⦿ @millsandboonuk

🐦 @millsandboon

Or get in touch on 0844 844 1351*

For all the latest titles coming soon, visit
millsandboon.co.uk/nextmonth